THE SCREAMING SKULL: THE CHRONICLES OF ELBERON, VOL. I

Copyright © 2018 Rick Ferguson

All rights reserved. ISBN-13: 978-1-7325662-1-7

Published by Mr. Phabulous, LLC dba Phabulousity Press, 2018

Cincinnati, Ohio, USA

This is a work of fiction. Any similarity between the characters and situations within its pages and places or persons, living or dead, is unintentional and co-incidental.

Cover image and interior illustrations by Obsidian Abnormal and are used with permission.

THE SCREAMING SKULL

THE CHRONICLES OF ELBERON, VOL. I

RICK FERGUSON

PHABULOUSITY PRESS

"Though much is taken, much abides; and though
We are not now that strength which in old days
Moved earth and heaven, that which we are, we are;
One equal temper of heroic hearts,
Made weak by time and fate, but strong in will
To strive, to seek, to find, and not to yield."

—*Ulysses*, Alfred, Lord Tennyson

For Andy, Chris, John, Wa, and Wam,
who helped a young man dream.

BOOK I

They Call Me a Hero

1

They call me a hero. They call me a leader of men. They, in this case, are my loyal subjects, all 850,000 of them, spread across the grottos, harbors and sparkling blue shores of a chain of islands no bigger than Hawaii. Shipwrights, fishermen, blacksmiths, nobles, commoners, men-at-arms—all drink to my health at their local taverns and regale each other with tales of my exploits, when I was a young man wandering the Woerth in search of fame and fortune. They wonder at my strength and courage. They spend coins with my profile stamped on them. To their eyes, they live in the most enlightened monarchy this side of Kenwood. They go to sleep at night convinced that they rest under the watchful care of a courageous and noble king.

Bloody fools.

You want titles? I got 'em. King Elberon, Lord of the Tradewind Isles, Defender of the Faith, President of the Southern Shield, High Admiral of the Seven Fleets, Protector of the Iron Coast, and Friend of the Dolphins. Likely I have other titles of which I am not aware, honorifics bestowed upon me by one High Council or another at elaborate ceremonies at which I may or may not have been present. Who knows? None of them mean shit to me. My Trophy Hall is filled with the dusty relics of my past triumphs. Tapestries recount great battles at which I led my armies and fleets to astounding victories. The hall holds rare and powerful magical items: glowing armor that can turn a frost giant spear, shields that can withstand white dragon breath, swords that burn lustily with arcane powers. My private reserve holds more powerful and dangerous items still. I hardly look at them anymore.

My father, the illustrious and well-storied King Olderon, once told me I have more wisdom than intelligence. It was the closest he ever came to paying me a compliment. When I first received my adventurer's license, a lifetime ago in Redhauke, the Guild measured both attributes, assigning each a number value: fifteen for my wisdom and eleven for my intelligence. I never quite understood what those numbers measured, or where upon what scale they lay. Wilberd told me to be thankful I hadn't tried to be a wizard.

"Wizards need at least a fifteen intelligence to stay alive," he told me.

I never wanted to be a wizard; I was always a fighter by trade. The Wizards' Code forbids spellcasters to wear armor or wield any weapon but a standard-issue dagger, so they can only lurk in the back of a raiding party, hiding from whatever monster is trying to disembowel them, and then waiting for the right moment to launch a *Mystical Missile* or a *Flamethrower* spell and run like hell. It's not my style. Nothing pleases me more than the trembling *thunk* of my blade as it bites into the skull of an imp warrior. Always first to wade into battle, I stood like an unfaltering sea-cliff as waves of enemies crashed and broke against the great rock of my strength. I cut a wide arc of death around me. Sometimes I'd roll a critical hit and send some fucker's head spiraling from his shoulders. If I got into trouble, the great sword of Amabored or the singing bow of Lithaine would haul my ass out of danger. We were badass motherfuckers back then —and we knew it.

So, now I'm the King—even though, as the younger of two sons, I had no chance of inheriting the throne. To end up regent of some little kingdom that needed a man of stature to represent them at elven councils, to preside over feasts and revelries, to knock up a princess and produce an heir—that wouldn't have been so bad, would it? I never wanted the big chair. Who needs the aggravation? I renounced my father's kingdom to prove my worth, but it never occurred to me that he really was the smarter man. Now he's dead, and my ass is warming his seat. Irony is a butcher's trade.

Olderon never saw it coming. Both he and my brother Eldernon were slain by Garrin, the Grimmreaper, whom I personally beheaded atop the uppermost spire of the Dread Keep to end the Dread Wars and save the Woerth. Even as I await the effects of the *Remembrance* potion, I can see my father's headless corpse, blood flowing from his severed neck to mingle with the rain puddling on the stone battlements. The barbed tongues of memory lash my soul like a scourge.

OF OUR CONFRONTATION AFTER HE MURDERED MY FATHER, I RECALL every detail. Garrin and I stood facing each other across the flat roof of the South Tower of Castle Kraken, he wielding the black blade Soulreaver, and me gripping the haft of my notched battle-axe. Garrin wore the cursed colors of the Hand: black leather lined with tanned human flesh, died blood-red. Even unto that night, no one living had ever seen his face. His hooded cloak framed nothing but darkness, negative space where his features should be. In his left hand, he clutched by the crown of its hair my father's severed head. Fresh blood, ruby-red, streamed from the neck to run with the rivulets of rain on the stones. Olderon's wild eyes—the eyes that had long ago regarded me most often with cold disapproval or contempt —stared at nothing. They were the eyes of a fish dying in the bottom of a boat.

Curtains of rain swept over Garrin and me. Jagged lightning scarred the black sky. Thunder roiled across Hydra Bay and the port city of Tradewind, huddling below the castle. Around us, the Multiverse came apart at the seams—the chrome mountains and ghastly violet skies of the Last Universe bleeding into our own Woerth, shimmering into being and then vanishing as fast. Moments later, the

greensward and turquoise dome of the First Universe winked in and
out of being. The pipes of the Machine Elves, blanketing the sky with
the music of creation, dissembled into cacophony. Reality itself was
worn as thin as parchment. Somewhere close, the Violet Queen was
watching.

The bitch had very nearly won, thanks to this worthless turdloaf
standing before me. One of us would die that night, I vowed. But first,
I needed the truth.

"Who are you?" I snarled, my voice broken by the howling wind.

Then came his laugh—a laugh so familiar that it shattered
my mind.

"Don't you know?" asked Garrin, sounding the doom of my heart.
"Haven't you guessed? Are you so great a fool?"

"All right. We'll do this the hard way," I said, and charged.

Yet neither of us died that night. Another year would pass before
Garrin got got, and I got my revenge. Somewhere in Valhalla, Dad is
wondering why it took me so long.

2

You must think I have it soft: sitting on the throne of one of the most progressive kingdoms on Woerth, secure in my glory, basking in the love of my subjects, enjoying the carnal delights of my luscious queen. My sixty-fifth birthday is just ten days away, the celebration of which is the most anticipated event in all the Lordship, and maybe in all the Free Kingdoms. Why aren't I shitting gold bricks of delight?

Well, here's what I found out, only two days ago: how long I'm going to live. I even know the exact date of my death. How would you handle that knowledge? Exactly how I'm handling it, I'll warrant.

I swear to Odin that Wilberd secretly despises me. He's some kind of Buddhist, I think, although if most monks are as useless as this one, then I weep for Buddha. When we first met, he browbeat me for days to get a religion of my own.

"What in blazes for?" I asked him.

"Who are you going to praise after battle?" he asked me. "To whom will you dedicate your conquests? To what afterlife will you commend your soul?"

We spoke at a back table of the Suds 'n Shade Tavern in Redhauke. It must have been forty years ago now. I had lived in

Redhauke for six years by then, enjoying the fruits of a comfortable adventuring trade, and saw no need to rock the boat by involving the gods. Wilberd had saved my ass from the Hand a month earlier, however, so I owed it to him to listen. He was under a vow of silence, and so technically not permitted to speak. When we were alone, he never shut up.

"Who says I have to dedicate anything to anybody?" I asked. "Why should I live by rules concocted thousands of years ago by some prophet on a mountaintop who doesn't know dick? I'd have to go to temple, sacrifice the fattest rams in my flock, tithe ten percent of everything I bring in—it's a giant pain in the ass. No thanks."

"What alignment are you practicing?" Wilberd asked.

"Neutral Good," I said. "God bless you, but don't fuck with me."

"There are perfectly good religions that will let you be a practicing Neutral. Pick one that fits your image. Something with a good God of War. What about the Greek pantheon?"

"Zeus and that lot? Don't make me laugh."

"Well, you'd better think about it," Wilberd said. "It could save your life. You can call on your deity once per battle, and he has a five percent chance of blessing your victory. That's across the board, no matter who you worship. Your god is obligated to save your neck."

"No kidding?"

"You'd have to go on a side-quest afterward, but that's a small price to pay. Think it over."

And so, I did. Taking a stroll down the Godsway, I wandered with my nose in the air through the pressing throng of supplicants winding their way amongst the fluted marble columns, past the shrines, temples, mosques, and cathedrals representing a buyer's market of faiths spanning thousands of years and dozens of universes. You couldn't swing a cat without hitting a messiah. Feigning disinterest, I collected the pamphlets pressed into my palm by old men who rent their garments, bathed in ashes, and flagellated themselves with cats-o-nine-tails when they weren't pooling their money to catch the Saturday night donkey show over at the gnome whorehouse. Piety has its rewards.

The truth was that I didn't really buy any of it. The bit about having a god around to pull your nuts out of the fire appealed to me, however, so I shopped around. The Melnibonean gods, Arioch and that crowd, interested me, but I couldn't deal with the angst. The Romans were mythology-stealing pricks, and who wanted to speak bloody Latin, anyway? Finally, I settled on the Norse pantheon. Their gods had style: Odin with his two ravens and eight-legged steed, Thor with his mighty hammer. If I pretended to believe in the whole song-and-dance, perhaps valkyries would one day descend from Valhalla to lift my broken corpse from some blood-soaked battlefield.

So, I received my blessing from a staff cleric, paid the membership fee, and received, along with my ID card and pamphlet, a nicely-carved hickory staff that I still have to this day. Aesir and Vanir alike have served me well, and it's easy to show fealty to a god like Odin whose only commandment is *Thou Shalt Kick Ass and Take Names*, who expects you to take his name in vain, and who will fuck up your life big time if things are going too well. Is there a flagon of ale reserved for me in Valhalla? Thanks to Wilberd, I now know exactly when I'll find out.

3

This was just two days ago. Minding my own business, I was pruning the azaleas in the main courtyard of the Kraken. A well-tended garden soothes my restless heart, and my dotage affords me the time to indulge myself. Planting, weeding, pruning, mowing—I do it all. Astrid has hired gardeners behind my back, but I always smoke them out and kick their asses into the moat. The odor of freshly shorn grass, the line of well-trimmed shrubbery, the come-hither chaos of a flowerbed: I crave it all. And don't get me started on the vegetable garden.

I was wrestling with the azaleas when Wilberd appeared from around a hedgerow. His expression foretold trouble.

"Go away," I said.

"I have good news," Wilberd said.

"War has broken out?"

Did I mention that Wilberd has a unicorn horn sticking out of his forehead? Not a fake one, either. It's a standard-issue magical unicorn horn, fused irrevocably to his skull. He got it by opening the wrong magic egg in the Temple of Pain Eternal, lurking on an island in the middle of the Sunless Sea. Most of the eggs were blessings—extra health, invulnerability, doses of speed. When

Wilberd cracked his egg open, damned if a spiral, pearl-hued unicorn horn didn't sprout right out of his forehead. Looked like it hurt, too; the poor bastard bled like a woman. At first, he took it poorly: sleeping on his back, suffering neck strain, and running into doors. He raced from one priest and wizard to another seeking a cure. It was a tough curse, though, and no one could figure it out. So, he learned to live with it. He was especially pleased to learn that it could split open an armored breastplate. Whenever I rib him about it, he lowers the horn as if he's going to ram me. If he ever tried that shit with me, I'd remove that fucking horn and shove it up his ass. End of curse.

Sensing my thoughts, Wilberd raised his horn. "Remember the Astral Telescope, the one you found at the Workshop? The one we used to search for Lithaine?"

"Of course," I said. "Probably should have destroyed it."

"Did you know that you can divine the future with it? You only get about ten seconds out of it before the image dissolves into an unblinking vagina-shaped red eye. But it does span all space and time —at least in this universe."

"Impressive. What did you see?"

"I saw the moment of your death."

For a moment, I felt as if I were on the deck of one of my quinqueremes. The ground lurched and swayed beneath me. Suddenly, the knowledge of my mortality, the inescapable conclusion that someday *I would die*, would no longer draw breath, eat, shit, piss or fuck came crashing down on me. Twenty seconds of silence passed before I spoke.

"Why the fuck would you look at that?" I finally croaked.

"Had to look at something."

"Why didn't you look at the moment of *your* death?"

"Are you kidding? The knowledge would drive me mad. I wouldn't even tell you what I saw, except that it's such good news."

"*Good* news?" Hot surging blood stung my face.

"You're going to live to be one hundred and thirty years old!" Wilberd said, his voice spiked with that bitter potion of wonder and condescension I had come to despise. "Your birthday is but the halfway point. You'll have the lifespan of two men!"

My legs felt like creamed spinach. Dropping my shears, I collapsed onto a nearby stone bench. Frightful thoughts caromed inside my skull. Another sixty-five years—that was good, right? Shit, the average human lifespan in our pre-industrial society was about forty-five years. By contrast, elves didn't even reach puberty until they were seventy-five. Dwarfs sometimes lived to be 250, as if anybody could stand to be around a dwarf for that long. Your average monkey's cousin, however, was fortunate to see his grandchildren born. If the Telescope was correct, then I'd likely outlive my own son. My wife would be forty years in the ground.

Who wants to live that long?

If I could be thirty-five for an extra sixty-five years, then sign me up. Instead, I face another sixty-five years of decrepitude, of gazing with tragic longing at my cobweb-draped battle-axe, as impotent in battle as I'll no doubt be in the sack. Meanwhile, my hair will fall out, my teeth will rot, my skin will shrivel, hair will sprout out of my nose and ears, and my brain will slowly putrefy in my skull. I'll end up right where I started when I first arrived on this godforsaken rock, requiring caregivers to feed me and wipe my ass. Who wants it? Who needs it? Why live at all, when the greatest tragedy of life is to be born? We're forced into the world against our will, we spend our lives utterly clueless, and finally, just when we manage to accumulate a little wisdom, Death bends us over the table without the courtesy of a reach-around. It's all a steaming bowl of shit soup.

For some while, I sat on the bench gathering my wits. The thought of wrapping my hands around Wilberd's throat gave me passing solace.

"Did it show you *how* I'll die?" I finally asked.

"Yes," Wilberd said, now looking away. "You might not want to hear that part."

"Look, you've gone this far. I may as well have the rest of it."

"You die sitting down," he offered.

"Sitting down? Where?"

"On the toilet."

I lurched upright. Bestial noises clawed my throat. Wilberd took a step back.

"On the *toilet*?" I cried.

"I told you, you wouldn't want to hear it."

"That's swell! That's perfect! When I arrive in Valhalla and Odin asks me, 'How many men did you send to Hell before you came to stand before me?' I'll have to say, 'None, my lord, because I died on the *fucking toilet!*' I'll be laughed out of the afterlife!"

"I'm just telling you what I saw," Wilberd said. "I thought you'd be happy about it."

"I'm as happy as your mother when I pay her in cash!" I paced like a caged ferret. "What if I pull a sword down from the wall and cut my own throat with it five minutes from now? Where would your Astral-fucking-Telescope be then?"

"Don't be dense. The Telescope reveals the end of your current path through the Multiverse, but it doesn't eradicate free will. You can always step off the path. Every heartbeat creates a new universe."

My shears lay on the ground. The azaleas turned to other business. What now? Intimations of mortality hung around my neck like a petrified dragon turd. The urge to flee—out of the castle, through Tradewind City and down to the harbor, commandeer a ship and keep sailing until I had outrun my fate—flooded me with hot desire. No matter how far I ran, my end would still loom before me: rising with the sun, shining with the stars, a bright comet scarring the sky to herald my demise.

In truth, it isn't the method or date of my passing that gets to me. It's the simple certainty of death itself. I'm not immortal, as I had always secretly hoped. Fate is a fisherman, and none escape his net.

Now, I sit my throne, unmoved since the day Wilberd dropped his bombshell. My wife, my ministers, and my priests ply me with food, with counsel, with ointments and salves. I refuse all ministrations. I crave only solitude and dwell mostly in the past. So, I've called in my scribes to take down this dictation in the hopes that you understand why I did what I'm about to do. To know why I do this thing, you need to know my story, as painful as that might be for you. My story is, after all, not some garden-variety *bildungsroman*. It's an epic tale of high adventure, with the fate of the Multiverse at stake. I've stepped through the Black Mirror and lived to tell the tale. I've been to Hell and back. I've fought arch-devils, extra-dimensional Chaos queens, dragons, pirate lords, giants, the undead, aliens, hellspawn—you name it, I've slain it.

Saving the world always requires sacrifice. Some of the good guys must die, or there was never really much at stake. It could have been me just as easily as Malcolm, or Redulfo, or Bellasa, or Cassie. Why, when I've spent my life seeking Death, do I so despair now that Death has come to call? That I need not answer the door for another six decades is cold comfort indeed.

My birthday party is nine days hence. There will be parades, a fleet processional, feasts, speeches, and revues. Even now, heads of state from across the Free Kingdoms undertake long and perilous journeys to sit at my table and toast my good health. Those survivors of the Quest who still draw breath will attend as well. Shouldn't I simply bask in the love of my family and subjects, secure in the knowledge that I've lived, against all the empty clockwork of this dangerous and incalculably heartless Multiverse, a good life?

No. Fucking. Way. I have scores to settle, markers to collect, and debts to pay. My birthday guests are in for a shock—especially Wilberd, that smug bald bastard. They'll learn that this decrepit hero has a few surprises left in him yet. My oldest and dearest friends will be here: Amabored, James, Andrigan, even Melinda, whom I betrayed. And when I finally get them all together, I'm going to kill every last one of them.

4

efore I continue, a point of order. Does the mere mention of elves and dwarfs, of swords and sorcery, mark me as a mere Tolkien rip-off artist? Allow me to point out that, by his own admission, Tolkien was the translator of the *Red Book of Westmarch*, not its author. How can you rip off history? In the Multiverse, Middle Earth is no more or less real than my Woerth. Even if Tolkien was lying, and he did make up the whole thing, then he cribbed most of his ideas from Celtic and Norse mythology. Hell, I could have done that. Could I hide behind faux conceits by calling the elves Fairies or Eldar, and the dwarfs Squats or Stunties? Sure, but could you be fooled so easily? I assure you that the arrogant, hemp-wearing, lute-playing, rope-smoking, herbal-tea-drinking elves in my tale are quite real, as are the smelly, avaricious, beer-swilling, gas-passing, gluttonous dwarfs. Middle Earth may reside a mere universe or two away from mine, but I'm a lot farther away from it than some other universes I could name. If Woerth is in the same neighborhood as Hobbiton, then the Four Lands can be found on fucking Bagshot Row.

If I could create my own universe to inhabit, it would be more *Star Wars* than Middle Earth—modern plumbing, grooming, and medical science aside, it would be a lot easier to slay a dragon with a lightsaber than the heavy metal I had to lug around. You think it's fun to live in the equivalent of Sixth Century Europe? No sanitation system, slop from the chamber pots falling like rain on the city streets, medical practices that would pass for torture in any civilized society. Try living through a case of the flu. Try getting an abscessed wisdom tooth pulled. Try dating a girl with hairy legs and summer teeth who doesn't bathe. You didn't hear about any of that stuff in Tolkien because he cleaned it all up. Hobbit holes don't exactly smell like freshly shorn rose petals, you know. Mostly, they smell like outhouses.

Such was the world in which I found myself. When I came into manhood, I dreamed only of journeying to the far city of Redhauke to seek my fortune. As a prince, I was entitled to my own fleet, my own castle and men-at-arms, and my own vineyards and flocks. It would have been a good life, but it wouldn't have been *my* life. It was all very well for Elderon, my brother and heir to the throne, to beg at the table for my father's scraps. One day, he would run the show, and he could toss down the nearest shithole all the wisdom our father had drummed into his thick skull. But me? I faced a lifetime of watching Elderon walk into doors, take credit for my accomplishments, and lay siege to the last crumbling castle of my self-respect. No thanks. I packed my bags the moment I was old enough to understand the reason for my brother's smug, shit-eating grin.

When I found the Girdle of Gargantua, the mild unease I felt at the course of my life became a fever. Still, it wasn't until my nineteenth year that I worked up the courage to tell dad that I wanted to try my luck in Redhauke. He looked like a man who had just had his worst suspicions confirmed.

"Did you fall out of your tower window again?" He asked.

"No. I've thought this through."

"Thought?" Olderon gave what passed on his face for a smile. "Is that your hobby these days—thinking? You think it's sensible to throw away your birthright to scour dungeons?"

"I can beat any sailor in your navy. I'm a better fighter than Elderon. Maybe even better than you. There's a world out there that could use my help. There's evil to be vanquished. Kingdoms to be won. Maidenheads to take."

Olderon rose from his throne. Having married late in life, he was nearing decrepitude by the time I reached manhood, but even now his presence imposed. He had the torso of a rhinoceros, the legs of a mastiff, and the grin of a wolf ready to tear the hindquarters off an unlucky deer. He gave me the full effect, as it were, fixing his heavy brows into a battlement overhanging his gunmetal eyes.

"Now you listen to me, boy," he said. "Don't tell me about winning kingdoms. Who civilized these islands? When we first settlers landed on Hydra Rock, there was naught here but a flourishing Stone Age civilization with an advanced knowledge of astronomy and a fondness for human sacrifice. Do you think it was easy to slaughter their men, enslave their women and children, destroy their culture, and usurp their land? Why, if it weren't for Manifest Destiny, you and I would be toiling still in the copper mines of the Talony. I stacked bodies like cordwood while you were flinging shit on the walls of your nursery. I built this Lordship with my own two hands, over the bones of the dead, and for what? To have my own son spit in my face? I'd sooner feed you to the sea drakes!"

We stood nose to nose. I held my ground, though he terrified me still. His idea of parenting was to lock his sons in a maze with a hired Minotaur.

"I want what you wanted," I said. "To forge my own destiny!"

"If your destiny needs the forge, then I'll fetch my hammer!"

"You'd better forge shackles if you expect to keep me here!"

"I'll shackle you myself!"

"You and what army?"

That did it. Olderon found the haft of his broadsword and swung the blade in a broad arc aimed straight at my skull. Usually, he stopped the blade before it cleaved me in two. Just the same, I grabbed a buckler from the wall to absorb the blow. Better safe than dead.

For a charged moment, we glared at each other. Fortunately, I had come prepared for this impasse.

"There's only one way to settle this," I said.

Olderon raised a furry brow. "You don't mean..."

"Crush the Kobold," I said. "One match. If you win, I stay and polish your brass. If I win, I go with your blessing."

"No strings?" asked Olderon, his gaze narrowing.

"Would I ever take advantage of you?"

This broke his mood. Chuckling, he lowered his sword and thumped my shoulder with the flat of his hand.

"You are an arrow from your old man's quiver, my boy," he said, "however crooked the shaft may be. Very well—you'll have your game. Three days hence, when the cock crows. My steward will make the arrangements. But I'll hear no pleas when we fish you from the moat."

"I'll have the alligators removed."

My father's vanity now duly served, I could turn my attention to winning the match. Lucky for me that I had an ace in my codpiece.

5

Crush the Kobold is the family game. Our ancestors have played it for generations uncounted, long before my father's kin were enslaved by the Talony, and it's a rite of passage for every male child in the Lordship. There are few rules to speak of. There's a studded iron ball. There are two goals, one at either end of the field. The ball carrier must reach one of the goals before the other players beat him stupid. If he makes it to the goal alive, he chooses the next man to carry the ball, who runs for the opposite goal. There are no teams, and any number can play. Sometimes we played Greek style, with our banners flapping in the breeze, as it were. Sometimes we played in full plate armor, sometimes on horseback. The last man standing won the day. Never mind the property damage, broken bones, and murderous grudges—that was part of the fun. What can I say? We're a primitive people.

Now, about that ace. Three years earlier I had been camping out at Chasm Falls, a 1,200-foot torrential wall of water that swept into Hydra Bay. The land was craggy and forested, and you could lose yourself in the wilderness for days, as you traversed old trails or blazed new ones. Whenever I got the urge to murder my father or beat the piss out of my brother, I retreated there. On my third morning in country, I came across a cave tucked away at the base of the falls. Though I had passed that spot a hundred times before, I'd never before seen it—a recent rockslide had revealed the entrance. I struck flint to steel, got a torch going, and crept inside.

The cave became a tunnel. Waste deep in cold bay water, I waded deeper into the cliff face until I realized how far I had come and froze stiff. The tunnel walls pressed closer. Nothing stirred but my torch flame, shuddering in the breeze from deep within the tunnel. There was another entrance somewhere on the other side of the cliff.

Thoughts of sunlight spurred me forward. At last, the tunnel ended in a small antechamber. I swung the torch around for a look. There was another tunnel opposite the one I came through, blocked by fallen debris. The walls arched overhead into a rough dome. To my right was a ledge, waist high, upon which grew a plush carpet of phosphorescent moss. Upon the moss lay—

—a corpse.

A skeleton, actually; it hadn't been a corpse for centuries. It was missing a skull. Now, I've stumbled upon thousands of stiffs in my day, and I assure you that they always stink. The fresh ones reek like spoiling melons. If they've gone over a week or so, they smell like a thousand skunk carcasses rotting in one of the pits of Malebolge. When they're as dead as this fellow was, which was at least a thousand years, they just smell... like Death. It was a wicked, poisonous stench, like the breath of a crazy witch who welcomes children into her gingerbread house—a visit that begins with sweetcakes and cider and ends in screaming agony inside an oven.

It was my introduction to death, and I couldn't have been more excited if I had stumbled upon a pot of gold guarded by a couple of comely elf maidens. I dipped the torch closer, and the sputtering light revealed a leather girdle draped across the skeleton's ribcage. Not a woman's girdle, but rather a protective warrior's girdle: thick, black leather strap and belt, studded with gemstones and girded by a skirt of bronze bands fastened with beaten gold rings. There were runes— elvish or dwarfish, who really cared?—stamped on the broad golden buckle. It was an impressive piece of equipment.

Rest assured that I wanted it off that rotten pile of bones faster than you can change your mind. It sure wasn't doing that bloody bugger any good.

I reached for it—and how surprised was I when the thing thrust out a bony claw to seize my grasping hand?

6

My bowels turned to tapioca. I had encountered a few magical creatures in my day—when I was a kid, my father hid actual monsters under my bed to toughen me up—but nothing to prepare me for the pants-pissing shock of an inert pile of bones springing to life just as I was collecting a little treasure. It would one day become old hat; I've vanquished enough skeleton warriors to populate Atlantic City. But that first time was something else.

The thing now towered over me. Its ancient bones were held together by some fell cartilage of molten evil. Perched atop its spine was a skull-shaped black hole of negative space, limned in red light. From that skull-shaped void came the distant, reverb-laden music of pipes and flutes playing the mad songs of idiot gods. Capering pupils of flame gleamed with malice and delight. It pulled me up in its bony grip, and I braced for disembowelment.

"*WHAT ART THOU?*" the thing roared, its gibbering voice issuing from that negative skull-space like whispers from a tomb.

I couldn't answer. The spine-freezing voice seemed to issue from deep within my own brainstem, flooding my body with lunatic terror. Where it gripped me, my flesh froze and burned simultaneously.

"THOUS HAST FREED ME," it said. *"THOU MUST NOW BECOME ME."*

Before my eyes, the skeleton underwent a blizzard of transmogrifications: wrapped in capering black flames, crawling with obscene puss-filled worms, dripping with hideous green demon-snot, the bones swelling and bursting with blood and semen and maggots from the rotting carcass of Beelzebub's dead dog. I wanted the thing to rip out my heart, just so I would never have to look at it again. Little did I know that this episode was merely the antipasti. I had just ordered the entrée, and I didn't even know it.

The skeleton rose to its full height, still clutching my wrist as it swelled with Hellfire. Then, in a booming explosion that shook the cavern to its bones, it vanished. I was flung backward, hit the cavern wall at high speed, landed in a pool of muck, and lay there for a long while.

Finally, I stirred. What dim light the cavern had afforded was now gone. Only the glow of the phosphorescent moss protected me from utter darkness. Was I dead after all?

As the young are certain of nothing if not of their own immortality, my fear soon dissipated. The former owner of that skeleton had been slain by a wizard, I supposed, who then booby-trapped the corpse with a *Fear* spell to protect treasure long since stolen. It put me through the fucking ringer, all right, but I was more interested in the girdle that still lay on the mossy shelf. Here was a prize for the shock I had suffered.

I ran out of that tunnel before my luck could change, broke camp, and rode back to civilization that same night. Once back in Tradewind City, I took my discovery to a pawnbroker of passing acquaintance.

His name was Ronald. He ran his fingers over the girdle approvingly and smelled the leather.

"Nice," he said. "Good workmanship. Probably dwarfish. It has a rude sort of charm."

"What do the runes mean?" I asked.

"I don't recognize them. Let me check the database." He hauled up an impressively dusty tome from beneath his desk and dropped it loudly on the table. He thumbed through it for a long while. Then he looked up.

"So, you looking to sell?" he asked. He tried to act nonchalant, but his gaze was fixed on mine.

"What's it worth?"

"Oh, you know, it's a nice piece, I can sell it to one of the guards. I'll give you two hundred and fifty auratae."

Big mistake. If he had offered me fifty for it, I might have sold. His immediate leap to 250 told me that it was worth much more.

"Two hundred and fifty?" I laughed. "You wouldn't pay that much to bail your mother out of the toll booth. What aren't you telling me?"

"Okay, I'll give you four hundred. Give me until tomorrow to come up with it."

"If you don't level with me, I'll take it to that one-eyed gnome down the street."

"All right," he said. "Keep your codpiece on." He went to the rear of his shop and took down a thick iron bar upon which had hung a mess of copper pots. He brought the bar over and tossed it onto the table.

"Try to bend it," he said.

He knew I couldn't. I tried anyway, to help him make his point.

"Now put the girdle on and try it."

I donned the girdle. Gripping the bar with both hands, I brought it up to chest level. At that moment, the girdle *moved*—it tightened itself around me as if trying to get a better grip. A current of energy bolted up my body, surged through my shoulders, and raced down my arms to my fingertips. It was a more powerful high than any opium I would ever smoke. I felt good, and strong. Almost without trying, I bent the iron bar like a sapling in my hands.

"Holy smoke," I said.

"It's enchanted, all right," said Ronald. "No curse on it, either, unless it afflicts you with leprosy or something that you won't know about until it's too late. You know who made that? Stone giants. Have you ever seen a stone giant? Spend some quality time with those fellows, and tell me you don't discover your feminine side."

"So, what's it worth?" I made no move to take off the girdle.

"It's worth twenty-five hundred auratae if it's worth a pfennig. You're lucky you're the King's son. Otherwise, you'd be dead before sunrise. Word gets around."

Though I was only a gangly sixteen, I was already tall enough to place my hand in a comradely way on Ronald's shoulder. With minor effort, I squeezed his deltoid enough to make him squeal.

"Christ, that *hurts*," he said.

"So, I can rely on your discretion."

"What am I going to do—rat out a prince?" He jerked his shoulder away from me and resumed an air of indifference. "Wear it in good health. That kind of strength will impress the chicks."

And so, it did. If I had known then who put the girdle there for me to find, and why, and down what hellish roads finding the thing would send me, I would have taken the 250 auratae and skipped off merrily down the lane.

Still, the Girdle of Gargantua has always been my ace; it cemented my reputation as a modern-day Hercules. Invariably, I was the strongest sword in my adventuring party. I was the guy called upon to take out the door, to lift the sarcophagus lid, to square off against the biggest, baddest motherfucking imp chieftain blocking our road to one epic adventure or another. I enjoyed the notoriety. Let those pointy-headed magicians copy incantations until their hands cramped. Let the priests shake their beads, and the rogues climb walls or blend into shadows like the skulking rodents they were. Me? I was always in the middle of the fray, taking my medicine and then dealing it out. So what if I had a little help? We were all looking for an edge. Adventuring is a dirty, dangerous, cut-throat business, which is why most of the poor and downtrodden don't attempt it. We used to dice over the enchanted items we recovered from our dungeon sweeps. They became so plentiful that we would turn up our noses at all but the most potent weapons of mass destruction. Rune-covered swords that burn with Hellfire? I have two dozen of them. I could step

into my Trophy Hall right now and outfit myself with enough
enchanted weapons and armor to stop Hitler at the Polish border. Of
all the Phylaxes we collected and destroyed, none have saved my ass
like the Girdle. The Horrible Heart, the Awful Orbs, the Mace of
Malice, the Crown of Chaos—you can have them all with my compliments. I'll take the Girdle every time.

I was smart enough, too, to keep it a secret from the old man. Let
Dad give me his best shot—I had something waiting for him. And I
had no qualms about cheating, either. He would have done the same
thing if he had found it. You think he got where he was by playing
fair?

7

Indeed, playing fair was not my father's strong suit. When the day of the grudge match dawned, I learned that he had stacked the field with twenty handpicked marines paid handsomely to see me carted unconscious from the field. The news left me holding the moral high ground as I strapped on my magic girdle in the Kraken's gymnasium. As he tightened the straps around me, my steward eyed it with suspicion.

"Never mind about that," I said. "Just fetch my gauntlets."

In Tradewind City, a game of Crush the Kobold is cause for celebration. The nights before a match are filled with feasts and revelries. Across the city, tavern doors burst open, and throngs of hard-drinking citizens of the realm spill into the streets. Wags roar their allegiance to this or that player, while pouches bursting with coins change hands as often as the bookies changed the odds. That day, the odds against me closed at eight to one. I sent my man into the street to wager coin on my victory—if this thing went down the way I hoped, then I'd need some spending money.

Instead of the stadium, Olderon had chosen the Kraken itself as the field of battle. As the appointed hour drew near, a parade wound its way from the harbor, into the city, along Pelican Way, and up the hill to the castle. The players rode on horseback—all except my father, who waited on his throne in full regalia for his guests to arrive. I rode at the head of the column on a steed borrowed from my brother, who savored the irony of loaning me the beast that would carry me to a beating from our father.

The castle grounds were thrown open to a random lottery of citizens who got to watch the match up close. No one could say that the old man didn't provide entertainment. "All they want are bread and circuses," my father used to say, though he cribbed the line from the Romans. The battlements, courtyards, and grand halls of the Kraken were thus lined with 5,000 screaming hooligans who had been swilling beer for three straight days. Players made a point to avoid the crowd, as any of this lot with money on someone else might shank you in the ribs. From the lowliest deck-swabber to the King himself, we were a nation of hard-ass survivors—and we were, every last one of us, always looking for a score.

Rocking my leather battle armor and ready to do business, I strode into the Coral Hall. As big as three soccer fields, with scarlet and pearl columns of real coral mined from the Drakespine Reef, the hall is supported by a massive vaulted ceiling that is itself the inverted hull of one of our prized quinqueremes. That day, the ravenous horde lined the balcony thirty feet over our heads and screamed for blood. The other players ranged far around me in every direction, three yards' space around each man. Big, burly bastards they were, with noses broken in foredeck boxing bouts and hands that looked like bundles of link sausages.

At the far end of the hall stood the Coral Throne, which is every bit as ostentatious as its name implies. Before the throne stood King Olderon, Conqueror of the Isles: scepter in one hand, the other hand gripping his small oaken shield, iron helm on his head, beard bristling with regal authority. He raised his scepter. The mob went wild.

I couldn't help but smile. The old man knew how to work a crowd.

"Let it be known," Olderon began, his baritone booming through the cavernous interior, "that this royally sanctioned game of Crush the Kobold will hereby begin upon the crowing of the cock. Let it also be known that the rules agreed upon by these just men and true are set down henceforth: leather accouterments, no metal bands or studs; small hand-shields or bucklers, no spikes; leather gauntlets, studs of which must be rounded and no more than one-eighth finger in height. No hand weapons, blades, staves, or chains permitted. Match is to the last man upright. Release the Kobold!"

And here was a surprise—a live kobold. He came scurrying out of a side door at the end of a poleax to take his position at center court. Kobolds are a lot like imps, only smaller, fouler-smelling, and easier to slay in vast quantities. They also have a grasping love of money, which they spend like sailors in the taverns because no one will let them in unless they buy. This unfortunate bastard had no doubt been promised a chest of gold coins for this morning's command performance. Had he any idea how bad it would go for him, he would gladly have stayed a pauper.

The Chief Steward, stationed at a safe distance behind the throne, pulled the hood from the head of the cock he had been carrying under one arm. It stretched out its neck, shook itself awake, and let loose a defiant cockcrow. The match had begun.

Technically, the only man open for punishment was the one who grabbed the kobold first. It was customary, however, to get in a little action at the starting crow. Lunging for my nearest opponent, I got him in a headlock and drove my fist into his eye. From the girdle, I felt a small charge—it seemed to sense how much strength I required. The marine crumpled. Sure, it was dirty, but there were no penalties in Crush the Kobold. Even if there were, who would be foolish enough to referee? Howling like a werebeast, I dove after the sorry bugger now leaping away with the kobold tucked in his arms like a football.

The day grew long, and still the match dragged on. You might wonder how it could, with twenty-odd players doing their best to beat each other to a bloody pulp. The trick was that any man who made it to a goal with the kobold still alive could take a fifteen-minute break.

These breathers gave us time to stitch up our cuts, bandage our wounds, guzzle a few flagons of ale, or make time with the maidens in the gallery. At noon, the castle bells signaled the lunch break. The survivors gathered around long tables in the adjoining hall and tore into haunches of meat and loaves of bread like ravenous weasels. Sneaking a drink from the *Health* potion tucked in my boot, I dug in.

The bells rang again. Bloody and bruised but still standing, the kobold ran for cover. From one end of the Kraken to the other, the battle raged on. We shattered pottery, destroyed furniture, trampled the carpets, and tore the tapestries into confetti. One by one, the marines came after me, and each time the girdle gave me exactly the power required to take out my opponent without breaking something that wouldn't heal. When I had whittled the field down to five men, the remaining players kept their distance. So, I went after them. The last man tried to escape by crawling into one of the kitchen chimneys, but he fucked up by trying to shove the kobold in ahead of him. Kobolds don't like to be crammed into tight quarters—a favorite imp pastime known as "Cram the Kobold" involves trying to shove the kobold up your opponent's ass before he stabs you in the heart. This kobold did my job for me; in fact, I had to pull the little psycho off the guy.

That left the old man and me.

8

How many of you have squared off against your own father in mortal combat? Perhaps more of you than I think. If so, you'll agree that it's a moral pickle. Had it really come down to him or me, I wouldn't have hesitated for a second—I wasn't about to let him deny me the pleasure of pissing on his grave. Was he really trying to kill me, there in the moat? For months afterward, I thought so—but, as I later learned, doing so made little sense, given to how much trouble he had gone to send me on a quest of his own devising.

That he was taking the match personally, I had no doubt. He wore his Death Face: the same expression, I am told, he wore when driving the native island tribes into extinction forty years earlier. Now, with a son of my own, I understand how a man might feel about losing a contest of wills to his offspring. Still, I hadn't bet the old man for his kingdom. All I wanted was my freedom, a diluted version of the same desire that propelled Olderon from the slave pits of the Talon Empire to the Coral Throne. Dad never made the connection.

Spectators of the match's climax were not disappointed. They saw my father in the moat, trudging along the muddy edge of its southern bank with the kobold crammed under one arm, hoping to reach the base beneath the drawbridge before I found him.

Then they saw me appear at a window in the South Tower, a good sixty feet above the moat—the same tower upon which Olderon would years later meet his grisly end. Spotting Dad, I planted a foot on the windowsill and launched myself from the window like a falcon. The old man went sprawling as he broke my fall.

We untangled our limbs, locked hands around each other's throats, and rolled together into the moat. Spying his chance, the kobold crawled away up the bank. Wanting to wait to unveil my strength at the most dramatic moment, I refrained from calling on the girdle to help me finish the old bastard.

Before I knew it, however, Olderon had me submerged in the cruddy moat water. His thumbs drove into my esophagus. I saw stars, and there suddenly appeared in my panicked mind the notion that he might not let go until I stopped moving. I wanted nothing more than to beat him square, to show him that I wasn't afraid of him—but I was afraid. Should the old man sniff so much as a molecule of that fear, he would strangle me to death in that moat before he'd admit to himself that he had a coward for a son.

So, I took him out. Calling up the girdle's power, I flipped him around and shoved his head into the drink. I let him flail about for a moment. Then I yanked up his head so he could hear me.

"Yield, old man!" I cried.

"I'll see you in Hell first!"

I gave him another taste of the moat. "Yield! You are finished here!"

"You'll have to kill me!"

I flipped him over, so I could see his face. "I don't want to kill you!" I bellowed. "I want my freedom!"

We locked gazes. For a moment, I thought I saw the cold light of triumph in his eyes. Then he threw up his hands.

"I yield!" King Olderon cried. "Prince Elberon is the victor!"

The crowd went berserk. As the cheers rang across the common, only I could hear the words my father spoke to me.

"Your freedom is well won, boy," Olderon said as he twisted the water out of his beard. "You will leave the Lordship with only what you can carry on your back. You may take a good sword from the armory, and whatever armor you like. But know this: From this moment forward, I have but one son. That son shall be heir to a kingdom that you may no longer call home until his message reaches you with word of my demise."

Despite my victory, I burned with shame for relying on the girdle after all. By beating the old man, I had crossed a line from which his pride would never allow me to return. Why then, did I detect that hint of triumph? For a long moment, I gazed upon him with no presentiment that it would be the last time I ever laid eyes on him. Had I known, I would have left anyway.

Thus would I come to dwell in the Free City of Redhauke, just another pauper in a city of paupers, looking for dangerous work that no one of right mind would dare attempt. Heroes are born of desperate times. After a couple of weeks of enjoying my hard-won freedom, I was as desperate as they come.

9

A few hours ago, Astrid came to me with news that I'm still trying to digest.

Over the long years of our marriage, the Lady Astrid has played more roles in my life than either of us ever thought possible when we married impulsively during our long leisure cruise around the Hydra Sea in the autumn of my forty-third year. She has played my lover, confidante, therapist, harasser, haranguer, life coach, mortal enemy, goddess, rock 'n roll warrior princess, and many more besides. She became to my son a better mother than I've ever been a father to him. Throughout the storm-tossed sea of our marriage, hers has been the one steady hand on the rudder, the one person in all the Woerth who cared enough to put up with my shit. She's seen me at my worst, and she loves me anyway. She's seen me weep like an old woman. She's endured my apoplectic rage. I've given her not a single reason to stay married to me for one year, let alone twenty-five. And yet here she is, as unfathomably beautiful as she was when first I awoke to find her luscious, naked body next to mine. She's still a great lay, too; being faithful to her has been a snap. Not that a king is not tempted. If sitting atop the brashest and most progressive young kingdom this side of the Everdeep doesn't make you a chick magnet, nothing will. Whenever I craved forbidden fruit, I had only to think of her, back in the day: running my kingdom with a firm but gentle hand; spending long hours poring over Alderon's lessons with him; praying to Odin for my safekeeping after I had cursed that unconscionable prick from stem to stern. And if that didn't work, I had only to think of Cassiopeia, whom I lost.

Now? Let's just say that little Elberon has trouble getting up off the Barcalounger. Once, I had one of my wizards concoct a *Virility* potion, and I quaffed it only to suffer from an erection that lasted for four days. I could have made some epic porno films during that period, but it was difficult to sleep with my pecker as stiff as a pole-arm. If Astrid has taken a lover, then she's kept him out of my sight; if she has, I can't really blame her. A woman has needs, after all. Not that those needs would stop me from cutting off the fucker's head.

What about love? Is there still room, in a marriage as old and entrenched as ours, for such a narcissistic, vampiric, and costly emotion? Perhaps Astrid still loves me, after her fashion. We've been at war for many long years, she and I. Our grievances have grown calcified and immutable: she convinced that I've perfected the art of tuning her out; me convinced that her goal is to wear me down to a useless little nub. Even now, Astrid believes that my melancholy is cover for my secret plan to oust her for a younger queen. So, she's been plotting a preemptive strike. She thinks me clueless, but she forgets that I've survived this long by virtue of my brains, as well as my brawn. My own spies have witnessed dark meetings in her chambers, whispered conversations with low men who promise her a painless end for me in my sleep. Phoebes reports of her secretly assembled fleet, of the army, ensconced at Castle de Aur on the neighboring island of Cormorant, awaiting her command to move against the city.

Would she ever go through with it? Probably not, but who the fuck really knows anybody else? Even after twenty-five years, I have no more idea of what goes on in that chick's mind than I do the mind of Odin himself. This much do I know: Astrid enjoys such love from her people that if we ever become true enemies, the Lordship will be torn asunder by civil war—with me the likely loser.

In truth, I still love her desperately, even as I sometimes fantasize about feeding her to my dogs. If true love does exist, it has the shelf life of cottage cheese. True Love implies effortless bliss. True Love requires no sacrifice. Astrid and I have worked the hard soil of our marriage season after season, through drought and flood and bitter winter, so that we might enjoy whatever harvest the gods deem fit for us. Or, to use a less hackneyed metaphor: Love is not a right, nor a gift, nor an excuse. Love is a paycheck. You work your ass off for it, and then you spend it as quickly as you can.

My depression is therefore seasoned with guilt for brooding on my throne like some spoiled child these past two days. Wilberd, my counselors, and my people—they can all go fuck themselves. I don't give a gnome's ass what they think. Astrid, however, deserves better. If only I could give it to her.

When she came with her news, I could barely look her in the eye.

"I still don't want to talk about it," I said.

"I have news," Astrid said. Her back was stiff. If I made the first move and embraced her, would her defenses collapse? Perhaps—but I couldn't bring myself to do it. "Have you eaten?" she asked.

"No."

"If you don't eat, I'll have Phoebes force some stew into you."

You may have noticed certain etymological inconsistencies in the names you've heard: Astrid, Cassiopeia, Phoebes. I'm not making them up; Woerth is a chamber pot of competing cultures and religions from dozens of different universes. We have our Greeks, our Romans, our Norse, our Indians, our Celts, our Chinese, our Egyptians, our Aztecs—and those are just the cultures you recognize. Early in Woerth's history, the Free Kingdoms were continually laid waste from one religious or ethnic conflict or another. Romans slaughtered Celts, Muslims slaughtered Jews, Christians slaughtered Muslims, elves slaughtered dwarfs, and everybody slaughtered the gnomes. After centuries of it, the religious conflict became tedious. There was held a Council of the Wise, at which it was decided that, as all religions were most likely bullshit anyway, there was no reason to hold any particular faith higher than any other. Besides, we humans are most likely descended from ape-like ancestors—at least that's what our time-traveling wizards tell us, and boy, don't the elves get a kick out of pointing out *that* whenever they have a chance. Odin, Zeus, Saturn, Jehovah—when you get down to it, what the hell's the difference? I pray to Odin, sure. Sometimes, I even believe in him. But gods are like assholes: everybody has one.

"So, what's your news?" I asked my wife.

"Lithaine has returned to Woerth."

Astrid might have her plots, but she would never dissemble about Lithaine. She had heard the stories, and she was as terrified of that fucking lunatic as I was.

"When?" I asked, stiffening on my throne.

"I don't know, exactly," she said. "Word came in from a merchant vessel from the Were Coast. Rumors of a White Demon that has assumed the form of an elf lord. Tales of a Chaos army from Helene burning villages to the ground. The last reports had him heading for the Daggerlands. It sounds like Lithaine. We knew if he ever got out, he'd come after you."

"Let him try."

"Should we call off the party?"

Now, there was the question: the party. I dreaded it. There I sat, grievously certain of my own mortality, paralyzed with horror watching my youth spiral down into the Abyss like a turd flushed down the privy. Was I supposed to celebrate? Whoever invented birthday parties was a sick, perverted misanthrope. To put the cap on the kobold, my former adventuring partner, whom we betrayed by using him as a cork to seal the breach between Hell and Woerth, had returned to exact his revenge. Was I number one on his list of paybacks? You bet your ass I was. Best to call off the party and prepare for war.

"Let me think about it," I said to Astrid.

So I did, for a few hours. I called for my pipe and smoked it. Here's what Astrid didn't know: over the past two days, I haven't merely been brooding; I've also been formulating.

Over the years, whenever my soul hurt, my mind sought out Jo Ki-Rin, the keeper of answers—but he had gone silent. Just yesterday, I had searched for him via the Astral Telescope but could find no rumor of him. Did he even exist, I wonder, or had I just imagined him? Yesterday, as I sat ruminating over my pipe after a long, wearying night gazing through the Telescope, I heard that familiar, faint, plaintive call of the pipes, and I heard the Ki-Rin's voice come unbidden to my mind. The past came flooding back, and I was struck dumb with understanding. From deep within my amygdala came a single name.

Xingo.

That was all it took. The entire plan sprang fully formed in my mind, a dark golem of my own making. It was a plan of either perfect good or perfect evil. The moment I conceived of it, I knew it was my destiny. What was it that Redulfo had said, so long ago? Success only becomes probable when you have no other choice.

Calling for a torch, I headed for the dungeons. It was the first time my ass left the throne since Wilberd dropped a dime on me. Down the stairs, past the guards, down more stairs, through the gates, and down into the dank stone corridors where no light shone. Xingo's cell crouched at the end of a long row of cells—mostly empty, but for the few still holding traitors and spies, the names of whom I had long since forgotten. The gaoler handed me the key on a rusted metal ring. I turned key in lock and swung open the cell door. Torchlight fell on the emaciated frame of the gnome, hanging from manacles bolted to the stone. He stank of piss and shit. When the torchlight hit him, his dangling hairy feet twitched.

"A year have you languished in my dungeon, shitbird," I said. "How'd you like to earn your freedom?"

Xingo lifted his head. His beard made him look more dwarf than gnome. His little rat-eyes gleamed in the shadows of his brows.

"Suck my asshole, fuckface," croaked the gnome.

"Enough small talk," I said. "I have a mission for you. Should you choose to accept it, I'll release you from those shackles right now."

A low groan came from the gnome—not of pain nor sorrow, but of anger. He was furious at his own weakness. He'd no choice but to accept my offer, and it sickened him. His despair notably improved my mood.

"What do I have to do?" Xingo asked.

What indeed? I could tell you my plan, but I think not—not yet, anyway. Every tale needs a modicum of suspense, lest it becomes mere dry recitation. Suffice it to say that it has a decent enough chance of failure that I'm in suspense myself—not least because I am forced to entrust it to the squirrelly little piss-bucket who has been trying to kill me for the better part of forty years. Despite his year of degradation, the gnome seemed to grasp the plan quickly enough.

"I'm in," Xingo said.

Calling for the guards, I remanded Xingo into their custody with instructions to clean him up and give him a meal. Then I returned to the Coral Hall, sat the throne, and called for my wife.

"No need to call off the party," I said. "In fact, send a ship back to the Were Coast with a message for Lithaine, if it is him. Tell him that Lord Elberon of the Isles would be delighted if he would attend my Birthday Jubilee as my honored guest."

Astrid gave a half-smile and turned to go.

"And fetch my scribe," I called after her. If that pointy-eared magic boy wants a fight, I'm ready to give him one.

10

As the *Remembrance* potion takes hold, I recall my first meeting with Lithaine, now forty-five years gone, with terrifying clarity. I was newly arrived in Redhauke: that great, teeming, free city hugging the shores of Lake Everdeep, where would-be adventurers from across the free lands flock to seek their fortunes. In its 500-year history, Redhauke has undergone many permutations, both before and after I first arrived there as a cocksure ex-prince. Marauding armies have conquered it. Fire has leveled it. Evil arch-mages have cursed it. The city has seen plagues, riots, gang wars, political corruption, and garbage strikes; once, the entire city was teleported into another universe and its inhabitants enslaved by a race of sentient, spacefaring squid. One wonders why anyone in their right mind would step foot in the place. I can answer in one word: action. It's the action that brings them in.

Redhauke, you see, is like New York City, Casablanca, ancient Rome, Alexandria, the Barbary Coast, and Deadwood, all squashed into one gigantic freak show occupying a parcel of land no larger than downtown Las Vegas. In Redhauke, the word *action* is both instantly grasped and yet still undefinable; it describes a pervasive current, if you will, of money, power, sex, and drugs that can find a man wealthy beyond comprehension or staring at a steaming pile of his own intestines right before the lights go out. You're limited only by your own reserves of strength, cunning, and imagination.

You can play it straight if you want. You can apprentice yourself to one of the great guildhalls and become an artisan of wide renown. You can become a merchant baron, with a fleet of ships and acres of warehouse space at your disposal. Innkeepers, shopkeepers, barbers, apothecaries, artists, and musicians—all are welcome. Those of a military bent can muster with the Redhauke Guard, at once a formidable army and a police force with which you don't want to fuck. The faithful find their homes on the Godsway; more religions have been borne here than at any spot in the Multiverse, and the Apocalypse has come and gone so many times that nobody even notices anymore. Nerds and geeks can enroll in the School of Thaumaturgy, the greatest college of magic in the Free Kingdoms. If crime is your bag, then hie thee to the Thieves Guild, which presides over a smorgasbord of illicit trade in gaming, drugs, spices, slaves, and women. Over the infinite variety of commerce and crime in Redhauke, there rules the omnipresent threat of death—the chance that someone smarter or luckier than you will stick a figurative, or a literal, knife in your back. Redhauke is a city of addicts hooked on the naked adrenaline rush that only the action can deliver.

I would have to wait, however, for my first fix. When I arrived at the outskirts of the city, having just undertaken an arduous journey from my former island home some 400 leagues southeast, I discovered that I came at a troubled time.

There were wars, rumors of wars, and damned lies about wars to the North. Thousands of refugees were streaming southward along the western shore of the Everdeep—hungry, desperate peasants from such obscure kingdoms as the Duchy of Kent and the Folstaff Barony. Their squalid homes had been burnt to the ground, their women violated, their men lined up and shot with arrows or hung and then dumped into mass graves. While there were rumors of Plague Knights, no one really knew exactly who was waging war on whom or why. It didn't matter much, really. Through hardship and horrors, thousands of starving refugees had made their way to Redhauke, where they camped in vast, makeshift shantytowns around the Outer Walls. I hadn't known what to expect when I arrived, but I sure as hell hadn't expected this.

Soon, I had to face facts: I was a refugee myself. My winnings from the Crush the Kobold match had vanished with alarming rapidity, most of it spent on the boat ride across the Hydra Sea, the rest spent losing at skullbones to the merchants with whom I had hitched a ride up the Were Coast. Any hope I had of waltzing into the city and landing a plumb swordsman's job drowned in a sea of stinking, sweating peasants hoping to find food, work, and shelter before winter arrived. I was as expendable as anyone else.

Redhauke was a free city but not an open one. Even when there weren't ten thousand supplicants outside the walls, only those with legitimate business, such as traders and the merchant caravans of great cartels, could count on free passage. The rest of us had to take a number and wait. Some of those lost souls in Doomtown, as the locals had taken to calling it, had been waiting so long that their stomachs bloated with hunger. Crime was rampant, justice swift; be caught thieving, and the Guard would give you five minutes to plead your case before forcing your head onto the chopping block. The best for which a refugee could hope was short work hauling wood or bailing hay on the outlying farms for a loaf of bread or a quick shag with a farmer's daughter. Life outside the city walls was reduced to its essentials: one meal a day and a dry place to sleep made you rich beyond the dreams of avarice.

And so, I found myself sharing the courtyard of an abandoned onion farm with a dozen other cutthroats from the North. They had a well that needed protecting, while I had a sword and knew how to use it. We dug wild onions out of the earth for food and withered the trees with our non-stop farting. I slept on a reed mat in the one-room farmhouse next to a barbarian who picked his teeth with one horny toenail. After a week of such luxury, I was ready to crawl on my knees back to Olderon and beg him to take me back.

11

Once a month, refugees could enter a lottery to win an appointment with a clerk, who would take your application for immigration into the city. On a good week, fifty immigrants were admitted; on a bad week, none. There were more bad weeks than good ones. Only those supplicants with employable skills were considered. I had an admirable set of skills to offer: I could fight with sword and staff, I could mend armor and blade, could pilot any seagoing vessel, and could make rope blindfolded.

The problem was, so could everyone else. Six weeks passed as high summer turned to the first blush of Fall, and I still couldn't get an appointment. At last, I scored one, and I waited anxiously in a winding line of refugees outside a clerk's tent before finally having a chance to tell my tale.

"From where do you hale?" the clerk asked as he scribbled notes on his tablet.

"From the Tradewind Isles," I answered. "The greatest kingdom south of the Hydra Sea."

The clerk snorted. "That provincial backwater? They're barely out of the Stone Age and rife with cannibalism, from what I've heard. You're lucky to have escaped."

I resisted the urge to snap his neck. "So, my application is in order?"

"Your skills are adequate, though we've no shortage of brawny men in Redhauke," he said. "Perhaps if you paid the application fee in advance..."

He regarded me from beneath a raised brow. No need to wonder where this was headed. Fortunately, I had come prepared. Olderon had given me leave to take what personal effects I could carry; since he didn't preclude it, I took his offer to include my own store of the Crown jewels. Specifically, I had taken my fleet ring—an impressive bauble with intertwining gold anchor chains wrapped around a tiny platinum sea drake. It was the only item I dared pinch that Dad wouldn't immediately miss.

I held it up by its chain so the sunlight reflected off its enticing contours. The clerk's reaction was much as I had expected.

"Let's get to the Devil's business," I said. "This ring isn't stolen, though you'll have to take my word on that. It's worth one hundred and fifty auratae if it's worth a copper. Give my application full consideration, and we'll take it to a broker of your choosing, sell it, and split the profits."

Sometimes you can hear the bells ringing in the head of a man who learns that his ship has come in. The clerk asked where he could meet me that evening, and I told him.

"I'll be in touch," he said, closing his book and leaping from his stool.

That evening, the clerk and two guards found me at the onion farm and laid a mace upside my head when I wasn't looking. So much for my fleet ring. It was a hard lesson, but I learned it—always assume the worst about people, and they'll never disappoint you.

Hours later, I awoke with blood caked in my hair, a headache the size of Mount Doom, and the urge to vomit every few minutes. I took a quick personal inventory: no prospects, and nothing to my name but a sword and thirty copper pennies. Concussion notwithstanding, I decided that a good drunk was in order. That was Doomtown's one saving grace: you might not find food, but you could always find drink. I needed a fire, a flagon, and some company.

All three requirements lay just a few camps to the west, where I settled in with a mixed bag of swarthy men, a few dwarfs, and a loud-mouth half-imp who couldn't hold his liquor. Normally, no one at the fire would have suffered any contact with the imp-spawn; on the social ladder, his type was considered one step below sewer rats. With a strict prohibition against brawls or duels within sight of the city walls, however, we had little choice but to give him a spot at the fire. Fortunately, he was already in the bag. He snored loudly while the campfire talk turned to the latest rumors around Doomtown—particularly the rumor that refugee children were being kidnapped. The stories were all hearsay. The dwarfs claimed to have seen masked and hooded men stealing through the camps one night, snatching up children in sacks and spiriting them away. If children were disappearing, I was more inclined to blame dysentery than kidnappers, but what did I know?

After several hours of such talk lubricated with countless flagons of ale, I found myself staring at the embers of the waning fire. Only the hardcores were left—the dwarfs showing off their tattoos to a buxom gnome wench, a minstrel plucking out some forgettable tune on a lyre, and the half-imp. I was lost in thought, attuned to that elemental, symbiotic connection between camper and campfire present since the dawn of time. I scarcely noticed the cloaked figure that stepped up just outside the ring of firelight.

"You," said the newcomer, in a voice soft but of deadly intent. "Imp-spawn. Stand up."

Raising his head, the half-imp revealed a dull gaze addled with drink. "Oy?" he asked.

"You heard me," said the stranger.

The half-imp lurched to his feet as if constructing himself out of spare parts. Locating a passable center of balance, he glared at the stranger across the campfire.

"You want to have a go with Arty?" he asked, snorting with derision. "I've had bigger shits than you after breakfast. Elves—good only for slavery. I'll have you cleaning my dirty bits with yer tongue before the next bell."

The stranger pulled back the hood of his cloak to reveal the pale, angular face and pointed ears of an elf. And a young one at that—he couldn't have been a day over forty. His hair was the color of new wheat, pulled back in a simple ponytail. Filled with fell purpose, he leveled his gaze upon his prey.

"You?" said Arty. "Back to your tree-house, magic boy."

"Draw your weapon," the elf said.

"My pleasure, mate." The half-imp reached for the haft of the pockmarked scimitar fastened to his hip. How surprised we all were when, a split second later, the poor bastard fell dead with two arrows piercing his heart. He had only a moment to stare incredulously at the two shafts before giving up the ghost.

"Nice grouping," remarked one of the dwarfs.

The elf might have made a clean getaway—but as luck would have it, a patrol of guards swung by on their midnight rounds. Three beefy soldiers wielding broadswords stepped up to the fire. The elf studied their approach. If thoughts of his head in a basket rattled him, he didn't show it.

"What's all this then?" asked the patrol sergeant.

12

W hy I did what I did at that moment, I can't precisely say. Perhaps it was my innate understanding that a good bowman would make a valuable ally. I know what you're thinking—an elf with a bow, how clichéd. Like all good clichés, this one is rooted in truth; elves learn the bow before they're weaned from the tit. It's the only way their armies can prevail on the battlefield, as they tend to pussy out when the slaughter gets personal. In my youth, I disdained the bow as an unmanly weapon; after a few years of adventuring with elves, I learned wisdom. Never close with an enemy you can dispatch from a safe distance.

So, I leaped up and presented myself to the sergeant. "I saw the whole thing, sir," I said.

"Let's have it, then."

"He fell on them."

"Fell on what?"

"The arrows." I pointed at the two shafts stuck in the half-imp's chest. "He fell on them." I looked to the two dwarfs for help. They glanced at each other, then at the sergeant.

"Right," they said. The elf said nothing.

"Fell on them, did he?" asked the sergeant. The guards chortled

48 RICK FERGUSON

together. "Poor blighters fall onto arrows all the time, don't they? Why, just the other day me mum-in-law tripped on the sofa and got a bolt right up her cooze. Unlike this bloke, I'd say she fancied it!"

As the guards exploded in laughter, I stepped closer to the sergeant. "Look here," I said, intending to slip him a few of the pennies I had left in my pocket. "There's no harm done. What's one less imp-spawn in the world? Why don't we just—"

An arrow shaft sprouted from the sergeant's right eye. Two more arrows pierced the throats of the other two guards. The three shots took less than two seconds. The sergeant looked right at me with his remaining eye, his gaze laced with wild surprise and annoyance. Then he dropped dead.

I wheeled around to face the elf. "Why the hell did you do that?" I bellowed.

But the elf was gone, bounding toward a nearby hay barn with a flaming brand from the fire clutched in his hand. He lobbed the brand through the barn's open loft, then fled into the darkness. Within seconds, the barn was ablaze.

There's gratitude for you, I thought. No wonder they were a dying race.

13

I took off after the elf. A nearby gang of Southrons saw him torch the barn, which prompted them to leap up from their own fire and start torching other buildings. Vaulting over another campfire, I plowed straight into the two dwarfs, who were now beating the bard with his own lyre. More fights broke out. Mobs formed. Gangs of filthy, underfed refugees clashed, wailing on one another with fists, staves, and blades. I got caught up in it and had to deal out punishment myself just to stay alive. That bloody elf had started a riot.

For a half-hour or more the raging mobs surged, until the Redhauke Guard emerged from the Chimera Gate in full riot gear. They formed up behind a pair of dwarf-designed street cleaners— fearsome steam-powered battle tanks fronted with whirring scythes that took limbs and heads without mercy. Close behind these mechanical beasts followed the guards, firing crossbows liberally into the crowd, aiming for the biggest targets they could find. That's when I took cover under a capsized hay wagon. No magic girdle was going to protect me from a crossbow bolt in the heart.

Experienced as they were in such matters, the Guard soon had the crowd under control. Bucket brigades formed to douse the bigger fires. A few smaller outbuildings burned the rest of the night, lifting

their oily coils of smoke into the starless sky. As a lesson to trouble-
makers, the bodies were left to lie until morning.

When the carnage at last abated, I picked my way through the
bodies and rubble back to the campfire. The elf sat alone on a stump,
roasting a potato on a stick as if nothing had happened. His bow lay
handily nearby. I took a seat near him.

"That was some diversion, elf," I said, "but it was overkill. I could
have paid those guards off for five coppers each and been done
with it."

"I didn't ask for your help," the elf said, keeping his gaze on his
potato.

"If a man only receives help when he asks for it, then he lacks
character," I said. "Let's just say I was in the mood to make a friend
tonight. What did you have against the imp-spawn, anyway?"

The elf looked up, and his eyes were the crystalline blue of a
frozen Northern lake. The rumor of a smile brushed his lips.

"He called me a pointy-eared magic boy," he said.

That got me—I burst into laughter. I hadn't laughed that hard
since my brother fell down a well. The elf's smile crept closer.

"My name is Lithaine," he said. "I have no drink, but I have potatoes and bread. Make a meal, if you wish."

"I have the drink," I said, reaching for my flask. "Let's toast our
homelands. Where's yours?"

The elf's smile fled, and his mood changed from overcast to
threatening rain. His eyes narrowed to slits.

"Let's get one thing straight," said Lithaine. "You ask me where I'm
from again, and I'll kill you. Got it?"

I shrugged. "Don't worry about me, elf," I said. "I like you—you're
uncomplicated."

Then we both laughed, together. His friendship was won. That's
how I met Lithaine, my oldest and dearest friend. Now, he's coming to
kill me. From his perspective, I certainly deserve it.

14

From the earliest days of my legendary career, Lithaine and I were inseparable. Wilberd I met several years later. Then there was Amabored: the most ferocious, bloodthirsty son of a bitch with whom I ever had the pleasure of campaigning. The wizard Redulfo completed the original quartet, long before he made the unfortunate decision to open an enchanted egg in the Temple of Pain Eternal on the Sunless Sea, absorbed the Bad Brain, and had his alignment transformed from Neutral Good to Lawful Evil. We sort of avoided him after that. People change, sure, but within reason, and who wants a fucking evil mastermind around anyway? Tough break for him, especially after we incinerated his corpse and the Crimson Hand transferred his soul into the body of a big, stinky black dragon. Was it our fault that we had to kill him twice?

Cassiopeia came along just in time to for me to fuck over Melinda. There was the paladin Malcolm, a standup warrior who didn't deserve what he got from Lithaine at the end. The ranger James wound up living the good life after marrying the Queen of Kenwood. The half-elf Lindar and the dwarf Andrigan joined the team late; they were both skilled adventurers, though I seem to remember keeping Lindar's corpse pickled in a barrel for a few weeks until we could get him to a cleric for a proper resurrection. Others, names too numerous to mention, came and went. Some came to a bloody end. Those of us who survived did so by finding an edge and exploiting it. I had my magic girdle and my double-bladed battle-axe. Amabored bore the sword Stormcrow, Lithaine his bow and angel-haunted blade. To prosper as an adventurer, you must deal death swiftly; those who fail to develop this skill soon become fertilizer. When you see a Gelatinous Cube bearing down on your ass in some dank dungeon corridor, it's time to put on your big-boy pants.

By the time we were tasked with saving the Woerth, the lineup of heroes was set: Amabored, Lithaine, Malcolm, James, Wilberd, Andrigan, Lindar, Cassie, and me. Together, we formed the Second Quest of the Dread Plain: each one of us essential to the success of this Quest, each destined to bear a piece of Koschei's unbearable soul. Not long after Koschei fell and the acclaim died down, our egos got the best of us. We argued, split into factions, and talked shit about each other. And in our own way, each one of us went mad.

TAKE AMABORED, FOR INSTANCE. LAST YEAR, I HAD OCCASION TO MEET him again. I hadn't seen him for two years prior, at least. I was in Kenwood attending some ceremony or another at the invitation of James, who had served as the country's regent since the fall of Koschei. Kenwood is a land of rolling hills and hedgerows, sheep country, the sort of green and pleasant land that people think Ireland is, until they arrive and see what the Irish have done to it. James had it soft: The Queen was a knockout, the kingdom was at peace, the gentry was landed and prosperous, and the peasants knew their place. He spent most of his free time roaming the back forty with his Ranger crew, slaughtering the occasional imp raiding party and holding forth with tales of high adventure at the border pubs. He enjoyed peace of mind that I could only admire from a distance.

When we sat up late one night in his study smoking cigars and drinking good single-malt Scotch, however, James looked troubled. We hardly ever found it necessary to reminisce about the old times.

We had both stared into the Abyss, had both seen our naked souls exposed before us like quivering jellyfish. What was the point of scratching at old scars? Something was bugging him, but he was too much of a stoic to spit it out.

"What's the matter?" I asked. "Queen Arianna won't give your pecker a rest?"

"We're fine, thank you." James sat facing the fire, his boots resting on the haunches of one of his sleeping mastiffs. Years of weathering had given his face the look of a ruddy hillside; his bushy gray mustache adorned his lip like a lion lounging on a rock. The haunted look in his eyes from the Dread Wars was mostly a memory.

"What is it, then?" I asked. "You look like my grandfather's ball sack."

James poured himself another dram of scotch. He held the glass to his eye and watched the firelight caper through the amber prism.

"Amabored is in country," he said finally.

"Mother of God! Amabored? When? Where?"

"He's camped out in the Beradon Forest. Been there a fortnight. Him and about two hundred men."

"Then why the hell isn't he here drinking with us?"

"You haven't seen him lately, Elberon. He's changed, and not for the better."

That wasn't news. We had all changed, each of us damaged in some irreparable way. But Amabored was always the best of us: the strongest, the quickest wit, the bravest, the most dependable. In his youth, he bore the air of a proud archangel come to Woerth to stir up shit for the mortals. The Bronze God, we called him. Men feared him; women spread their legs for him. In battle, his trusty broadsword whirled overhead like a helicopter blade, slicing through bone and sinew at will. Stormcrow was its name; when it took a life, it rent the air with a teeth-rattling thunderclap, a white-hot net of lightning arcing along its tempered length as our enemies evacuated their bowels. There were several kings' ransoms offered for his death or capture, but they never touched him. Some thought him demon-possessed.

To me, however, he was just Amabored. Around the campfire, he used to fart loud enough to set the wolves howling. He undertook epic drunken benders that lasted for weeks. He and I nearly came to blows more than once; although I was supremely confident in my abilities, I was never certain that I could take him. He was a badass son of a bitch, and I was glad to have him on my side.

Who knew how he had changed since? It had been ten years since I'd laid eyes on him. Time is a toilet, and our lives spiral down the bowl.

"So what?" I asked. "None of us have changed for the better. Mostly, we're just parodies of our younger selves."

"He's found religion," James said.

"Really? You mean, beyond the usual lip service?"

James stood and reached for his cane. He had nearly lost a leg at the hand of the undead knight Eckberd in the great siege of Helene—the same leg that was crushed into jelly during the bugbear ambush in the Shadow Pass. Cassie did the best she could for him at the time, but those black blades don't just hew flesh and bone—they leave a scar on your soul. Just ask a certain famous halfling I could mention.

"This is wild-eyed, scroll-thumping stuff," James said. "He's preaching the Awakening. The Millennium is bringing the crazies out of their caves, but I never thought Amabored was the type. There has to be a score in it somewhere."

I stroked my beard. "Odd. Self-destructive. Does he pose a threat?"

"Not yet. But he's building a cult—or an army. The peasants I can handle, but he's converted a few of my Rangers. I need my Rangers. The borders are getting dangerous again."

"Did you tell him to knock it off?"

"Not in so many words. He's a mate, you know. What can you do?"

"He has to be playing an angle. We just need to figure out what it is. You've invited him to the palace?"

"Yes. He won't come."

"Then we'll ride out to see him," I said. "Have a couple of horses ready at dawn."

15

The ride through Kenwood took two days. We spent the night at an inn near the Royal Turnpike, where we signed a few autographs and posed for a few pictures with the innkeeper. The barmaid was a comely lass with huge tracts of land, and in my younger days, I would have happily sheathed my sword in her warm scabbard. But my younger days were a lifetime ago.

We set out on the road again at dawn with James' small band of retainers trailing us along the Turnpike. Having the opportunity to study James at length, I found that he lived a life of rare equanimity. What had he ever wanted but a forest clearing and a star-strewn sky? The fame, the adulation, the chance to stamp his imprimatur on the wealthiest kingdom south of Redhauke—he could toss it all in the shitter without a second thought. His association with Kenwood bought him security and freedom. We had cashed in, he and I, as a reward for the terror we had endured. Yet, even as James found contentment, the same eluded me. I could only chalk it up to some fundamental flaw in my own character.

Toward evening of the second day, we rode down from a range of low wooded foothills into a shallow river valley a few marches across. Draped in valley mist lay the river, which curved around a forested peninsula before slipping off into the foothills. There were no bridges in sight.

"That's the Beradon," James said. "The ferry will take us across."

I recognized the landscape—we weren't far from the site of my epic battle with Redfang the Terrible, so many years ago. Amabored had chosen a strong defensive position; if I recalled the map correctly, there was marshland on the other side of that forest. With two hundred men and the river at his back, he could hold out against a siege indefinitely. Or at least until James called down his war barges.

When we had crossed a third of the valley, we were met by a team of five outriders—hardened campaigners with notched blades, pitted armor, and scarred flesh. They might once have been mercenaries, but now their eyes burned with the illuminating light of the one true faith. Whatever Amabored was feeding them, they were gorging on it.

Their captain, a sweaty brute with a deep scar splitting his face, nodded his welcome. A loaded crossbow swung from his saddle.

"Lord James, Lord Elberon," the captain said. "Lord Amabored sends his regards. If you'll follow us, please."

James and I exchanged a look. The lands for a thousand miles were at peace. No imp horde would dare show its colors within the Kenwood borders. And yet, by the look of this crew, you'd think there was a war on. As we picked our way along the path, the guards were all appropriately deferential. Behind their deference, however, they were jovial, arrogant, and unimpressed with our celebrity. James and I could slay every man-jack without breaking a sweat, but they didn't care. They grinned at us, and they grinned at each other. It was disconcerting.

A short ride later found us at the ferry. "You'll need to leave your mounts and retainers here, my Lords," said the captain, "and turn over your weapons to us."

James and I exchanged another look.

"My ass," I said.

"Lord Amabored's orders, I'm afraid," said the captain, taking a step back to stand with his men. "No weapons within the camp."

"Amabored giving orders in my own kingdom?" snorted James. "You tell him to shove those orders up his ass!"

There came the familiar sound of a metallic snake slithering swiftly around us. We had heard that snake a hundred times before, and our reaction was instinctive. James' sword sliced open one guard. My axe sent another's arm spinning from his shoulder. Then came a flash of multihued light and some music, and I found myself toppling over, my every muscle turned to concrete. I couldn't move an eyelash.

A guard rolled me over, and then the captain loomed over me with an unrolled scroll in hands. A *Paralyzation* charm, no doubt— and, thank Odin, not the fatal kind, since my heart and lungs still worked.

"Forgive the sorcery, my Lords," said the captain, "but I can't have you slaying any more of my men before we get you to your quarters. If Lord Amabored permits, you may then slay as many as you like."

The outriders buried their dead, picked us up like sacks of wheat and delivered us to another armed escort on the ferry. I was livid. *Paralyzation* charms wear off—and when this one did, I was going to kill every armed man within fifty leagues of this valley. Starting with Amabored.

Across the river, we were transferred to a third team, who loaded us onto litters and dragged us onto a path flanked by a pair of wooden guard towers topped with trebuchets on swiveling mounts. The crest of the ridge overlooking the river had been converted into breastworks. I had laid enough sieges in my day to know how tough this place would be to assault; those trebuchets could hurl a spear through a suit of plate armor.

The charm had degraded enough to allow our mouths to move. "He's just visiting, you said?" I whispered to James.

"He's a mate," James said. "What can you do?"

Given the number of armed men camped along our route, I began to wonder if James's Rangers could take them in a pitched battle. The figure of 200 men was obviously outdated; there were easily 500 soldiers camped in the forest. They were seasoned veterans, bearing the arms and armor of a dozen kingdoms, their past crimes and grievances forgotten for the opportunity to serve at Amabored's pleasure, whatever that was.

Soon enough, we had our first clue. Amabored's men dragged us to a glade dotted with tents, dropped to their haunches, and lit pipes while they waited for us to regain the use of our legs. Another hour passed, and we could walk again. The captain ordered our hands bound. I cast a beckoning glance at James. He shook his head —not yet.

Leaving behind the soldiers' camp, we passed through the civilian campsite. The woods on either side of the trail were pimpled with more tents, smoldering campfires, and hammocks lashed between trees. There were no campers in sight. Had Amabored gone Kurtz on us? Was he now ensconced somewhere deep within the forest building altars to himself out of human skulls? A mile further in, we heard the faint sounds of percussion, pipes, and lutes playing. A festival, then. I relaxed a little. Amabored could always throw a good party.

Then we saw the crosses.

16

There were a dozen of them reaching skyward on the north side of the trail, as incongruous as a pile of horseshit in the Kraken. Over each cross flapped a blue banner emblazoned with a winged sword—Amabored's latest heraldry, we surmised. From each cross hung a crucified wizard. That they were wizards, there was no doubt; after you've been around them enough, you can pick them out of a crowd. They're fond of facial hair and flamboyant dress, though they're not as effete as you might think—I've known wizards who could break me in two, magic girdle notwithstanding. With their billowing, multicolored silks, now soiled with dried blood, these wizards looked like they might have hailed from up North, perhaps even from Amabored's home in the land of the Tiger Nomads. They had been dead perhaps three days. The crows had already taken most of their faces.

The guards waited while we paused to have a look at them. It took a lot to get James riled up. Crucifying men within his borders was a good way to do it.

"That's just great," James said. "Who does he think he is, Pontius Pilate?"

"Maybe he found them like this," I offered.

"Fat chance."

Fat chance indeed. We moved on. The music grew louder. We heard the buzz of a crowd, and the trail dumped us into a wide meadow, across which was spread a vast throng of young revelers. I dug the scene immediately. It was high summer, so the heat of the day had prompted most of these kids to drop trou, as it were. Topless young maids lounged in the flattened grass, twisting their hair into French braids or painting one another's faces with crushed berries. Shirtless young men, their hair long and unkempt, their bodies bronzed, played hacky-sack in small groups or cooked veggie burritos on small hibachi grills. The pungent odor of pipeweed drifted out of the myriad tents dotting the meadow. Along the south edge of the clearing, a line of makeshift vendor stands sold everything from glass beads to hemp clothing to crude hand-painted portraits of Amabored in beatific poses playing the guitar or gazing reverently at the sky; every portrait included the winged sword motif. A stage near the opposite edge of the meadow supported a lively band of minstrels, noodling out melodies that drifted across the field as a crowd of dancers twirled in endless circles nearby.

"It's worse than I thought," said James.

One of the guards pointed at a sprawling, wooden-walled, multi-room tent on the far side of the meadow. "He's in there," the guard said. "He's expecting you."

With that, the guards loosened our bonds. With no more reason to start any shit, we wended our way through the crowd towards the tent, stepping around the spun-out partiers sprawled on the ground. As men of stature, we were used to drawing wary stares from passers-by. No one here gave us a second look, however, unless it was to offer us "sheets," "shrooms," "molly," a toke on a pipe, or a hit off a hand-rolled smoke. James was nonplussed, but I thought of how nice it would be to hang there awhile, enjoy the naked girls, and get bent like the old days in Redhauke. We were so poor back then that guarding drug shipments was one of the few ways we could make any money. Of course, we partook whenever we could. Being Lawful Good, James was opposed to mind-altering substances. We Neutrals could do as we liked—and believe me, we did.

When we reached Amabored's tent, I saw that little needle-dicked bug-fucker Xingo. That's when the situation nearly got out of hand.

From the old man, I inherited a short fuse. Since a short fuse leads often to a short life, I tried to keep my temper reigned in—but that gnome cocksucker had stuck a fucking poisoned dagger in my back, and I defy you to forgive somebody for that. When I saw his oily complexion and cheesy handlebar mustache, I was on him like a dwarf on a ham sandwich. He was lounging on a divan and pawing at a young maiden too stoned to care that his hands were in her pants. A nano-second after I laid eyes on him, I had pulled a small hand-axe from a stand near the tent's entrance and sent it whistling toward the gnome's skull.

Age, unfortunately, had not slowed Xingo's rat-like reflexes. He launched himself off the couch as the hand-axe thudded into it. The comatose maiden flopped to the floor. I whirled toward the gnome, and three daggers slammed into the doorframe a few inches from my head. He'd have to do better than that.

"Let me trim that mustache for you, gnome scum!" I bellowed.

"Sit on this, asshole!" Xingo answered, saluting me with his stubby middle finger.

Left unchecked, the two of us would have leveled the tent trying to murder each other and killed a dozen innocent bystanders in the process. Fortunately, James tackled me before I could take another swing.

"Turn me loose!" I cried. "I'll pop his head like a pimple!"

"This isn't the time!" said James, holding me back. "Do you want to start a shooting war?"

Xingo had scurried behind the bar, where he watched me with his beady rat-eyes. "You can't touch me, fuckwad!" the gnome cried. "I'm under Amabored's protection! Lay a finger on me, and he'll part your hair all the way to your prick!"

"Amabored protect *you*?" I scoffed. "Fat chance!"

"The gnome's right," said a familiar voice from behind me. "He's with me."

17

"I t's like this," Amabored said after order had been restored. "Anyone who pledges himself to my banner has his past sins utterly wiped away. 'Plenary indulgence,' I call it. A lot of people want the chance to start over."

Xingo had made himself scarce, which meant that I could relax my guard enough to enjoy a flagon of ale from Amabored's private stash. Still, I kept my back to the wall. Never trust a gnome; if they weren't all conniving, backstabbing little shits, they'd have been wiped out long ago.

"That little puss-filled boil has tried to kill us both more times than I can count," I said, "and you've forgiven him?"

"Why not? He's smart enough to stay close to his enemies, and I'm one of them," said Amabored. "Besides, gnome assassins are useful and hard to come by. He's promised to start rubbing out wizards for me."

"Speaking of wizards," said James, "what about those poor bastards at the head of the trail? We're trying to attract trade to this kingdom. Crucifixions are fine for the Romans, but they don't play well in the Midwest."

"It was unavoidable." Amabored set his ale aside and stood,

stretching his white wings with a luxurious rustle of great feathers. When I say wings, by the way, I mean *wings*—Amabored had a real pair sprouting out of his back.

He wasn't born with them. For most of his life, Amabored was a garden-variety human swordsman. Then, when we took our sojourn with the Cloud Riders during the Quest for the Sunless Sea, he met Bellasa. She was the Cloud King's daughter, naturally, so he could marry her only by agreeing to enter the Sky Temple and take the wings to become one of her people. Sporting a pair of wings sounds cool, but to Amabored they were often a curse. They smelled like the flanks of a wet sheepdog, for one thing. He was always shedding goddamn feathers all over the place, for another. Lice were a problem. Seriously, there was almost nothing cool about them.

He could really fly, though. I never understood the aerodynamics —to generate that kind of lift, you'd think he'd need a thirty-foot wingspan, but his spanned no more than ten. While he couldn't take off from the ground, if he threw himself off a cliff, then he could soar with the eagles. He kept the wings as a tribute to Bellasa, but he stopped flying. As far as I know, he's never been back to the Greensward.

Shortly after he gained his wings, Amabored encountered another curse that temporarily turned his skin fluorescent green. Imagine for a moment that you're an illiterate peasant residing in some messy border village, your head full of superstitious mumbo-jumbo, and a flying, glowing, green-skinned warrior with a sword that speaks thunder and hurls lightning bolts comes swooping into town. No wonder the peasants thought he was one of the Fallen. Though he no longer glowed green, he still cut an impressive figure, even in his advancing age. All three of us were used to attracting men-at-arms to fight under our banners. Amabored's armies did more than follow him—they worshiped him.

"Unavoidable?" James asked. His mustache bristled like a wall of spears. "You *unavoidably* had to nail those wizards to crosses?"

"Ah, but these aren't just any wizards," Amabored said. He allowed the thinnest of smiles. "I finally caught him."

James and I exchanged glances. "You don't mean—" I said.

"Jaspin Spellbinder himself."

"Spinning Korean fuck chairs!" I cried. "Seriously?"

"Didn't you recognize the foul stench of donkey semen when you walked past the crosses?"

Jaspin-fucking-Spellbinder! We had chased that fu-manchued hemorrhoid from one end of the Multiverse to another, and always he had slipped the noose—even in our moment of triumph, when Koschei lay dead before us, the Deathless One's triumphant comeback tour cut tragically short when my battle-axe parted his hair all the way down to his throat. Who knew, way back when in those halcyon days of yore in Redhauke, that a nondescript if marginally shady tavern proprietor and retired mid-level illusionist would turn out to be the key guy fucking up our program? From the moment we first stumbled into the Suds 'n Shade in search of cheap libations, that asshole was working for the Hand—when he wasn't working for my father, that is. When we faced down the lemming imps, he was there. When we nearly came to ruin in the bowels of the Blue Falcon, he was watching. When the Empress Wilomina took up the Mace of Malice and became the Black Countess reborn, he stood beside her. His machinations nearly capsized our quest a dozen times, and always the wizard had escaped our clutches. Now here he was, lashed to a cross and drawing flies. Still, I felt little of the blue blaze of cold triumph I might have expected to feel at the sight. Mostly, I was disappointed that Amabored had gotten to the douchebag before I had.

"I don't believe it!" James said. "I thought Jaspin left this universe?"

"He came back," Amabored said. "The rest of them are his apprentices. They were working for the Sultan right before he razed my capital. Greedy motherfucker must have needed the dough. Let's just say he never saw me coming."

"You lost your *capital*?" I cried.

"The Sultan sent a fucking skeleton army backed with werewolf mercenaries. How was I going to stand up to that? Then Jaspin's crew sent Nightshades to murder my clerics so I couldn't send the lot of them back to Hell. The Sultan's men sat on their asses and watched while the undead tore us apart. I saw the best soldiers in the Nomad Kingdoms eaten alive. Had to flee my lands with my tail tucked. Now, I find myself in need of a new army. So, here we are."

"Bloody Hell," I said. We'd all witnessed such massacres in the past. For James and me, it was thirty years ago. While I'd been keeping my throne warm down South, Amabored had been fighting for his kingdom. Even for trained heroes like the three of us, the undead are a pain in the ass. Your average illiterate foot soldier shits himself at his first sight of a skeleton warrior, which leaves your veterans to face alone the red-hot anvil of death. Without a phalanx of priests to turn the Infernals, Amabored's army never stood a chance.

"You started a religion just so you could rebuild your army," James said. It wasn't a question. "I'll be damned. But you might have asked me before you started cherry-picking my rangers. You know I'll give you a wide berth, but that's the kind of thing I can't let go."

"You started a religion?" I asked.

"What choice did I have?" asked Amabored. "I was broke. My country was gone. My army was decimated." He took out pouch and pipe, and a moment later the pungent bouquet of pipeweed filled the tent. "There's naught left in the Nomad Lands but boys and old bastards. And when you have no tender, declaring a jihad is the quickest way to recruit. The Sultan may be sleeping in my bed, but I'm still here. He couldn't kill me. And he knows I'll be back."

"You're an evil genius, I'll give you that," said James. "So, what's your angle?"

"The Seven."

"The Seven are a myth," snorted James.

"Some of your rangers think otherwise," said Amabored.

To most scholars, the Seven Dragons of World's End are an urban legend, like the old story where the guy picks up a fabulous elf maiden in a tavern and later wakes up in a bathtub full of ice with both his kidneys gone. Others claim they're real, that they sleep in a cavern leagues below the Dread Keep surrounded by magma, and that their dreams create the Chaos music that powers all sorcery on Woerth. The Seven are said to be the Proto-Dragons, the spawn of Tiamat and the progenitors of each dragon species: Red, Black, White, Green, Blue, Silver, and Copper. The Time Lords Gygax and Rigsby—Koschei's former apprentices and members of the original Quest that took him down—claimed to have vanquished and imprisoned them at Koschei's behest. They even recorded the entire battle for posterity with Rigsby's Staff of Seeing, although the authenticity of the recording remains in dispute. Naturalists examining ancient dragon skeletons, meanwhile, have pretty well established their evolutionary heritage; supposedly, they're descended from prehistoric cockatiels. Either theory sounds plausible to me. After all, dragons are magical creatures, not trilobites. What do I know? I'm just a simple swordsman.

"I always thought the story was bullshit," Amabored said. "But then I had a vision."

"I told you he was nuts," said James.

Amabored grinned in acknowledgment. "As I stood knee-deep in werewolf limbs on the battlefield of Oxcipius Plain, watching the Sultan's undead army slaughter my men, I was struck blind and dumb by a lightning bolt that descended from a clear starlit sky. It lit my ass up, and I fell to my knees. I was sure that I had been nailed with a Force Hammer by one of the Sultan's clerics, and that werewolves would soon be fighting over my intestines. Then the sky was rent as if a great door opened between our universe and another—and I beheld, ringed with the holy light of *logos*, the winged and unbearably majestic form of Metatron, the Herald of El, He who dreams the Multiverse."

James and I exchanged glances. *Time to get the butterfly net*, James' eyes told me.

Amabored stood and cast his gaze heavenward. His eyes burned with righteous fire. If it was an act, then it was a good one; the guards near the tent entrance knelt before him and cast their gazes to the ground.

"I feared that the Herald of the Word might turn me to stone right there," Amabored continued. "When Metatron spoke, his voice seemed to issue from my spine and fill my head with exploding thunderbolts.

"'*My child,*' spoke Metatron. '*In one year hence, the Seven Children of Barbēlō, she who is called Tiamat, the Mother of Chaos, will destroy the Woerth with Hellfire. Only thou may prevent this. Wilt thou take up the Sword of El?*'

"'But how?' I cried. The sounds of battle, the devastation around me, the very ground on which I stood, all fell away as if I had slipped off a cloak. I stood naked, exposed before the majesty of the Throne. 'Why me? What must I do?'

"'*Thou must not allow the keepers of knowledge to open the Seven Gates. Slay the keepers, and the doors will close forever. Fail in this task, and the Hour of Chaos will arrive. The Woerth will be devoured.*'"

"You've told this story more than once," said James.

"And then, a vision of a shield, emblazoned with a winged sword, appeared before me," Amabored continued, ignoring James. "The earth shook. Fearing that my life had ended, I collapsed on the ground. The sky split again with a blast of mighty trumpets, and Metatron vanished in a flash of blinding golden light. For a long while, I lay prone, convinced that I was dead. Hours later, with the sun approaching noon, I finally awoke. Around me lay my devastated army, their bodies already picked clean by poachers. Fortunately, so covered was I in blood and entrails that the Sultan's men had left me for dead. The vision had saved my life."

"So, you had a vision," I said. "What's that got to do with nailing wizards to crosses?"

"Everything. Don't you see? '*Slay the keepers of knowledge,*' he said. Wizards are the keepers of knowledge. '*The Hour of Chaos,*' he said. That's the turn of the Millennium, when the Bug kicks in and all Hell breaks loose. The Proto-Dragons sleep behind the Seven Doors; I have to slay enough Chaos wizards to ensure that the good guys can patch the glyphs guarding the doors. I've already taken care of the Spellbinder and his crew; there are only a hundred or so Chaos wizards left of high enough level to keep the Doors open. That limits the field considerably. Once I've rubbed them out, the Woerth will be saved, ushering in a new Millennium of peace—made possible by yours truly, the chosen Sword of El. Who wouldn't join such a noble quest?"

James and I stared flabbergasted at our friend. If this was simply a scheme to raise an army and win back his kingdom, then it was overkill by a wide margin. Hell, James would front him the money for an army just to get him out of Kenwood. It couldn't be that simple. Was it a long con of some kind? Amabored has the best poker face I've ever seen; he's so inscrutable that you're better off taking what he says at face value. If he tells you that he's attempting to prevent Armageddon by murdering Chaos wizards, then you're better off believing him. It's the safe play.

"You're out of your mind!" James said. He stood up so abruptly that Amabored's guards leaped to their feet and grasped their sword hilts. As if.

"I've never been saner," Amabored said. Rather than answer James's challenge, he sat back down on his sleeping silks.

"You call slaughtering wizards to satisfy the whims of some battle-field hallucination *sane*? Do you have any idea what the Council of Thaumaturgy will do once they get wind of your little jihad? They'll send down a rain of death on this place that'll make the Siege of Helene look like a game of touch football!"

"I caught them up North, so you're in the clear. But make no mistake: Those motherfuckers deserved death—the Spellbinder most of all. Either of you would have greased him if you'd had the chance, so spare me the sanctimony. We're doing the Lord's work."

"The Lord's work?!" I had never seen James so angry. He stood there red-faced, too livid for words. Then he turned on his heel and stormed out of the tent.

I reached for Amabored's pipe, which he had placed on a table next to a cheesy ceramic bust of Elvis Presley that made the King look strangely like a Filipino waiter. I lit it and took a long drag, letting the smoke work its magic. When in doubt, self-medicate.

"He's right to be angry," I said. "If you tried this foolishness down in the Lordship, I'd have to flush you out. You're a brother, Amabored, and we love you. But this is beyond the pale. I hope you're playing an angle."

"Maybe I am playing an angle. Maybe I'm not," Amabored said. His eyes flashed with wry humor, as if he wondered whether I knew more than I was letting on. "If he's worried that I'm going to bring ruin to his country, he shouldn't. He offered his hospitality and I took it. When he wants me to leave, then I'll leave. While I'm here, I'll defend myself. Once the Chaos wizards get wind of my plan, they'll come after me."

"When will it end? How many more are you going to string up before one ends up using your skull for a spittoon?"

"It will end on the last day of next year. That's when the Millennium Bug is supposed to strike, and we find out if I'm right or not." Amabored took the pipe from me to pack it full again. After a pause, he looked up from beneath his brows. A grin creased his weathered face.

"Say, isn't your birthday on New Years' day?" he asked.

18

And so it is. In nine days, we'll be celebrating two propitious events: my sixty-fifth birthday, and the end of the world.

Could Amabored be right about the Millennium Bug? If so, what a colossal fuck-up. Peasants might still work the land with ox and plow and light candles at night, but city-dwellers rely upon sorcery for conveniences upon which they've become alarmingly dependent. Your typical Redhauke hipster switches on magical glowing orbs to light his flat, takes magical lifts to get to the upper floors of buildings, goes to bars to swill magically cooled beer, and watches minstrels play magically amplified instruments. The countryside, meanwhile, is pitted with thousands of dungeons, depthless caverns, underground cities, enchanted castles, towers of spider-haunted mystery, elaborate ruins, crashed spaceships, deadly labyrinths, and monstrous lairs, all of which are filled to the brim with magic arms and armor, potions, rings, tomes, cloaks, and wands. Magical tricks and traps guard these treasures. Wizards write and cast these enchantments, and they get rich doing so. Wizards are also lazy, with a pathological aversion to labor of any kind, and this slothfulness extends to their sorcery. When copying time-sensitive spells into their tomes and grimoires, for example, wizards follow the example of Gygax the Great, who commonly omitted the first two digits of any dates encoded into his spells: writing 99 instead of 3999, for example. This little shortcut was dandy until some wise guy asked what would happen when the date rolled over from 3999 to 4000, as it will in just nine days.

"Don't ask us," the wizards replied.

No one knows what will happen when the date rolls over. Will spells suddenly cease to function? Will the monsters, demons, dragons, and undead sorcerer kings now held at bay by glyphs of warding suddenly find themselves free to terrorize the countryside? Will some spells hold while others fail with tragic consequences? Or will everything just keep humming along? To weather the apocalypse, end-timers have been digging holes in the ground and stocking them full of supplies. The skeptics tell us not to worry, that it's all horseshit concocted by those selfsame wizards who caused the problem, and who have since been landing fat Y3K contracts to rewrite spells at the behest of the petrified rulers who fear the worst.

Will any of these charms, spells or enchantments work after the first of the year? According to Amabored, while most wizards are working to solve the problem, Chaos wizards still loyal to the Hand— all disciples of Jaspin Spellbinder—are working to undo the fix to ensure that the Seven arise and destroy the Woerth. Will they succeed? Who knows? The prudent are taking no chances. I've had my own wizards working on the problem for six months; I even threw a couple of them into the dungeon to light a fire under the others.

So, you see my dilemma. The Astral Telescope tells me that I'll live another sixty-five years. Amabored's prophecy tells me that, unless he can stop the Seven from waking, in nine days I'll be dead along with everyone else. They can't both be right. The thought that keeps me slumped on my throne, too terrified to eat or shit or touch my wife, is that I'd rather Amabored be right—and that I hope he fails.

You heard me. Rather than face another sixty-five years of decrepitude, I'd prefer to face the end now. It's better to burn out than to fade away, somebody once said. I pray that I'll be consumed by dragonfire, thereby avoiding the coward's death of dying on the fucking toilet. I'm too much of a pussy to kill myself. If the only way I can ensure my timely demise is to take the rest of the Woerth with me, then that's a deal I'm willing to make.

AFTER JAMES CALMED DOWN, ASSURED BY AMABORED THAT HE HAD NO intention of bringing down destruction on Kenwood—at least not for another eighteen months—we spent the night in our old friend's company. We drank excellent Trappist ale, feasted on pheasant and wild berries, and smoked the peace pipe. Xingo made no more appearances. It was a good night, but something was missing; the years apart had made us stiff and wary around each other.

At the first bell, we prepared to bed down in a pair of nearby tents arranged for us by Amabored's men. Before we departed his digs, Amabored took me aside. From his belt pouch, he produced a smooth black stone and tossed it to me. It was obsidian or even brimstone, and I knew at once that it was a charmed relic of some kind.

"What's this?" I asked.

"It's a Time Stone," Amabored said. "I'm supposed to give it to you before you leave. I'm told you'll need it."

"Who asked you to give it to me?"

The wry, fierce humor returned to Amabored's gaze. "You did," he said.

19

I sure as hell didn't remember finding a Time Stone, nor asking Amabored to hold it for me. Time Stones are nothing to trifle with. They're fashioned from pure brimstone, and only the most powerful wizards dare attempt to manufacture them without unleashing proverbial forces beyond their control. As much as I wanted to grill Amabored about it, he would brook no further questions and kicked me out of his tent. I placed the stone in my backpack and promptly forgot about it.

Not long thereafter, a pair of plush peasant girls, their hair like corn silk and their bodies ripe with patchouli oil, crept into my tent and burrowed into my bedroll. They were a gift from Amabored, and I was tempted to let them try. Had I been prepared to forgo my vows, the same curse that has kept me from accepting my wife's ministrations would have found me here just as cold and unresponsive. So, I sent them away.

Telling you this gives me no pleasure, especially since my profession is replete with phallic symbols that serve to remind a warrior of whatever he might be packing, however unimpressive. What is a broadsword, after all, but the lethal extension of what swings between a warrior's legs? I knew many a swordsman who compensated for his shortcomings with an oversized two-handed battle blade. My most prized phallus was a nifty magical battle-axe called—I'm not kidding—the *Rod of Lordly Might*. The very mention of its name would send my adventuring comrades into spasms of laughter. Countless times, our crew would wander into a strange town, find a welcome tavern, start knocking 'em back and, sooner or later, Amabored or Lithaine would shout *Hey Elberon! Show 'em your Rod of Lordly Might!*

It was a handy device nonetheless, the Swiss Army knife of enchanted weapons. It was a +4 battle-axe on the Adventurers Guild's Enchantment Index. It could expand into a fifty-foot telescoping pole, which came in handy whenever we fell into a dungeon pit, which was nearly every day. It could turn into a javelin or disguise itself as a nondescript walking staff. It was also a perfectly balanced weapon that could send imp heads popping from their shoulders like champagne corks. I loved it—and as my wives would once have told you, I wasn't compensating for anything.

I found it early in my adventuring career, somewhere in my Fourth Level as a Guild fighter, during one of our endless succession of imp tower sweeps. The lands outside of Redhauke are pimpled with abandoned keeps, castle ruins, and guard towers, all of which are infested with imp squatters who use them as bases from which to launch raids on the surrounding peasantry. Numbers range anywhere from a dozen to a couple of hundred imps. A party of five mixed adventurers, including a couple of fighters, a wizard, a cleric, and a rogue, can perform a clean-and-sweep in an afternoon.

We'd be sitting around the Suds 'n Shade, bored out of our skulls, when someone would eventually get hammered enough to suggest a tower sweep. Most of the time, the imps were sitting on a stash of booty—usually, a couple of small chests filled with coin and a few magical weapons, scrolls, or potions. Sometimes we'd give the Guild their cut, sometimes not. Sure, there was always the risk of a bloody death if you ran into an Eighth-Level imp chieftain on the top floor, but we were fucking nuts in those days. We didn't know from death. Spending a day killing imps was like playing a round of golf.

On one of those tower sweeps, I found the Rod hidden in a booby-trapped chest that, when opened, fired a poison dart straight at your jugular vein. We found the chest on the top level of the tower, after a pitched battle in which we sent twenty-five imps to their hellish reward. With no rogue in our party that day to check for traps, we took a chance and opened it anyway.

Sproing! Wilberd took the dart in the throat. We were all hosed with his blood. The monk dropped like a drunken dwarf.

"Holy shit!" I cried. *"Medic!"*

Adventurer's Rule Number One: Never leave home without a cleric. They're worth their weight in platinum. It didn't matter what god the cleric worshipped—Athena, Quetzalcoatl, Osiris, or L. Ron Hubbard—we didn't give a damn so long as he had a goodly supply of *Heal Wounds* blessings. Clerics are handy in all sorts of scenarios. Though generally forbidden to use edged weapons, they'll happily bash in skulls with maces or morning stars. They double as field surgeons. They can detect evil, turn away the undead, and inflict opponents with curses. They also believe in a higher power of some sort, which makes them humbler than wizards, who think their shit smells like lavender potpourri even though they're usually cowering in the back of the party hoping not to get filleted by an imp scimitar.

Like cats, clerics tend to die horribly, however, and we went through a lot of them. Our cleric that day, Father Frito of Lay, was still alive, so he could lay hands on poor expiring Wilberd and heal the fatal wound. As a First-Level blessing, the *Healing* spell is short on theatrics but nonetheless impressive: Bathed in the holy light of whatever deity Frito worshipped, the wound was cauterized, disinfected, and stitched as if by an invisible thread. If ever you wonder whether a faith healer really has the goods, just cut off your arm, wrap it in ice, carry it into the revival tent, and ask him to put it back. If he does, then pony up.

My unfortunately-named Rod of Lordly Might still hangs above my throne, though long years have passed since its blade last tasted blood. It still works like the day I found it. If only my real phallus worked as well as my metaphorical one, I might still be married in more than name only.

20

That's enough about my dick. The next morning, James and I awoke to find that Amabored had split shortly before dawn, leaving a cryptic message about receiving a hot lead on another Chaos wizard fleeing Kenwood.

"I'll have to throw him into my dungeon," said James as he stewed over the plate of fruit, hummus, and pita bread brought forth by a gaggle of hippie girls.

"Good luck," I said, longing forlornly for a slab of bacon. "They haven't invented the dungeon that can hold him. Do you think you could take him?"

James mused for a long moment over this question. Finally, he grinned, the first genuine smile I had seen from him since arriving in his lands.

"Hell no," he said. "I've gotten soft. But if it's a fight he wants, I can give him one. I've the wealth of a kingdom at my disposal. What's he got? A few cultists and a cockeyed story."

There was the difference. After returning in triumph from the Dread Plain, we were treated like rock stars. Amabored was thus afforded the same chance to sell out that we all enjoyed; he had his pick of beautiful princesses, elf maidens willing to sacrifice their immortality for his love, knighthoods, endorsement deals, acting offers, and empty thrones looking for regents. Instead of cashing in, he immediately scraped together the remnants of his army and marched north to win back the lands that Koschei had handed to the Sultan.

Five years later, he finally won back his kingdom—but at what cost? He spent every dime he'd ever made. Scorched-earth tactics ruined his reputation; people stopped calling him eccentric and started calling him crazy. His reign as Grand Warlord of the Nomad Kingdoms was short-lived and disastrous, with civil war, famine, flood, and the occasional plague decimating his people and depleting his resources. He lost and won back his lands so many times that they put a revolving door on his palace.

Meanwhile, James and I grew paunchy signing proclamations, entertaining foreign dignitaries, and cutting ribbons at ceremonies dedicating statues of ourselves. I always suspected that Amabored held us in contempt for giving up the fight. James seemed to believe we deserved the good life; perhaps we did. It was the difference between working harder and working smarter. Hadn't we already done our part? After you've saved the world, what do you do for an encore?

We were beat. It was time to hang up the spikes.

That Amabored and James nearly came to blows demonstrated how far apart we had all drifted. Once, we were each instrumental to the success of the Quest: James functioned as our eyes and ears; Lithaine our spirit; Malcolm our Faith; Andrigan and I as our brute strength; Lindar our intellect; Amabored our heart; Cassie our conscience. Once the war was over, it was head-spinning how quickly we found ourselves at odds. Nothing fucks up your head like victory.

I wasn't sure what our journey had accomplished, but James seemed satisfied to learn that he needn't act immediately against his old friend. I considered riding back with him to Castle Darien to hang for a while longer, but I sensed that he was ready to see me off. He had his life to attend, and I had mine. We would always be brothers, but that intense bond of comrades in arms, the utter surety of our friendship—that was gone. Perhaps it was never meant to last. Hell, the James I knew back in the day hardly existed anymore, no more than the Elberon he once knew still existed. Every morning, you look in the mirror and see the same face you saw the day before. You don't feel or look any different. Nevertheless, in some subtle and yet irreversible way, you've changed. Five, ten, or twenty years slip away, and you can't even recognize yourself anymore.

So, we bade farewell to Amabored's Camp Jihad, crossed the river, gathered our horses and retainers, mounted up, and headed west. A half-day's ride found us at the Long Road, where our paths parted. We watered our horses at a burbling stream and stood together for a final smoke as our men tended the beasts near the road.

"If Amabored gives you any trouble, send word to me through the aether," I said. "I'll send reinforcements. I love the guy, but you just can't tell with him. He's either the sanest man I've ever met, or he's out of his fucking mind."

"I can handle him," James said. "If he nails up one more wizard in my kingdom, I swear I'm going to napalm that for—"

A dart no bigger than a hummingbird beak sprouted out of James's throat, a hair's breadth above his jugular vein. His sword hand lurched upward, his fingers grasping at the offending projectile. His gaze locked onto mine.

"Bloody hell," James gurgled. He dropped to the ground in a heap.

"Holy fuck!" I cried, wheeling around, my body flooding from stem to stern with adrenaline and rage. I dove beneath my grazing horse. Three more darts bloomed on the horse's flank. It bolted, and I had to roll into the brook to avoid getting my skull bashed in. Of course, my battle-axe was still lashed to the saddle.

Weaponless, dripping wet, I crouched in the middle of the brook. No need to wonder who had attacked us.

"XINGO!" I bellowed. "Show yourself, you dickless worm!"

Blowguns had an effective range of about twenty-five chains. The little bug-fucker had to be close. If I could reach our men about a hundred chains away on the road, I might have a shot. I'd need to smoke out the gnome first, though.

"Suck my asshole, dickwad!" came the tinny reply.

His voice came from a line of sycamore trees paralleling the brook at the crest of a low rise. Xingo's curses had startled a pair of robins nesting in the upper branches; a quick trace of their flight path led me to him. He was holed up in the crook of one tree wearing a gillie suit decked out in branches and leaves. He must have been tracking us since we broke Amabored's camp. Dirty gnome bastard.

His location made him vulnerable. Although my horse had bolted, James's horse stood placidly tethered to a fallen ash tree within arm's reach. Xingo was reloading, which gave me a second—had to think like a young man if I wanted to live.

Although I don't take naturally to horses, I have learned a few tricks in my day, as horsemanship is prerequisite to Adventurers Guild mastery. Belly-crawling to James's horse, I slid under its flank, flopped myself over, and hooked my boots in the stirrups. Then I reached for the reigns, untied them, flipped them over the horse's left flank, and pulled them tight. I gave the horse a taste of my spurs.

"*Yeeahh!*" I cried. The horse broke up the hill at a full gallop with me hanging from his belly. The *Hi-Ho Blow Me* move, we used to call it, because the position left you staring right at the horse's johnson.

The horse rocketed up the hill. When I reached the tree line, two of Xingo's daggers hissed past my ear and thudded into the ground. With at best a half-second until he reloaded, I launched myself from the horse and slammed into the thin trunk of Xingo's tree at about twelve knots. The force of the collision popped the gnome out of the branches. He landed hard on his head and then lay there groaning.

As did I—my middle-aged body would soon make me pay dearly for this tomfoolery. For now, rage stood me well. Grabbing one of Xingo's own daggers, I pounced on him and thrust the tip of the blade under his jaw.

"One move, gnome, and I'll ventilate you," I hissed.

While Xingo was still too groggy to resist, I hog-tied him with a belt and then raced back to James. The ranger had turned a distinct shade of blueberry and his breath was shallow, but the poison had yet to reach his heart. As an old campaigner, I still traveled with the essential adventurer's travel pack, which included such necessities as tinder and flint, lantern oil, a six-pack of pitch-soaked torches, a coil of rope, a week's supply of hardtack, and several handy potions stored in sealed clay jars: healing salves, invisibility ointments, magical Molotov cocktails, poison antidotes, and Sterno. You can buy the whole kit-and-caboodle at most Guild-approved merchants; don't leave home without it.

I forced two *Antidote* potions down James's throat. He'd puke his guts out, but he'd live. Then I turned my attention back to the gillie-suited gnome, who had recovered enough to regard me with a mixture of bile and fear. I grabbed him by the scruff of his hair.

"Who put you up to this?" I demanded.

"Go fuck yourself!"

"Spit it out, creep, or I'll geld you."

"You can't touch me!" the gnome squealed. "I'm under Amabored's protection!"

The gnome was right. Though I couldn't fathom why Amabored wanted to protect the same oily runt who had tried to murder us a dozen times over, I knew the rules. As Lords, we were entitled to offer sanctuary under our banners. No Lord could harm a man protected by another Lord's banner without risking war. To execute Xingo, I'd have to arrange a sit with Amabored, read a list of grievances, call witnesses... it was a hard slog through fetid bogs of red tape and paperwork before I'd have the pleasure of separating this louse's head from his shoulders, and who had time for that? Besides, with Amabored convinced that Ragnarök was nigh, who knew how he'd react?

There was nothing in the Code that prohibited me from neutralizing a threat, however. Offering Xingo a grim smile, I placed my boot on his throat.

"That's true," I said. "But I'm not about to leave you to try your luck again. You're coming with me. If Amabored wants you, he can come and get you."

I'd regale you with the stream of inventive profanity spewing from the gnome before I stuffed the gag in his mouth, but I'm sure you've heard it all before. A few hours later, James was done puking, Xingo was safely trussed to the back of my horse, and we were finally able to say our proper goodbyes.

"Thanks again," James said, rubbing the horrid purple bruise on his throat. "The little turd got the drop on me."

"With the number of times you've saved my carcass over the years?" I asked. "Forget it. The question is, why is that little shit still trying to murder us? You have any enemies you've forgotten about?"

"None that I'm aware of. You?"

"Too many to count. You don't think Amabored put him up to it, do you?"

James considered this point. "I don't dare believe it. He may be nuts, but he's not crazy. Are you sure you don't want to turn the gnome over to me? A few hours sitting on a short stake, and he'll talk."

That one made me smile. Lawful Good or not, James had a mean streak. He could carry a grudge longer than any man I knew.

"I don't doubt it," I said. "But we can't touch him without Amabored's leave. Let him cool his heels in my dungeons for a while. Something will break."

We stood up and stared past each other during a few moments of awkward silence. *What the hell*, I thought, and wrapped James in a bear hug. He gave me the bro-pat, and we pulled back.

"Let me know if that throne of yours starts putting too many calluses on your ass," I said. "I'll start a war and call you for help. It'll be like old times."

"Will do," James said. "Keep your powder dry."

That was the last time I saw both James and Amabored. In one week, they're both due to arrive here at the Lordship for my birthday celebration. It's supposed to be a joyous reunion—the Musketeers together again. Xingo was still rotting in my dungeon until I let him out. I kept the little cockroach on ice for a year now. Has he spoken a word about who hired him to kill us? Maybe he has... maybe he hasn't. I'll tell you later.

In any case, Amabored has certainly figured out what happened to the gnome—and you might imagine that he's sore about it. Lithaine may be coming to kill me, but what about Amabored? Am I to face the bloody wrath of my two dearest friends? With the Millennium approaching? With the fate of both my life and the Woerth at large hanging in the balance?

That's the funny thing about life: It's never so bad that it can't get worse.

21

T hat lesson quickly dawned on me during my first few weeks outside of Redhauke, lo these forty-five years ago. After a month of cooling my heels with the rest of the proles, I had yet to so much as sniff the inside of the city. The stream of northern refugees had slowed to a trickle. For the denizens of Doomtown, that collection of filthy shantytowns sprawled alongside the Outer Walls, desperation was setting in. The wind shifted, and the air assumed the crisp clarity of approaching autumn. After the summer harvest, food had become scarce, and thoughts of winter began to caper in our minds. The refugees began to size each other up and to contemplate, in the dark recesses of their souls, the merits of cannibalism.

It was tempting to blame the city elders for the pervasive misery, but what could they do? Open the gates to the mob and watch them storm the granaries and empty the larders? The city had to take care of its own. Guards tossed sacks of grain and potatoes over the wall whenever they could spare them, but the manna hadn't fallen from heaven in weeks. Now, a hunk of bread and the occasional bowl of cabbage soup was the most a refugee could hope for to keep starvation at bay. Just to rub it in, once a fortnight the city gates swung open to admit the long cattle drives that came up from the Were Coast led by posses of lariat-twirling cowboys. The city had a ravenous appetite for beef, milk, cheese, and leather, and of the thousands of cattle that shuffled inside the walls of Redhauke, not a single heifer or bull made it out alive. We envied them.

Meanwhile, rumors of child kidnapping continued apace, forcing groups of parents to band together to guard their grimy urchins while the men foraged for food. Further rumors that only children outside the walls were being snatched, while those within the city remained safe, made things worse. Traumatized parents flung themselves at the feet of the Guards, begging entrance to the city; some even attempted to smuggle their children inside. Anyone who looked even slightly suspicious was tagged as a potential child-snatcher and targeted for a beating or worse. Doomtown became as flammable as a pile of dry tinder, lacking only a spark to ignite the blaze.

As for me, I had lost twenty pounds. When I happened upon a reflective surface, I saw in my eyes the same flinty, haunted, down-trodden stare that I saw in everyone else. It was time for the würm to turn. Either I got inside the city gates before winter, or I crawled on my belly back to Dad and presented my balls to him on a platter.

FORTUNATELY, *BON CHANCE* WAS IN THE AIR. ONE LATE AFTERNOON IN mid-September, as I was cleaning and dressing a dog that had unwisely wandered onto the onion farm looking for food, Lithaine bounded over from his own campsite. The bloody elf never walked anywhere; he bounced and leaped about like some swashbuckling ballet dancer or a Broadway Tarzan, and I sometimes had to fight the urge to beat his head against a tree.

"You're just in time," I said, stacking up a meager supply of dog steaks on the tree stump that served as my kitchen counter. "Get a fire going."

"Drop that mess and come with me," said Lithaine. "There's somebody you need to meet."

I packed the dog steaks in salt, grabbed my sword, and scurried after the elf. Trying to pry details from him along the way was like trying to pry a chicken leg from a dwarf's hand. Winding our way through the shantytowns, we passed everywhere the hopeless, the terrified, the swell-bellied, the blind, the lame, and the old. Eventually, we came to a cluster of tents and shacks near the southwest shore of Lake Everdeep. This immense, freshwater inland sea spanning a hundred leagues long and fifty wide provided a livelihood for the scores of fishing villages squatting on its shores. Redhauke itself, nestled on the bay through which the lake flowed into the Whitehorse River, was home to the vast commercial shipping fleets that plied its waters. Legend tells of a sprawling merman city hidden miles beneath the surface. Can you imagine life as a merman? Fish swim in their own shit. Think of a merman city, and you might imagine a magical undersea paradise of coral and shell. It's probably more like a rancid aquarium.

Even the mermen themselves, I imagine, have no idea how deep the lake is or what manner of beasts dwell at the bottom. No one, not even Gygax the Great himself, has ever fully plumbed its depths. The lake intrigued the seaman in me, and I couldn't help but stare at it in dumbstruck wonder as we entered the campsite.

My attention was soon diverted, however, by sounds that I only half-understood.

A man's voice. "No, move it over here. *Over here.*"

Then a woman. *"Oh, god, don't stop, oh god, oh, oh ooooohhhh...."*

And then an animal, braying. Or *baah*-ing. What the fuck was that? A sheep?

These dulcet tones issued from a ramshackle cabin constructed out of several rough-hewn logs, driftwood, and the hull of a small fishing boat. A leather tarp nailed to the hull served as a front wall and door. A breeze caught the edge of the tarp, lifting it to reveal the ghostly apparition of a white male ass bobbing up and down between a pair of plump female legs splayed wide. Outside the cabin, three malnourished, toothless inbreeds had gathered to watch the show. Lithaine chased them off at the point of his sword.

The elf pounded on the driftwood doorframe. "Amabored! Finish up! We have business!"

The ass stopped bobbing. Whispered nothings commenced—whether to the woman or to the sheep, I couldn't say. A few moments later, a fat, happy, and red-faced peasant woman scurried out of the cabin, pulling up her bloomers as she ran. Then out jumped the sheep, skittish but none the worse for wear. Behind the animal emerged a tall, bronzed, chiseled fighter wearing the loincloth, bandoleer, and breeches of a Northern barbarian. Though he appeared to be around twenty-five, his mullet and goatee were white. His gaze bore the easy regard of a young man certain of the world, and his place in it. He slapped the girl on the ass as she ran away.

"Don't forget, I'll be here at eight. *Eight!*" the barbarian called after her. "And don't forget the wine!"

He turned to us, still grinning, and extended his hand to me. "Amabored of the Nomad Kingdoms. You must be Elberon of the Isles. The elf tells me you're handy with a blade."

"I know a few steps," I said. "The Nomad Kingdoms, you say? You're a barbarian?"

"Yes," said Amabored, sizing me up. "But I wipe my ass with toilet paper."

"Fair enough. So, what's up?" I asked, turning to Lithaine.

Lithaine led us around to the back of the lean-to, where the three of us crouched together. The barbarian produced a wooden dugout pipe and a pouch stuffed with gnome pipeweed. He packed a bowl, fired up a hit, and then passed it to me. I sheepishly declined. Lithaine took a puff, and then passed his gaze over the two of us.

"If either of you tells anybody what I'm going to tell you, then I'll kill you both," he said. "I don't even care which one of you blabs, I'll still kill both of you. Got me?"

"Try it, donkey-puncher," said Amabored, "and see where it gets you."

Taking this comment as acquiescence, Lithaine commenced his tale. I wouldn't have believed it but for the deadly gleam in his eyes, which told us that any skepticism would be met with immediate disembowelment. The previous night, Lithaine had been awakened at his camp, which lay within a starlit clearing hidden behind a small copse of ash trees, by what sounded like distant chimes. The sound echoed along the chill autumn breeze ruffling the treetops. He sat up, seeking the music's source—and found himself staring at the ghostly, glowing, neon-limned form of a child.

She stood watching him at the edge of the clearing. She looked human, no more than eight years old, with shoulder-length raven hair, a white gown, and no shoes. Lithaine grabbed his quiver and bow, set shaft to string, and approached the child warily. As he closed with her, he found that he could see the tree trunks through her shimmering form.

"I'm an elf, so I'm used to this shimmering-in-the-forest shit," Lithaine told us, "but this was different. The music seemed to come from within her. And she seemed to know me."

"I told you to lay off the wild mushrooms," said Amabored.

Rather than run frightened from the armed elf, the child instead beckoned him closer. Lithaine approached to within arm's length and stood staring down at her with his bow at rest.

"Who are you?" he asked.

Like the chimes, the child's voice seemed to reach Lithaine from the opposite end of a long tunnel. *"We have yet to meet, my beloved,"* said the child, *"but in due course, we shall. Until that blessed day, I beg your aid in righting a great wrong."*

"I don't know you," Lithaine said. "And I don't care about your troubles." He turned on his heels to walk away. He was immediately stopped short—for the girl now stood before him again.

"It feeds on the children," the child said. *"I am not yet manifest fully in this universe, and so cannot stop it. But you can, your Majesty. You and your friends. First, you must get the children of this place inside the city walls, for out here, none are safe. In three days must you do this. Fail, and doom them you shall. Fail, and you may doom the Woerth."*

With that, the apparition of the child faded away, borne on the night wind along with the keening of the chimes. The last Lithaine saw of her was her eyes. Her gaze was full of hope, and longing—and something akin to love.

"'*Your Majesty*'?" Amabored said. "What are you king of besides your dick and your right hand?"

"Shut your hole or I'll shut it for you, you goddamned savage. I'm not fucking around."

"Do you believe what this ghost was telling you?" I asked. "That something is 'feeding on' children? And that we can stop it by getting them inside the city in three days?"

Lithaine paused to consider his answer, which we could already read in his eyes. "Yeah, I do. I don't know why she picked me. But I believe her."

"If we play this right," I said, "it could be our chance to become heroes."

"Who wants to be a hero?" asked Lithaine.

"Not me," Amabored said. "I want to get rich. And I can't get rich until I get into that city. If helping these kids will get me there, then I say we try it."

"I'm in," I said. "Say, do you think that ghost was revealing the future?" I asked Lithaine. "Maybe you'll be a king someday."

"If I ever become a king, remind me to kill myself," Lithaine said.

"Nobody in his right mind wants to be a king," said Amabored, clapping the elf on the shoulder. "That's why the world is so fucked up."

22

The next day, the three of us scattered, each looking for some hidden entrance, tunnel, or airborne drop that we might exploit to get into the city. For my part, I walked the length of the Outer Walls from stem to stern and back again, looking for a culvert, a cistern, a loose block, sleeping guards—anything that smelled like a hole in the city's defenses. I even hiked down to the where the walls met the shore of Lake Everdeep, near the city's massive harbor. I saw only an exposed cliff that led down to the depthless waters, and towers bristling with bowmen.

It was Amabored, of course, who found an angle. He explained it to Lithaine and me, and then the three of us approached the leader of a group of about two hundred refugees who were guarding the thousand or more children currently camped outside the city walls. Their vigilance had slowed the vanishings to a trickle but hadn't sealed the breach; three more children had disappeared the previous night, leaving their mothers in hysterics and their fathers with their throats cut.

The vigilantes' leader, a short and burly farmer from Kent named Barlan, called together ten of his trusted mates to meet us at Lithaine's clearing. When they arrived at dusk, we built a campfire and passed around the elf's last flask of mead. Then Amabored addressed the men.

"We've heard what's been happening to your children," Amabored said. "Like you, we've also heard that children within the city walls aren't being snatched. We think we can help get your kids inside."

"Do you mock us?" Barlan asked. "I lost my youngest daughter, only three weeks gone. Some here have lost their entire families. And you say you can get the other children inside? How? Will you grow wings and fly them over the walls?"

If only he knew. Thus far wingless, Amabored crouched down with a stick to draw a rough diagram of the city in the dirt.

"It's like this," he said. "A wizard acquaintance of mine is being held captive in a chapel near the Dragon Gate. A gang of half-imps is guarding him. During the evening watch, there are only two mongrels on guard while the rest are out looking for drink. If we can bust him out, he has a spell that will help us all get inside."

"A wizard? Why did they pinch him?" one of the men asked.

"He got in a few days ago, and the hellspawn grabbed him for ransom," Amabored said. "They think his family has money."

"If it only took a few half-imps to bring him in, then he's not much of a wizard," said Barlan.

Amabored towered over the farmer and jabbed a finger at his chest. "If I vouch for him, then he's vouched for. Got it?"

To his credit, the farmer stood his ground against the tall barbarian. He regarded each of us in turn and then nodded. "So, we form a posse and fetch your wizard?"

"We'll bust out the wizard," replied Amabored. "You need to confiscate every wagon, mule, and wheelbarrow you can find in Doomtown. Gather the kids, get them into whatever transport you can muster, and then line them up near the Chimera Gate, about a quarter-mile back and well away from the road. Do it piecemeal, throughout the day tomorrow, so as not to draw attention. Be ready by dusk. When the spell goes off, you'll know it. The gate will open, and the guards will be occupied. Just get the kids into the city as quickly as you can."

"What happens if you fail, barbarian?" the farmer asked. "Whoever is taking our children will see what we've done. We'll have angered them."

"Winter's coming," said Amabored. Still young and largely untested, he cut an imposing figure even then; with his chin jutting just so and arms akimbo, he looked like the leader he would one day become. "The food's running out. The city fathers won't let us in voluntarily. If this doesn't work, your children are going to die one way or another. What choice do you have?"

"Then godspeed, barbarian," said Barlan. "I pray your plan succeeds."

"Nothing succeeds like success," said Amabored.

23

The next evening, Amabored, Lithaine and I wound our way along the perimeter of the great city, the western Butcher's Wall of Redhauke looming large over our right shoulders. I was wild with excitement and fear. Back in my own land, I had been afraid of neither man nor beast; I was afraid only of my father, who fell somewhere between the two. Out here in the world, following felt safer than leading. Amabored already seemed the most natural-born leader I had ever met, while Lithaine knew his own mind better than I could ever hope to know my own.

Along the walls of the great city, tiny hamlets and villages had sprung up over the centuries like patches of weeds at the perimeter of a garden. In normal times, these villages housed servants and laborers who worked within the city walls by day but couldn't afford rooms at night. Since the influx of refugees, however, the villages had become home to gangs of mercenaries hired by the city to police Doomtown and dispense their own form of rough justice. The village we now approached had become such a place: emptied of peasants, pitted with military tents, and lit by smoldering campfires. At the near end of the village square, a rough banner snapped against the wind—a cartoonish scrawl on a red field showing a yellow smiley-face with pointed ears and an arrow piercing the round head.

We crouched behind an overturned hay wagon to scope out the scene. Lithaine peered at the banner through the spokes of a shattered wagon wheel. His eyes narrowed to black slits.

"Bully Boyz!" he hissed. "You were holding out on me, Amabored."

"I didn't want you leaping over here to start the killing before you had heard the plan."

During the Quest, I would introduce hundreds of Fourth Reich Bully Boyz to my axe-blade. Imp-spawn couldn't get work in decent society, but they were always available for killing. Consequently, a dozen or so half-imp mercenary bands had risen to prominence as a cheap alternative to fielding a regular army. The Bully Boyz, Lithaine told me, were particularly fond of gutting elves. This lot had rampaged up from the Daggerlands and through the neighboring elvish kingdom of Helene, burning fields and putting the occasional elf village to the sword. Now they had joined the fray outside of Redhauke in the service of a city noble who carried a grudge against elves. The half-imp that Lithaine had skewered the night of our first meeting had, in fact, been a Bully Boy. Too bad for him.

"I'll execute every motherfucking last one of them," said Lithaine.

"In due time, honey-bunny," said Amabored. "First, we need the wizard."

The chapel, Amabored told us, stood at the far end of the village beneath the shadow of the Butcher's Wall. We needed only to sneak in, dispose of the two Boyz guarding the wizard, free him, and then use his spell, whatever that was, to blow down the Chimera Gate. If Barlan and his boys had done their jobs, they'd have the children lined up and ready. They'd need to get the kids inside before the guards rallied or the mob realized that the gates were open. The window between calm and chaos would be maddeningly short.

We slunk like wharf rats around the squalid huts made of straw and mud or cow shit dried hard as cement. As we crept past the half-imp mercenaries sprawled drunk in the offal or drawing steel over a knucklebones dispute, the anger smoldered off Lithaine like steam from a bog. Creeping past the open maw of a deserted blacksmith shed, we slunk into a crouch behind a moldy woodpile.

Across a sodden expanse of muddy alleyway, we spied the chapel. What we saw nearly sent Lithaine's head spinning from its shoulders. There weren't just two guards, as Amabored had promised, nor five, nor ten. It was a full platoon—fifteen half-imps gathered in a semicircle, cheering on a pair of starving dogs locked in a death-dance over what I could only guess was a human thighbone.

Amabored grinned. "I was misinformed."

"If this wizard is so powerful," I whispered, "then why doesn't he blast himself out?"

"Who said he was powerful?" asked Amabored. "I said he had a spell. He's First Level, just an apprentice. That'll be enough."

"*We're* only First Level," Lithaine hissed. "Those fuckers have eight health points apiece!"

"You have enough arrows. Just don't miss."

"From this range, I can put two into your eye socket."

"Not before I shove my sword up your asshole."

"Will you two put a sock in it?" I said. "Maybe we should just hide out until nightfall. They'll have to thin out sometime."

"No dice," said Amabored. "We need to spring the spellthrower in half a bell, or we'll miss our chance. What we need—" and at this, he threw us a sidelong glance that I would come to recognize as inevitably preceding a great bloodletting— "is a diversion."

The Adventurer's Manual devotes a whole chapter to creating a successful diversion. Diversions require an alchemical blend of skill and luck; in your calculations, you must consider the number of your foe, their strength, the terrain, the weather, and the potential for collateral damage. If you have the means, one diversionary tactic has become *de rigueur* for all adventurers looking for the shortest distance to their goal: a big-ass fire. Start a big-ass fire, and like gnomes to a Chinese buffet, your foes will go running to it. We used the tactic so often we even had a code name for it: Old Reliable.

At this moment, however, we were merely three greenhorn

fighters who didn't know dragon shit from Shinola. A fire was simply the only thing we could think of. Creeping into the smithy shack, we uncovered a still-smoldering forge, threw some wood chips on the coals, nursed them into a few infant flames, and then tossed in some pitch-soaked rags. When the flames snarled and crackled, we kicked the whole mess over into a stack of hay bales lining one wall. Soon the shack was ablaze.

"Run for your lives!" cried Amabored. We scattered. The barbarian bolted for the tavern across from the chapel, Lithaine went long, and I ran behind an empty cottage. The arduous process of half-imp brain chemistry commenced, and the platoon of mercenaries began wandering over to stare slack-jawed at the blazing smithy. Bracing my back against the cottage wall, I peered around the corner. Three soldiers remained behind to guard the chapel—one apiece unless somebody got greedy.

By prearranged signal, Amabored leaped out of the tavern door directly in front of the three soldiers.

"Hey, zipperheads!" Amabored shouted. "Feast on this!"

With that challenge, Amabored whirled around, bent over, and flipped up his loincloth. If there's one thing that can send hellspawn into spittle-flinging apoplexy, it's a full pair of white, pimpled, human *glutei maximi* mocking him to his face.

The sight had the intended effect. Howling blood-oaths, the Bully Boyz raced forward, scimitars at the ready. One fell promptly into a tumbling heap with three of Lithaine's arrows piercing his back. The other ran headlong into the wide arc of Amabored's broadsword; the dogs would later find his head.

That left one for me. As a teenager, I had slain scores of kobolds, which infested our island kingdom like termites. I had fought and killed wolves, bears, cougars, sharks, and even a were-boar—my father's personal chef, whom I speared with a fireplace poker while Dad was out campaigning. Never had I purposefully confronted an enemy, however, with the intent of sliding steel into his belly before he did the same to me. The thought of slaying another intelligent being, of depriving him of all possible futures by violating his body with my sword, struck me momentarily stupid. We pass our lives both certain of our own end and paradoxically convinced that we'll live forever. All the while, Death creeps ever closer behind, waiting to drown us in four inches of dirty water, explode a blood vessel in our brains, choke us on a chicken bone—or stop our hearts when we're squatting on the fucking toilet. The noose is already around our necks the moment we leave the womb.

Is it really this poor bastard's fate to meet eternity at the end of my sword? I wondered in those few seconds. *Is it mine to die at the end of his?* Why were we trying to kill each other? What was in it for this guy, other than the chance to serve as an arbitrary obstacle between my goal and me?

The half-imp saw me leap from behind the wall with knees knocking, and he charged. *Can I take him?* I wondered. I wore the girdle, but strength alone is of middling importance in a melee. More important is speed, and brains. I had a little of both, but not a lot of either. Then introspection ceased; instinct took over. Bellowing like a bull moose, I charged him with my sword whistling above my head.

My foe raised his buckler to meet the blow. The girdle tightened around my waste. Power surged from my belly, flowed up my torso, and raced down my sword arm. My blade split the soldier's buckler in two, then bit into flesh and bone. The half-imp's shield arm flopped into the mud. He had only half a second to stare in horror at the blood spurting from the stump before my sword sliced through his breastplate and into his heart.

Okay, so the girdle did tell the tale. What of it? The moment I realized my blow had been true, I understood my true purpose: To seek out evil and send it back to Hell. I have lain with all manner of women; I have taken every drug known to man, elf, and dwarf; and I have quenched my blade in the blood of the Violet Queen, who can turn your heart into cinders and your brain into ashes. None of it compared to the moment when my blade claimed its first hellspawn. It was better than any orgasm I'd ever have.

The corpse fell back so abruptly that I lost my sword grip. I stood there dumbfounded, watching the hilt vibrate in the poor bastard's chest. Amabored, his own bare chest dripping with his enemy's blood, came up and clapped me on the back.

"Fine sword work, my friend," he said. "But don't admire it so plainly—it looks like masturbation."

Lithaine approached, and the three of us high-tailed it into the chapel.

24

W e found the wizard Redulfo asleep in a man-sized steel cage on the second floor. He made a poor first impression: drab gray robes, a slight and frumpy frame, a face you couldn't pick out of a lineup. So average was he in every respect that we would soon dub him Redulfo the Redundant. His only distinguishing feature was a pair of round-rimmed spectacles, which were distinguished only because no one had invented them yet. Later, after he opened the wrong magic egg, became irrevocably evil, died, and was reincarnated into the body of a 300-year-old black dragon, he became quite distinguished indeed. From the moment I saw him snoring in that cell, however, he was just Redulfo—a good friend who was handy in a pinch.

"Redulfo!" Amabored called, rattling the bars of the cage. "Wake your ass up!"

The wizard's eyes blinked open. He stretched. He stood. He took his time.

"You paid the ransom?" he asked Amabored.

"Yes. They asked for a pair of nickels and a chicken. Is there a key?"

"It's a Cage of Keeping," Redulfo said, his eyes rotating dolefully around his cage. "Galerian has a wizard on the payroll. You need a charm of opening."

"Why don't we drop the cage from the belfry?" asked Lithaine.

"Let me try," I said, approaching the cage. Redulfo stepped back, and I took a grip on two of the bars. Over time, I would learn that it was dangerous to pit two enchanted items directly against each other. Wizards are a vindictive lot, known to code booby traps into their spells that do something unpleasant when encountering a rival's spellcraft. Nothing ruins your day faster than an enchanted item that explodes in your face.

I called up as much power from the girdle as I dared. My heart filled with molten lead, my veins with lava, my head with hot steam. The cage bars burst into flame. There was a flash of light, smoke, and noise, and I found myself resting a good ten feet away, singed but alive.

I had opened the bars a good six inches, but the wizard was still trapped inside. Amabored looked askance at me; he probably realized then that I was packing.

"You're wasting time," said Redulfo, as I clambered to my feet. As if on cue, we heard a sudden chorus of bellowing half-imps down below.

Lithaine bounded over to the shattered remains of a stained-glass window now open to the elements. "The cage will fit through here," he said. "Let's toss him out."

"That's not a bad idea," I said.

"Now, hold on a minute—" said Redulfo.

We ignored him. Lithaine clambered out the window, down the protruding stones in the chapel wall, and leaped to the ground to stand watch. Then Amabored and I picked up the cage with Redulfo in it, got a running start, and heaved both cage and wizard through the window. The resulting crash was masked by the hubbub of the crowd that had gathered to watch the smithy burn. Amabored thrust his torso through the window.

"Is he free?" Amabored called down.

"No," we heard Lithaine call back, "but he is unconscious."

"Fucking hell!" Amabored looked back at me. "We've got ten minutes to wake him up and get him to the gate."

So, it was a bad idea to toss the wizard out the window. He lived, didn't he? Next, Amabored and I both attempted a Lithaine-style gambol down the church wall. As we were not lithesome elves, we both fell on our asses. We untangled our limbs, and then the three of us made it to Redulfo's battered cage just as the remainder of the half-imp platoon, having tired of staring at the blaze, wandered back to the chapel in time to see us stealing away with their charge.

The platoon captain shouted in our direction. "*Oy!* What's all this then?"

"Grab the cage, you slack-jaws!" Lithaine shouted to Amabored and me.

We grabbed the cage. As we ran with it, Redulfo's dead weight careening from side to side like a marble on a roulette wheel, Lithaine leaped atop the cage roof. Balancing himself as if on the prow of a trireme dancing in the sea, he rained bowfire upon the charging mercenaries. Two of them dropped with arrows through their throats.

"That's giving them the fucking business!" Amabored cried. Lithaine continued to drop hellspawn until the remainder broke off the pursuit. We kept running toward the outer Shield Wall, the smithy fire receding behind the horizon, then dropped the cage with a jarring thud near the Chimera Gate now looming large before us. Lithaine hopped from the cage roof as Amabored and I bent over, wheezing.

"What about the wizard?" I asked. "He's in a coma!"

"I'll wake his ass up." Amabored motioned with his chin toward the way we had come. "Look, we're right on time."

For a moment, I couldn't figure out where Amabored was pointing. Then I saw them, coming down the broad dirt avenue that passed through the village toward the gate: the last cattle drive of the season. Somewhere near 5,000 head of cattle, herded between several dozen mounted cowboys armed with short swords and crossbows slung at their backs. Both cattle and horses shuffled wearily, kicking up immense clouds of dust as a starving mob gathered on either side of the avenue to cast ravenous gazes upon the mooing slabs of meat. Some of them were ready to skip the cattle and start straight in on the cowboys.

Somewhere nearby, we hoped, Barlan had gathered the children together. As the herd drew near the city wall, the full thirty-foot height of the Chimera Gate began to swing open. Redhauke Guards lined the walls and stood at the gate entrance, ready to let in the herd but kill anything else that dared to pass through.

I tried to piece it together. Unconscious wizard plus a massive herd of cattle plus us equaled—what? There was no time for questions, however, as Amabored motioned for us to hoist up the cage again.

"Head for the rear of the herd!" Amabored called. As we cut an arc around the rumbling beasts, we saw that a squad of Bully Boyz had rallied and were now bearing down on us. Lithaine resumed his perch on the cage and let fly, and two more half-imps went tumbling with feathered shafts piercing their vitals. Then the elf's bowstring snapped. His bow sailed from his hands.

"Fucking hell—I rolled a one!" Lithaine called to us. "Keep going!" With a snarling stream of elvish invective, he drew his sword, launched himself from the cage, and flew crashing into the hellspawn.

Amabored cast an admiring look over his shoulder. "He may be a poncy magic-boy," he called back, "but he has style!"

25

That was the last we saw of Lithaine. Hauling the cage around shacks, through crowds of peasants, and over campfires, we soon found ourselves standing in the middle of the road directly behind the herd. Cow shit lay everywhere, the smell of which filled my wheezing nose as we dropped the cage again.

Amabored wasted no time. He stepped up to the cage, lifted his loincloth, and started pissing on the wizard's head. If you've never been pissed on, then you're lucky. It's not pleasant—unless that's what you're into. After a second or two of this golden shower, Redulfo started. He rolled upright.

"All right, all right, ALL RIGHT!" he cried.

"You're on," Amabored told the wizard as he lowered his loincloth. He produced a small hickory wand from his belt pack and tossed it into the cage. "Check your target at twelve o'clock."

Redulfo fumbled for his glasses with piss still dripping from his nose. He found them, quickly assessed the situation, and reached for the wand.

"Stand back," the wizard told us, his voice barely audible over the mooing din of the cattle. "I'm not sure what this thing will do."

He aimed the wand out of the cage and directly at the tail end of the shuffling herd. *"Anál nathrach, orth' bháis's bethad, do chél dénmha!"* he chanted.

There came a brief flurry of flute-like notes from the wand, and then its business-end exploded. A house-sized mushroom cloud of napalm condensed out of the atmosphere, balled itself up into a miniature sun, and surged forth with a massive sonic boom. Every man-jack within fifty yards hit the deck. The concussion threw Amabored and me back a good twenty feet. The recoil flung Redulfo through the now-demolished cage and halfway down the road.

The fireball exploded at the rear of the herd. Several hundred cattle were incinerated instantly. Several hundred more were now aflame, their hides burning lustily. A few dozen of the cowboys found themselves on fire, and they leaped from their flaming horses to roll screaming in the dirt. A score or more of the surrounding huts were now also ablaze. The sky was a roiling chaos of smoke, cinders, and flame.

Redulfo's fireball marked the first time I had witnessed truly badass sorcery. It would eventually become old hat. I've seen magic that would turn your hair white, your brain into banana puree, and your balls into raisins. But, man, that first time really sticks with you. Good or Evil, Lawful or Chaotic—no matter your alignment, once you get a taste of that kind of power, you want to get your hands on it. Later, I learned that Redulfo's wand, which he claimed to have purchased at a pawnshop on the Were Coast, held a Level Twelve fireball—and since he was only a First-Level mage, he was in violation of Wizard Guild policies and subject to summary expulsion. Redulfo later told us that the wand shouldn't have worked for him at all, although he didn't seem too curious as to why. The recoil flung him so far away that no witnesses could ever pin it on him.

And the cattle—Jesus. I've been in the middle of a few massive earthquakes, but never again would I feel the earth move with anything like the force of those 20,000-odd hooves beating the ground away from that fireball. The terrible trembling tossed us around on the road like scallions sautéing in a frying pan. Five thousand head of cattle, terrified beyond all bovine reason, thundered with a brain-hammering roar toward their only means of escape—through the Chimera Gate's long tunnel and into the city. Like the wrath of the Hebrew God, the herd demolished everything in its path: carts, huts, barns, wagons. Had Odin himself descended from Valhalla and taken a massive steaming dump outside the gate, he could have done no more damage. None of us dared contemplate the human cost.

Amabored and I eventually found our feet. Unconscious again, Redulfo lay in a heap. A singed, maddened horse raced toward us up the road, and Amabored made a flailing leap for the saddle. He caught the stirrups and was dragged a good ten yards before he managed to swing up onto the animal's back. He yanked back hard on the reins and dug in the bit. The horse screamed and reared until the barbarian fought the beast to a tense standoff on the road.

"Grab the wizard!" Amabored called to me.

I ran for the supine Redulfo, slung him over my shoulder like a sack of laundry, and then loped toward Amabored, who rode to meet me. He hauled the wizard up and over the saddle. Then something caught his eye, and he pointed to the rear of the herd.

Following his gaze, I saw Lithaine balancing atop a racing cow in the middle of the thundering herd, his arms extended as if surfing the breaks around Hydra Rock. We watched him until the herd reached the open Chimera Gate. The surging tsunami of cow flesh sent the thirty-foot-high gate doors spinning like dinner plates from their massive hinges, which twisted free from their stone moorings as brick and mortar shrapnel exploded onto the street. The elf was lost in the churning maelstrom of dust and the hailstorm of debris. The herd had entered the city. *The gods help those inside*, I thought.

Amabored threw back his head and laughed. "I love it when a plan comes together!" He motioned for me to get on the horse. "Let's get inside."

I shook my head. "We need to make sure Barlan gets those kids inside."

Amabored considered this, then nodded. "Fair enough. You find the farmer. I'll stay near the gate and take care of any trouble coming from the other side."

The barbarian rammed his heels into the horse's flanks. The horse leaped forward and galloped into the swirling hurricane of dust. Through the choking clouds, I could see the remains of the Chimera Gate yawning open. Turning away from my salvation, I ran back down the road to find Barlan.

I found a long, irregular column made up of carts, wagons, and wheelbarrows, most pulled by men but for a few oxen and mules, and upon all of which were perched terrified children clutching each other. Pulling on handles and hauling at reigns, their parents and guardians were dragging the makeshift transports forward toward the ruined gate. When I saw that Barlan had roped every piece of transportation together in one long daisy chain, I silently toasted him—for a peasant, he was surprisingly competent.

Barlan had posted himself at the head of the column, where he led a single emaciated ox lashed to a hay wagon burgeoning with swaying children. He waved to me—and then an arrow slammed into his chest, fired by one of the guards topping the Shield Wall battlements. He fell to his knees. More arrows dropped around him, narrowly missing the kids. I ran to him.

"Never mind me!" Barlan croaked, blood spurting from his lips. "Get them inside before any more die!"

I could do no less. Expecting an arrow in my heart at any moment, I lifted the heavy wooden yoke from the ox and hoisted it onto my shoulders. Summoning every ounce of strength the girdle offered, I hauled on the yoke. My muscles burning, my lungs swelling like the bellows of an iron forge, I hauled the caravan forward. Stone giant strength—if this was how strong they were, I hoped never to meet one.

Arrows rained down, but the dust was so thick that the marksmen atop the Shield Wall battlements couldn't make out any clear targets. I trudged forward, dragging the caravan behind me. When at last the dust cleared a bit, I finally saw it: the ruined Chimera gate yawning wide open to reveal the city of my dreams. Even better, Lithaine stood atop a pile of charred cow carcasses firing arrows up at the battle-ments. With his infrared elf-o-vision, the dust presented no hindrance to his aim.

The elf's cover fire drove off the few remaining guards, and I was finally able to drag the caravan unmolested through the blood-streaked debris, around the scores of cow carcasses, and into the city. Since my father had banished me from his kingdom, a full four months had passed: four months of malnutrition, dysentery, and despair; four months of hardscrabble survival, with only the vague promise of better times to come. Now, my every hope for the future was embodied by the sight of those wide-open gates beckoning me within. Tears stung my eyes—from the dust or from relief, I couldn't say. I felt as if I were returning to the womb.

So I entered the Free City of Redhauke.

BOOK II

Let Me Tell You About My Prostate

1

Let me tell you about my prostate. Until age forty or so, I never thought about this infernal organ. Why would I? I'm still unsure of exactly what it is or why I have one; apparently, it's the organ that connects your dick to your balls. You never notice it until it goes bad. Once it does so, you're hard-pressed to think of anything but the ostrich egg-sized piece of hot lead shoved up your asshole, the urge to piss every fifteen minutes, and the humiliation you feel at the pathetic dribbling that passes for said urination. A prostate infection is a minor *fuck you* from the gods: not sexy enough to garner any sympathy from friends, but painful enough to fuck with your mood, your job performance, and your sex life. In the eyes of your mates, you become a pathetic whining asshole, and you catch glimpses of their secret desire to cut you loose. So does the herd range ahead of the lame.

And don't even think about getting cured. Wizards have crafted potions, unguents, and salves for me. Clerics have blessed my hindquarters. Apothecaries have shoved their arms, up to their elbows, into my rectum. Nothing has worked. After a trip to the healer, I feel like a prison bitch. Imagine the inner life of a man who spends his days looking up assholes for a living. As the man once said, proctology isn't a science; it's a calling.

2

I bring up my prostate for two reasons. The first is that this swollen organ contributes to my current malaise. I have become a brooding, inconsolable, immovable monarch; ass glued to his throne, powerless before his kingdom, impotent before his woman. My albatross isn't hanging around my neck—it's shoved up my colon. My asshole is swollen and sore. My balls feel like they're being squeezed in a vice. Fuck it—I'll I just sit here until I fall over dead, or the Seven destroy the Woerth. Either outcome is all right with me.

My prostate also reminds me of how we finally killed Redulfo the second time, after he had returned to Woerth in the form of a fully mature black dragon. Poor bastard died not once, but twice, and both times he was fucked over by his friends. So what if the Bad Brain turned him Lawful Evil, and he conspired with the Crimson Hand to kill us all and give the Woerth over to the Violet Queen? Every friendship has its ups and downs.

This was after Lithaine began to wield Starfall, after the Siege of Helene, and after Jo Ki-Rin had warned us that defeating Koschei the Deathless would destroy our fellowship and send at least one of us to his death. We ignored all the warning signs. All we knew was that we needed the Bad Brain to complete our Quest—and since said brain currently resided inside Redulfo's dragon skull, we were prepared to slaughter anything that stood in the way of us performing a craniotomy on our unfortunate friend. We were all around Tenth-Level adventurers at the time—badasses, but still vulnerable to something with a lot of hit points and special abilities. Like a black dragon.

REDULFO HAD SET UP SHOP IN THE FORMER DIGS OF GYGAX AND RIGSBY: the Valley of Sorcerers, a highly defensible piece of real estate in the Shadow Mountains accessible only by a treacherous pass guarded by cloud giants, bugbears, and spiders big enough to eat a Buick. The Quest reassembled, we set out into the Valley—Amabored, Lithaine, James, Malcolm, Wilberd, and me—to send the wizard once again to his reward. We were all fighters, rangers, and paladins, with only Malcolm's few spells to combat Redulfo's sorcery, and only the monk to heal our wounds. We could kill anything that moved, but we were at a serious disadvantage against a wizard. So what? We were still young and headstrong, and we didn't know from death.

Our first night in the Shadow Pass, we ran into trouble. Weather was setting in; it was October, and the snow had already begun to fall on the lower mountain peaks. As we scaled the pass, we left the deciduous forests behind, and began to encounter the hardier whatever-bushes and don't-know-what-they're-called trees that meant we were entering bugbear country. Soon enough, the bugbears ambushed us.

It happened just after the pass narrowed into a steep-walled gorge. The bugbears had scouted us from the top of a superior position until we passed one of their preconstructed traps. With his handy elf-o-vision, Lithaine was the first to spot the scout.

"Two o'clock," Lithaine said. "Behind the boulder. You know what that means."

"It means hit the fucking dirt!" cried Amabored. Then the avalanche struck.

3

For barely sentient half-imp, half-bear man-eaters, bugbears were clever. They had disguised the trap as a tree-lined rock crown on either side of the gorge. When we came within range, their scout gave a rumbling bellow that echoed from the canyon walls. His fellows kicked out the supporting logs, and the entire top of the gorge collapsed in a thundering avalanche of rock and wood.

We bolted for cover. The raven-haired, elven paladin Malcolm thrust his +4 Force Blade into the air and let loose with a war cry. The sword burst into cold white flame.

"To me!" He cried, as the gorge collapsed around us. Malcolm took heroism seriously—unlike the rest of us, he wasn't just in it for the money. As children seeking their mother's skirt, we ran to him. A thunderclap rolled as the air around Malcolm hardened into a Force Wall extending in a wide hemisphere around the blade. We all reached the interior of the force field safely—all but James, that is, who only managed to get three-quarters of his body inside before the avalanche struck. He screamed as the collapsing rock crushed his left leg into powdered jelly.

There was no time to help him. Malcolm's force field dissipated, and we braced for what we knew was next. Down the new tumble of rock, concealed by the immense cloud of choking dust, the bugbears came. Not a few dozen, either; they came by the score. From somewhere off in the dust-shrouded distance, I heard Amabored's battle cry:

"COOOOORRRRNNN-HOLE!!!"

The first bugbear hit me with the force of a charging rhino. Bugbears are big fucking beasts that wear whatever scraps of armor they can find. You aim for the neck or the gut, and you hope for the best. I had long ago given up swords for my trusty battle-axe; what the axe lacked in speed, it more than made up in smiting ability. I simply found a defensible position to protect my back, and I let them come. Attacking me was like raping a buzz saw.

Spearing the bugbear in the belly with the spike-end of my axe-haft, I hoisted its stinking, flea-ridden carcass over my head. Behind it came a dozen more. To my left, Lithaine pumped arrows into the mob, then switched deftly to Starfall as they closed within claw-and-fang range. To my right, Amabored and Malcolm stood backs together, severing limbs and cleaving skulls. Behind me, Wilberd covered my back with his whirling staff and unicorn horn.

It doesn't get any better than that.

After an hour of battle, the remaining dozen or so bugbears ran squealing for the hills. We were all drenched in blood. Amabored had taken a slashing wound across his chest, while Wilberd had been tossed down a sliding fall of jagged rocks. The rest of us emerged from the fracas with only minor claw marks, scrapes, and bite wounds. Wilberd administered a few *Cure Wounds* blessings and rationed a few vials of *Health* potions to those who took the worst of it. We managed to heal James's leg—he'd walk again, eventually—but he wasn't going anywhere now.

As we gathered to smoke the ceremonial pipeweed victory bowl, Amabored scowled into the middle distance.

"That was too coordinated an assault for bugbears," he said. "They had help."

"Redulfo must know we're coming," I said.

"Then this is just the first of it," said Malcolm. "Gird your loins, gents."

Lithaine turned a semicircle and extended a one-finger salute. Since losing his kingdom, his already-short fuse had burned down to a black nub. "We're on our way, Redulfo! You hear me, you fat fucking lizard? We're coming!"

"I'll drink to that," I said, reaching for my flask.

4

I miss that son-of-a-bitch Redulfo. In those first desperate days inside the walls of Redhauke, I was drawn to both his unflappable demeanor and his unshakeable pessimism. Amabored was larger than life, craving chaos the way some men crave women or drink. Lithaine existed at a continuous slow boil. Redulfo, meanwhile, could stare down Lord Eckberd himself and dismiss him with a single, exquisitely-timed retort laden with withering sarcasm. He became a badass wizard, and one of my truest comrades—but former comrades make the most implacable foes.

Back in the day, however, he was just Redulfo: a First-Level wizard clinging to a rung on the social ladder somewhere between privy-cleaners and customs agents. Apprentice wizards were laughed at, spat upon, shoved around, de-pantsed, beaten and humiliated, and they had to take it like the pencil-necked geeks they were. Woe be unto anyone, however, who got on a wizard's bad side; those who survived their apprenticeships to become powerful sorcerers invariably returned to settle old scores. You could be sitting in a tavern chatting up a wench when some scrawny mage to whom you gave an atomic wedgie ten years prior would appear at the door to vaporize you. Me, I always made friends with wizards. I've only beheaded the ones who had it coming.

In those days, Redulfo seemed like a shrimp who needed protecting—particularly in those first weeks inside the city, when the Redhauke Guard scoured the streets searching for the rogue wizard who had caused the Great Stampede. Perhaps you haven't seen what five thousand head of terrified cattle can do to a city: buildings reduced to rubble, cobblestones slick with gore, gnome scum and imp-spawn looting every shop and stall from the Bazaar to Hundred Fountain Square. The looting brought out the Guard in force to cordon off entire city blocks and pump crossbow bolts into anything that moved.

For weeks afterward, cows roamed the streets shitting on everything. They wandered into pubs, upset apple carts, chewed their cud in the middle of the street, and lumbered into churches. Finally, the Lord Mayor appealed to old Sklaar, the Grand Thaumaturge of the Wizard's College, for help. Sklaar sent faculty and students into the city to fry the cows, which were then scooped up by roving posses of butchers and turned into steaks, roasts, and hamburger. The tanners came after.

We felt bad about the destruction, but we sure as hell weren't going to spend winter outside the city walls. That was for chumps.

Besides, we had tempered the destruction with the good deed of getting those kids out of Doomtown. The kids turned out okay; afterward, the child snatchings seemed to stop. Years later, I'd occasionally pass by a gaggle of teen street-urchins regaling their younger companions with tales of the fierce young giant who had dragged a thousand wagons full of children into the city.

And the rest of Doomtown? Once the herd passed through the Chimera Gate, about half of the refugees came flooding in before order was restored. At the Lord Mayor's orders, guards lined up in regiments ready to mow them down with crossbow fire. Fortunately, cooler heads prevailed. The site of the Chimera Gate lying in ruins seemed to snap the city awake; maybe it wasn't a great idea to attack a

starving mob. So, Redhauke rallied. The High Council ordered the
construction of a refugee camp near the Pit, the Godsway churches
opened their granaries, and the newcomers settled in. I hadn't known
Barlan, but I wished he were around to see it. The refugees were
unemployed and homeless, but at least they'd live—most of them,
anyway.

It might have been the terrifying rumors that finally awakened
the city's sense of compassion. Word had come from the North that
more refugees were fleeing before an army led by Plague Knights. At
the head of this column, rumor had it, rode Lord Eckberd the Pestilent, he who had slain the kings of Kenwood, Helene and Varnalla in
the Dread Wars some five hundred years earlier. Survivors recounted
a skirmish line of rats that flooded into towns and villages to infect
the population before the Plague Knights sallied forth to murder
every living thing that remained.

In his famous treatise *The Balance*, Sir Michael of Moorcock
argued that the wars of the Multiverse were waged not between Good
versus Evil, but rather between Law and Chaos: *Logos* and Hellfire,
the two fundamental and unalterably opposed forces in the Multiverse. Every universe was a manifestation of this war. When the
cosmic scales in any universe tipped too far to one side, an Eternal
Champion would arise to restore the balance. Five hundred years
ago, the Dread Wars had found Chaos nearly triumphant. To restore
the balance, the legendary warlord Arturus had led a quest including
Koschei's former apprentices Gygax and Rigsby, dwarf warrior Storm
Stonegorm, Eckberd the Bold—before he was slain and reincarnated
as Koschei's warlord—the elven priestess Gemalatel, and the Cloud
Rider Wanbli to cast down the Deathless One and restore the
Balance. If Lord Eckberd had indeed risen again, could Koschei be
far behind? If we wanted to see an entire tavern full of drunks shit
their pants, we need only mention Koschei and wait for the minor-
key chords followed by the ominous silence. We did it often, just for
laughs.

When we weren't rumor-mongering, we were trying to figure out our next move. The only topic off-limits was the apparition witnessed by Lithaine. Anyone who mentioned the ghost found the elf's dagger at his throat.

"You better keep a low profile," Amabored told Redulfo, as we sat nursing ales at what would become our regular haunt, the Suds 'n Shade. The proprietor, a retired illusionist named Jaspin Spellbinder —yes, *that* Jaspin Spellbinder, the goddamn shit-stained asshole— didn't ask any questions, provided that you didn't start any shit.

"No kidding," said Redulfo, sulking in the corner. "Right now, I'm as useful as tits on a walrus."

"Walruses don't have tits?" I asked.

Together, the four of us had enough coppers to pay for a single room and a week's worth of short rations. We needed jobs, and soon. Once the heat died down, Redulfo planned to take his letter of recommendation from the noble lord of his hometown and apply for entrance into the School of Thaumaturgy. He couldn't go near the place, however, until the residue of enchantment wore off. If the College detected any Twelfth-Level magic on him, he'd be out of the city on his ass.

While Redulfo laid low, the rest of us explored our new home. Even on the cusp of winter, the sensory assault was overwhelming. The smells hit you first: the deep, sultry aroma of a hundred spices hovering in a lurid cloud over the Bazaar; the briny stench of the fish markets; bread baking in the bustling kitchens of the Merchant Quarter; those were the welcome smells. In contrast, there was the hallucinogenic cloud of body odor radiating from 100,000 citizens from a dozen different races—if you could bottle the stuff, you could napalm villages with it. With no sanitary system to speak of, raw sewage and offal was tossed into pits and poured into the sewers. You could tell when a rat-catcher was nearby the wide swath his smell cut through the crowd—not even the cutpurses would get near one. There was the giant cat-box smell wafting over from Gnome Row, and the unnamable horror emanating from the Pit near the Mere Wall. Have you ever sat across the table from an arch-devil cutting a juicy fart after a meal of sauerkraut and boiled eggs? I have. The Pit was worse.

Amabored, Lithaine and I were all fighters. If we wanted work, we had to apply to the Fighters' Chapter of the Adventurers Guild. Because any half-wit with a notched sword and a buckler could call himself a fighter, the waiting list was long. The turnover rate, on the other hand, was the highest of any Chapter. Send ten First-Level fighters into a dungeon, and maybe two would come out. We were cannon fodder, and we knew it.

Here's how adventuring works in Redhauke. As an aspiring fighter, you take any work you can get—bouncer at a brothel, dock-worker, stable boy, message runner, census taker—whatever manner of humiliation you can endure. Your goal is to get apprenticed to one of the adventuring trades. Blacksmiths, armorers, fletchers, and swordsmiths all must grease the Guild to land a contract supplying the thousands of adventurers who funnel through the city. After suffering through one shit job after another while avoiding a shank in the ribs or some gut-rotting disease, you begin to figure out who's who. You chat up flea-ridden dwarfs in alehouses, bang homely wait-resses, or suffer the sweaty advances of swishy nobles until you get word that Bob the bowmaker or Sam the swordsmith is in the market for an apprentice. If fortune smiles, you might land a decent guild-master who doesn't beat you or whore you out. After a year or two, he might nominate you for Guild membership. At that point, you're put through the Exam.

The Exam happens twice a year and draws apprentices from all over the Free Kingdoms. Designed by guildmasters and administered by journeymen, the Exam consists of fifteen highly diabolical and dangerous feats of skill designed to test your intelligence, strength, wisdom, dexterity, and constitution. You're dropped into pits filled with scorpions. You're forced into corridors filled with collapsing ceil-ings, whirring scythes, swinging pendulums, and springing spikes. You're thrown down a chute naked into a water tank full of baby dragon eels. The final contest is usually against an ogre, a giant cave spider, or a dire wolf—to the death, of course, with clerics standing by to heal mortal wounds.

Only a congenital idiot would subject himself to such torture. No way were we going to play it straight. Winter was setting in, we needed jobs, and Amabored had contacts. There was a black market in Guild memberships, and we were going to tap into it. Who got anywhere in life without cutting a few corners?

5

It was during this period that I first met Melinda the Blade. Although I have much to atone for in life, she tops the list. No one goes through life sinless—that is, if you believe in sin. I believe in it because I can't figure out the evolutionary purpose of guilt. Is guilt merely the state of conflict between the ego and the superego that our mind-melding wizards say it is? Guilt over big crimes, like murder or adultery, may indeed have evolved to ensure social cohesion and the survival of the species. But what about guilt over everyday, petty sins? What biological purpose does it serve? Why feel guilty because you fucked someone over? Who gives a shit but the person you hurt?

Melinda the Blade was her *nom de guerre*; I never knew her real name. I first encountered her while guarding pipeweed shipments imported by Saggon, Over-Boss of the Thieves Guild, on midnight smuggling runs by barges plying the vast underground canals that serve as Redhauke's circulatory system. It was deadly dull work, mostly sitting around rolling knucklebones with whatever lunk-headed swordsman with whom you happened to be paired that night. Back when organized crime was run at the family level, drug shipments were hijacked as often as the sun rose. Once Saggon the

Large consolidated underworld power in the Thieves Guild by simultaneously executing twenty-three key crime family heads during the Feast of the Fountains in 3930, the resulting monopoly effectively ended hijackings. Lately, drug heists had ticked back up again, which set Saggon's teeth on edge. Armed guards began accompanying the barges, while swordsmen oversaw unloading on the Under-Canal docks.

For Amabored, Lithaine and me, petty thug-work for the Thieves Guild represented our best chance of gaining Adventurers Guild admission; save up enough scratch, and we could bribe our way past the Exam. Saggon paid shit, but working for him gave us an excuse to act like big swinging dicks instead of the tiny tadgers we were.

On one particularly dull and freezing night deep in midwinter, Lithaine and I were minding our business, smoking a phatty on the dock with Barry and Tim, a pair of mouth-breathers whom Saggon's man picked up at the marina. A barrel filled with burning refuse passed for warmth.

We were guarding a one-horse dray upon which sat piled high dozens of barrels stuffed with the finest gnome leaf this side of the Brandywine Bridge. As we smoked, the barge from which we had unloaded the shipment slipped along the canal and into the darkness; our orders were to stand by until a charlie arrived to drive the wagon through the Warren to the subterranean warehouse earmarked for storage. Though noble and commoner alike smoked pipeweed as often as they could get their hands on it, it was nonetheless illegal, for no reason other than the barrels full of cash made by the Guard and the Thieves Guild as they respectively enforced and broke the prohibition laws. Only gnomes could smoke it legally. The corresponding resentment resulted in many of them getting stomped on—especially the ones who sat smugly in front of their quaint little round doors smoking their ridiculous long-stemmed pipes.

The dock stood about one hundred chains below Hundred Fountain Square, within the massive vaulted tunnel through which ran the Grand Canal that bisected the underbelly of the city from Mere Harbor to the Whitehorse River. The Under-Canals were miserable places to spend your time—the air wretchedly cold and clammy like a bucketful of fish heads, the canal water brimming with the offal of the city, the stone walls glistening with poisonous slime and the Rat King's army continually massing for attack. It took a week of shivering down in those godforsaken canals before I started dipping into the pipeweed with the rest of the boys. To stay sane in this line of work, you had to stay stoned.

"Let me get this straight," I was saying to Lithaine. "You really haven't hit puberty?"

One of the most enjoyable ways to pass the time was to get Lithaine fired up and watch the flaming magma ooze out of his ears. The surest way to get him fired up was to question his elfness.

"It doesn't work that way," he said, blood rising to the tips of his pointed ears.

"So how does it work? You're too young to knock up an elf maiden, right?"

"I don't want to talk about it."

"Then I'm right. You're still in short pants."

"If you know what's good for you, you'll shut your fucking pie hole."

"What about whacking off? Do elves pull the taffy? Shake hands with the bishop? Groom the wookie?"

"Groom the wookie," repeated Tim the swordsman. Tim might have laughed, had a pair of throwing-stars not thunked into his forehead and sent him to his reward at that very instant.

"Jesus, Mary, and Joseph!" I cried. Before my pipeweed-addled brain could signal my sword hand to draw steel, Lithaine had drawn his bow and launched a pair of feathered shafts at a cloaked, masked figure perched on the high catwalk that ran the perimeter of the canal. The second shaft pierced the man's throat. He flipped over the railing and plunged into the fetid canal water.

Three more throwing-stars—two buried themselves in Barry's throat, dropping him, while the third bored into my cheap boiled leather cuirass directly above my left nipple. A stab of pain, and then blood dribbled down my chest. A quick calculation quantified the danger: throwing-stars did one to four points of damage, and I had twelve health points. I couldn't take much more of this.

Out of one eye, I saw Lithaine take aim at two more would-be ninjas crouched on the opposite catwalk. Out of the other, I saw the horse rear up and lunge forward. Someone had grabbed the reigns. A lost shipment would be a mere prelude to the loss of our heads beneath Saggon's knife. There was nothing for it: I launched myself at the dray just as the hijacker sent the horse flying up the long, curved ramp twisting high into the darkness.

Hanging on to the dray was a chore. If the driver had noticed my crash landing, he wasn't letting on. Creeping forward atop the barrels as the wagon rattled and thumped up the brick ramp, I could barely discern the slight cloaked figure hunched over the reigns. All I needed was a hand around his neck, and that would be the end of him.

As I crept forward to make my move, the driver whipped around —revealing the flat, heart-shaped face of a woman. I had time only to note a pair of burning emerald eyes and a nimbus of curly auburn hair before the woman planted a mailed fist in my face. I went flying. An extended pratfall down the ramp found me battered, bloodied, and glaring at the dray as it disappeared into the gravelike darkness.

Fucking hell, I thought. Three months in Redhauke and already I had to hightail it out of town.

Lithaine approached, wiping the blood from his sword. He helped me to my feet.

"Did you get a look at the driver?" he asked.

"I did," I said. "And I'll see her again."

6

Probabilities collide, sending other people careening into our lives: siblings, friends, lovers, rivals. If you live long enough, a lot of them hurtle right back out. When I watched Melinda walk out of my life for good, back into the sewer tunnel beneath Redhauke after the gory demise of the Rat King, I understood that I'd never see her again. What I didn't get was how quickly everything I knew about her—her face, her voice, the smell of her hair, her laugh, her smile, her sex—would rush away from me, as broken waves surge back to the sea. When I think of her now, I see only the faintest of phantasms, memories as wisps of smoke, white fractals spiraling upward in the dark. We're all ghosts to someone.

Now, I recall every detail, and I'm here to tell you that it's a hell of a lot better to forget. I need only cast my gaze inward to stand once again in Hundred Fountain Square as two bronzed, bare-chested Cloud Riders, their hair streaming in dark ribbons, their white wings outstretched, descend in a flourish through the bitter February cold. High above Redhauke, a phalanx of Riders herds the thunderheads piled in tall purple columns above the city spires. It is three years after I entered Redhauke; nearly a year has passed since Melinda stepped through the Hellmouth and was seemingly lost to me forever.

Legend had long told of the winged warriors who bent the weather to their will. That day, seeing them in the flesh reminded those of us in the Square that we really didn't know shit about anything. Between these two descending riders, they held the reins of four winged horses bearing a litter. They landed, and the steeds pranced fitfully, their breath steaming as if from a forge, their wings flexing fitfully. A crowd of gawkers filled the Square.

Any hope I had of blending into the crowd died when the Riders fixed me with their gazes. In those days, I couldn't pass a single day without one thing or another landing on me like a fucking cartoon piano.

One of the Riders, a woman with skin the color of polished oak, thrust a spear under my nose. "Be you Elberon of the Isles?"

"Who wants to know?" I asked.

"Answer, earthbound, or you'll taste my spear," said the Rider.

"Okay, then. Yeah, I'm him."

The woman gestured back to the horses, their wings now folded across their flanks. "This woman bade us bring her to you."

Inside the litter, a figure slumped against a pillow. I stepped forward, exposed to the invisible pressure of several hundred pairs of eyes now turned toward me. I pulled back the curtain, and there she was.

Her eyes were closed. Her ringleted auburn hair, strewn across the pillow, was now run through with a streak of white. A lump leaped into my throat. Relief—pure, blessed relief, ambrosia straight from the goblet of Frigg—flooded my heart. *Alive*, I thought. Ten months of crushing guilt vanished in an instant.

SHE HAD BEEN THROUGH SOME SHIT SINCE I HAD SEEN HER LAST, WHEN I cried out her name as the mighty obsidian doors of the Hellmouth slammed shut, trapping her in Hell. Talk about getting the dirty end of the stick.

"Come back!" I cried that night. The Screaming Skull, which I had worn in place of my own head long enough to vanquish Malacoda, was now gone—tossed by me into a lake of Hellfire with the blessing of King Minos of Limbo. Above my head, the Blue Falcon shook in its final death throes; soon the deep dungeons themselves would collapse, entombing me within. The fleshy walls of the Hellmouth writhed and twisted, the tortured souls within crying out in psychic agony. Separating Melinda and I were the doors of the Hellmouth itself, the runes carved into the brimstone glowing crimson as they began to swing shut again on their monstrous hinges.

"I have to save them!" Melinda called.

"You can't save them! They're dead!"

"Maybe I can still save their souls. I have to try!"

Then I understood: Melinda never quit. The fires of Hell itself held no power over her will. If she had to brave them to save the souls of the children we failed to save in life, then through the black bones of Tartarus, into the bottomless pits of Malebolge, and across the frozen plain of Cocytus itself would she journey to save them. In her own way, she was ten times the hero that I ever was. Her balls were ten times bigger than mine.

"Then I'm coming with you!" I called, racing toward her. A geyser of flaming Hellfire and brimstone erupted before me, the force flinging me backward. The Hellmouth shuddered. Then, I heard a voice both familiar and terrifying.

"I think not," came the figure's voice, filling my head like a tumor. "You have a date, I'm afraid."

I didn't turn to face that voice—not yet. My gaze was fixed on Melinda, standing within the Hellmouth, prepared to sacrifice everything for the sake of seven doomed children.

"Melinda!" I cried. The Hellmouth doors slammed shut, their massive hinges groaning so loudly that I could only read her lips as she uttered what I would come to think of her final words—*I love you.* Then came the high, keening screams of the souls trapped in the doors as they were pulled into the Void.

Some men wait their entire lives in vain for a woman to utter those words. I should have run after her that day. I should have beat on the doors of Hell with my head until they opened again.

Before I could make a move, I saw him—the assassin Garrin Grimmreaper, my dark counterpart, my negation. Suddenly he was there, the black cowl masking his face, his black scythe drawn. It was our first encounter. At the time, I knew shit about the Quest, or Koschei, or the Grimmreaper, or any of it. I knew only that I was terrified of him. Even so, I might have mistaken him for some garden-variety tool of Saggon—until I heard his voice again, caroming around inside my head.

"Too late for the Skull," came the dark figure's voice. "But I'll have that girdle off your stinking corpse, shitstain."

"Come and get it, assclown," I said.

THAT WAS TEN MONTHS EARLIER. UNTIL I SAW MELINDA ASLEEP IN THAT litter, I thought she was dead. So, you may forgive me if I mistook relief for love. When I scooped her into my arms, soaking in her reality, and when her eyes opened to find mine, and she smiled, it sure as fuck felt like love. Chemically, what's the difference?

"Hey, stranger," Melinda said. Her face was pale. There was a new scar near her left ear. "Buy me a drink?"

"Sister, I'll buy you the whole bar," I said.

7

B ack when I first met Melinda, I didn't know from women. They were alien creatures, as exotic as the rarest of dryads. My mother Lisandra died from lung-fever barely six months after my birth, and the nurses, nannies and *au pairs* who raised me are nothing to me now but a blur of sagging breasts, sour breath, silent farts, and cold porridge. So, I didn't exactly grow up comfortable around women. You'd think that being a prince would give you an edge with the ladies, and you'd be right—about my older brother Elderon, who was banging chambermaids in junior high. It wasn't just that he was the oldest, that his jaw jutted a little more than mine, that he stood a hair taller, or that his dimples were placed just so. He also seemed to intuitively get women in a way that I never could. I was a gangly dorkwad of a kid, underweight and struggling with personal hygiene; once old enough to crave the attention of girls, I had as much success as a mouse at a cat party. So, I wallowed in self-pity and spent long, stolen moments staring into the mirror. It never occurred to me that if I simply cleaned up my act, dressed a little better, and stopped acting like such a fucking dipshit, then maybe my luck would change. No dice. As I stumbled into manhood, I focused on my swordplay in the hope that a steel phallus would grant me the confidence I so sorely lacked.

When the woman on the cart planted her fist in my eye, she therefore struck a hornet's nest. I couldn't get that chick out of my head. As I sat swilling beer in the Suds 'n Shade, sparring with Amabored outside Saggon's armory, or writhing on my cot at Lady Hagg's Boarding House on Lamplight Street, I pored over the fleeting image of her flat, pug-nosed face burned into my brain. In a city of 100,000 souls, I had to find her again.

"It was an inside job," Amabored whispered as he, Lithaine and I cooled our heels outside Saggon's office the next day. The Thieves Guild headquarters, a lavish, legendary, decaying freak show of a hotel and inn named the Blue Falcon, stood brazenly in the Thieves Quarter at the corner of Halberd and Chainmail Streets. The Blue Falcon was built, so the legend told, by Storm Stonegorm as a gift to Arturus after the end of the Dread Wars. The Falcon was legendary because, to put it simply, the manor's interior did not match its exterior. Without, the Falcon was a fantastically ornate inn and manor house, the sprawl of which covered two full city blocks and included copious entrances, tall spires, myriad carved beasties, stables, courtyards, gardens and outbuildings, all towering behind a ten-foot-tall stone wall topped with wrought-iron spikes. Within, the Falcon seemed far larger and more sprawling than its exterior footprint could possibly allow. Corridors ran for scores of yards before angling into tangled mazes of narrow passages. The inn's Great Room, renowned for hosting what most wags believed to be the longest continuous party in existence, seemed about three sizes too large for the building. It was not uncommon for guests to wander into a room and, when they wandered back out, find themselves in another part of the building altogether. Some doorways, rumors told, led to different universes entirely.

The approach to Saggon's office, lurking at the top of his personal tower, was straightforward enough. Squirm through the Great Room past the ever-evolving horde of cutpurses, scallywags, rapscallions, button-men, grifters, gypsies, tramps, and thieves gathered to swill the cheapest beer and rye whiskey in the Free Kingdoms; speak the password to the one-eyed ogre who guarded the tower with spiked club at the ready; ascend the dank staircase into the tight stone labyrinth that squatted near the top of the tower, being careful to flip the hidden levers that prevented poison-tipped darts from sending you into a mouth-foaming death rattle; skirt the hidden pit of sentient Black Sand that lay in wait to squeeze your internal organs out through your orifices; offer a hello to Saggon's hot Shadow Elf secretary—who kept a hand-crossbow cocked and loaded beneath her desk—and you were in.

In the reception area sat the dark elf, her sublimely long teal legs driving us to distraction as she studied her carved black nails. That yesterday we were mere hired cogs in a vast thrumming engine of vice and crime, and today were moments away from an audience with the Man himself, was not lost on us. Amabored saw it as an opportunity, Lithaine as a threat. I saw it as a reason to piss my pants.

"Inside job? Get the fuck out," Lithaine whispered back. "The bats down there work for Saggon, for fuck's sake. Who would cross him?"

"Maybe it's one of the old families trying to muscle their way back in," I offered.

"All I know is it stinks like a dwarf's sweat socks," said Amabored. "Yours wasn't the only shipment hijacked last night. I heard five shipments went down, and each one lightly guarded. Somebody sang. If he thinks it's you two, then the gibbet will be the least of your problems."

"Let him try," Lithaine said absently, as his gaze traversed the blue-green curves of the shadow-elf.

"Good luck with that," Amabored said. "I'll bet she prefers an elf with hair between his legs. Or is it spun silk you lot grow?"

With a metallic *snirk*, Lithaine's knife swung against Amabored's throat. The barbarian's grin widened, and then it vanished as the receptionist loosed a crossbow bolt that buried itself in the wall a quarter-inch from Lithaine's skull.

At that moment the door to Saggon's office swung open, and a blast of frigid air hit us in the face. The Over-Boss hailed from the Fordal Wastes, some of the most inhospitable country on Woerth and a thousand leagues north of Redhauke, and thus kept his quarters as cold as a witch's tit—or so we had heard. Had we known what he really was, we'd have fled his office and not stopped running until we reached the Pustiu Waste.

The receptionist motioned us into an alcove, where two body-guards relieved us of our weapons. Then we were shoved into Saggon's office.

We found the Over-Boss waiting behind a desk in a simple, well-appointed office hung with bearskins. The desk was laden with food and drink. From two carved stone bear heads snarling on the wall opposite the desk blew twin streams of chilled air, while on the wall behind his desk a great stone fireplace stood unused. Along the curved tower wall hung the stuffed and mounted heads of what we took to be the bosses of the seven crime families who once ran the Redhauke underworld. On the fireplace mantle rested on a pedestal the scimitar-shaped, petrified red dragon phallus that we would later use to send Redulfo the Black to his reward. Had we the foresight to sneak it out of Saggon's office that day, we would have saved ourselves a passel of trouble.

As for Saggon the Large himself, the man did not disappoint. Like my father, he bore the aura of a man who had learned to bend other men to his will. His head was bald, his nose Roman, and what had once been a lantern jaw now struggled to support the weight of multiple chins. Saggon had once been a powerful man, in the physical sense of muscle, bone, and sinew—a fierce warrior possessed of boundless ambition and ruthless cunning. Now, his sobriquet referred solely to his disgusting Jabba-like girth. Sure, he could still squash our skulls like peanut shells, but he'd have to catch us first.

"Boys," Saggon said, motioning us inside with a wave of a sausage-fingered hand. "Come on in, have a seat. Have some mulled wine. From a little gnome tavern I know. They make the best. And here, some crab cakes from the wharf. And the little cheeses there. Try that one there, the Camembert. I get a shipment in from Arrendell. They age it in gryphon skulls."

We sat. We partook. I tried to keep my hands from shaking. For minutes, there was no conversation as Saggon attacked his own plate and poured two goblets of spiced wine down his gullet. With a belch that set the candles to swooning, he wiped the wine from his greasy lips and gave us the once-over.

"So, Manny. Moe. Jack," he began. "Here's the thing. On any other day a shipment gets pinched on your watch, then I'm afraid you leave our employ by the swiftest means available. No offense, that's just the way I do business. But today, I'm feeling magnanimous. Frankly, I need your help."

"At your service, my lord," said Amabored, bowing from the waist.

Saggon seemed surprised that one of us had dared to speak. He let it pass. "Yes, you are. It's the woman, you see. One of you saw her last night?"

"I—I did, my lord," I stammered.

The Over-Boss leaned forward in his chair, his fur-shrouded fat sliding forward. "Did you speak to her? How many men were with her?"

Lithaine and I told the story. From Saggon's reaction, we learned that he knew her—and that he was afraid of her. The moment passed, and the Over-Boss creaked backward in his chair.

"So, here's how it is," he said, taking a hand-rolled cigar from a case and lighting it. "You two swells are bait. She got the drop on you once, so she'll be back. You let her snag another shipment, one week from tonight. When she does, our barbarian friend here will be waiting inside the false bottom. She gets to where she's going, and you find out where she's holed up. Whatever you do, don't you dare take her out. Leave that part to me."

"Could be a suicide mission," Lithaine said.

"Life is a suicide mission, my pointed-eared friend," Saggon said. "My man downstairs will arrange the details. Be at the Falcon at midnight on the twenty-third. Any questions?"

We had no questions. The Over-Boss dismissed us with a wave. Once back in the lobby, I took Amabored aside.

"Let me have the spot in the wagon," I said. "I have a score to settle with this broad."

"Sure, you do," Amabored said. "Be my guest."

8

That there was more to this story, we had no doubt. Saggon had dozens of thugs on his payroll smarter and more talented than us. Why send us to get close to a woman who seemed to have his number? He had to be playing an angle—one that would most likely result in us being dead.

"Saggon's not that smart," said Jaspin Spellbinder—yes, still the same Jaspin Spellbinder who fucked us as hard as it's possible to get fucked—proprietor of the Suds 'n Shade tavern, tucked on the corner of Specter Lane in the Guild Quarter of Redhauke. Suds was the premier watering hole for Redhauke adventurers, the place to see and be seen, to pick up rumors about deserted towers filled to the brim with booty and doubloons, about forgotten catacombs strewn with emeralds and rubies, about a certain necropolis outside the village of Hightower in which every other crypt held enough jewelry to buy the finest mansion in the city. On any given night, the place was packed to the rafters, knee deep in body odor and bullshit as swordsmen, sorcerers, rogues, and priests of every race, stripe, and denomination traded war stories, scars, women, and blows. A former adventurer himself, Jaspin kept the drinks cheap and a bottomless supply of anecdotes, insults, and quips at hand. He asked only that you not fuck with him or his livelihood. Cross him, and he'd unleash some mind-melting spectral illusionist shit on you that would leave you gouging out your own eyeballs or swallowing your tongue.

Jaspin liked us because we only showed up when we had cash on the barrelhead. During the frequent slow afternoons when we had naught to do but nurse our beers and watch the flotsam and jetsam of the street drift past the front door, he'd regale us with tales of his old adventuring days—like the time he was captured by the Negali tribesmen on the Serpent Islands, who lashed him to a tree, tortured him, and forced him to drink hallucinogenic Beholder blood before sending him into to the Pit of Dagal, from whence no man returns. I don't know who the hell Dagal was, but then again, neither does Jaspin. When the tribesmen bound his hands, they failed to gag him, which allowed him to cast the one spell in all the Nine Books of Thaumaturgy that doesn't require a hand gesture or a material component: the First-Level illusionist spell *Blind Enemy*. Suddenly every tribesman within a hundred-foot radius saw the lights go out. While they fluttered about like headless chickens, Jaspin worked his way out of his bindings and walked away. Any other adventurer would have braved the Pit of Dagal and its dozens of chambers, ten-foot-wide corridors, secret doors, clever traps, and hordes of killable monsters, all for the chance to rack up treasure and Guild experience points. Not Jaspin. Above all else, he treasured his own hide—which was why he retired from adventuring to tend bar. That he was up to far more than bartending, we had no clue.

"Seriously, the guy has more earwax than brains," Jaspin was telling us as our asses were once again wearing out his bar stools. "I have hemorrhoids smarter than him."

"How do you run a criminal empire with no brains?" Redulfo asked.

"By surrounding yourself with smart people who have an interest in seeing you do well," Jaspin said. "The Over-Boss is always a target. Better to be the guy whispering in the Man's ear than be the Man yourself. This woman—she's highly placed, or she possesses skills that Saggon has found useful. For some reason, she's turned on him."

"Enough shop talk," Amabored said. "Come on, Jaspin, batter up."

"You'd better warm up with a couple of beers. It's going to be a while."

Saggon had given us a bonus to arm up for the work ahead. We were supposed to spend it to repair our patchy quilted armor, sharpen our blades, and fill our quivers. Instead, the three of us— Redulfo liked to keep a clear head—pooled our argentae to purchase three Flaming Telepaths, Jaspin's specialty cocktail. We had been itching to try one for weeks, but it was too pricey for those of us living in abject poverty. That day, the argentae burning holes in our breeches found us racing straight for Jaspin's place to have our minds blown.

The drink had to be ordered two hours in advance. Jaspin needed two assistants to help him mix it. While much of the process took place in the tavern's cellar and had never been witnessed by patrons, I did later learn that, besides containing equal parts Shōchū, triple-sec, and Everclear, the drink also contained wyvern milk, dryad nectar, and green fairy sweat—three of the more powerful hallucinogens on Woerth. There was a blowtorch involved. Jaspin also cast an enchantment of some sort on it, which was possibly the real source of its power. He served it *flambé* in an imp skull. The *coup de grâce* required the would-be imbiber to chant, in High Elvish, *Nothing good can possibly come of this.*

When Jaspin and his apprentices finally emerged from the cellar with the flaming imp skulls in hand, the ten or so other patrons in the bar fell silent. All eyes were on us. My feet went ice-cold, and I found myself glancing sideways at Amabored. We had heard tales of Telepath drinkers who returned from their trips less than whole; some were now sprawled in the gutters of Redhauke screaming in terror from unseen horrors. Had either of my companions given me an out, I would have taken it.

Then again, the money was spent. How could I expect to brave monster-filled dungeons if I couldn't handle a stiff drink?

"Bottoms up," Amabored said to Lithaine and me.

"Nice knowing you fellows," said Redulfo. He moved farther away down the bar.

9

With a final prayer to my ancestors, I thrust my face into the flames and poured the hot liquid down my throat. Immediately, I perceived a fantastic ripping sound, as if a sheet of parchment as large as the Woerth was being torn asunder. The Suds 'n Shade disappeared. I plunged headlong into a spiraling black tunnel filled with stars. My stomach rocketed into my throat; my balls felt as large as roc eggs. Filled with brain-exploding terror and elation, I fell through this cosmic wormhole for what seemed like hours as planets, stars, and galaxies swirled around me in a maelstrom of creation.

In the vast interstellar distance, I perceived a pinprick of green light. As I rocketed forward, the pinprick grew larger, filled my frame of vision, and resolved itself into what appeared to be a green meadow. It was adorned with yellow and white wildflowers, carpeted with thick-trunked trees, and canopied by a vast clear dome from which emanated a brilliant spectrum of pastel light. On the green meadow, creatures danced together in an undulating circle to what sounded like an ethereal chorus of pan flutes but wasn't.

I landed gently in their midst. The grass felt aware. My presence seemed to delight the circle of dancers, who twirled closer to me and continued their revelry. They looked like leprechauns—about three feet tall, ruddy-faced, bearded and apple-cheeked—but they could, bizarrely, trade body parts with one another. As they danced, they popped off their heads and lobbed them to each other, broke off their arms and passed them around the circle, and tossed their legs into the air. It's still some of the craziest shit I've ever seen.

All I could do was sit up on the grass and look around. The terror and elation were gone. The memory of the drink, the Suds 'n Shade, and my friends receded into the past. Then one of the detachable faeries danced a jig over to me and thrust his bulbous little face close to mine.

"*Xdvlvpad flgasvvee vidkisfavdkn,*" the creature said. It laughed. I laughed back.

"Say what?" I asked.

"*Skfe, veredskszf, sd sdfdavnfaf,*" it said.

And then, from behind me: "He's trying to teach you."

Twisting around, I beheld the most amazingly flamboyant creature I had ever seen. It was chimeran in nature, tall and powerful, with the head of a dragon, the antlers of a fourteen-point imperial buck, and the proud mane of a lion king. His thick, muscled hide was covered in iridescent fish scales, and he bore the tail of a lion to complement the mane. He sat before me sphinx-like, with forelegs outstretched. Even in that pose, he towered over me by a good eight feet.

"Excuse me?" I asked.

"This is the First Universe. This is where it all begins. The dance of these creatures creates the Multiverse," the creature said. "When someone like you shows up here, they tell you the secret of creation. The meaning of life. Why we're here. The Big Answer to the Big Question."

"I see," I said, not seeing at all. "But I can't understand them."

"That's the joke." The creature sighed. He appeared weary of the whole business. He glanced around disdainfully at the dancing sprites as they continued to chatter and trade appendages. "They know you can't understand them. No one else in the Multiverse can speak their language. It's the only irony available to them, apparently, and they never tire of it."

"But I can understand you."

"So you can. Do you find that point interesting?"

"Who are you?"

"Ah. Names." The creature rose on its hindquarters, and I noticed that it possessed an impressive pair of eagle's wings. "You can call me Jo. I'm a Ki-Rin."

"A what?"

"I'm a harbinger of good fortune," Jo Ki-Rin said, "but I left Fortune's employ aeons ago. Now I'm a free agent. I've been tasked with giving you a message. I knew you were coming here, so I arranged a meeting."

"A message? What message?"

The creature seemed pained by the conversation. "You are about to embark on a quest," Jo Ki-Rin said. "This quest will place your life in considerable and continual danger, as it will the lives of your friends. You will at first believe your quest is to save the Woerth. But you'll learn that the fate of this place, the First Universe, is at stake as well. If you fail, then the Multiverse itself will end, blah blah blah. Do I really have to go through the whole speech?"

"A quest? Fat chance."

Jo rolled his eyes. "Let me break it down for you. You're a hero. Heroes go on quests. You're part of the monomyth. You have to meet a wizened mentor—that's me—descend into the underworld, confront your *anima* and reconcile with your feminine side—"

"Seriously, what the fuck are you on about?"

"A-hah! See?" The Ki-Rin pointed a hoof at me. "You're refusing the call. Classic monomyth. Oh wait—maybe that makes me the Herald. I thought I was the Mentor."

"Say, wait a minute," I said. "If these leprechauns speak a language that no one else in the Multiverse knows, then how do *you* know what they're saying?"

Before the Ki-Rin could answer, that jaw-rattling, tearing noise returned, and I found myself hurtling backward through space and time. The same ball-crunching fear returned, too. After what seemed like several eternities, I found myself collapsed on the floor back in the Suds 'n Shade. The stench surrounding me came from the pool of my own vomit. Raising my dripping head, I saw the blurry figure of Redulfo hovering over me.

"How long?" I croaked.

"What do you mean, how long?" Redulfo asked. "You drank your drink, fell off your stool, and barfed up your lunch. You haven't been out for more than a minute."

I sat up, a feat made more difficult by the cannonball weight of my head. Nearby, Lithaine and Amabored rose uncertainly from their own lakes of alcohol and stomach bile.

"Now, that's what I call a drink," said Amabored.

10

That fucking Jo Ki-Rin. On the blessing-curse continuum, he ranked somewhere between a festering boil and a sucking chest wound. Had I really journeyed to the mystical First Universe and witnessed the Dance of Creation, or had I simply ingested too many drugs at once? Either way, I wasn't about to undertake some stupid quest when I hadn't even scoured my first dungeon. The Ki-Rin, I decided, must have been simply the manifestation of my unchecked Id.

"The Ki-Rin was the manifestation of your unchecked Id," said Jaspin Spellbinder, after each of us told the story of his Telepath experience. We had each experienced a vastly individual trip; Amabored had briefly found himself manifested in an alternate universe as an albino warrior-king wielding a demon-possessed black sword that drank souls, while Lithaine became, at some point in the future of a far-distant universe, a middle-aged human who smoked too much pipeweed and delivered pizzas for a living. Once you drank your first Flaming Telepath, why would you ever order another?

"What's an Id?" I asked.

"He means you're a raving egomaniac with delusions of grandeur," Amabored said.

"Or deeply insecure," said Redulfo.

"Or both," Lithaine added.

"How about taking the spotlight off me?" I asked. "Lithaine was a fucking pizza delivery guy. What does that say about his Id?"

"Maybe he's the pizza guy's Id," said Jaspin. "Maybe all of you are merely avatars of pencil-necked geeks and dorkwad losers in some other universe."

"If I'm somebody's idea of a fantasy, then I feel sorry for him," said Redulfo.

Amen to that. Not for a moment did I consider that the Ki-rin might be real—until I saw him again. About four months later, we had finally bribed enough bureaucrats to secure our Adventurers Guild membership cards and were now legally entitled to seek fortune and glory. My official stats were on file in the Guild office: 18 Strength, 12 Dexterity, 11 Intelligence, 15 Wisdom, 14 Constitution, and 12 Charisma—all above average numbers, they told me, although I never understood exactly what charisma was supposed to measure. Was it the ratio of the whiteness of my teeth to the depth of my dimples? Did it measure my ability to talk my way out of a jam? To score chicks? What if my charisma had been low? It can't help your self-esteem to be told you have the same charisma score as a hill troll.

Scouring the Guild bulletin board for jobs, we found in Hardcastle, a barony two days' ride from Redhauke, a noble who needed some hard boys to clear the catacombs beneath the family estate. A long-departed wizard had laid a curse on the place and trapped all manner of creepy-crawlies inside to protect his treasure hoard. It was strictly standard-issue dungeon-crawling. The noble offered us a straight split on the booty, with the Guild cut coming out of our end. We were ready to take the bit in our teeth.

The inaugural adventuring party consisted of Amabored, Lithaine, Redulfo, a Christian cleric we had hired named Father Kellogg of Battle Creek, and me. We lacked a rogue, but we had enough muscle to bash our way through most obstacles and a spell-caster to boot. Besides, the Guild had rated this dungeon suitable for adventurer levels One through Three. What could go wrong?

We geared up with seven days of hard rations each, parchment and ink to map out the dungeon, torches, tinder and flint, coiled rope, several quivers of arrows, oiled and honed swords, quilted armor, bucklers, and shields. We had even pooled enough money to buy a true extravagance: a *Health* potion, sealed in a clay flask and ready for the quaffing whenever the padre ran out of blessings. Having gained admittance to the Wizards College, Redulfo had his First-Level spell *Mystical Missile* locked and loaded. Our marching order was likewise set: Amabored and I in front as the offensive line; Lithaine behind us, ready to run routes as the wideout; Redulfo beside him as the quarterback; and Father Kellogg in the back as the halftime trainer ready to inject us with cortisone and dole out amphetamines like candy. The end zone was our destiny.

So it was with the utmost confidence that we entered the noble's manor house, found the secret wizard's chamber accessible only through the trapdoor hidden behind the ballroom fireplace, and confronted the ten-foot-high brimstone gargoyle that barred entrance to the dungeon proper. We had only to solve the hieroglyphic puzzle carved into the gargoyle's protruding stone tongue to learn the password, and we'd be shitting out gold auratae back at the pub.

An hour later, we still couldn't figure it out. As much I had hoped to keep my super-strength a secret, I figured a little demonstration would impress the boys. Move that big stone fucker five feet to the left, and we were in business.

"Step aside," I said to Redulfo, who had been studying the puzzle in detail over the bridge of his spectacles. "Let's do this the old-fashioned way."

"Maybe we ought to think about this for a minute—" said Redulfo.

"Thinking's for pussies." I searched the gargoyle for the right angle of attack. The rest of the party took a few steps back. As I rammed my shoulder into the statue's side and heaved, the familiar electric surge flowed from the girdle, through my limbs, and into my extremities. Brimming with giant-juice, I felt the statue give.

Then a savage, white-hot jet of flame roared from the gargoyle's lurid mouth and incinerated Father Kellogg where he stood. He went up like a scarecrow soaked in lamp oil. There was nothing left of him but a pile of ashes.

"That's just fucking swell!" Amabored roared. "What do you do for an encore?"

"Look, I was only trying to help!" I said.

"Next time you want to help, do us all a favor and stab yourself in the fucking heart!"

"Wait a minute—I got it," Lithaine said, sidestepping the departed Father Kellogg's ashes to gaze closely at the gargoyle's tongue. "It says, *What's brown and sounds like a bell?*"

"Dung?" Redulfo asked.

With the loud grumble of stone on stone, the gargoyle slid ten feet to the left. The movement revealed an open trap door and a set of rough-hewn steps that descended into darkness.

"What a lame riddle," said Redulfo.

"Let's go kill some monsters," Lithaine said, bounding to the steps with torch in hand. With a final wistful gaze at Father Kellogg's remains, the party headed for the steps—everyone except me. Lithaine turned to give me a questioning look.

"Fuck you, assholes," I said. "Go scour the dungeon without me."

Lithaine and Redulfo looked to Amabored, who only shrugged, hurled a wry grin back at me, and then leaped down the steps. The other two followed. *Fucking assholes*, I thought—but I followed them anyway.

Still pissed off at Amabored, I lagged behind. The steps dropped us into a small antechamber with an open steel-shod door at the opposite end. We crept through the door into what looked like a guardroom, through which we passed to enter a long corridor that hooked to the right. As soon as Amabored rounded the corner, the skeletons struck.

Racing to catch up, I found the others locked in battle with a dozen skeleton warriors. Animated skeletons are the pigeons of the dungeon world. They're easy to animate; all you need is a human heart, which you can find for sale in nearly every magic shop, and which you must eat. A necromancer with a treasure stash to guard need only hang a low-level *Animate Dead* spell on a pile of bones and be on his way. As we gained experience, we could eventually sweep away a skeleton horde like so many dust bunnies. To lowly First-Level warriors, they're nasty buggers: leering skulls, gaping eye sockets, clattering bones, and the choking stench of arrested decay. You can't slide a sword into a skeleton's belly because he doesn't have one. A mace or morning star will stave in the skull, but absent such weaponry you're forced to swat them with the flat of your sword or bash them with your shield. Bows are useless.

A skeleton scimitar bit into Lithaine's shoulder. The elf fell back, blood streaming, and dropped in front of me. That left Amabored to take on four bone boys himself. Having dispatched three skeletons with his only spell, Redulfo now cowered behind a barrel.

"Potion!" I shouted to Redulfo.

The magician produced the *Health* potion from his pouch and flung it my way. I uncorked it and poured the precious elixir past the blood bubbles forming on Lithaine's lips. We could only hope that the apothecary hadn't ripped us off.

Good news: Lithaine's mortal wound filled with a warm golden glow as the power of *logos* began to knit his savaged flesh together. Within two minutes, he was shaken but whole. Neat stuff, that. In my universe, we can't build an internal combustion engine, but we can heal mortal wounds in a snap.

I ran to Amabored's side, and the two of us made short work of the remaining bone boys by jamming our swords into their gaping jaws and twisting the blades. Amabored was nicked up, and I took a shallow wound in my shield arm—but everyone was alive.

"The padre could have turned those fucking things," Amabored said as he sheathed his sword.

"Look, what do you want me to do about it?" I asked. "I'm sorry I fried our cleric, and that's that."

"At least you made up for it," said Amabored. "Let's move on."

Proceeding on our dungeon sweep, we found what we'd come to know as the usual assortment of monsters and traps: were-rats, a nasty pack of kobolds, a cave spider, a couple of zombies, concealed blowguns, hidden spike-filled pits and the like. When you scour enough dungeons, you come to realize how little thought goes into most of them; it's as if some pimply teenaged loser sits in his parents' basement drawing them on graph paper and randomly inserting monsters, traps, and treasure. The booty included a random collection of precious gems, about a hundred gold pieces, a glowing +1 dagger, another *Health* potion, and a +2 battle-helm that Amabored won after we diced over it. We were stoked—until we stumbled onto the hydra.

11

That the hydra's presence was a clear message from my father occurred to me only after I learned that he was behind the whole fucking Quest. Hydra Bay, Hydra Rock; the Lordship was replete with geographic features named after the multi-headed beast. My father could be clever when he wanted, but he was seldom subtle.

We had found our first secret door in the dungeons beneath the manor house. Our "Intro to Dungeon Sweeps" class at the Adventurers Academy advised us that secret doors were often portals to untold riches that most adventurers passed blithely by. False bookcases, faux candlesticks, busts of Plato hiding buttons, sliding panels —we saw all of them. Why dungeon designers constructed so many hidden doors, when reinforced oak and a strong lock would serve just as well, was anybody's guess. They were so ubiquitous, however, that we spent twenty minutes looking for them in every room we entered.

We searched every square inch of this place with no luck until Lithaine spotted a mirror in the wizard's bedroom and stopped to shift it so he could see his own mug. From a small skylight leading to the surface 200 feet above our heads, a faint shaft of sunlight lanced down, refracted off the mirror, and struck the wall near Redulfo's head to reveal a hidden keyhole.

"Don't move that mirror!" I called to Lithaine.

"Thus, the key," said Redulfo, pointing to a key hung around his chest. We had swiped it from a hacked-up zombie right before setting a torch to it.

"Give it a try," Amabored said. "Everybody gear up. Kill anything that comes out."

We brandished our weapons as Redulfo inserted key into lock. With a low rumble and a shower of dust, a section of the stone wall shifted back and to the side, revealing a black maw of darkness that led—where?

"Fuckin' A!" Lithaine drew his sword and leaped into the black breach. A light blazed through the doorway. Then: a womanly scream, followed by the most bone-freezing reptilian screech we had ever heard.

Smarter men would have run like hell. We grabbed our ball-sacks and charged through the doorway.

Slaying a heavy-hitter like a hydra, or some other beast from the pages of the Guild's *Monstrous Manual*, was a goal of any adventuring team. Besides the bump in experience and treasure, you could count on a nice PR boost—a portrait in the Guild newsletter, sometimes an interview, toasts in your honor at the Suds 'n Shade, and the kind attentions of fortune-seeking wenches. Sure, you risked the Big Sleep —if I had a nickel for every two-bit hero I've seen incinerated, dismembered, or eaten alive by a big fucking monster, I'd have about a dollar-twenty—but once you slayed something huge, you were on the way to owning a keep in some green and pleasant land with a buxom noblewoman to knock up and your own passel of down-trodden serfs to work the fields.

There was only one problem: Most adventurers don't face a mature hydra until Fifth or Sixth Level. The Guild's dungeon ratings are strict; into each dungeon, the Guild sends a *Sphere of Seeing* to map the place and record the presence of all beasties within. The Leveling Committee then assigns it a rating designed to prevent high-level heroes from clearing out lightly-defended catacombs just for the fuck of it, and chumps like us from wandering into a mountain keep full of Twelfth-Level thunder giants. A hydra in this dungeon meant that either someone fucked up, or someone set us up. We were mosquitoes facing a bug-zapper.

We followed Lithaine into a vast, columned gallery with a broad stone catwalk lining the perimeter about twenty feet up. The gallery might once have been a gladiator pit or a bear-baiting arena; at present, it was the lair of a forty-foot-long, twenty-foot-high, six-headed, venom-dripping, roaring reptilian spawn of Chaos that looked to smother our adventuring careers in the crib.

The hydra had Lithaine cornered. Two of its heads worried the elf while the other four whipped around to spear us with eight rheumy yellow cat-eyes. Rearing back, the heads loosed a quartet of ball-shriveling screeches, then charged us with jaws snapping.

One of the heads snapped close, its hellishly hot stink-breath washing over me. Staring down the black gullet, I saw my doom. Terror flooded me. I swung my sword in a wild arc at the beast's neck —and the girdle helped me to hew through bone, sinew, and meat. Black blood geysered in a high loop as the severed head flopped at my feet.

"Did you see that?" I cried with joy. Turning to look for congratulations, I saw Redulfo drawn and quartered by two of the hydra heads. His ravaged torso slid to a stop at my feet, spraying blood and entrails across the stone floor. His legs landed elsewhere.

Across the gallery, Lithaine had spent his last arrow. The elf drew his sword and charged the beast—only to be engulfed by two heads that turned him into bloody hamburger meat from the shoulders up. His headless body tipped over the catwalk and plummeted to the gallery floor.

"Run away!" Amabored cried, but the barbarian was already being dragged by the legs back into the pit. Three heads pureed him, sending tissue and bone exploding in a red cloud from his mangled corpse.

Before I had even a second to ponder the bloody deaths of my friends, the neck I had decapitated whipped back around just as two new heads sprouted from the bloody horror of the stump. Dumbfounded, I stood watching until another head took me from behind.

It's a common misconception that beheading is a humane form of execution. In fact, decapitation is the worst way to die. Whether you lose your head to an executioner's axe or a hydra's maw, you have a good twenty seconds to stare at your own twitching headless corpse before the lights go out. It's a fucking trip.

12

S o, I was dead. Having not yet acquired the Norse faith, I harbored no dream of Valhalla, where a flagon of ale might await me in the All-Father's hall. Religion never did anything for me—particularly monotheism, an impossible ask of any god. At least polytheists divvy up their celestial needs. Need a healthy crop, or true love, or to slay the infidels? There's a god for each prayer standing by to take your order. There's no sense in praying to the same god for everything; facing such a barrage of contradictory supplications, what god wouldn't tell his creations to fuck off? Monotheism turns you into a tight-assed prick obsessed with admission to the Heavenly Kingdom, the most exclusive club in the Multiverse. Angels don't have genitals, for Christ's sake. What good is Heaven if you can't get laid there?

Too young and cynical to give thought to the life everlasting, I mostly expected the Big Nothing. Instead, I found myself naked in a small, bare, black room with doors facing each other on opposite walls. Ambient light bathed me. Before I could try one of the doors, I heard that familiar music: the reverb-laden chorus of instruments that sounded vaguely like pan flutes but weren't. Brilliant colors exploded in a spectral orgasm, and then: Jo Ki-Rin, perched proudly behind some sort of astral window. He stood atop a windswept, grass-covered hill. Cherubic white clouds skidded behind him. His mane rippled magisterially.

"You again?" I asked. "You're simply the manifestation of my unchecked Id."

"If only that were true," said the Ki-Rin.

"So, where am I? I was just decapitated by a goddamned hydra. This is the afterlife?"

"You're exceptionally dense, even for a human." Jo took a moment to regard one buffed and polished hoof. "You're not supposed to be dead—not for quite some time, anyhow. Somebody rigged the game."

"No shit. Hydras don't grow out of the dungeon moss," I said. "Who did it?"

"You'll figure that out soon enough," said Jo. "So, here's the deal. I can't force you back to the Material Plane; the choice is yours. The door before you leads to the afterlife; open it, and you're toast. The door behind you leads back to Woerth. Open it, and you'll live."

Here was a pickle. Standing in the small room, I attempted to think profound thoughts, but I mostly thought about dinner.

"Can't I, you know, peek at the afterlife first? Just crack open the door a little?" I asked.

"No."

"Well fuck. I guess it's back to Woerth then. I'm pretty hungry." Then the light bulb went off. "What about my friends? Do they come back too?"

"Of course not," the Ki-Rin said. "This is *your* story. They're just supporting characters. You can get more."

Then I realized that I had leverage. The Ki-Rin wasn't saying so, but he—or whoever he was working for—*wanted* me to live. The game was rigged indeed.

"Nothing doing," I said. "Those guys are my friends. They're integral to my story. Hell, it's *our* story. If they don't live, then I don't live."

The Ki-Rin glowered at me from beneath his fur-lined brows. Potent and deadly magic radiated from him; if I pissed him off, he could vaporize me. As old as the Multiverse itself, Ki-Rins are guardians of the Law with whom even the gods know better than to fuck. That parties unknown had enlisted this one to serve as my guardian would later strike me so profoundly that I would spend an hour vomiting into the privy. For now, I had the fucker over a barrel.

"All right," Jo said. "They live. But you are now sworn to them in bonds of fellowship, and they to you. Your Fate lines are one. The Doom of Koschei is now their doom as well."

"Whatever," I said. "If you're going to send me back, do it soon."

With that, the door behind me swung open—and I found myself back in my own body, now standing on the gallery walkway. My head was back on my shoulders, which was nice, but I was cut, bruised, battered, and drenched in hydra blood. Sprawled across the gallery floor, the hydra's body smoldered like a pile of burning tires. Its six necks were headless, the stumps themselves sealed with what looked like flaming pitch. The corpse was riddled with arrows. Bloody hydra heads lay here and there with tongues lolling, their yellow eyes staring at nothing.

"Holy fucking Christ, how did we do that?" a blood-soaked Amabored called from across the chamber.

"Looks like we made that thing our bitch," said Lithaine, who stood nearby bearing a bloody gash on his shoulder. His quiver was empty. "Wish I could remember how we did it."

Redulfo stood near an open barrel of black pitch. In one hand he held the blackened remains of a torch; that arm was coated in pitch up to the elbow. "We should be dead," the wizard said. "Especially me —I have four health points."

"What can we say?" I asked. At the sight of my three bosom companions alive and breathing, I couldn't help but grin. "We're damn good."

By way of celebration, we filled our rucksacks to bursting with the hydra's horde of gemstones, gold and silver coins, candlesticks, all the usual swag. Amabored found a *Raise Dead* scroll, which he tossed to me.

"Something to remember him by," Amabored said. I stuffed the scroll in my backpack and forgot about it until years later, when it saved my life.

Then we scurried out of the dungeon and back to Redhauke. Two days of riding and hard drinking later found me creeping into Melinda's subterranean room, deep beneath the Golden Gryphon Inn on Foundry Street. I squirreled out of my blood-soaked togs and tossed them into the fireplace. Just past midnight, I slipped into bed, where Melinda lay curled up naked under the quilt hugging her goose-down pillow. I spooned her. She stirred like a snoozing housecat.

"How'd it go?" Melinda purred.

"It went great," I whispered. "It was to die for."

13

Yeah, that's right—I was boning Melinda. The terminal virgin got laid at last. Would I lie to you? I have nothing to gain. In a few days, I'll most likely be dead again, no matter what Wilberd's Astral Telescope says. This time, there will be no competing offers, and that's fine with me. If the Woerth is consumed by dragonfire, at least it beats dying on the toilet.

One week after Saggon assigned us to spy on his mystery woman, and six months or so before I died, I was thinking quite a bit about death. We were back in the dank underbelly of Redhauke, waiting for a barge to dock at one of the Under-Canal piers so we could unload the pipeweed barrels onto the waiting dray. As the horses stamped and chewed their oats, I scoped out the wagon's false bottom. While the barrels would prevent egress from the top, a spring-loaded trap door in the undercarriage would provide a quick escape, should I need one. Was sealing myself in a potential coffin a bad move, especially if the wagon plunged over an embankment or was struck by flaming arrows? Of course—but lust knows no fear.

"You sure you want to do this?" Lithaine asked as he poked his own nose around the wagon. "She's just a chick. Besides, she might cut off your balls."

"Good advice from someone who hasn't seen a vagina since he squirted out of one," said Amabored.

"I heard your mother shit you out in a stream of bloody diarrhea."

"Right into your mom's mouth."

"For fuck's sake, give it a rest," I said, as a bobbing bow light emerged from the darkness of the canal tunnel. "The barge is here. You know the plan?"

"If the woman shows, put up a light show of force before we let her run," said Amabored. "You know the meeting place?"

"I do. See you on the other side."

I crawled into the dray's false bottom and gave a thumbs-up to Amabored, who sealed me in. The crawlspace allowed me only to lay on my back with about four inches of air between nose and wood. Torchlight glowed from the air holes in the floorboards. Nothing for it now but to wait for my cue.

Next: the slow lapping of waves against the pier and thumping of oars as the barge arrived; Amabored conversing with the barge master; the tattoo of boots on the dock; and then a terrifying series of bassoon crashes as the crewmen dumped barrels onto the dray. I prayed to no particular god that the false bottom would hold.

And then, chaos: shouts of alarm and the clatter of arrows against the wagon. A cry of pain, and the singing of Lithaine's bow. Barge crewmen running back up their gangway to draw anchor—they weren't paid enough to fight. Then a rocking thump as someone landed on the headboard, grabbed the reigns, and gave the horses a taste of the whip. The wagon leaped away from the pier and up the stone ramp towards the city surface. I could only brace myself; what a bad idea this was.

If temporary, blindness can be cool. Tracking the wagon's route through the city worked for about four intersections before it became hopeless. Creaking to a halt, we idled for nearly a watch; The hubbub of voices and stamping hooves told me that we were stuck in the nightly traffic jam at one of the city gates—possibly the Dragon Gate, though I couldn't be sure. That the hijacker had chosen a public checkpoint, rather than one of the scores of secret exits, told me that Saggon's men were a bigger threat than the Guard.

At last the wagon lurched forward. Echoing hoof-falls through a long stone tunnel, and then we were on the open road. Panic briefly seized me—what if I couldn't get back in the city again? I had little—a few friends, a room, some coins in my pocket, and the chance to become a player if I lived long enough—but compared to starting over with nothing, I was a rich man.

An hour passed. Then two. When we finally wheeled to a stop, I surmised that we were a good three leagues outside the city. So frozen from the midwinter cold was I that my fingers couldn't feel my sword pommel.

There came a sudden chorus of raucous shouts and oaths. A steel-tipped crossbow bolt, dripping with black goo, pierced the wagon an inch from my nose. The peal of clashing blades rent the air. That sealed it. I couldn't let this woman die before I had a chance to see her again.

14

I opened the false bottom of the dray and thumped to the frozen ground. The sounds of battle echoed. Rolling out from beneath the wagon, I surveyed the terrain. The wagon sat on an immense stone bridge spanning a deep river valley. It was the Stonesong Bridge, another one of Storm Stonegorm's famous constructions, unless I missed my guess. The pregnant moon revealed forested, snow-covered hills and the glint of a frozen river far below. On the ground before me lay a headless corpse.

A short distance away, the woman and her remaining ally were locked in combat with a circle of freakish dwarfs garbed in metal-banded bugbear skulls, giant horned helms, spiked shoulder plates, shrunken heads dangling from belts, and bucklers emblazoned with leering demons and the eight-pointed sigil of Chaos. Their faces were pockmarked, their teeth filed to razors. In place of a left arm, one dwarf bore a scorpion's stinger.

As I leaped up, one of the dwarfs slid steel into the man's belly. He dropped. That left the woman alone to face ten foes.

"Half-pints!" I cried, brandishing my sword. "Supper's ready!"

I crashed into the fray. My compound attack sent one dwarf head

flying. I parted two more arms from torsos before the first axe blade
bit into my forearm.

Ignoring me, the woman launched into her own furious assault
with short sword and dagger. She took out two more dwarfs, slick-
ening the narrow stone bridge with blood.

We had the dwarfs beaten—until the odds changed. The semicircle parted, and another dwarf stepped forward: blazing red
mohawk, gold eye fixed with a gleaming ruby pupil, beard threaded
with copper rings, and a double-bladed axe bolted to his right arm in
lieu of a hand. In his left hand, he held a chain leading to the collar of
what you might call a muscled black dog. Then again, you might not
call it a dog—for, in place of a dog's head, the thing bore a ring of
dripping gray tentacles around a snarling, fang-filled mouth. A green
cloud of pestilential stink drifted from the beast's open maw. The tip
of each tentacle sported a single, red-limned eye.

"*What the fuck is that?*" I whispered to the woman. She ignored me
still. Our exhaled breath mingled together in a sinuous cloud—a
strangely thrilling detail.

"By Beelzebub's cock, it's Melinda the Blade!" the mohawked
dwarf growled. "All those stolen shipments, that was you—Saggon's
bitch. He'll pay us five barges for the news, I'll wager."

"You won't live to bring him the news, squat," Melinda said.

"I'll bring your head to his table," said the dwarf. Behind him, his
men chortled.

"Draw steel, and let's dance."

I brandished my blade. "Mind if I cut in?"

"So, you needed a man's help after all, eh bitch?" the dwarf
growled. His hellhound snarled and snapped. "It won't make a soul's
difference. You'll die tonight."

"Maybe," said Melinda, "but not before I toss this bauble into the
river." Over the bridge wall, she held forth a jewel-encrusted skull
depending from a silver chain. Two small horns protruded from its
forehead. An implicit threat, it dangled over the river valley
far below.

"The Skull!" the dwarf snarled. "How came you by this treasure?"

"I found it in an outhouse down at the Pit," Melinda said, her voice calm. "Saggon will pay you ten barges of gold for it. You want it? Come and get it."

Laughing a demon's laugh, the dwarf clasped an amulet at his breast. Dwarf and hellhound both vanished in a thunderclap, accompanied by blazing scarlet light and cheap special-effects fog. The bridge shook. The remaining dwarfs pulled hand-crossbows from their belts, fired grappling hooks into the stone, and then leaped from the bridge trailing rope behind them into the chasm.

I raced to the ledge, but they had already disappeared into the night mist. Whether they reached the river valley, vanished into the aether, or were dashed on the rocks below, I couldn't say. Turning from the precipice, I found Melinda's dagger at my throat.

"Who the hell are you?" she asked.

"I'm a friend—" I began. Before I could finish the sentence, the woman swung the skull on its chain and bashed me in the head with it. Then she clocked me with her sword pommel for good measure. I dropped. Be miserly with your wishes, the bard said.

15

I didn't know from trouble until Melinda bashed me upside the head with that fucking skull. According to Redulfo, I never had a choice; I was meant to find the Screaming Skull, to possess the Girdle of Gargantua, the Crown of Chaos, and the other relics that would collectively draw Koschei's soul back to Woerth, and not only because my father arranged it. *The Book of Fate* is said to contain the record of all events that occur in the Multiverse: past, present and future, all written in permanent ink. If our future is already written—and time is not, as some elven philosophers propose, merely a mental fiction that prevents us from experiencing our entire lives all at once—then why try to change it?

"Free will is an illusion. A fairy tale we tell our children," Redulfo proclaimed during one of our late-night bull sessions at the Suds 'n Shade. We sat swilling beer while Jaspin tended bar and chimed in when appropriate.

"Fuck you, it's bullshit," said Amabored. "No force in the universe can tell me what to do. I write my own tale."

"If causality is a basic construct of the universe, then so is determinism," said Redulfo. "You think you write your own tale, but your actions have been predetermined by forces set in motion since the dawn of Time. Choice itself is an illusion—your mind is simply justifying fate before it occurs. The future is just the past coming at you from the opposite direction."

"What the fuck are you talking about?" asked Lithaine.

"The wizard has a point, and it's not just the one under his hat," I said. "Either everything is predetermined, or nothing is. Maybe we're all just part of the machinery of the Multiverse. I glimpsed the First Universe, remember. I've seen the little fuckers that set the whole thing in motion."

"That was just the Flaming Telepath talking," said Amabored.

"Which I drank because the Multiverse preordained it."

"You're both taking causality on faith," said Melinda. "Who says every result needs a cause?"

"Are you claiming that causality isn't a natural law?" Redulfo asked her. "If you prick me, do I not bleed?"

"Well, yes, but—"

"If causality isn't a fundamental force of our universe, there must be some case in which you can truly originate your actions," said Redulfo. "Can you think of one? What action can you take that isn't presupposed by an event outside of your control? By the time you choose to act, electrochemical activity in the brain has already made it happen. Again, the choice itself is an illusion."

"So, our entire lives are predetermined?" Melinda asked. "Why would El create a universe of automatons?"

"You're implying that El has a plan," I said. "Maybe he's just making up the universe as he goes along. And he's writing our dialogue as we speak it."

"Then he needs to write us some better lines," said Lithaine.

"You're all forgetting that this particular universe, as boring and derivative as it is, is but one of an infinitude of universes," said Jaspin as he brought over another round. "The Multiverse teaches us to be compatibilists. Every action in the universe, however small, influences every other action. The movement of a single electron orbiting the nucleus of a single hydrogen atom begins a chain of events that leads to great natural disasters, mighty wars, and decisions that seemingly change the course of history. That electron itself was acted upon by outside forces. Causality isn't a chain of events, you see. It's a web of interconnected events."

"Now you sound like a Buddhist," said Redulfo. "Compatibilism is weak sauce. Free will and determinism can't peacefully coexist."

"Perhaps they don't, in this universe. In the Multiverse, they must coexist. Think of the Multiverse as an infinite skim of soap bubbles. Every choice you make spins off a new universe. Turn left, and you create one universe; turn right, and you create another one. Your actions are predetermined only in the universe you inhabit at this instant. Because the number of possible universes is infinite, the future is always mutable. That's why Amabored can perceive free will in a universe that Redulfo views as deterministic. The soap bubbles collide, connect, and then break apart again. Eventually, they burst."

"So, each of us is the center of his own universe," I said. "We should be high instead of drunk."

"And free will is a prerequisite of the soul," said Amabored. "We have it; animals don't. When a dog licks his balls, it's because he has no choice. When I lick my balls, it's because I'm extremely flexible."

Jaspin brought over another round. Handing Redulfo a beer, the illusionist-turned-bartender eyed the young wizard with puzzlement.

"I feel like you and I have had this conversation before," Jaspin told Redulfo.

"We have," said Redulfo. "Just now. The Time Lords tell us that time can be traversed just like space, and that *déjà vu* happens when we accidentally remember the future. You're not a Time Lord, are you?"

"Just call me Dr. Who," said Jaspin.

16

S o, if I shit my pants right here on the throne, then I create one
universe. If I get up and head to the can, then I create another
one. Soap bubbles, my ass. The Multiverse is more a sea of
snot bubbles expelled from the nose of a blind, idiot god. In this
universe, my only concern is which of my two possible ends will
come to pass. Will I live well into decrepitude, as the Astral Telescope
promises? Or will the Woerth be destroyed in ten days by the Seven?
When will my bubble burst?

I'm not the first member of the Quest to receive a sneak preview
of my fate; Redulfo received his during the showdown at the Blue
Falcon. Unlike me, he refused to alter his behavior in the slightest. He
was such a determinist that if you told him opening a door would
result in his certain death, he'd just shrug, say, "That figures," and
open it anyway.

His cynicism could be a downer, but his ability to think around a
problem often came in handy. For example, we were high up in the
Wyvern Mountains, caught in the icy grip of the Sorrowful Pass,
when he nearly came through for us again. This was after we had
slaughtered two-dozen snow giants in the Pellucid Palace and found
the map that would lead us first to the Magma Hall, and thence to

Mormant, city of the shadow elves, and ultimately to the Sunless Sea. Our cleric, Father Jethro of Tull, had slipped on a patch of ice midway through the pass and plummeted over the cliff-edge. It was a good two thousand feet to the foot of the mountain, which meant we'd hear his screams for long seconds before he vaporized on the rocks below.

"For fuck's sake—not again!" Amabored cried. Like the rest of us, he was bundled up in the fur-lined parka and trousers we had purchased at a premium at the gnome village we had freed from snow giant enslavement. Ungrateful rodents. Xingo was with us now, fulfilling our long-vacant rogue position, and even he agreed that those particular gnomes deserved extermination.

"It wasn't me!" I cried.

Redulfo leaped to the edge of the precipice. He blew a short arpeggio on his flute. A wall of wind burst forth from the wizard like a dwarf shock grenade and blew down the crevasse. Within a second, it had caught up to Father Jethro and stopped his fall. The cleric now hovered a good seven chains below us, still screaming.

"Nice work," Amabored said. "Can you bring him back?"

"It's a *Hover* spell. Won't last more than a minute. Lithaine—" Redulfo said, spinning towards the elf— "tie your rope to an arrow, and put it through Jethro's back."

One of Lithaine's finer qualities is his lack of introspection. Without hesitation, the elf lashed the end of his +3 elven coil to an arrow and set shaft to string. Before he could let it fly, I grabbed his arm.

"Hold on," I said. "You want him to put an arrow through our cleric? Are you mental?"

"Do it!" said Xingo.

Redulfo only looked at me with that blank, hang-dog expression. "Lithaine, how many health points of damage does an arrow do?" the wizard asked.

"One to six, unless I put it through his eye," said Lithaine.

Redulfo then called over the cliff-edge to Jethro, who hovered face down and focused on his impending doom. "Hey, Friar, how many health points do you have?"

"Uh...thirty-eight!" came the distant, terrified reply. "For the love of Apollo, bring me back!"

"The wizard's right," said Amabored. "A single arrow can't kill him without a critical hit."

"You're going to put an arrow *through his back*," I said. "In what universe *won't* that kill the poor bastard?"

"Even if Lithaine hits a vital organ, the cleric has ten combat rounds before he bleeds to death," Redulfo said. "Plenty of time to get a potion down his throat."

"Right," Lithaine said, and let the arrow fly. The rope accordioned out behind the shaft. The arrow drove through the cleric's leather cuirass and out through his belly. He shrieked in pain.

"Hey padre, grab hold of the shaft tightly below your belly, or your weight will yank it out!" Amabored called down. He motioned me over, and together we took hold of Lithaine's rope and pulled. Each time we hauled up another length of rope, the cleric screamed. We raised him one chain, then two, then three. For a moment, it looked like we might succeed.

Then Lithaine's knot unraveled. A +3 elven rope is supposed to hold a knot through fire and flood—but you need to tie a good knot. We could do nothing but wince as Father Jethro plummeted into the crevasse. His screams echoed against the knife-edges of the mountain peaks and were carried away by the winds.

"Oops," said Lithaine.

Redulfo stood firm against my rueful gaze. "Did you have a better idea?" he asked.

"Yeah—we should have put three arrows into him," I said, clapping the wizard on the back. "Next time, think bigger."

17

T hat episode was a node in the network of events that would become the greatest campaign of our early years, before the Free Kingdoms anointed us as saviors and the Talon Empire marked us for death. Ostensibly, we embarked on the campaign to track down the Bad Brain after receiving a hot tip. In truth, my Quest began when I boarded the *Bilge Rat* and left Redhauke for good—not to save the world, mind you, but rather to score points with a chick.

Or perhaps it was the Screaming Skull itself that set this intricate machine of nefarious plots, blind chance, and foolhardy heroism in motion. What a pain in the goddamn ass *that* thing was.

Melinda and I had been shacking up for nearly five years. I saw a little less of the droogs in those days. Amabored was busy with a buxom barmaid from the Suds 'n Shade named Kirabelle. Redulfo was busy stirring Eye of Newt and Frog's Breath into a big cauldron, or whatever the fuck it is they do at the School of Thaumaturgy. Lithaine would simply vanish for a few weeks, only to return in time to scour another dungeon. During these years, we progressed in adventuring levels steadily—once every fortnight or so, we snagged a dungeon opening from the Guild bulletin board, rode out of town, and spent the weekend slaughtering imps, trolls, basilisks, wraiths, dire wolves, mummies, skeletons, troglodytes, goblins, blood puddings, giant centipedes, and zombies with abandon. Apart from the hydra episode, we encountered nothing that we couldn't handle. We had the occasional close call; with no rogue in our party, we were vulnerable to traps, and one of us would occasionally stumble into a spike-filled pit or a swinging pendulum. Thankfully, Redhauke apothecaries were stocked with *Health* potions.

Meanwhile, we were hauling in so much treasure that we had to rent one of Jaspin's vaults below the Suds 'n Shade to store our loot. We weren't rich, but good meals, soft beds, copious drink, and sturdy equipment were no longer the stuff of dreams. I had long since traded in my smelly leather armor for a set of chain mail with plate pauldrons and a stylish fauld with brass rivets. I had also traded my longsword for a new weapon specialty, which I practiced religiously at the Guild gymnasium five days a week: the double-bladed battle-axe. I took a +2 charmed one off a dead imp chieftain and never looked back; until you've buried an axe blade in your opponent's breastbone, you haven't really lived.

And then there was Melinda. After our initial meeting of the minds, we fell into such an easy rhythm that we were a couple before we even realized it. Like me, she came to Redhauke with nothing; and like me, she turned to the Thieves Guild out of impatience. Blades, garrotes, and crossbows weren't her only tools. With her flat face, pug nose, and wide hips, she had the look of a farmer's wife, if not the vocation—but her smile was bright and disarming, her heart honest and open. She made friends easily, a trait which complemented my general misanthropy. Our sex life soon settled into a comfortable routine: she did most of the work, and I got most of the pleasure. Weren't regular blowjobs my birthright?

Did I love her? Hell, I don't know. I sure told her I did.

So, life was good. As a pessimist, however, I knew better than to trust to good fortune. The dam burst in midwinter of my fifth year in Redhauke. Four months had passed since the lemming imps had attacked the city. Since that dark time, the days had been fruitful and mostly pleasant; my mistake was to allow myself a momentary lapse into satisfaction. As I strolled one morning through the hubbub of the Godsway, the day was brilliant: as cold as a dawn swim in the Everdeep, with the sky blazing blue and the sun a bright copper plate fixed in the sky. The crowd around me pulsed and bustled, but I paid no mind to the humanoid stench. I had a woman at home, a profession I loved, and money in my pocket. What more could I ask of life? I dared to whistle.

Big mistake. Odin waits for moments like this to take the piss out of you. I had just passed the fluted marble columns fronting the Temple of Athena when a fire-bearded dwarf slipped out of an alley bearing a leather-clad box wrapped in buckled straps. He stopped before me, bowed low, and presented his parcel with outstretched arms. It wouldn't occur to me until much later that the dwarf get-up was a disguise—and not a great one, at that.

"Be you Elberon of the Isles?" the dwarf asked.

"Who's asking?" I said.

"Delivery for you, sieur," said the dwarf. He knew me, all right. "Sign here."

"What is it, Frenchy?" I asked as I signed the receipt.

"None of my affair, sieur. Have a good day." The dwarf bowed, spun on his heel, and scurried away.

A shadow befell me as serried ranks of bruised storm clouds overtook the sun. *That's funny*, I thought. Hadn't been a cloud in the sky before.

Pausing in the street, I loosened the straps and removed the box lid. When I saw the gleaming white dome tucked inside, I recognized my doom.

With as much strength as the girdle provided, I heaved the box in a high parabola over the Temple of Athena. It was too late. Inside the box, the Skull had already started to scream—that ball-shriveling wail of the damned I had come to dread. Around me, passers-by startled and looked upward as if bracing for a Luftwaffe strafing run.

I knew what would follow. Unstrapping my battle-axe, I braced myself to face the crucible of death.

18

I heard the lamentations of the wolves before I saw them. Around the corner of St. Cecelia's they came bounding—a dozen of them, each one as big as a nose-tackle, muzzles contorted in snarls, yellow fangs dripping with hot spittle, black merciless eyes limned in red. Passers-by screamed and scattered. One leaped upon an unlucky washerwoman, tore out her throat, and then came for me.

Fight or flight? I was tired of running. *Fuck these beasts*, I thought. This was the best the Skull could throw at me?

Naivety is charming in review but deadly in the moment. As the first wolf crashed into me, a figure hooded and cloaked in scarlet rounded a corner before me, stopped, and began to shake violently. As three wolves clamped their fangs into my arm and leg, the figure's right arm split open like a blood-filled sausage. From the torso emerged a black, segmented insect leg topped by a jagged-toothed claw of bone. His jaw separated from his head in a crimson gout to reveal a pair of clacking mandibles.

The insectoid was soon joined by a half-dozen cloaked men, each of whom transformed into some biological monstrosity built of segmented bodies, oily translucent wings, ragged claws, and prehensile stinger-shod tails. When one hooded woman's skull exploded like a suppurating melon and a giant, gleaming mantis-head sprang from her shoulders, I screamed. You wouldn't?

The double-assault of dire wolves and insectoids fell upon me. With no axe room, I was forced into close sword work, opening the bellies of two more wolves before the horde brought me down. Claws and fangs pierced through my mail rings and bit into my flesh. When a wolf sank his teeth into my throat, I succumbed. Unless Jo Ki-Rin had another offer for me on the other side, this was it.

Then, salvation. A whirling dervish of limbs barreled into the horde and scattered it like a stand of bowling pins. When the horde regrouped, my new ally—a bald human in a robe of simple home-spun—set upon them. He bore no weapon, but he didn't need one. As I collapsed onto the cobblestones with blood running into my eyes, he snapped a wolf's neck, pulled an eye from a socket, and drove his leg through the torso of an insectoid. Within moments, he slew five insectoids and sent the remaining two battered wolves loping away with bitter yelps in their throats.

I lay in a pool of warm, copper-scented goo. My breath was shallow in my lungs. A bald head blotted out the sun. Then, a feminine voice: "Step aside, monk, or he'll die."

An angel hovered over me. Her hair was spun gold, her skin Italian alabaster, her lips the ripest of plump red strawberries glistening in the dew. Her eyes sparkled with blue faerie fire. Her gaze met mine, and I was lost.

"Mommy," I said, and passed out.

19

Sometime later I awoke to find myself surrounded by gleaming marble. My nostrils were filled with the scent of fermented grapes. There was a down pillow under my head. A hand held a goblet before me.

"Drink this," said a woman's voice.

She helped me to a few swallows of wine. My vision clearing, I discerned marble columns, wooden pews, and an altar laden with olive branches. The marble likeness of a warrior woman with spear and helm towered over me. I lay on a soft divan, naked but for a silk sheet draped over my midsection. Beside me sat the angel who had appeared in the street—an angel now disguised as a mortal, golden-haired woman with a laughing gaze. I loved her instantly.

"You have me at a disadvantage," I burbled.

"Don't flatter yourself. The monk disrobed you, not I," the woman said. "I merely saved you from death. By the grace of noble Athena, you are healed. Your wounds were grave."

"Athena, eh? You're a shield-maiden, then?"

"I am her servant, Cassiopeia. You are...?"

"Elberon of the Isles," I said. I took the goblet from her hand and drained it. My strength was returning quickly. "Cassiopeia—I've heard that story. You've a sister chained to a rock somewhere, right?"

"I was named after the constellation, not the queen," said Cassiopeia. "My father didn't read much. But he loved the stars."

"Obviously," I said, "since he sired one himself."

20

That was smooth, wasn't it? Show me the woman who wouldn't fall for that line.

The reappearance of the Screaming Skull marked the onset of several imminent crises. The most obvious problem—that whoever delivered the Skull to me knew I had once possessed it—wasn't even the worst one. The worse problem was that, although I had been living with one woman for five years—and married to her for four months—I was now in love with another one. Or at least in lust. What's the difference? Either way, I was obsessed.

After Melinda clocked me upside the head with that fucking skull five years earlier, she became my first obsession. What I had only glimpsed when she drove her fist into my eye on that first night, I had now seen in full flower: her bravado, her strength, her skill with a blade. She was like me, but with tits.

I awoke hours later, prostrate on the Stonesong Bridge and suffering from a hangover the size of Mt. Meru. A thin layer of snow covered me. Dawn was breaking over the mist-shrouded hills. I was alive, intact, and still possessed of both sword and purse. Melinda the Blade, as I now knew her to be, was gone, as was the jeweled skull with which she had cold-cocked me. The bodies on the bridge were gone. The frozen pools of blood remained. But for the distant cawing of crows somewhere in the valley below, I was alone.

The journey from on-my-back to on-my-feet was long and arduous, and still I faced the bone-freezing trek back to the city. Two hours by wagon became six hours on foot: over hill and dale, past farmhouses farting chimney smoke into the blue sky, skirting the occasional bundled-up travelers to whom I gave curt nods even as my hand found my sword pommel. A league outside the city, I finally scored a ride with a pot-maker who sat a mule wagon rattling with cookware. The pot-maker's merchant pass got him through the Dragon Gate, saving me from another stint in Doomtown.

Once inside the city, I stopped off at Lady Hagg's for a hot bath administered by her ancient gnome manservant. After a good tongue-lashing from the old woman for leaving the privy a mess, I headed for the Suds 'n Shade to rendezvous with my mates. I found them breaking fast, the barbarian hunched over a slab of bacon and a side of grits, while the elf worked over a bowl of spiced oatmeal.

"There he is!" said Amabored as I took a seat while Trilecia, one of Jaspin's barmaids, brought me coffee and bread. "So, you fucked her, right? How'd she like it? Could she find your cock without a magnifying glass?"

"Shut the fuck up."

"Maybe he wants to take her on a date first," said Lithaine. "Just because you'll screw anything with a hole doesn't mean the rest of us will."

"Damn straight. Bend over this table and I'll fuck you too."

"You couldn't handle a prime cut of elf meat. I'd make you my bitch."

It felt good to hear such civilized discourse. While we ate, I recounted the night's events. We were in a thorny thicket. I hadn't located Melinda's hideout, but I knew her name. What else did I know? That some badass dwarfs, apparently wanting that wagon full of pipeweed for themselves, had attacked her. That she had some sort of jeweled skull of potential value to Saggon. Was this information worth enough to save our asses? Or was it so worthless that Saggon would throw us from his tower window?

"Let him try," said Lithaine, when I mentioned this possibility. "I say we march into the Falcon, cut off his fucking head, and blow this shithole."

"We don't want that fat bastard on our asses yet," Amabored said. "Let's tell him what we know, and then we'll decide our next move."

Heading for the Blue Falcon, we wound our way along the crooked byways of the Guild Quarter, pushing our way through the afternoon throngs as the high, moss-draped towers of Saggon's lair loomed ever closer. Fingers of ice gripped our spines as if the Falcon itself was filled with malevolence and brooding upon our approach.

At the entrance to the inn's main courtyard, we found two centaur guards, their dark skin stretched taught over rippling muscles. Alerted to our arrival, they lowered their fencepost-sized crossbows to allow us inside. The Falcon's courtyard itself sprawled as large as a rugby field and crawled with all manner of cutpurses, pickpockets, ruffians, second-story men, grifters, gamblers, and hedge-fund managers gathered in various clots to strike deals and manufacture plots. Once inside the inn's massive granite-columned Great Hall, we penguin-walked through the crowd to the bar, where we were promptly set upon by a murder of tiny wood-elf hookers who pushed their tits into our bellies and angled for drinks. Before we could shoo them away, a gargantuan eight-foot-tall hill troll stomped over and did it for us. He hooked a meaty thumb over his shoulder.

"This way," the troll grumbled.

We followed. The troll led us out a pair of barred and chained double doors, down a long stone corridor ramping downward, through another pair of doors, and into a lavishly wide hall lined with ten-by-ten-foot pits. The pits were presided over by masked and leather-bound men wielding whips and chains: lictors from the Torturers Guild, under contract to Saggon. Dangling over several of the pits were screaming men, their limbs splayed wide by ropes lashing them to posts anchored at the corners of the pits.

We had heard of this place. Saggon called it the Confessional, for it was in this room that his prisoners confessed their sins. At the bottom of each pit grew a colony of piranha fungus, its hundreds of savage fanged mouths snapping and snarling amongst the purplish moss, waiting for the torturers to cut the lashes and send down fresh meat. We exchanged glances—and in that fleeting moment, each of us understood that none of us was going into one of those pits. We would die instead, fighting back-to-back.

The troll motioned for us to sit at a table near the stoves, which suited us fine, as Saggon kept the Confessional as frigid as his office atop the high tower. After a moment, we saw the Over-Boss himself turn away from a table upon which lay the gory remains of a prisoner. He trundled over to us, wiping his bloody hands on his bloody smock, and dropped into a chair opposite ours. Something grotesque passed over his face that might have been a smile.

"You boys hungry?" he asked. "Some quail eggs maybe? Some sandwiches?" He called over to his shadow-elf secretary, who lounged nearby, cloaked in wolf furs and filing her nails into sharp points. "Get a tray of sausages in here for the boys, would you? There's a girl." He gave us another once-over. "So—Mo. Larry. Curly. About the woman. What do you have for me? Something good?"

I got through the story as quickly as I could without telling him that I hadn't learned the one thing he had asked me to learn. As I spoke, the torturers continued their dark work on the men dangling over the pits. Soon the food arrived; Saggon dug in while we tried to keep our breakfasts down. It took everything we had not to cut and run.

"Interesting," Saggon said. He licked the sausage grease from his fingers. "Dwarfs. Crazy octopus-dogs. Melinda. A skull on a chain." The Over-Boss leaned forward, his swollen forehead hovering inches from my own. "Tell me about that skull, my young friend. Tell me everything."

There wasn't much to tell, but I told him. He listened with feigned insouciance.

"You did good, kid," Saggon said, motioning for me to stand up.

He did so as well, hauling his prodigious girth around the table. He gave me a fatherly embrace—one that soon became a headlock.

"Here's the thing," said the Over-Boss, his muscled arm wrapped around my neck like a python. "You left out one very important detail, the detail that I just happened to send you out there to find out for me, the very small detail of where this woman is holed up. You didn't find that out for me, did you, Shemp?"

It felt as Saggon was trying to squeeze my brains out through my asshole. Outside of his lair, I would have used the girdle to do as much to him, but trying it now would only invite his henchmen to kill all three of us. So, I could only surrender as Saggon dragged me over to one of the pits. He hoisted me up by a leg and dangled me over the edge. Later, I would have cause to wonder at his strength, which seemed far too great for such a fat tub of goo. For now, the snapping fangs of the piranha fungus swaying beneath my inverted gaze left me too terrified to think.

Lithaine and Amabored didn't dare move—any attempt to save me would find them drawn and quartered. I could pray only for a quick death.

"What if I just dropped you into this pit, my son?" Saggon snarled. "And then maybe drop your friends in after you, just for knowing you? You think I should do that, Gomer?"

"No, my lord!"

"Then tell me what that bitch wants! What's she hiding from me? Where's the skull? Did you make a deal with her? Spit it out!"

"I've told you everything, my lord! I swear it!"

Screwing my eyes shut, I waited for the end. Instead, Saggon hauled me back, dropped me onto the sawdust-strewn floor, and then helped me to my feet. He clapped me on the back and bellowed laughter.

"I was just fuckin' witcha!" He cried. "I had ya, didn't I? I had him, boys, didn't I?" He said to my companions. "Naw, you did all right, Frankie. You did what you could."

Saggon motioned me back to the table. My legs felt *al dente*, but I managed to collapse into a chair. Thank the gods I hadn't pissed myself.

"This is what I want, Elvis," Saggon said, leveling his gaze at me. "You get me the location of that gal's hideout within twenty-four hours, or I sell pieces of you around town like Girl Scout cookies. You got me?"

A frozen sheath of doom formed around my heart. Mother-fucking bad luck. I would have to bug out of town after all.

"Consider it done, my lord," I said, with no conviction whatsoever.

To our blessed relief, Saggon motioned us out the door. The troll led us back through the Great Hall and Grand Foyer, and then out to the courtyard.

"That was fun," Lithaine said. "What now?"

"I'll be out of town by nightfall," I said. "No reason why you boys can't stay. I'm the one who's fucked."

"If you split without giving him what he wants, then we're all fucked," Amabored said. "Time to ply our trade on the Were Coast. We'll meet at Jaspin's place at dusk."

It appeared that our lives in Redhauke were over—but fate was destined to yank us by the balls in a different direction. A watch later found me back at Lady Hagg's to pack up my meager possessions. When I stepped into my third-floor room, the skull with which Melinda had clobbered me on the Stonesong Bridge sat leering on my nightstand between a fat red candlestick and an oil lamp. It looked utterly benign—and I might have considered it so, had I any inkling of who put it in my room, or why.

I considered the skull less benign still when suddenly—and, may I say, unexpectedly—it started to scream.

21

I hadn't even time to wrap my brain around the horned skull shrieking in my room before Melinda and two masked henchmen burst through the door behind me. The woman spun me around and thrust her dagger at my throat.

"Do what I say or die!" she shouted. So loud was the skull's keening wail that I could only read her lips. I nodded. Grabbing the still-wailing skull from the nightstand, she wrapped it in the thin bedsheet from my sleeping mat and dropped it into a shoulder bag. Then she flung open the door and yanked me into the hall.

At once, we saw the leaches. Dozens of them, each the size of a bull terrier and as black and slimy as a devil's tongue, slithered on the walls, hung from the ceiling, or writhed on the floor. At the business end of each one lurked a puckered maw lined with a double row of needled fangs.

"What the holy fuck—?" I cried.

"We're too late," Melinda said. "Swords!"

A scream behind us, from one of Melinda's men. A leach had dropped from the ceiling and sank its fangs into the poor bastard's head. The henchman screamed and caromed off the walls. Throbbing obscenely, the leach sucked pinkish-gray goo from his skull through the hollow straws of its fangs. A scarlet flood poured from the man's eyes, nose, and ears. In five seconds he lay twitching on the floor, a bloody horror.

"Crom's beard!" I said.

The leaches launched themselves at us. They were blind and slow; by timing our swings, we could bisect them in mid-flight—which didn't kill them but did slow them down.

Soon, the other henchman had his face pulled from his skull, and Melinda and I found ourselves back-to-back near a window at the end of the hall. Still the glistening, black abominations came. Behind closed doors, the other boarders cowered beneath their beds; I envied them. I also felt the old familiar rush of adrenalin at once again doing the death-tango, with the crone's fingers around my throat and her cold breath on me like the horror of an open tomb. My nuts felt like cannonballs.

Catching Melinda's gaze, I saw the same hunger in her eyes—she felt it too.

"Out the window, then," she said, her gaze locking on mine.

"You read my mind."

Still clutching the bag holding the screaming skull, Melinda launched into a headfirst dive out the third-floor window. I followed, and a push from the girdle sent the window frame exploding ahead of me over Lamplight Street.

A three-story fall rarely ends well. Fortunately, even in midwinter Lamplight Street is lined with thatch-covered vendor stalls selling wormy fruit, knockoff roc-feathers, worthless aphrodisiacs, and the like. We crashed into a pair of them, sending the stall proprietors running for cover.

Then we heard the sirens: Sklaar's ornithopters, piloted by gnomes and drawn by whatever powerful magic had summoned those leaches. Swooping towards us, they darkened the streets like the shadows of owls hunting field mice. They were zeroing in on the skull's muffled wails. Unless we could quiet the thing and then vanish, in moments they would cordon off the block with Force Shields and clamp us in irons for unauthorized use of sorcery.

A pair of ornithopters dropped low to hover over the street before us. "Follow me!" Melinda cried. She bolted for the nearest alley.

I followed. Crossing over Fountain Avenue, we were soon lost in the maze of the Guild Quarter, leapfrogging over piles of refuse and pools of sewage, losing ourselves in the bowels of the city. The skull had stopped screaming, opting instead to concoct new deviltry from its hiding spot in Melinda's purse.

We stopped short in a cramped courtyard lined with barrels. Melinda crouched before one barrel and depressed a hidden latch. The barrel sprang back to reveal the maw of a well and a ladder descending to the catacombs below. Without a look back, she started down the ladder. I dove in after her just before the spring-loaded barrel snapped back into place. Wherever Melinda the Blade was leading me, I was at her mercy.

22

Dropping from the ladder into a narrow rock-hewn tunnel, I raced after Melinda. Despite my shock and terror, I fixated on her ass bobbing before me in the feeble torchlight. My thoughts lingered upon that mystical nexus where her ass, thighs, and abdomen all merged into a fantastical, goddess-touched landscape. If ever I found myself sniffing around that landscape, then I'd have to fake not needing a map.

For a good while, we jogged through the slime-coated tunnel as it twisted and branched, coming at last to a rusted sluice gate anchoring the end of a narrow tributary. Melinda gestured over it, and hidden runes carved in the metal awoke into a dim ruby glow. She touched the runes with her finger. The gate dissolved into the aether, replaced by a portal that led into a chamber plump with warm firelight. Melinda looked back at me.

"Saggon will pay dearly for the location of this place," Melinda said. "But you'd better spend the money quickly."

"Fair enough," I said.

"Then come in," she said. No sooner did I slip into her silk-draped apartment than I found myself slammed against a stone wall with her dagger once again at my throat.

"How did you get the skull?" Melinda growled. "When did you steal it? Tell me now, or I'll show you how I earned my name!"

"I—I don't know about any skull!" I stammered. "I never saw it before until you bashed me in the head with it! I didn't see it again until I found it in my room!"

"You're lying!" She took the knife from my throat and pressed the blade against my balls.

"Do I look like I'm lying, lady?"

That stopped her. For a lingering moment, she stared hard into my eyes. Then she removed her blade from my balls. I allowed myself a small swallow.

"No," she said. "You're not lying." She sheathed her knife, took the still-quiet skull from her pouch, and unwrapped it. Raising its leering countenance to her own face, she regarded it as the bard's gravedigger might.

"I don't know what this thing is," she said. "I only know that Saggon wants it. It's the only leverage I have against him."

"How did you get it?" I asked. Relief finding me at last, my questions spilled out. "Why does it scream? What does it have to do with those fucking leaches? I mean, what the fuck?"

"Later," Melinda said. "We need a drink first." She dropped the skull back into her purse and set it aside. Then a grin supplanted her scowl like the sun muscling its way through a fog bank. She wasn't beautiful, but she had a beautiful smile.

When she dropped her cloak on a fall of pillows and disappeared into the kitchen, I took a moment to survey her apartment. Though the city above shivered in midwinter, Melinda had warmed her rooms with shallow brass bowls piled with dwarfen firestones—an expensive luxury. The sitting room lay redolent with color: tie-dyed tapestries dancing on the stone walls, couches bursting with pillows, bookshelves stuffed and groaning with tomes and scrolls. Tucked away on one shelf was a ceramic bust of Elvis Presley, looking for all the world like a Filipino waiter. A map of the city hung over the hearth. Off the main room lay the kitchen and a bedchamber. The décor stood in contrast to the woman herself, who favored grades of umbra and penumbra in her dress.

A moment later, she emerged with two goblets of brandy. "Your name, swordsman? I'll forgive you if you don't give your real one."

"Elberon of the Isles," I said. "And you're Melinda the Blade, I gather?"

"Not my real name, though I answer to no other," she said. "To your health." She clinked my glass. Her eyes were blazing emeralds.

I eyed the glass. "I hope you aren't being ironic."

"It was more like sarcasm."

We drank. It was good, expensive stuff, warm liquid gold.

"I'm safe as long as I don't become one of your henchmen," I said. "In the three times we've met, I've seen a half-dozen of them die. You should dress them in red shirts."

"Make light of them at your peril, swordsman," Melinda said. "They paid dearly for their loyalty."

"They must have loved you dearly to pay so dear a price."

"Perhaps they did," she said, lowering her gaze. "Why were you in the bottom of that dray? Did Saggon set you to it?"

"Now *you* have questions?" I asked. "I guarantee you that I have more. Shall we trade?"

"Of course."

"Yes, he set me to it. He wanted to find out where you were holed up. He seems to think you're a threat."

"I am a threat. Three months ago, I left him." She raised her gaze to meet mine. "I was his Second."

"His *Second*?" I felt like a three-year-old attempting to master the obvious. Saggon's Second—that meant she was in line to become the Over-Boss. It meant she had outfoxed every captain in the Guild, that she had amassed enough power to run the whole enterprise, that she had survived a dozen assassination attempts. It meant she was a badass.

"I've worked for him since I was thirteen years old," Melinda said. "He's the closest thing to a father I have."

"You had a falling out?" I asked.

"What did you think was in those barrels I hijacked?"

"Pipeweed."

"Did you ever open one? Pick one up?"

"Look, I've only been in town a few months. I don't ask questions. If they didn't hold pipeweed, then what did they hold?"

"Drugged children," Melinda said. "One child per barrel. The first night you saw me, there were twelve children in the cart. There were ten children in the cart on the Stonesong Bridge."

"Get the fuck out!" I said. "Children? Why?"

She soon convinced me it was true. Saggon was importing child slaves into the city via the Chaos Dwarfs, then enslaving them to dig in the catacombs beneath the Blue Falcon. Melinda, meanwhile, had been hijacking shipments to smuggle the children to safe houses hidden in the hinterlands. Saggon had set the dwarfs on her trail— and the night I rode out with her, they ambushed her. Only her threat to the skull had kept the dwarfs at bay.

"Why is Saggon digging beneath the Falcon?" I asked. "Why kids?"

"I asked those questions myself," Melinda said. "He was digging for that thing, of course," she said, pointing to her purse.

"The skull? Why? How did you get it?"

Melinda refilled our glasses and told her tale. The excavation had been going on for a year, she said, although she only learned about it six months ago. At first, Saggon had set adult slaves to digging in the catacombs—only an idiot would rely on children to perform hard labor—but the slaves dug too deep. They broke into the prison of something ancient and abominable entombed beneath the Blue Falcon, and the sight of the gibbering fiend drove the slaves mad. Whatever it was, no slave could get near it and live. All work stopped.

"And then Saggon sent me down there to find out what it was, and treat with it," Melinda said.

"Jesus," I said. "What was it?"

"Do you recall the legend of the first Quest of the Dread Plain?" she asked.

Who didn't? The tales were told to every schoolkid from Hydra

Bay to the Northern Wastes: tales of that first generation of heroes, the Heroes of Old, as essential to any epic tale as dark lords or relics of great power. Woerth's particular Heroes of Old had each become legendary: Arturus, the warlord who would later found Redhauke; Koschei's apprentices, the arch-mages Gygax and Rigsby; the dwarf prince Storm Stonegorm, who designed the Blue Falcon for Arturus; Eckberd the Bold, later turned to the dark side; the elven warrior-priestess Gemalatel; and the Cloud Rider Wanbli, slain horribly by Eckberd. It was this group who retrieved the Black Mirror from Hell, closed the Hellmouth, and threw down Koschei. Arturus himself cut off the asshole's head. For five hundred years, the Free Kingdoms had been at peace, secure in the knowledge that the threat from the Deathless One had been banished forever from Woerth.

Fat chance. Of course, the first Quest was a mere prelude. In what part of the Multiverse isn't that true?

At my nod, Melinda continued. "The legend tells of a portal to Hell itself, buried deep beneath Redhauke—and that the Blue Falcon itself was designed to seal the breach between Hell and Woerth."

"You're not saying—"

"I am saying. I've seen it. And I've seen the creature that dwells there to guard the Hellmouth. It's one of the Fallen—a devil straight from the pits of Malebolge. It eats children, Elberon of the Isles. It feeds on their souls."

I let this bit of news sink in. If she was playing me somehow, she belonged on the stage; the haunted look in her eyes was utterly convincing.

"You say Saggon sent you to treat with it," I offered.

"The slaves uncovered the Hellmouth," Melinda said. "The original portal from which Beelzebub attacked Woerth. I'm convinced of it. Whether the devil down there is set to guard Woerth from Hell, or Hell from Woerth, I can't say. Fortunately, it's bound by chains of brimstone—by whom or by what, I still don't know—or it would have already destroyed the city. The devil is a liar, and it offers no sure answers."

"So, you did talk to it?" I asked. "Why aren't you a dribbling idiot?"

"Malacoda is a very particular devil. He says that no man can see his face and remain sane—and he means it literally. Women aren't worth his time."

Continuing her tale, Melinda told of Saggon ordering her into the catacombs, his eyes strangely blank as she pleaded against it. Left with no choice, she descended to confront whatever evil lurked there. I've battled both demons and devils, and I can assure you that shitting your pants is the least of your worries. Nevertheless, Melinda crept into the hot, stinking tunnel glowing with lurid Hellfire, its walls writhing from the tortured souls entrapped within, with as much intestinal fortitude as any Fifteenth-Level adventurer. She crept close enough to speak to the creature while avoiding its gaze.

"WHO GOES THERE?" the creature asked, its voice laden with bass and heavy-metal distortion.

"Melinda the Blade, of the Thieves Guild," Melinda called to it. "My master, Saggon the Large, sent me to parlay with you."

"PARLAY WITH THEE," the creature corrected her. *"IF YOU'RE GOING TO BLATHER ON, AT LEAST EXTEND THE PROPER COUR-TESY. THE NAME'S MALACODA. DIRE MALEBRANCHE OF THE EIGHTH CIRCLE, AT YOUR SERVICE. IF YOU MUST ADDRESS ME AT ALL, TINY MORTAL, YOU CAN ADDRESS ME AS 'YOUR SATANIC HIGHNESS.' IT'S BEEN MILLENNIA SINCE I'VE HEARD PROPER TALK."*

"I come to parlay, your Satanic Highness," Melinda tried again. "My master desires to treat with thee."

"GET ME OUT OF THESE CHAINS, AND WE'LL PARLAY," the devil said.

"Such is beyond my power, my lord," Melinda said. "But if thou desirest anything within my meager grasp, thou hast only to ask."

"I NEED TO EAT," the devil said. *"I HAVEN'T HAD A BITE IN FIVE THOUSAND YEARS."*

"Of course, my lord. What is thy desire?"

"THAT FAT COCKSUCKER BOSS OF YOURS KNOWS. TELL HIM

NOT TO INSULT ME WITH HIS PATHETIC SLAVES. I CRAVE FRESHER MEAT."

"Very well, my lord. Saggon desires only that he be allowed to continue his work in these tunnels."

"QUENCH MY HUNGER, AND HE CAN DIG AWAY."

"Thou art high amongst the Fallen, my lord. It shall be as you command." With that, Melinda backed away, bowing low as she retreated down the obscene, fleshy tunnel. But the devil stopped her with a command.

"HOLD ON A MINUTE," the devil said. "SAGGON'S LOOKING FOR THIS, I THINK. IF I WERE YOU, I WOULDN'T GIVE IT TO HIM."

Malacoda tossed something down the tunnel. It bounced toward Melinda until it came to rest at her feet: a head-sized, copper-banded chest with a ruby-encrusted rune fixed to the curved lid. Without another word, she picked it up and ran like hell.

She reported back to Saggon, who merely nodded and dismissed her. Of the skull, she said nothing. The next day, the Over-Boss sent forth emissaries to establish trade in child slaves with the Chaos Dwarfs from the Brimstone Hills west of Redhauke. A fortnight later, the first children were suffering under the lash far beneath the Blue Falcon. Saggon made them dig, their small hands clutching hand-shovels, their thin backs breaking under the hard labor of moving piles of rock until they collapsed—and then he gave them to the devil.

"They die in terror, Elberon," Melinda said. Her eyes shone with tears. "The moment I learned what Saggon was doing, I vowed to kill him. I'll end this evil or die trying."

I took her hand. You might think it a calculated gesture, but I didn't realize I had done it until she squeezed my hand with hers. "But why the trade?" I asked, after a moment. "Why not just snatch kids from the streets?"

"It would draw too much attention," Melinda said. "At least, once the well of street urchins ran dry. Children from the villages are missed by none but those who love them."

Suddenly it came to me—a bolt from the blue, as two frazzled synapses in my brain connected at last. "Holy shit! So that's what the ghost was trying to tell Lithaine! That's why we had to get those kids into the city!"

"Excuse me?"

Now it was my turn to spin a tale to beggar belief. I told her everything—my arrival in Doomtown, my introduction to my friends, our realization that children were in danger, the appearance of Lithaine's ghost, and the cattle stampede into the city. She listened without interruption.

"Now we know why the kids were disappearing," I said. "A devil's gotta eat."

"I believe you," she said, regarding me with naked appraisal. "So, it was you who nearly leveled the city with a stampede. You'd best not mention it to Saggon—that event cost the Guild a lot of money."

"If Saggon wants that skull," I said, "why not just give it to him? He'll stop digging, and he won't need to keep replacing his slaves."

"I thought of that, of course," Melinda said. "Now that the devil's awake, I reckon he'll want to keep feeding, regardless of whether Saggon keeps digging. Besides, whatever that skull is, I don't think it's Saggon who wants it. He wants only to eat and fuck and count his money. Someone else is paying him to find it—and that means it's dangerous. I need to find out what it is."

"And the leaches, back on Lamplight street? What the hell was all that about? How did you find me in the first place? You didn't know me from a peasant."

"The skull's case. It's drawn to the skull like a magnet. Since I've had the thing, it's screamed like that twice. Both times, it summoned creatures of Chaos to attack me. So far, it's stayed quiet down here."

For a long moment, we sat in silence, lost in the burnt-umber iridescence of the brandy in our goblets, absorbing the news we had just shared. I stole a look at Melinda the Blade, studied the swell of her breasts, the languid curve of her hips, the fiery copper sheen of her hair. The rubescent glow from the firestones revealed that my initial reaction was wrong: She was beautiful, after all. Her achievements marked her as cunning and ruthless. Behind her wide, apple-cheeked face and emerald eyes, there flowed more than cunning; there flowed honesty, determination, and no small measure of hope.

"I want to kiss you," I said. "But first, I want you to know that I'm with you. I'll help you take down Saggon. Fuck that fat fucking fuck."

"I accept your offer because I need a friend," Melinda said. Her green eyes found mine. "I'm fresh out."

23

Saggon had been looking for the Skull all along, of course, and only much later would we learn which piece-of-shit retired illusionist put him up to it. With a little digging, Melinda learned that the Over-Boss had promised the Chaos Dwarfs ten barges full of gold if they found it for him. The dwarfs asked around, and a few months later they told him that the Skull was buried right beneath his feet.

Why was he looking for it, Melinda wondered? What power did it hold? And why did the devil throw it away so casually? To question a devil's motives is to invite madness. Most likely, he did it to sow discord. On the other hand, some Fallen can divine the future, so maybe Malacoda foresaw that giving it to her would get it into my hands, offering the best chance to resurrect Koschei. Fallen angels are the worst fucking pain in the ass.

You might also be wondering if I got laid, that first night in Melinda's apartment. Let's just say we had a meeting of the minds. So desperate was she to end Saggon's abominable trade that she would have taken any chance—and I was the only tool at hand. No one had ever needed me before. I loved her a little, right away.

That morning, I awoke with Melinda's arm draped around my neck. I squeezed the sand out of my eyes and found myself staring at the Skull. Somehow, it had teleported out of its casket and now rested on her nightstand as if it had always been there. Before I could wake her, it started to scream.

24

"If this is what I think it is," Jaspin said, ruminating over the skull with a scrying glass, "then you fellows are in for a spot of trouble."

Three weeks had passed since Melinda took from me the one thing I longed to have stolen. When I slipped into her that first time, it took me a second to believe it was really happening. Then, instinct took over. Afterward, we lay entwined together, sticky in all the right places. I felt like the first man ever to walk the Woerth. My cock felt like it was carved from granite. That I should concern myself with Melinda's reciprocal pleasure never occurred to me.

After several more nights of that action, I was to Melinda as a fish is to the dappled sunlight gleaming through the water's surface. As joined to her as I became, however, I became joined equally to the Skull. Wherever I went, the fucking thing showed up.

To see it twice was ominous. To see it a third time made it my doom, and I bent every thought to ridding myself of it. I locked it in a closet; the next morning, I woke to find it resting on my nightstand. I threw it down a well; within an hour, I walked into Jaspin's place to find it sitting on the bar. I rode back to the Stonesong Bridge and tossed it over the side; by the time I returned to Redhauke, it was resting comfortably in my saddlebag. Each time it appeared, I was attacked by an increasingly heinous array of monsters. Sometimes they were recognizable—say, a dozen cave trolls. And sometimes not —as in a homicidal Blood Cloud, a creature every bit as disturbing as you can imagine. Each time, I'd run screaming into an alley or an abandoned building lest the ornithopters find me again. After two weeks of this horror, my fate became clear. One night, Amabored took me out for a beer.

"Look, dude," Amabored said, "You're a brother and all. But come on. Maybe you should, you know—"

"Get lost?"

"I knew you'd understand."

And so, I was sent once again into exile. Packing my few belongings, I slunk out of Lady Hagg's, moved into Melinda's subterranean apartments, and didn't move out again until I was forced to flee the city. Two weeks of courtship, and Melinda and I became, essentially, man and wife.

I was losing my mind, sure, but Melinda was happy to have me. We fucked like rabbits, which took my mind off my troubles. We found that if we kept the skull always where I could see it, tucked away safely in its case, then it didn't scream—as much. I perceived in the thing a pulsing malevolence. Its black gaze sought me always. For long hours, I stared into the gaping hollows of its eye sockets, searching for some ember of life. I talked to it.

After a time, I suspected that it might be a relic, which gave me a small thrill; an encounter with one of those ancient and powerful magical items can make a career. Sure, to carry out its requisite destruction and save the Woerth—usually by flinging it into the inevitable volcano, crevasse, or magical cave—entails a long and arduous journey haunted by war, mind-melting horror, and the constant specter of death. So what? A relic is your ticket to fortune and glory. Simply hire some ink-stained scribe to write your trilogy— for some reason, it's *always* a trilogy—and hit the speaking circuit. An illusionist might even option the rights and create a big-budget shadow play to immortalize you forever. Who wouldn't risk certain death to make a little scratch?

If the skull was a relic, then I needed to know, pronto. That need brought me to Jaspin, who was the only high-level adventurer I knew. When I showed it to him, that first time in the Suds 'n Shade, he gave a convincing performance as a guy who had no idea what the hell the thing was.

"But why me?" I asked Jaspin. "What does it want?"

"Why *not* you?" asked Lithaine.

"Go piss on a blue dragon, ass-hat," I said.

Lithaine, Amabored, and Redulfo kept their distance from me at the other end of the bar. As far as I knew, Jaspin was doing me a huge solid; word of my troubles had hit the street, and the moment I stepped through the door, every man-jack inside the bar walked out. Even the kobolds gave me a wide berth.

"Curses and enchantments are often one link in a larger chain of magic," Jaspin said. "Have you any other relics that it might be reacting to? Perhaps a magical scepter? A piece of magical armor or clothing that you found on your travels?"

"Not at all," I said, lying through my teeth. I thought of the girdle, of course, but what the hell did it have to do with this skull? That was my business. "I haven't seen so much as a plus-one blade."

Curious." Jaspin picked up the skull. He stroked his beard and peered into its eye-sockets. "You should give it a name."

"You can call it Aloysius if you want. If this thing doesn't shut the fuck up, then I'm done for."

"I'm afraid he really is," said Redulfo.

"Perhaps the same force that sparked the Chaos hordes to move south again has also activated its powers—hello... what's this?" asked Jaspin. Holding up the glass, he peered through it into the left eye-socket, then motioned me over to look as well. Deep inside the eye socket I saw, outlined in the tiniest of ruby-red jewels, a rune:

<

"That's the same rune carved onto the box this thing came in," I said. "What is it?"

"It's the old dwarf tongue. The rune *Kaunan*," Jaspin said. "*Kaunan* means *pestilence*."

Ominous shadows filled the tavern. The temperature plummeted.

"Knock it off, Redulfo," I said.

"Sorry."

"It's Koschei's rune," said Jaspin.

"*Koschei!?!*" We all cried out simultaneously. "Are you fucking kidding me?" I added.

He wasn't fucking kidding me, as it turned out. It was the second time in two weeks I had heard that accursed name uttered in my presence. Six hundred or so years ago, the wizard Koschei of the Verdant Vale, the legends told, once ruled his lands as a noble philosopher-king. Koschei was a Twentieth-Level sorcerer, a man of staggering intellect, rich in wisdom, his vision far-reaching and true. His personal interests led revolutions in alchemy, architecture, astrology, magic, and medicine. Koschei's reign coincided with a golden age in the Free Kingdoms, the Age of Light, when the dwarfs advanced knowledge of minecraft and weaponry, the elves advanced knowledge of music, art, and philosophy, and the gnomes advanced the twin arts of brewing and marijuana cultivation. What human advances came during this time? Not much, I'll warrant. Advances in the art of the Seven Deadly Sins?

The only dark stain on the age: an open Hellmouth, burning on the southern shore of Lake Everdeep—the very one, Melinda believed, that she discovered beneath the Blue Falcon a few months earlier. From this open wound in the Woerth, hellspawn spooged like Lucifer's money shot across the countryside. No one knew from whence the Hellmouth came. Did the spells of some dark necromancer summon it forth? Or had it always been there, a malignant pimple on the otherwise unblemished face of the Woerth?

After more than a century of warfare between the Free Kingdoms and the forces of Hellfire—a war that saw Koschei become the primary defender of Woerth against Chaos—Koschei's only child, the

Lady Cataline, was murdered at the direction of Beelzebub, King of the Eighth Circle of Hell. The wizard went mad with grief, and he bent his thaumaturgical arts towards gaining the power to resurrect her. For years, he delved into the arcana, going farther and deeper in his exploration of the Multiverse than any wizard had gone before. To gain the power of resurrection, he had first to conquer Death itself—and so he did, the legends told. Koschei of the Verdant Vale was no more; in his place was Koschei the Deathless, the Dark Foe now allied with Beelzebub in a mad desire to enslave the Woerth. Such power did his black sorcery require that Koschei withered every leaf, flower, blade of grass, and stalk of wheat in his lands. He enslaved his people, dug deep pits beneath his fortresses, and filled them with foul hellspawn. In his quest for vengeance against El, he sent forth his armies to conquer the Free Kingdoms. For six more years, the Dread War raged—until the First Quest cast him down.

There are, of course, infinite Koscheis scattered throughout the Multiverse: Sauron, Voldemort, Lord Foul, Thulsa Doom, or Vladimir Putin—who gives a fuck? They're a dime a dozen. There was nothing special about our own Dark Lord, other than the peculiar brand of suffering he caused. Such suffering was fine with us, so long as it was consigned to the sepia-toned past. Only when it became clear that we were going to star in the sequel did we give a shit.

"The legends tell of the Ten Phylaxes: pieces of Koschei's physical body, as well as his most powerfully cursed relics," said Jaspin. "They've been scattered these long centuries, lost to time and chance. If ever they are all brought together, then Koschei's soul will return from the Void, and the Dread War will begin anew." The illusionist placed his hand on my shoulder. "You, my friend, are in possession of the skull of Koschei the Deathless—the Screaming Skull, legend has named it."

I collapsed onto a barstool. My mind was filled with raging turmoil, a river overflowing its banks. No one spoke. Everyone moved farther away from me.

"Is it worth anything?" Amabored asked, after it was clear that I was too stunned to speak. "This could be our ticket."

"Oh, now it's *our* ticket?" I cried, snapping out of my stupor. "Fine fucking friend you are!" I turned desperately to Jaspin. "How do I get rid of it? I don't want the goddamned thing—but every time I try to lose it, it turns up again! For fuck's sake, don't tell me I have to toss it into a volcano. I couldn't bear it."

"Why it's attached itself to you, I can't say," Jaspin said, placing the Skull back on the bar. "It will be drawn to other Phylaxes. You say you never saw it before you found it sitting on your nightstand. Quite curious. You're certain that nothing in your possession might be attracting it?"

I considered telling Jaspin the whole story—about the girdle, about Melinda finding the Hellmouth, about the devil Malacoda, about Saggon's child slaves, everything. This was Redhauke, however, and it was best to trust no one, not even a friendly bartender who seemed to have your best interests at heart. Besides, Melinda had sworn me to secrecy. I opted instead to play my hand tight until the illusionist proved a friend.

"No sir," I said. "I have no idea where the thing came from, or why I can't get rid of it. I only know that I want to, as soon as possible."

"Why don't we just go see Sklaar or the Lord Mayor?" Redulfo offered. "They're the city fathers, aren't they? We should punt this thing over to men who can handle it."

"That sounds about right," said Lithaine. "It shouldn't be any of our business."

"Damned straight," said Amabored.

"I'd advise against it," Jaspin said. "At least, not yet. There are forces searching for these Phylaxes. They have spies everywhere, some of them highly placed, and some of them right here in Redhauke. If they find out you have it, they won't just take it from you —they'll kill you, just to tie up whatever loose end you represent."

"What then?" I asked. "Spend the rest of my life looking at it until I die horribly?"

Jaspin made a show of considering my options for me. "In the cellar, I have a safe room, which I rent out to adventurers in need of a place to store enchanted items. Inside this room, no sorcery will work. Neither can any magic, no matter how strong, pierce its walls. The room was a gift to me from a sorcerer who valued my counsel. You can store the Skull there. If this room can't contain its power, then you're dead already."

"Okay—thanks," I said. "But for how long? Surely you don't want it down there for a second longer than it needs to be."

"I'll make inquiries. Perhaps Sklaar will know what to do—but before we approach him, we want to make sure that he's not working to bring Koschei back again."

Tension flowing out of my body, I slumped over the bar. I couldn't trust anyone—but I'd have to trust Jaspin, at least for now. The thought of being rid of that fucking Skull, even for a moment, was sweet ambrosia to my tortured mind. As the Screaming Skull rested ominously on the bar, its black eye sockets seemed to fill my frame of vision until I was lost to the darkness.

Amabored approached and handed me a beer. "If this doesn't work," he said, "and you need somebody to... you know..." He made a slicing motion across his throat.

"Brother, you'll be the first one I call."

25

So began my long association with the Ten Phylaxes of Koschei the Deathless. We learned their names soon enough: From the Awful Orbs to the Mace of Malice to the Scythe of Souls, we chased these ten motherfucking MacGuffins from one end of the Multiverse to the other to save the Woerth from Koschei. Our naivety was a liability; had we known that Jaspin was working for the Hand all along, we'd have run him through at the first opportunity. The cocksucker must have tried to turn the Skull over to the Hand that very night, only to find it back in his panic room the next day, which was exactly where it wanted to be. As Jaspin also had to pretend to my father that he was aiding me on the Quest with which Olderon had paid dearly to saddle me, his options were limited—he couldn't kill me, for instance. There were layers upon layers of bullshit surrounding the Skull, and I would have to eat all of it.

BACK IN THOSE INNOCENT DAYS WHEN MY ONLY WORRY WAS THE Screaming Skull—from which I had been momentarily relieved—I had the luxury of concentrating on my own life. The day after my first night with Melinda, I high-tailed it back to the Falcon to lie my ass off to Saggon about what I had discovered. That night, a dozen armed men burst into a room on the top floor of a safe house hidden deep in the Merchant Quarter, the address of which I had provided to Saggon at Melinda's request. When the door opened, six spring-loaded cross-bows unloaded on them, killing four; when the remainder tried to flee, hidden trap doors dropped them into pits filled with twelve-inch spikes. Within the hour, two of Saggon's larger oafs dragged me into another dungeon deep within the Falcon and shoved my face two inches away from a cauldron of molten lead, at which point I duti-fully cried for mercy and swore my oath that I had tracked the woman to that very address.

So it went until Saggon finally bought what I was selling, and he ordered me to continue boning Melinda as a double-agent. The Over-Boss feigned concern that Melinda still had the Skull, which meant he didn't dare assault her directly for fear that she had someone poised over a crevasse deep in the Shadow Mountains, ready to toss it into an abyss with one word through the aether. That fear was simply another layer of subterfuge. Jaspin, Saggon's puppet master, must have suspected that either Melinda or I had another one of the Phylaxes in our possession, which was why he couldn't get the Skull out of Redhauke to turn it over to the Hand. Everyone was watching everyone else, waiting for someone to tip a hand.

For my troubles, Saggon even promoted me; I was now a Soldier, Second Class in the Thieves Guild. Imagining Olderon hearing the news, I spent that night inside a whiskey bottle. The promotion also put me in command of Amabored and Lithaine; I imagined giving either of them an order, and then spent the next night there, too.

Following Melinda's ambush, she and Saggon thus entered a period of détente. Within Redhauke there stood four main sources of power: the Lord Mayor and his High Council, the Redhauke Guard, the Council of Thaumaturgy, and the Thieves Guild. The three former power centers suffered the latter's presence because of the tribute Saggon paid in gold, slaves, and contraband. The Over-Boss's strength, meanwhile, rested in the hands of his five Captains, each of whom oversaw an army of loosely-knit gangs with names like the

Energy Vampires, the Piledrivers, Painful Discharge, and Ding-Ding-Here-Comes-the-Shit-Mobile. The Captains supported Saggon with muscle; in return, he gave them political cover. If they should learn that Saggon's Second—his handpicked successor, who rose from a teenaged message-runner to captain the Merchant Quarter in just ten years—had declared a challenge, then his patrons in the Noble Quarter might murder him simply because they smelled disorder.

Though no agreement was ever inked or spoken between them, Saggon and Melinda thus found themselves in an uneasy truce. Melinda need only lay low and forgo building an army, and Saggon would forgo trying to waste her—at least until Jaspin gave the order. Meanwhile, I got laid and got to live. My friends, the Tree of Life bears no sweeter fruit.

As I was quickly learning, however, fruit rots. Despite Melinda's continued attempts to hijack shipments of children and spirit them safely away from Redhauke, the dam was foreordained to burst—and the following spring, it did. The shipments increased until the lands outside the city were nearly barren of children. We couldn't figure out why. Saggon knew that Melinda had the Skull; why was he still digging?

"The devil must be getting hungrier," Melinda said. "Saggon's no longer using the children as slaves. They're just food. If he doesn't keep feeding Malacoda, it will start to eat souls that matter to him—including his."

The five of us—Amabored, Lithaine, Melinda, Redulfo and I—sat nursing beers at the Suds 'n Shade. It was mid-morning, and the place was mostly empty. Trilecia stood behind the bar polishing candlesticks, paying us no mind; somewhere unbeknownst to us, Jaspin was spying on our conversation. Fucker.

"What are we supposed to do, kill an Arch-Devil?" Lithaine asked. "We're only Fourth Level. That thing would use our bones for toothpicks."

"What else can we do?" asked Redulfo. "Ask it to go on a diet?"

"We have to stop it," said Melinda. "We have no choice."

I had heard enough; Melinda's occasional waxing of my joint was not worth my life. "Are you out of your fucking mind?" I cried. "Forget the dead certainty that we'll all die horribly. That devil is the only thing stopping up the Hellmouth! We kill it, and this city might be overrun with hellspawn!"

"Maybe we don't have to kill it," Melinda said, forgoing whatever desire she might harbor to shank me in the belly. "Malacoda knows me. He might be willing to treat with me again. While I distract him, some of you can free whatever children are inside. If we can figure out how to do it, someone can open the Hellmouth long enough for us to shove the devil through it and trap him in Hell."

"No offense, my lady," Amabored said as he lit his pipe, "but that's the most fucked-up plan I've ever heard. How are we supposed to know how to open a Hellmouth, let alone close it again? We try that shit, and we're deader than fried chicken."

"Maybe not," Redulfo said, and so surprised were we to hear him espouse any degree of optimism that we all turned to stare at him. The wizard only blinked like a turtle behind his spectacles. "I work in Sklaar's library, remember? Everything about the original Quest is on record there. If I can find a way to control the Hellmouth, we might have a shot. And here's another angle—Elberon, if we get the Hellmouth shut again, you can toss the Skull into it while we're at it. You can rid yourself of that thing for good. The certainty of our deaths notwithstanding, it's not an impossible plan."

The bar fell into silence. Finally, Amabored drained his beer and belched loudly enough to rattle the glassware behind the bar.

"Fuck it," he said. "I'm in. It's just stupid enough to work."

Lithaine shrugged. "Why not? It'll be worth it just to watch Amabored get disemboweled by a devil."

Everyone looked to me. I found Melinda's gaze and saw in her green eyes the certainty that she was going through with the plan, whether I crapped out or not.

"Okay," I said, sounding defeat. "I've got nothing better to do than die."

Melinda took my hand. "This is your chance to be the hero I

know you can be," she said, smiling. "Besides, if you die, then I'll kill you."

"If we're going to face hellspawn, then we need a professional," said Amabored. "While Redulfo is geeking out at the library, I'll try to find us a paladin. Let's go."

We agreed to split up. Melinda and I would purchase supplies for battle, Amabored would rent a paladin, Redulfo would hit the library, and Lithaine would spend the day scouting the Falcon. As we headed for the street, I clapped Redulfo on the shoulder.

"You're the last guy I'd expect to believe in this cockeyed plan," I said to him.

"Oh, the plan itself has almost no chance of succeeding," said Redulfo. "But any other scenario likely ends with our deaths, as well. Success only becomes possible when we have no other choice."

That was Redulfo for you—pessimism as an art form. You had to admire it.

26

T he next morning, we were gathered once again at the Suds 'n Shade, slurping coffee as we reviewed our progress. We were all present but Redulfo, who had yet to return from his all-nighter in Sklaar's library. To our surprise, Jaspin was absent as well; having asked him to retrieve the Skull from his safe room, we expected the illusionist to show up to learn why. Instead, one of his bouncers, a small but surprisingly ass-kicking gnome we knew only as Sig, arrived with the Skull tucked inside its case. He handed it to me.

"My master sends his regrets," Sig growled, chomping on a wet stogie. "He's away visiting a supplier on the Were Coast. He bade me tell you that he trusts you all to your plans, whatever they might be. He'll return in a fortnight."

Curious—but the guy had a business to run, so what did we care? The gnome vamoosed to the kitchen. We turned quickly to the news, which was both good and bad: good, in that Amabored's perusal of the Guild bulletin board had indeed scored a paladin, who agreed to join our raiding party for one-fifth of any booty recovered, sight unseen; bad, in that Lithaine had spent the night scouting the Blue Falcon, only to find it crawling with bad guys.

"Imps, at least," the elf said, drawing on his long-stemmed pipe. "Other hellspawn as well, I suspect. I didn't see anybody come in the main gate or any of the service gates, so whatever's inside must have come from underground. The usual crowd is gone, other than a few hangers-on for show. We're supposed to think it's business as usual in there, but the whole place says, 'go away.' That means—"

"—we've been set up. Somebody dropped a dime on us," said Amabored.

"But who?" Melinda asked.

"Nobody was here but Trilecia," I said. "Could she be on Saggon's payroll?"

"Anything's possible," Amabored said. "We'll worry about that later. At least we know what we're up against."

"Yeah, and it means we're all going to die," I said. "Tonight. This is it."

"You got anything better to do?" asked Amabored.

"We might die, yes," Melinda said, her gaze boring into mine. "But this is something worth dying for."

She was right, of course—if you aren't willing to lay down your life to save innocent children, then what's your life worth? During the darkest days of the Quest, when it seemed a lot easier to turn tail than to face whatever horrors beset us, I would think often of her words that morning. They gnawed at me during those years when our Quest lay fallow, and every day of our inaction brought more darkness to Woerth. We were reluctant heroes—what else is new—but we were more than that; we were lazy ones, too. Had Melinda not been present in the bar that morning, I'm certain we would have called off the whole thing.

As we sat silently absorbing Melinda's words, Redulfo burst into the tavern carrying a pile of scrolls in his arms. He was unusually animated, nearly tripping over a chair on his way to dump the scroll pile onto the bar. He sat a barstool to catch his breath while Amabored poured him a coffee and spiked it with whiskey. Redulfo drained it in one go.

"Settle down, there, Punchy," said Amabored, his hand on the wizard's shoulder. "What's the rumpus?"

"I've been locked up in the Restricted section of the library all night," Redulfo huffed. He motioned to Amabored for a refill. "You wouldn't believe the stuff that's in there. It was almost as if I knew where to look, which was weird. Maybe Sklaar was giving me a hand. Turns out that the wizard Rigsby wrote the definitive work on the Ten Phylaxes of Koschei the Deathless. He teleported the tome to the School of Thaumaturgy right before he and Gygax had their big blow-up in the Shadow Mountains. Rigsby apparently disappeared afterward. If what I've read is true, Elberon, then it's only a matter of time before you find more of them. The Phylaxes are drawn to each other, like magnets. Once the first one is found, the others will be, too."

"They won't be found if I don't go looking for them, no matter what your books say," I said. "Besides, if we succeed in chucking the Skull into the Hellmouth, then it won't be my problem anymore."

"Never mind the other Phylaxes," said Amabored. "How do we get that Hell-door open? And how do we shut it again?"

"I was getting to that." Redulfo grabbed one of his scrolls and unrolled it flat on the table, securing the corners with pint glasses. He motioned us over for a look. The scroll was inscribed with a series of ink sketches. The first one showed what I took to be Arturus, legendary Warlord of the Free Kingdoms and leader of the first Quest, holding the Screaming Skull aloft like a trophy. A second sketch showed him atop the Dread Keep, swinging his sword Truth as it decapitated Koschei the Deathless before some sort of ornate black mirror. The third sketch showed him banishing a horde of huddled hellspawn through the Hellmouth door, which appeared to be swinging shut—only this time, Arturus was wearing the Skull, ringed with Hellfire, in place of his own head.

My stomach plummeted at warp speed until it landed hard on my balls. I could feel the gazes of my mates on me. I felt Melinda's hand take mine.

"Not a chance in fucking hell," I said. "Not even if I end up *in* Hell."

"Don't be a pussy," said Amabored. "What's the worst that could happen?"

"If you're so sure it's worth doing, then you put it on."

"It's the only way, I'm afraid," said Redulfo, rolling up the parchment. "At least, it's the only way I could find. The Hellmouth can only be compelled with a Word of Command from a Twentieth-Level sorcerer, which Koschei was. The Skull is powerful enough to command the door to Hell—but the only way to wield the power is to wear it."

"How do I fucking wear it?" I cried. "Like a hat? What happens to my own head? What if I can't get it off again? What the fucking Christ!"

My voice grew shrill as I backed away from my mates. *Fuck this*, I thought. Children or no, there was no fucking way I was wearing that thing. Dying was one thing. Wearing a dark lord's skull forever was quite another. Would *you* wear it? I thought not.

Once again, it was Melinda who talked me off the ledge. Taking my hands in hers, she pulled me to her and kissed my lips. The effect was like standing on the deck of a trireme when the storm finally broke, and the sun returned like a long-lost lover.

"You can do this," she said. "And you won't do it alone. We'll do it together."

I swallowed, hard. "I can do this," I groaned.

"You can do this."

"Look, this is touching and all, but we've more work to do," Amabored said. "Elberon, if you put on that Skull and can't get it off, I'll cut it off your shoulders myself. You have my word."

"That may be the nicest thing you've ever said to me," I said.

27

The rest of the day found me stumbling around the city as if through a thick fog, with Melinda leading me everywhere lest I stumble into a ditch or walk into a wall. I could think only of the Skull, now lurking quietly in my bag. That day, it did not scream; perhaps it was saving its strength for the big show scheduled for that night. It seemed to fill my vision, its leering grin mocking me, the black voids of its eye sockets beckoning me into their depths. Melinda fed me some soup for lunch, which I promptly vomited into the privy. I could think of no outcome that didn't involve Amabored slicing the Skull from my shoulders.

Somehow, I survived the day's terrors. That night found us all crouching behind a low courtyard wall on Halberd Street, one block away from the Falcon. The early spring breezes were cutting and chill, forcing passers-by to burrow deeper into their cloaks as they hurried along to their destinations. Assembled, armed and ready, we waited only for the paladin. We had no plan other than to storm the building, kill everything that moved, kill Saggon, send Melinda to treat with the devil, save whatever children remained in the pits below the manor, trap the devil and the Skull in the Hellmouth, and then blow. Never mind that the Falcon was packed with enough hellspawn to sack the city entire; we daren't let cold reality douse the fires of our fever-dreams.

"I have to take a piss," Lithaine said after we had spent an uneventful hour watching the Falcon. He bounded over the courtyard wall and around the street corner.

"Where in hell is that paladin?" asked Melinda.

"Here, my good lady, and not yet in Hell—although the night is young," said a voice behind us.

We whirled around. Before us stood the most impressive elf I had ever seen: a head taller than Lithaine, with a long, thick mane of raven-feathered hair and a noble, hatchet-shaped face flanked by a pair of flint-colored eyes. He was resplendent in silvered plate mail so polished that you could see it from space. The only visible sign that he was more than an actor trodding the boards was the notched and pitted broadsword strapped to his back.

"It's about time," Amabored said, bouncing to his feet. "You have I.D.?"

"Malcolm of the White Rose is my name, and my blade is my calling card," the paladin said. "Shall we waste time bandying words, or shall we spend it killing those that have it coming?"

"Good man," Amabored said, clapping him on a pauldron. "Let's go."

As we rose to our feet, Lithaine bounded back. Spying Malcolm, he stopped dead in his tracks. Pallid shock seized his face. A lightning bolt of recognition leaped between the two elves. Then Malcolm dropped to one knee and bowed his head.

"Your majesty!" said Malcolm. The paladin raised his head, his eyes shining with love and gratitude. "I dared not hope to see your face again. This is a blessed day!"

Still frozen in place, Lithaine said nothing. Amabored's face burst into a broad grin.

"'Your *majesty*?' Is he kidding?" the barbarian asked Lithaine. He turned to the paladin. "Are you kidding?"

"Surely you cannot deny the presence of King Elomiel, Lord of the White Rose, avatar of the Star Maiden, and anointed High Priest of the blessed realm of Helene?" Malcolm asked. He turned to face Lithaine. "My lord, all thought you dead—but never did I lose faith. Blessed be the Star Maiden!"

"Maybe he should wear the Skull," I offered.

BOOK III

Embrace the Suck

1

We were more than a little stunned to learn that our grouchy elven friend was regarded by his kinsmen as the living avatar of the Star Maiden on Woerth. He refused to say a word about it; the first time Amabored tried to fuck with him, Lithaine disappeared for two weeks, making it clear that any further broaching of the subject would mean that we'd never see him again. After that, none of us mentioned it again—until not mentioning it became impossible.

The elf summed up his life philosophy in a single phrase: "Embrace the suck." It was more than a battlefield mantra; it was his life's work. Embracing the suck means rejecting the good life, rejecting ease and comfort, and seeking hardship and suffering as the path to enlightenment. What else would drive a man to cast aside life as an elven Priest-King for a life of hardscrabble adventure? We all felt that way, more or less. By casting aside my father's wealth, I had likewise embraced the suck; by waging war to win back his own kingdom, so too did Amabored. Lithaine's was simply the purest expression of the credo by which we all lived.

There's no better way to embrace the suck than to become a father. My own father was both an absentee parent and a terrifying force of nature, and I long avoided siring a child myself for fear of emulating his woeful example. Finding those poor, terrified kids outside the Hellmouth, however, planted a seed in my mind: What if our only real purpose in this world is to pass on our genes? Besides, what else was I going to do with them? If there was one thing at which I knew I'd be better than the old man, it was parenting.

So, I warmed to the idea. Still, I was unprepared for how grasping and Gollum-like would be the love that I felt for the little alien that emerged, slimy and squalling, from Cassie's womb. After Alderon was born, in the wee hours I would creep into his nursery, kick out the nursemaid, and spend long moments watching him sleep. I craved his touch and his smell. It was a struggle not to hold him every waking minute. On a planet with nearly one billion souls, childbirth is no miracle; even so, I felt like the only man in history ever to sire a son.

Inside every besotted parent, however, there lurks a terrifying notion: What if, despite your best efforts, your child grows into an irredeemable shitbird? What if he becomes a total zero, and there's nothing you can do about it?

These thoughts come to me unbidden as the fruit of my loins now stands before me fingering the ring in his nose. The Lark, he calls himself, and indeed does he resemble a big brainless bird in his gaudy silks, feathered cap, and harlequin tights. A rapier depends from his hip, even as his callus-free hands mock his ability to wield it. His face is full of sardonic good humor that I long to erase with my fist in his teeth. So diametrically opposed is he to my aspirations for him that I'd challenge Cassie to prove that he's mine, were she here to challenge.

"Honestly, father," Alderon is saying as he regards his fingernails, "why so glum when the wildflowers are blooming on the heath? Ariel, Cecil, John and I have a trip to the Diamond Bank on tap for this weekend. If the Lady Astrid makes me stay to look after you, it'll be a bad weekend for us both."

He steals a glance at me from under his brows. Beneath the stage-powdered face of his irony, he's concerned only with the degree to which my mood will cramp his style. Not for the last time, I reconsider my own father's methods; if there's one thing this kid could use, it's a good ass-kicking. On the few occasions I've tried, he simply runs away, laughing at me.

"Go live your life," I tell him. "I require no ministrations. Give Ariel, Cecil, and John my regards."

I found out that I was going to be a father just a few hours before the Quest entered the Coldsoul Abyss to confront Koschei, the wellspring of Chaos on Woerth.

"I'm pregnant!" Cassie shouted as we crouched on a rock ledge overlooking the Abyss, into which Malcolm had mere hours ago fallen to his doom. Around us, the dreaded Harvesters bobbed and weaved, their shrieks filling our heads with madness. Their writhing eye-stalks blasted us with spectral rays that threatened to turn us to stone, ash, or molten goo. Our spiritually spent crew fended off the assault: Amabored swung Stormcrow in wild arcs; a devastated Lithaine, his mentor dead by his own hand, pumped arrows into the enemy; Andrigan bashed a bloated Harvester with a mailed fist; Lindar shredded a pair of the obscene orbs with glowing blue spectral blades. We were badasses, but these Harvesters were messing with our program.

"Now you tell me?" I asked Cassie.

"We're going to be dead in five minutes!" shouted Cassie. "I thought you'd want to know!"

"You couldn't let me die in peace?"

"I'm carrying your child, you fucking asshole! You expect me to suffer alone?"

"Yes!"

"Hey, congratulations, you crazy kids!" Amabored called over.

I raised my mirrored kite shield in time to avoid incineration from a Harvester death-ray. The blast caromed off the shield and flash-fried a pair of the Chaos creatures. Pulling Cassie to me, I held her as we crouched behind the shield.

"Look, I'm sorry," I said. "You were right to tell me."

"It's terrible timing," Cassie said, her eyes tearing. "But I love you, you goddamn fuckstick."

"I love you too, you crazy fucking bitch. Now let's finish this thing so you can pump out that kid."

And so, we did. Little did we suspect that the Harvesters were merely an appetizer on the full menu of horrors that Koschei had devised for us. We lived—and seven months later, Cassie pumped out the kid. The moment I laid eyes on him, I was lost.

LIKE MOST LAYABOUT SONS OF ACCOMPLISHED MEN, ALDERON HARBORS no ambition other than to spend my money on a life of casual hedonism—surfing the Diamond Banks, skiing the Horst Mountains, shopping in Gorm, crawling the pubs in Tradewind. He dabbles in the adventuring trade, which gives me some hope, even as he limits his gigs to Were Coast raiding parties and the occasional art heist. If he covets the Coral Throne, he keeps it to himself. He could impress me most by staging a coup, a move I worry about far less than I long for it. What would he do if he knew that my ass will occupy this throne for another sixty years? Time tests all men.

2

Just a few years ago, for example, Andrigan and I tried to track down Lindar. The half-elf joined the team after the entire Order of the White Rose fell to the Plague Knights during the Siege of Helene. He survived the sack of that fair kingdom only after we packed his corpse in a pickle barrel and dragged it around for six weeks until we found a priest in Kenwood who could resurrect him. The experience of death made him a little jumpy, and James's wedding was the last time any of us saw him in the flesh. Soon after, he disappeared. Since then, he's become pure dark matter, present by inference but impervious to observation.

Still, I always liked the spindly twerp. Common belief holds that elves are granola-crunching, androgynous tree-huggers who lounge about and pluck on delicate stringed instruments, eschew technology for esoterica, grow rope and smoke it—which they are and which they do. When provoked, they can be fierce warriors. Getting them to join a fight, however, is like coaxing a deer out of the woods. You could choke on the stench of refined liberal sensibility hanging in the air around your typical elven enclave.

LINDAR WAS THE EXCEPTION TO THE RULE. SOME NIGHTS HE WOULD HIT the mulled wine hard, and then run his mouth about politics. We wanted to argue politics like we wanted an acid enema, but what can you do when you're sharing a campfire? Lindar supported the Talon Republic, for Christ's sake, and he never shut up about it. When we reached Gorm to deliver Malcolm into Empress Wilomina's hand for marriage, I'll be damned if Lindar didn't offer her his sword.

"I despise that fascist shithole," I told him, a fortnight out from our fateful descent into the wreckage of the Sky Ship that had crashed in the Pustiu Waste. "My father spent twenty years in the Horst mines, so don't tell me about the Talony. They flog you looking crossways. They burn gays at the stake. They rape the peasants and give tongue baths to the nobility. They spend every dime they have on wars while their infrastructure falls to ruin. Wilomina is ruling over an ash heap."

"Nice military uniforms, though, one might add," said Malcolm, who sat nearby nursing a flagon of warm milk. "If one likes birds, that is."

"The Gnome Kingdom will get wiped off the map, and rightly so," said Lindar. "The Free Kingdoms ordered them to lay down their Chaos weapon. They refused. What's the Talony supposed to do— wait until an Ur-imp vaporizes the Imperial Promenade? If there's even a one-percent chance of a Chaos breach, then it was worth invasion."

"But they're funding the war with dwarf gold, and the juice is running," I said. "Meanwhile, they can't keep the street lamps on at night. A ruler should keep taxes low, the streets clean, and the pubs full. If anybody starts any shit, finish it. Give the vassals a wide berth. Provide a basic social safety net. And keep your fucking hands out of my business. You're a guy who likes cock? Go for it. You want to shoot heroin into your eyeball? God bless. You like to fuck donkeys? Have at it. Life is hard enough as it is."

"Citizens of a great nation must pay a price for its greatness," said Lindar. "And a great nation must be a moral one."

"Listen to yourself. You worship a massive imperial state that coddles the rich, runs the military on credit, and fucks the middle class. You're a goddamn oligarch."

"Or a plutocrat," said Malcolm.

"Don't dare to include the Talony among the Free Kingdoms," said James. "Free republics don't lock up and torture citizens without due process, even if they are gnomes. Now take Kenwood, for instance—"

"You admire Kenwood only because you want to dip your quill in Princess Arianna's inkpot, ranger," said Andrigan. "And piss on your republic, besides. A strong monarchy is the only sensible form of government. King Hammershield has ruled the Highlands for eighty years, and we enjoy more wealth and freedom than any land south of the Waste."

"Hammershield is paid for by the Baronies," I said. "He does what he's told. He can't even launch a sea pickle without permission."

"Shall I introduce my mace to your colon then, fighter?" Andrigan growled, his eyes glowing like coals in a forge.

"Bring it, stunty."

"You're all barking out of your asses," said Amabored, as he emptied the last of his wine flask into his flagon. "The only government I trust is a dictatorship with me in charge. I sure as hell wouldn't trust any of you ass-hats to run anything but your mouths."

"The Talon Republic is the greatest country on Woerth, and Malcolm should praise the Star Maiden that he'll help guide that blessed nation into the new Millennium," Lindar said. By way of punctuation, he thunked his dagger point-first into a nearby tree stump. "Would anyone else dare say a word against her?"

"Long live the Talon Republic," said Amabored, raising his flagon.

3

Even after Wilomina declared herself the Black Empress and launched her final solution against the Gnomes, Lindar stuck by her. Only when her true master was revealed did he come to his senses. His worldview imploded, and he filled the resulting vacuum with madness and depression. Now twenty years had passed without any of us seeing the crazy bastard in the flesh.

Then one day, Andrigan got word to me that his cousin Fordigan was opening a new gold vein in the Horst Mountains and had spotted Lindar in the foothills. My interest was piqued; Lindar was a still a brother, after all. Might it be possible still to bring him back amongst the living? What had twenty years done to the crazy bastard? With these questions in mind, I put out word on the aether asking for volunteers to help us track him down. With Amabored embroiled in war, James taking it easy, and Lithaine still plugging up the Hellmouth, Andrigan was the only taker. In early September of my sixty-first year on Woerth, Wilberd and I met him in Kenwood. James was roaming the outback somewhere, but he had left word to his steward to house and provision us.

"He'll never come voluntarily," I told Andrigan. "We'll have to black-bag him."

"We'd best hope he hasn't kept up with his sorcery," said the dwarf. His beard, now white and lengthened with age, was bound in so many elaborate knots and braids that it looked like an afghan blanket.

"If he tries anything, good luck to him. Christ, what the hell? He could've picked up the phone. The rest of us have stayed in touch."

"He was always as crazy as a vine-chewing hobgoblin, fighter. We simply found his madness useful. It's not as if the rest of us can lay fair claim to sanity."

"Fair enough. Let's push off."

Accompanied by a small band of retainers, we took the Long Ferry east up the Beradon for fifty leagues or so, drinking James's parting gift of Kenwood bourbon from the deck as we watched the rugged hills east of the kingdom drift past in a lazy processional. Rather than cross the Wyvern Mountains via the Sorrowful Pass, where we had nearly come to grief so many years before, we chose to travel under them via the Rockway, the new subterranean highway carved by the dwarfs in the years after Koschei's fall. It ran for nearly a thousand leagues from the Gold Hills to Vulturmunte, the new mining settlement on the Talony side of the mountains.

After a month on the Rockway dodging caravans and coughing up the endless tolls, we found ourselves one mid-October evening surveying the spectacular wind-sheered peaks of the Horst Mountains from cousin Fordigan's deck overlooking the bustling mining encampment at Vulturmunte. Fordigan broke out the gnome leaf, and we packed our pipes while he updated us on Lindar.

"He's a curious sight," Fordigan told us as he lit his pipe. "Like a wildman or a prophet. We tracked him to a cave in the foothills. For days at a time, he'll hide within. Mysterious lights illume the cave mouth at night. When he leaves, it's to fish or hunt elk. What will ye do with him, then? Is it an old score ye aim to settle?"

"Just have a look at him, mostly, cousin," said Andrigan. "He was a brother in arms, and we don't forgo those bonds lightly. If his mind is gone, mayhap we can offer aid. If alone he wishes to be left, then alone we shall leave him."

"Maybe it was the pickling that broke him," I offered. "He was dead for weeks. Who knows what he saw on the other side?" *Hopefully not a Ki-Rin*, I thought.

"Being dead was the least of his troubles, brother," said Andrigan.

"No doubt," I said. "In retrospect, death seemed to agree with him."

Fordigan fetched two of his wives to ply us with beer and more smoke, and our thoughts turned aside from our cranky friend. Contrary to belief, dwarf women aren't necessarily hideous. They're short, but they're game, with tits that last for days and milky thighs the color of pistachio shells. If I told you that I'd tagged a few dwarf women in my day, who are you to judge? I fucked an elf maiden once, and she just laid there like a gunny sack.

4

The next day found the three of us crouching outside Lindar's cave with our retainers armed to the teeth. The cave lay well concealed at the bottom of a steep defile about a half-day's ride from Vulturmunte. By way of preparation, we had spent a few hours hanging glyphs of warding, charms of protection, and magic dampeners. As we waited for a sign of our long-lost friend, Andrigan and I passed the time rolling knucklebones. Wilberd, the wiseass, said nothing.

Day passed into evening, and still we saw no sign of life in or around the cave. At last, a lone elk appeared, picking his steps smoothly down the jumbled rocks of the defile. The elk stopped upwind of us and displayed a noble profile, his majestic silhouette limned in dying scarlet sunlight.

"Ah—supper," said Andrigan. He reached for his crossbow.

"We shouldn't attract attention," I whispered. "What if he's set traps?"

"Then let's spring 'em and draw him out. In the meanwhile, I aim to eat that beastie."

At that moment, the darkening defile was pierced by a shaft of white light that streaked from the cave mouth and drilled a smoking hole the size of a grapefruit clean through the elk. The beast collapsed dead. The light vanished.

"Jumping Christ!" I cried.

"We'd best rush him before he recharges," Andrigan said.

Vaulting over our cover, we ran serpentine for the cave mouth with our retainers spread out ahead of us in a rough skirmish line. We heroes gather men-at-arms under our banners not so much to fuel our egos, but rather as an insurance policy: The more swords at your command, the less likely you'll die in battle. Super-villains surround themselves with nameless henchmen for the same reason —the smart money always sets the odds. I never understood what was in it for your typical red-shirt, who seemed to have no inner life, no reason for existence besides serving as cannon fodder. Why is there never a shortage of them? Beats me.

Sure enough, we made it no more than five yards into the narrow cavemouth before half our squad fell dead to sorcery: this one incinerated by a fireball, that one sucked screaming into a Soul Vortex, two more pulverized by a Force Hammer. Those remaining simply tucked tail and ran, and who could blame them? That left the three of us crouched breathless within a rock alcove as strobing purple light pulsed from deep within the cave. The cave walls thrummed with powerful sorcery.

"Has he shot his wad, do you think?" asked Andrigan, clutching his mace.

"Hell no. He's been hanging spells in here for years," I said. I chanced another glance around the wall. A hail of spectral bullets exploded the rock in front of me. "Lindar!" I shouted. "If you're back there, show yourself! It's us!"

He answered with a Sonic Tsunami that nearly took off our heads. We'd never take him by frontal assault. Then Wilberd tapped me on the shoulder; with his index finger, he made a twirling motion in his palm.

"The Dervish?" I asked. "You can still do it?"

The monk nodded. As troublesome as I found that prick, his skills had proven decisive in many a dire situation in which swords were useless, like this one. While Andrigan and I crouched against the wall, Wilberd stood, linked his thumbs and forefingers in a diamond shape, and mouthed chants to his mystery god. After a few minutes of this stuff, he began to rotate: slowly, then picking up speed; faster, then whirling in a tight circle like a figure skater on crystal meth. He became a deadly blur, his speed such that his horn would slice through plate armor as a knife through Neufchatel. Then he spun out like a human cyclone into the cave tunnel.

"Impressive trick, that," said Andrigan. "No wonder you haven't killed him yet."

We raced behind the monk, now kicking up a tornado of cave dust and debris, and advanced down the tunnel. Balls of scorching plasma, spectral laser beams, and forks of blue lightning caromed off his whirling form. Entering a widening chamber, we glimpsed a wretched, twisted form wrapped in a cloak and wielding a knobbed staff—and then the figure vanished in a gout of smoke and flame. The concussive effects of the *Teleportation* spell flattened us. Wilberd careened around the cave before tumbling into an exhausted heap.

"By the seven beards of the First Fathers!" Andrigan said as we picked ourselves up. "Did you see him? Like a twisted wraith, he was. What deviltry is this?"

"The worst kind," I said. The low torchlight revealed evidence of a mind savagely consuming itself: the cave walls hung with imp skins, various humanoid heads thrust onto spear points or depending from hooks, shelves stacked full of moldy tomes, cloudy jars in which unspecific organs floated. On a small table sat a ceramic bust that looked like Elvis Presley, except when it didn't. In one corner, a small mountain of pheasant and fish bones lay carelessly tossed. The place stank of offal and madness.

Wilberd tapped my shoulder and pointed up. We craned our necks to find giant, ragged, red elvish script scrawled across the rock above our heads. We could all read it, so no one spoke aloud what the script spelled out:

GYGAX MUST DIE

"Gygax?" asked Andrigan, stroking his ringed beard. "Isn't he dead already?"

"As far as I know, yes," I said. And so he was, if the stories were true. Gygax the Great, who had helped found modern sorcery as Koschei's apprentice; Gygax, who had saved the Woerth by joining Arturus's quest to slay his former master; Gygax, who, with his life-partner Rigsby, had founded the School of Thaumaturgy to train generations of wizards. No one knew what sparked the final row between the two wizards, long ago in the Valley of Sorcerers. Once the local barons finally worked up the nerve to send a search party into the Valley, months after the very Shadow Mountains themselves quaked from the force of the wizards' sorcerous duel, they found only one burned corpse in the Workshop of Telescopes, which they identified as Gygax's—but let's face it, the local yokels weren't exactly experienced forensic investigators. Maybe it was Rigsby's corpse, or the gardener's, or a stable hand's. There was, in fact, no hard evidence that Gygax was dead. Had Gygax faked his own death? If so, why? I mean, what the fuck?

"But even if he isn't dead," I continued, "how the hell would Lindar know anything about it? And why would he want to kill him now?"

"We missed our chance to ask him, fighter," Andrigan said. "If Lindar it was, then he has no desire for our counsel. And seeing this place, he was right to seek solitude."

As we spoke, Wilberd noticed something tall and oval-shaped concealed under a blanket in a shallow alcove off the north wall. The monk sidled over and pulled the blanket away, revealing a mirror—but not just any mirror. Oh, no.

It was the accursed Black Mirror itself—a relic of the Penultimate Universe and a gift from the Violet Queen to Koschei, given long centuries ago. We recognized instantly its contours, its polished obsidian frame, the leering abominations carved into it. We quailed before its utterly dark, featureless negative space reflecting nothing but the Void. Oaths sprang unbidden to our lips.

"Fuck me!" cried Andrigan.

"Holy jabbering monkey-Christ!" I cried.

"!" exclaimed Wilberd.

"So, there's the source of his madness," Andrigan allowed, after another long moment of stunned silence had passed. "That crazed elf must have braved the Dread Keep itself to retrieve it. We may have to take him out, fighter."

"Brother," I said, "If it comes to that, I'll dice with you for the honor."

5

We first encountered dimensional mirrors on our way to kill Redulfo the Black, the reincarnated black-dragon version of our friend holed up somewhere in the Workshop of Telescopes. After the Crimson Hand resurrected him, Redulfo flew from the topmost spire of the Crimson Citadel to the Valley of Sorcerers, where he claimed the Workshop as his own. The Hand's goals were opaque; for reasons known only to them, they were concerned mostly with sewing war between the Free Kingdoms and the Dread Plain. Redulfo throwing in his lot with those goddamned arthropods caused us a lot of grief. From that cesspool also sprang Garrin, the Grimmreaper, dispatched by the Hand to collect Koschei's Phylaxes before I could. I was in a race with that fucking asshole before I even knew who the hell he was. You might assume that when you look in a mirror, you'll recognize yourself. That notion isn't always true.

It took us a day to recover from the bugbear assault in the Shadow Pass. After that warm welcome, you'd have had a tough time convincing us that we had a chance to reach Redulfo. There's fucked, and then there's ass-fucked.

For example: With his jellied leg, James wasn't going anywhere.

We loaded him up with firewood, split our rations with him, and then bid him adieu. I gave him my wineskin and pressed a vial into his hand.

"This is a *Holocaust* potion," I told him. "If things look hopeless, you know what to do."

"Blaze of glory," said James with a grim smile. "Keep your powder dry, Elberon."

Parting from our friend for possibly the last time, we continued our march toward certain doom. By midday, the pass descended below the tree line, and the forest canopy thickened over our heads. The Rangers' Subcommittee of the Adventurers Guild had tagged this forest Lawful Evil; as we tromped along the winding ridgeline further into the forest's clutches, we could sense the malice in the trees as they loomed over us, threatening us with their grasping branches. The sun plunged below the high ridge walls, turning the sky into blood.

Then, we saw the first signs of the arachnids: thigh-thick strands of hairy webs draped over the higher branches. As we continued west, the strands gathered in numbers, coalescing at last into eldritch webs festooned with the shriveled corpses of birds, beasts, and humanoids.

"If Redulfo has promised them our blood," said Malcolm, "then it will be a long night."

We stopped to make camp. Knowing better than to build a fire, we sat circled with backs facing inward as we chewed venison jerky and fingered our blades, waiting for the hammer blow to strike. I drew first watch. While the others burrowed into their bedrolls, the sky blackened, and a wan half-moon limped above the horizon. Two hours of ominous silence passed. As I was about to raise Lithaine for the next watch, I spied along the tree line the first cluster of red eyes, burning like pinhole glimpses into the forges of Hell. There came another cluster, and another. Soon, we were surrounded by a phalanx of glowing crimson orbs. Segmented legs clicked and clacked as the creatures spun their foul webs in the dark.

I prodded Lithaine with my dagger. He sprang upright.

"Roust the others," I said. "It's on."

In a moment, the five of us stood backs together with weapons drawn. Malcolm cast a *Dispel Darkness* charm, and warm golden light glowed from his blade. The light threw the forest into stark relief. Their high voices cursing, the spider army shrank back into the shadows. Then their leader spoke, spewing black venom that pockmarked the tree limbs with smoking acid burns.

"Elf magic will avail you not, two-legs," croaked the spider. "We will feast on your juices this night. The Dragon Lord has commanded it."

"You can feast on my juices all you want, insect," said Amabored, "When I pump them up your ass."

"You dare call us insects?" hissed the spider. To an arachnid, there is no greater insult.

"I do."

"Then prepare to die!"

We weren't unduly worried. Giant spiders aren't that difficult to kill; you take out a few legs, dodge the mandibles and stingers, and fight with your back to something so they can't get behind you. We were unprepared for their numbers, however. Within seconds of Amabored's taunt, fifty-score of them vaulted out of the trees at us, screeching enraged spider-oaths and trailing thick slime-coated cables of web. We drew steel and went to work.

The battle raged for half the night. Soon we were waist-deep in arachnid corpses, befouled with entrails, slimed from head to toe with their stinking black blood. No one spoke. Periodically, a spider broke through the ring of steel to clamp fangs on an arm or a throat. If the unlucky bastard failed the proverbial saving throw, then one of us would leap over and pour an *Antidote* potion down the dying man's throat. Wilberd took a stinger in the heart, while Malcolm fell with a leg wound that nearly severed his femoral artery. We earned our fucking pay that night, and we ran through our *Health* potions in short order.

Still, we dealt more punishment than we took. After an eternity of battle, the remnants of the spider army fell back in a rough circle to spin webs of entrapment around us. It was a standoff.

"Is that all you've got, fuckrags?" cried Lithaine, brandishing Starfall. The elf was in high color. He was a refutation of everything that sensible people loathe about elves, which was why we loved him.

The spiders merely hung back and conspired in their clacking spider tongue. A violet haze began to fill the sky, emanating from a source just below the western ridge. The light grew brighter, accompanied by a throbbing vibration just out of the range of our hearing: a keening, off-kilter chorus singing somewhere deep within our skulls and filling us with vertigo. We were assaulted by a feeling of wrongness, a sense that reality itself had somehow splintered apart.

The unreality approached. The spiders scuttled aside to allow it passage. Light blinded us, the ground trembled, the chorus shrieked hate in our minds. The land around us seemed to quiver into nonexistence. Finally, we saw it—the biggest fucking spider we'd ever seen. It was the size of a jetliner, I shit you not. We couldn't truly grasp its size until it surmounted the ridge line and towered above us in horrid violet majesty, corrupting the Woerth with its impossible presence. The tree line wavered though its translucent torso. Around the beast, the purple sky and green cloud formations of some wretched alien landscape bled into our world.

It wasn't possible that such a thing existed, and yet there it was. When it spoke, it spoke with the voice of a woman.

"*THOU SHALT TURN ASIDE, OR PERISH IN THE VOID,*" the Violet Queen said, her voice invading our minds like a parasite.

We all knew about giant female spiders. Back at the Suds 'n Shade, we used to laugh about the two bosom halfling buddies in Tolkien's tale creeping terrified into a long, dark, moist tunnel to do battle with that horrifying eight-legged vagina. Odin knows that Tolkien had his hang-ups, but he didn't make that shit up. That's what giant spiders are: terrifying metaphors for female genitalia. Once you see one up close, and your balls shrivel into raisins, you don't give a Balrog's ass-crack about the subtext.

"So, what now?" I whispered to the others. "Run?"

"Fuck that," said Amabored. "How tough can she be? Slide steel into her belly, and she'll bleed."

The queen laughed, and the trees in a wide ring around her exploded into gouts of flame. The shockwave sent us reeling back.

"DO'ST THOU DARE TO STAND BEFORE ME?" the queen raved. *"I WHO HAVE TRAVERSED THE FLAMING DESERTS OF GROMM, TOUCHED THE RINGS OF BOLOCH, AND BOWED BEFORE SHE WHO WILL RETURN THE MULTIVERSE TO HER WOMB? STAND BACK, OR THE VOID AWAITS YOU."*

"See?" said Amabored. "She's all talk."

Then a curious thing happened. Lithaine, his eyes wide with shock, drew Starfall from her scabbard—or perhaps the sword drew herself. Lithaine raised her hilt. Cold white flames licked her blade. He took a step toward the abomination.

"My liege—what are you doing?" Malcolm shouted.

"It's the sword!" Lithaine cried. "I can't let go of the fucking thing!"

The blade rose higher, pulling Lithaine's arm with it.

The Violet Queen's reaction was unexpected. *"YOU!"* she spat. *"YOU DO NOT BELONG IN THIS UNIVERSE, CELESTIAL. WILL YOU DIE IN EVERY PLANE?"*

And then the sword spoke. Its voice thrummed like a bolt of lightning through our bodies. Lithaine stood with legs planted, sword held aloft, his silhouette limned in white flames, his blond hair a blazing yellow penumbra around his head.

"NOT BEFORE I SEND YOU BACK TO THE VOID, CHAOS-BITCH," the sword cried. Like the Violet Queen, the sword spoke in the voice of a woman.

"Catfight!" said Amabored.

6

Starfall, we called her, after the elvish phrase *Tahtidudai* inscribed in fine elf-o-mantium filigree on its white, jewel-encrusted pommel. When she took Lithaine into battle, the light of a galaxy entire shone from her steel. She drove her enemies before her, and Lithaine had only to keep a firm grip on her pommel to reap the glory.

Sentient blades are a rarity on Woerth, but not unheard of. Besides Starfall, Garrin possessed the only other one I ever encountered—Soulreaver, the black-bladed, soul-sucking, rune-covered, devil-possessed scythe that bears no resemblance whatsoever to Elric's Stormbringer, other than its nearly identical abilities. What can I say? Throughout the Multiverse there are echoes, and when you're dealing with universes as closely related as Woerth and Melniboné, the echoes can become deafening.

When Starfall chose Lithaine to wield her, however, we had no inkling that she was another avatar of the Celestial Madrigel, who first spoke to Lithaine about imprisoned children when we were still camped in Doomtown. That's how these things work. Not once have I encountered a relic that reveals its true import until it's far too late to drop it down a well.

LITHAINE ENTERED THAT DOOMED MARRIAGE WITH HIS SWORD DURING the winter of 3961. We spent the season on the Goldvale: a windswept plateau perched high within the Wyvern Mountains and warmed to a permanent midsummer's day by a network of hot springs. Bruised and bloody from the running fight through the Sorrowful Pass, we had been taken in by the Cloud Riders, *Daakos Hashkeeji* in their own tongue, the noble winged warriors and Pegasai who guarded the Celestial Stairway. Twice, Koschei came within a goblin's nose hair of throwing down the Stairway: once during the first Quest, when the Cloud Rider Wanbli was murdered by Eckberd, and once again during our Quest. That they didn't cast us out the moment they saw us coming marked them as true guardians of the Word—or as gluttons for punishment.

Their majestic nobility was belied, however, by prosaic reality. Wings are inherently unkempt; without regular upkeep, they resemble less angel wings and more a pair of moldy feather mattresses. The Cloud Riders themselves were largely a humorless race, devoted to cultivating an air of cultured superiority. Nothing got them more excited than a good compost pile. They sold dreamcatchers to each other and attended hot yoga classes regularly. Their smugness could be oppressive; after a month with them, I wanted daily to punch one of them in the teeth.

Most visitors would tell you that the Goldvale was a paradise. Certainly, Amabored would, since he fell in love there. Here was a guy who would fuck anything that moved, who never parked his car in the same garage twice, and suddenly he was swooning like a schoolboy over a skirt. Not that I could blame him; given how hard I had fallen for Cassie, I certainly understood the impulse. Bellasa had skin the color of molten caramel. Her eyes were the green of Elysium. Her body was as taut as a young fawn's at the dawn of the world. I don't doubt that she was a monster between the sheets. She was funny, cool, and a princess to boot. I'd have never stood a chance with her.

Amabored met her while hiking the trails that wound up behind the Cloud Temple and skirted high alongside the imposing face of Guardian Peak. A few miles traipsing up the mountain found him poised at the edge of a fog-draped valley carpeted with virgin forest and graced by a pristine mountain lake. A waterfall plunging into the lake from a hundred-foot cliff tossed rainbows into the air. As Amabored crested the ridge, a winged Cloud Huntress soared over the waterfall. She dive-bombed the lake, plunged in her head, and rocketed upward with water streaming out behind her dark tresses like a comet's tail.

Atop the ridge, Amabored watched her with arms akimbo and a grin plastered on his mug. The woman spotted him. She flew high over the lake, pausing in midair, majestic with wings outspread, then plummeted straight for him. His grin vanished. Then she had him, her strong arms lifting him by his armpits. Cruising twenty feet over the lake, she dropped him in.

He popped above the waterline, sputtering. "Try that again!" Amabored called, his grin returning.

"So may you dream, earthbound!" she called.

Anyway, that's how Amabored tells it. Meanwhile, I met my first wife when she punched me in the face, my second after I was nearly disemboweled by a Skull Horde, and my third while rotting in Empress Wilomina's dungeon. It wasn't all sunshine and bunnies after I met them, either.

7

If asked to pinpoint the moment I became a full-fledged asshole, I'd go back to that sultry summer night when Melinda confessed her love for me. Or rather, the night I forced her to confess.

It was the day that Amabored, Lithaine, and I finally received formal membership in the Adventurers Guild, a reward from Saggon for gaining Melinda's bed while remaining his spy. That I could be a double-agent never occurred to him. That I could join Melinda's side was beyond his comprehension. After all, feeding children to a pit devil was just business.

To Melinda, it was a crusade—and when I bent the knee to her cause, she melted. I had discovered a breach in the fortress around her heart.

Hers was a familiar tale. It began with a wicked stepfather, who had staked a claim on the beds of Melinda and her younger stepsister after Melinda's mother died. Creeping ever closer to deflowering both girls, stepdad ruled the tiny farmhouse with unique and perverse cruelty—until the night young Melinda stole a dagger from his rucksack and, when he slipped into her room to claim her maidenhead, stabbed him in the balls with it. Drenched in the vile pervert's blood, she fled her village that very night, never to return. Like most lost souls in the Free Kingdoms, she was drawn to Redhauke. She was twelve years old.

As a young girl in the big city, she found herself dependent on a series of men. When her luck was running, she was simply used and discarded; when it wasn't, she was beaten bloody or threatened with death. From each encounter, she took what she could, and she soon formed a hard exoskeleton of fierce determination. By the time she took her last lover, a bookie named Dwain, she had learned to use men in return. Through Dwain, she made connections in the Thieves Guild, gave out markers and collected them, until it slowly dawned on that dim-witted shit-sack that she was smarter than him.

Melinda took the beatings and bided her time. Finally, she sprang her trap. She hit a dozen of Saggon's drops, pinned the robberies on Dwain, fingered him to the Over-Boss, and took Saggon's charge to bring her abuser down. Dwain begged for his life—and, in a gesture of magnanimity, she only took his balls.

So did the young farm girl, who never told me her real name, earn her *nom de guerre*: Melinda the Blade. Here I was, just a kid but raised at court, possessed of some manners and at least a vague idea of how to treat a woman. In those first months we spent together, fucking every night and twice on Sundays, I could sense her giving in.

Never had I heard a woman tell me she loved me. I was determined to hear it from her. After a night of pub crawling with the boys, we returned to her flat and made love. Afterward, as we lay tangled up in her sheets, I could feel her glow. Rolling on top of her, I pinned her arms playfully to the mattress.

"Say it," I said.

"Say what?" asked Melinda. She didn't struggle.

"You know what I mean. Say it."

A long pause. Then: "I love you," she whispered. Her eyes shined in the candlelight.

"I love you too," I said.

8

That was the first truly douchebag lie I ever told. It would be the first of many. Why drop the L-bomb on her, when I knew in my heart that it wasn't true?

In my darkest hours of introspection, I tell myself that I meant it. As I sit here slumped on my throne, days before the grand fete to be held in my honor, I can tell you it was bullshit. I admired her, I cared for her, and I let her love me. For her sake, I maintained the charade, but I should never have said the words. There may come a time in your life when you find someone in your power—a lover who would die for you, a child who would die without you—and you'll find that you have the whip in your hand. Will you use it? Or will you cast it aside?

When Melinda put the whip in my hand, I used it without hesitation—and was irrevocably transformed into a giant, hemorrhoid-packed asshole. In less than a fortnight, after forty years apart, Melinda will have the opportunity to call me such to my face.

9

That's right—I invited her to my party. Why wouldn't I? Won't we have a lot to talk about, right before I kill her along with everybody else?

She's in her dotage now, long retired as the Grand Duchess of Redhauke. Her second husband is long in the ground. Have the years been kind to her, or have they ravaged her body as they have mine? Is her mind still sharp? Forty years gone, and all we have left are the bleached white bones of memories, thrust up from the desert of the past like the fossils of ancient beasts. Even now, I dare not ask for her forgiveness.

Besides, she already forgave me by helping me sneak out of Redhauke with my balls still attached—and with Cassie at my side. It was a neat trick, when you think about it, jumping from one wife to the next with no downtime. Amabored enjoyed the more traditional meet-cute, but we do share one thing in common: Love kicked us both right in the teeth.

FROM THE MOMENT I AWOKE IN THE TEMPLE OF ATHENA, I CRAVED

Cassiopeia like a drug. Cassie was everything that Melinda wasn't: blonde, slender, ethereal, ivory skinned, a knockout. She was the kind of woman you assume is out of your league, unless you're a douche who thinks that no woman is. If Melinda was an earth elemental, then Cassie was a woman of fire. Given the chance to explore a volcano, how could I stay down on the farm?

Before stumbling out of the temple battered but unbowed, I asked this stunningly intriguing priestess to meet me for lunch so I could properly thank her for saving my life. To my surprise, she agreed. Then I ran home and told Melinda everything about the return of the Screaming Skull, and not a thing about the priestess. The next day, I lied to her about where I was going. It would be the first of many bricks I would lay to build my cathedral of deceit.

First, I took the Skull back to Jaspin's vault and locked it down. If the illusionist was alarmed to see it again, he said nothing, only pursing his lips beneath his Confucian mustaches; I failed to notice the burning look of delight in his eyes. The fucking Skull wouldn't stay there for long, but the vault would buy me a day or so. Soon after, I sat facing Cassiopeia on the patio of a cozy bistro near Hundred Fountain Square. While I drank spiced rum, she put away five beers in an hour. Those Athenians liked to get their drink on.

"So, what's your story?" I asked Cassie. "How'd you end up at that temple? Enjoy the life of the mind, do you?"

"A life most foreign to you, I'd wager," Cassie said.

"You have my number. Go on."

"There's not much to tell. My family grows olives on the Verdance Hills near the town of Prasinakti, on the coast of Collanna."

"Collanna? You're part of the Shield Wall, then. Growing up, we were practically neighbors."

"With only the Hydra Sea between us," Cassie said. "My mother died when I was young. My father lives still. I have eight siblings whom I miss or not as they deserve. I'm here because I had a choice: marry a landed noble or become a priestess. So, I took up the Shield. The Oracle sent me here a year ago."

"Lucky for me," I said. I told her as much of my story as I dared. Desiring her confidence, I also told her the abridged version of the Skull's history. About Melinda, I said nothing at all.

"And you're convinced it's... a relic of *Koschei*?" Cassie asked. "Really? You haven't just taken too many blows to the head?" She leaned across the table toward me, a move that suggested she was amenable to approach.

"There's no doubt. When I find out who delivered the thing to me, I'll beat the truth out of him. I need to know what it wants from me."

"Then I pray for your strength, in contemplation and in battle, Elberon of the Isles," Cassie said. "May Athena grant you courage, first fighter. If our Shield Maidens may assist you in your struggle, please call upon us." She pushed her chair back.

"It may come to that," I said. "But before you go, I'd like to pay you a compliment. It's the least I can do for the woman who saved my life."

The priestess settled back in. "A compliment? Go for it, Slick."

"Even though I'm the king's son," I said, "I've never had luck with the girls at court. I was kind of a joke, really. One day, my mate Darlen told me that a fleet admiral's daughter, newly arrived from one of the outer isles, had a crush on me. I didn't believe him, because why would she? But he insisted it was true, and he arranged a court dinner so I could have a look at her. Any girl with a crush on me must look like the ass-end of a berserker, I thought, so I wasn't much excited. But when Darlen pointed her out to me—holy Moses. She was a knockout, the most beautiful girl I'd ever laid eyes on. And it was true—she did have her eye on me. Not because I was royalty, either. She hadn't even known I was Olderon's son until Darlen told her."

"And then she ran screaming for the hills?"

"No." *This woman has a mouth on her*, I thought. I didn't yet know the half of it. "We hit it off for a while until she dumped me for another admiral's son. I took it hard—but while it lasted, I dared to believe the world could be wonderful."

"Touching. How does it translate into a compliment for me?"

Leaning forward, I looked deep into her eyes and took her hand.

"I was getting to that," I said. "She was indeed the most beautiful girl I'd ever laid eyes on—until today. For you put her to shame, Cassiopeia of Collanna. You're the most beautiful woman I've ever seen."

10

———

That story had the virtue of being true. Not that the truth mattered; to be close to Cassie, I deemed no lie too egregious. The proof came at our next meeting when I stopped by the temple to deliver a spray of wildflowers for her altar. Noticing the lust in my eyes, she asked the obvious question.

"I'm not going to find out you're married, am I?" she asked.

For a moment, I thought of Melinda in the catacombs below the Blue Falcon, mouthing the words to me: *I love you.* And then a voice in my head, speaking words familiar and yet somehow foreign: *You've seen how much pain we cause Melinda. Don't you want the chance to save her from it?"*

Perhaps it was my conscience. If so, it took one look at Cassie for me to tell my conscience to fuck off.

"Not me," I said. "I'm free as a lark."

11

At least I married Cassie before I knocked her up. Not so with Melinda. What can I say? It's not like I'm Johnny fucking Appleseed. I am, within the meager subset of women who find me attractive, monogamous. Sure, I plowed my share of fields back in the day, but only when Cassie and I were broken up. For real, Amabored could field a fair-sized army comprised exclusively of his bastards.

Even now, I wonder how differently things might have turned out. If we each create and destroy an infinitude of universes every second, then there exists a universe near to this one in which Melinda bore my child. One in which we live, if not happily ever after, then at least in peaceful coexistence. In that universe, perhaps Cassie rose to high prominence among the Athenians. Maybe she even became the Oracle herself, and was counted among the wise—and, because she never got involved with me, she's still alive. Do I blame myself for her death, in this universe? You bet your ass I do. I would gladly have died in her place, and that I'm still alive is all the proof I need that Odin hates my guts.

Alas, we only know the universe in front of our noses. In this one, I wish I had treated better the three women whose only mistake was to love me. It's pointless to regret the past, which is nothing more than a probability wave receding from the knife-edge of the present. We can take comfort knowing that our worst sins only *probably* happened. Who needs a god to absolve you when the Multiverse will do it for you?

SOMETIMES, YOUR SINS CATCH UP TO YOU BEFORE YOU'VE SINNED—A certificate of deposit on karma, if you will. For example, the year prior to meeting Cassie, I stumbled into the Suds 'n Shade one brisk October morning for a planning session with the boys. Since Saggon's fall and Jaspin's disappearance, Melinda now used the place for her office. She kept Guild business out of it, however, which left it the *de facto* watering hole for Redhauke adventurers. I must have looked as ashen as I felt, because Amabored immediately called to Trilecia for more wine.

"You look like a dragon sat on your face," Redulfo offered.

"Melinda's pregnant," I said, slumping into a chair.

"No shit?" asked Lithaine.

"Knocked up like a cheerleader."

I waited for the boys to silently congratulate themselves for avoiding my fate. Then Redulfo patted my back. "Congratulations," said the wizard. "That is, unless condolences serve better."

"Thor's hammer, man, why didn't you just come on her tits?" Amabored asked.

"She was drinking the potions every week," I said, head in hands. "Lady Hagg mixed them herself. How could this happen?"

"Look, dude, there's the door," Lithaine said, hooking a thumb over his shoulder. "Make a run for it. Go live your life."

"What do you know about it, magic boy?" Amabored asked the elf. "Talk to us when you've seen a woman naked."

"I saw your mother naked. She fucks for fish heads down at the docks."

"My mother would be too busy laughing at your tiny elven dick to fuck you."

"I can't fucking leave her, man, not after all we've been through," I said. "She saved my life, for Christ's sake. She nearly died herself. Plus, she needs my help pulling the Guild together. She's in deeper shit now than when Saggon was around."

"Do you love her?" Redulfo asked.

"Love her? What's that supposed to mean?"

"It's a simple question. Do. You. Love. Her?" The wizard peered at me from over his round Lennon-specs. "If you do, then what's the problem?"

Amabored leaned forward, a cat regarding a cornered mouse. "You're going to be a dad. Shit, man, that's great. Congratulations, really. We should have a toast. Trilecia—the wine!"

All three of them, my only real friends in the world, regarded me with varying degrees of sympathy and bemusement. The mark of a devoted friend is someone who can see right through you.

"Fuck you, assholes!" I cried, and stormed out of the bar.

12

Of course, I stormed right back again, climbed the two flights of steps to Melinda's office, kicked out the supplicants, and begged her to marry me. She threw her arms around me and buried her face in my neck. At that moment, I *did* love her—didn't I? At least, I loved the idea of being in love with her. That she loved me, I didn't doubt. There was less dishonesty in her than in most honest women, even if she did run a vast criminal enterprise.

Her hold on said enterprise was tenuous, however, which precluded an open wedding. So, we risked a small one instead, held at the Suds 'n Shade and attended only by my mates and her few trusted friends. Lithaine was my best man; Melinda's Second, a feisty sparkplug named Fiona, served as her maid of honor. Afterward, we opened the bar to general merrymaking. It filled quickly with well-wishers and backslappers, most of whom were there to curry favor with Melinda. Outside, two-dozen handpicked Guild archers crouched on the rooftops surrounding the bar.

The boys shoved a flagon of ale into my hand, hoisted me on their shoulders, and paraded me around the room to the raucous play of the minstrels. They dumped me in front of Melinda. Laughing and dripping with ale, I shoved the flagon in her direction.

"Come, wife—a toast to the bambino!" I said, pointing to her stomach. "Let's give him his first hangover!"

To my surprise, Melinda shook off the flagon. As Fiona pulled her aside for a quick conference, Amabored clapped me on the back and stuck a cigar in my mouth.

"My sympathies, brother," he said. "The elf was right—you should have run when you had the chance."

Then the bar was rattled by an earthshaking explosion that thundered in from somewhere near the city center. Everybody hit the dirt. For a prolonged moment, we all lay prone, rafter-dust falling upon us in thick flurries. We heard distant screams, followed by the sound of a bone-jarring voice drenched in bass and reverb.

"Let's go," said Amabored as we all raised our heads. He leaped up, grabbed his sword from the rack near the door, and raced outside. The rest of the wedding party followed. Melinda took my hand and we ran out together, partners in whatever shit-tornado life was about to throw at us. Other than the tiny rodents of doubt gnawing at my guts, it felt good.

The explosion had drawn the crowds out of the pubs and tenements that slumped together on Specter Street. The curious and the alarmed alike spilled out onto the cobblestones and surged toward the source of the explosion, which appeared centered on Hundred Fountain Square some ten blocks away. That bystanders always move *toward* a source of obvious danger is a phenomenon I have yet to unravel, but there it is.

Caught up in the throng, we were wedged apart by the shuffling humanity. Amabored's snow-white mane bobbed ahead of us, while behind us Lithaine and Redulfo forced their way through the swelling horde crammed like a blood clot in one of the city's arteries. The crowd forced us into a shuffling penguin-walk. Near the square, the booming voice thundered and railed. Then a blast of hurricane-force wind roared around us, flattening everyone in its path for a good block. Melinda and I remained upright. Ahead of us, Amabored now stood clearly visible—the crowd around him had been blown over like stalks of wheat.

"Good work, wizard!" Amabored called back. Behind us, Redulfo gave a disinterested shrug.

We jogged down the now-clear street. Turning down this lane, sprinting up that one, we soon found ourselves at the back of another, larger throng gathered around the perimeter of the square. Hundred Fountain Square is a literal, rather than a fanciful, name: There really are one hundred fountains spread across the massive plaza, ranging in size from small cherub-carved birdbaths to the immense Genius of Waters, with its twin hundred-foot-tall marble sea-drakes bowing before an immense marble likeness of Arturus. As we approached, thick columns of steam broiled off the great fountain. Through the obscuring clouds of vapor, we caught glimpses of smoke and flame.

Then came that deep bassoon voice, bellowing with menace, and our hearts quavered. Melinda and I had heard that voice before.

"*YOU HAVE THREE DAYS,*" the voice boomed. "*MAY NOT THE DEATHLESS ONE CONSIGN THEE TO THE OUTER VOID? MAY NOT HE SEND THIS CITY TO PERDITION?*"

Glancing at Melinda, I was alarmed by her pale, stricken countenance. She gave my hand a reassuring squeeze. The last time we had heard that bellowing bass voice, three years earlier, I had been... somewhere else. My mind raced, trying to forge a connection to the past. We pushed forward for a clearer view, and there he stood: His Satanic Highness Malacoda, Dire Malebranche of the Eighth Circle of Hell and pledged vassal to Beelzebub, who brought us so close to grief.

The devil's immense torso rippled with taut muscle. His bull's head sported a massive pair of curved, pockmarked, and iron-shod ebony horns from which depended barbed chains festooned with the shrunken heads of children. His fur-bearing ram's legs ended in splayed, scaly hawk's talons. His skin, marbled red and black, was carved with runes borne with great malice and pain. Two clawed hands gripped a monstrous spiked iron mace upon which orange flames danced and capered. Ragged bat-wings beat the air. Hellfire spewed also from his nostrils, and he was wrapped in a poisonous black cloud.

The fog obscuring the past cleared, and I remembered: I had battled this devil in the bowels below the Blue Falcon. To vanquish him, I had donned the Screaming Skull itself. After the battle, Melinda sacrificed herself to save the souls of those doomed children. How had I beaten the devil? That part of our battle was shrouded in darkness.

Here, though, was something different: The devil was bound neck and wrist by manacles attached to heavy black chains. These chains were gathered in the hands of a figure wearing a knee-length cloak lined with leather died blood-red, black horseman's boots, and black leather gloves. The man's face was hidden, shadowed within the folds of a thick hood. From his belt hung a pair of wicked, curved daggers. Strapped to one forearm, the blackest of black kite shields, its surface so dark that no light seemed to escape it, carved out negative space. When the devil strained forward, the figure drew hard upon the chains, jerking it backward. There was something hidden in the shadows of this man's hood that was far worse than the devil. The hood turned toward me.

I felt the man mark me—and then I remembered, even as my memories of wearing the Skull had grown dark. He, too, had appeared beneath the Blue Falcon. When I had finished with the pit devil, I had done battle with him—I was certain of it. He had come there to murder me, to take both the Skull and the Girdle—and now here he was again.

Then a tinny, human voice near the front of the crowd dared to speak.

"Peace, Your Satanic Highness!" said the voice, which belonged to a portly noble bearing a ruby-topped staff. It was the Lord Mayor of Redhauke himself, who had come to treat with the devil. "Peace! Tell us your desire, so that we may grant it, and beg your leave!"

"PEACE?" the devil roared. His rumbling, roaring laugh set the crowd to wailing. Those of us still standing would have broken and run if we could. We were now all within the circle of the devil's glamour, however, and none could flee unless the devil willed it.

"PEACE?" Malacoda roared again. *"NONE HERE SHALL KNOW PEACE IN LIFE OR IN DEATH. THOU LIVEST AT THE PLEASURE OF THE DEATHLESS ONE."*

This certainly wasn't the devil's usual talk. Malacoda was in character, and clearly enjoying himself.

"YOU HAVE UNTIL THE NEXT SUNSET. DELIVER UNTO ME THE SKULL AND THE GIRDLE AND THOU MAYEST YET LIVE. REFUSE OR DELAY, AND BE DESTROYED." Then the devil turned to his captor and spoke in *sotto voce*. *"Look, is that good enough? I hate that fucking medieval pussy-talk. Get me a drink before I vomit."*

The figure said nothing, only yanked on the chains until the devil roared with rage. *"YOU OUT THERE, ELBERON? I TOLD YOU THIS WASN'T OVER, FUCKSTICK!"* Malacoda bellowed. *"SHOW YOURSELF, MORTAL!"*

Every friendly eye turned to me. Melinda took both my hands in hers.

"Oh Elberon," she whispered. "What do we do?"

Amabored thrust his face before mine. "I thought the Skull was gone for good?" he growled.

Before I could answer, the devil roared again, a wrenching snarl of fury drawn straight from Hellfire. The crowd screamed and quavered. Malacoda raised his flaming mace on high and brought the weapon down with a monumental crash onto the tiled plaza. The resulting shockwave flattened everything within a hundred yards. I flew backward through the night until I caromed off a marble basin and hit the ground in a flailing heap. With that crescendo, the pit devil vanished in an obscene gout of orange-red plasma.

The air was rent with rancid vapors and choking dust. Flames licked the rooftops of surrounding buildings. Citizens stumbled to their feet, either standing in a daze or administering to those with cuts and broken bones. Battered but intact, I picked myself up. Nearby, Amabored helped Redulfo to his feet. Lithaine staggered over, pressing a kerchief to his bloody nose. Everyone was alive and accounted for, except—

"Melinda!" I shouted, whirling around. I spotted her sitting upright near the remains of a dolphin-shaped fountain. She saw me and smiled. I ran to her.

"Thank the gods!" I cried, kneeling beside her. "Are you okay?"

"Yes, I think so." She tried to stand, then staggered and doubled over in pain. I grabbed her. Clutching me, she cried out and bent double again. What I saw then bent my mind permanently.

On her white wedding gown, a red rose bloomed. Melinda touched her fingertips to the stain, centered between her legs. They came away crimson.

"I'm sorry—" she said, and then fainted in my arms.

13

That was a kick in the ass, and no mistake, as Sam Gamgee might say. One moment, you're expectant parents; the next moment, you're not. To say Melinda was devastated doesn't begin to describe her sorrow; it was as if the devil had reached into her body, removed her beating heart, and laughed at her as he threw it into the dirt and stomped on it with his cloven hoof. The pain and trauma of the miscarriage were not limited to the necessary physical process of expelling the dead fetus from her body; it was also the external manifestation of her psychic pain. Unable to console her in any meaningful way, I wandered the city that following day in a daze, alternating between rage at the devil and his mysterious master for demolishing our lives, and depression at the certain knowledge that our loss was somehow my fault.

I had no idea where that fucking Skull was, either; as far as I knew, it had been lost forever in the Hellmouth. The Girdle, on the other hand, was now permanently fused to my torso; wherever the girdle went, my torso would follow, the rest of my body notwithstanding. Failure to deliver both to Malacoda by the next night, however, might find the devil abusing me like a truck-stop condom. I was in a pickle.

Y<small>OUR FIRST</small> M<small>ALEBRANCHE WILL SET YOU BACK ON YOUR HEELS; SO WILL</small> your first dragon. While you can't reason with a pit devil, however, most dragons are eminently reasonable. I encountered my first würm during the fallow years, after the fall of Helene but before we descended into the Valley of Sorcerers. At last, I had achieved Tenth Level in the Adventurers Guild—a momentous event in the life of a swordsman, one accompanied by copious perks and benefits. A Tenth-Level fighter can build a keep, attract men-at-arms to fight under his banner, and receive the title of Lord, which sounds pretentious until people start calling you one. Most importantly, you can tax the local peasants—the key to real wealth. Hauling sacks of coin and jewels out of some dank dungeon is fine as far as it goes, but I have yet to meet the hero who wouldn't rather sit on his ass instead. Maybe Amabored, but he had unfinished business.

You can't become a Tenth-Level fighter, however, without slaying your first dragon. It's damned arduous work unless you're packing an arsenal of enchanted armor and weapons that renders the contest moot—and goddamn it, that's another thing that pisses me off about the *Red Book of Westmarch*. Once that certain famous halfling bore the One Ring of MacGuffinness, the coat of magic chainmail, his magic short sword, and the magic phial given to him by the hot elf queen, he was invincible. What could have touched him? That fucking halfling was packing so much heat that he could have marched into the dark lord's tower through the front door and kicked his ass into the street. The wise know better than to make a sucker's bet.

The challenge of becoming a Lord is that dragons seldom wander around waiting to be slain. Fortunately, most dragons had learned long ago that the best way to avoid drawing against every gunslinger in town was to agree to the fix. A would-be Lord need only approach a dragon and negotiate the terms of defeat, which typically involved a stake in the hero's future income. Was it a pussy move? Sure, but it beats incineration by dragonfire. I would live, and the dragon would get paid. Everybody wins.

After six weeks of sending out feelers, I finally located a likely prospect: a young green dragon holed up in a rocky gorge near the Beradon Forest in the Kenwood—very near Amabored's future camp, in fact. It was customary to negotiate through intermediaries, so I called in my old shipmate Phoebes from the Lordship to proxy me. Riding out from Castle Darien with a folder full of my press clippings and a good-faith offering—two heavy chests full of hard-won booty from my stash—Phoebes returned a week later with good news: The dragon was willing to talk. Phoebes had even gotten a look at the beast: Its given name was *Formidabilus Quercus Viridans*, or Greenoak the Terrible. Young and undersized at only 500 years old, Greenoak possessed a treasure hoard far smaller than his appetite. Having drained the local villages dry of tribute and fair maidens, but not yet fearsome enough to assault any of the nearby castles, Greenoak saw that a deal was in his best interests. In exchange for swallowing a little pride, the dragon would stay flush without risking my blade in his heart. Where was the downside?

Phoebes, James, and I journeyed to an inn at the Valen Crossroads and met the dragon's proxies, a pair of rogues named Zereth and Tarkin, half-elven and gnome respectively. I introduced James as my second. We murdered a plateful of pork chops, swilled a half-dozen rounds of ale, fired up our pipes, and got down to business.

"The sticking point, as I see it, is the matter of the dragon's proposed death," said Zereth, drawing prissily on his slender elvish pipe as he studied the contract we had proposed. "Greenoak the Terrible has a reputation to uphold. It would irreparably damage his career to be slain by a mere Ninth-Level hero. Were you Eleventh or Twelfth Level, we'd have some wriggle room. The dragon proposes that, instead of slaying him outright, you merely wound him and drive him from these lands. Might not that outcome satisfy honor?"

"How can death damage his career?" I asked. "Wouldn't death end it?"

"Come now, sir," Zereth said, "Surely you can't think this matter would end his rampaging. The contract merely provides that he departs these lands forthwith. Should he settle in another land outside an as-yet-undetermined radius from his current lair to seek a similar arrangement with another hero, word of this matter might precede him. He simply can't die by an unsuitable hand."

"Sorry, I can't bend on this one," I said. "I can't reach Tenth Level until I've slain a dragon, and you're telling me I can't slay this one because I'm not already there?"

The half-elf stowed his pipe and made a show of gathering up his scrolls and papers. "As it appears we are at an impasse, may I wish you the best of luck in your quest, good sieur. I'm sure you will find a hatchling suitable for your purposes. Good day to you."

Before I could retort, Zereth and his sidekick bowed low before us and walked out of the inn to their waiting horses. I jumped up to grab them, but James stayed me with a hand on my arm.

"Don't cave just yet," he said. "They're bluffing."

"How do you know?" I asked. "For fuck's sake, it took me six weeks to find this lizard."

"The ranger is right," said Phoebes. "The dragon's hoard is light—big mistake on his part to let me see it. No self-respecting würm could show his face at the Gathering with such a hoard. They're playing hardball, that's all."

"That's right," said James. "Lay back and wait for your pitch. We'll bed down here. If they don't return in the morning with a counter-offer, then you can still take the deal."

James was right. As we were mopping up our breakfast the next morning in the inn's crowded common room, the gnome reappeared through the door bearing a fresh scroll.

"We told Greenoak that you were a man of stature," Tarkin told us. "He believes you can still work together. Please give this most generous offer your full consideration, with the understanding that it is indeed final. Should you choose to accept, you may call upon us at the Blue Balrog in Falcastle. Good day to you, sieurs."

The gnome backed out of the inn, and the three of us laughed at our good fortune. I clapped James on the back.

"You have a keen instinct for bullshit, my friend," I said. "Let's see the offer."

James perused the scroll. "Not too bad," he said. "They've upped the percentage from five to ten. You'll need to take a wound yourself, but that's not a problem."

"Is that all?" I asked. "Phoebes, tell those two limp dicks that if the dragon will take seven percent, they've got a deal."

14

You'll have noticed how cocky I was. Pride goeth before the fall, however, and a guy who steps in dog shit is likely to have shit on his shoes. One week later, I rode out of Falcastle on my rented horse, tarted up like a whore on the Sabbath in my gleaming chain mail, polished cuirass, and pressed tunic. My kite shield bore my personal coat of arms, a sea drake rampant on a blue field. My oiled and sharpened battle-axe hung strapped to my back. My beard was trimmed to perfection. James and Phoebes rode at a respectful distance behind me. Tilting my visor, I waved at the few huddled villagers lining the main drag to see me off. A couple of children blew noisemakers while the old women—there were no comely maids left in town—tossed a few meager flower petals before my path. A band played desultorily. We stopped at the edge of town, where the meager crowd gathered for a half-hearted chorus of "For He's a Jolly Good Fellow," and then quickly dispersed. I was left staring like a fool at the scroll bearing the speech I had written that morning.

"Is it so bloody obvious that the thing is in the bag?" I asked. "I thought these were goodhearted folk."

"You thought they were gullible," said James. "What's a little pride when you have a chance to stay in the clover?"

"Fuck you."

We rode off under a sky frowning with rain for Falcastle Gorge, site of the famous Battle of Falcastle, where King Margordon II came to grief with two hundred of his men against the imp warlord Bloodboil the Black. The king and his men were buried where they fell, in the Glittering Cave at the bottom of the gorge through which the Blackguard River flowed. As the fix was in, I had no chance of joining their boney sleep—or so I thought.

There was yet no sign of the dragon, but I was early to the show. We were supposed to tangle a little before he clawed me and I buried my axe in his underbelly, just deep enough to draw blood. As a precaution, I had quaffed the *Antidote* potion that Phoebes had procured for me. Dragons come in a variety of hues, and each breed boasts a terrifying breath weapon: red dragons breathe fire, black dragons spit acid, blue dragons hurl ball lightning, copper dragons ooze magma. Generally smaller than other breeds, green dragons breathe a noxious mustard gas that can melt the skin from your bones and turn your lungs into shredded wheat. Should the dragon get a little too method in its acting, the potion would counteract the worst of the effects. I'd probably vomit, but I could blame it on the pitcher of Bloody Caesars I downed at the inn that morning.

A cold drizzle began to fall as we traversed the wooded hills and dales leading to the proving ground. Around a bend in the trail, the gorge suddenly yawned open before us, its sides plunging steeply down into the twisting valley carved by the fog-draped Blackguard River, which wound through the gorge and into the Glittering Cave before flowing into the Beradon about twenty miles southeast. Across the valley, a few scores of peasants sat camped on Half-Moon Rock, a thin two-hundred-foot-high limestone peninsula thrust out from the opposite edge of the gorge. Some of the villagers had come out after all—which meant I would have to put on a respectable show.

"We'll wait for you here," James said, handing me his flask for a parting swig. "Don't take too long."

"No sweat," I said, and spurred my horse. Descending the winding trail, I was swallowed up by the mist, which was oddly warm for such a chilly day. The air was filled with a vaguely acrid, burnt stench as if somebody had struck the world's largest match. To either side of the trail, the flattened underbrush told of a deer herd that had fled in a hurry. No birds sang.

And then I saw it: a crimson bulk perched on a rocky outcropping near the river. The beast raised his long scaly neck to regard me with its gleaming cat-eyes. His stinking smog-breath boiled out before him. The valley mist wasn't mist at all—it was dragon breath. This was no green dragon, against the deadly breath of which I was safely inoculated; it was an honest-to-god, fully mature, fire-breathing red dragon, against which I had no protection at all.

"Sold out! Mother*fuckers*!" I cried out. "Where the fuck did *you* come from?"

"Greenoak sends his regrets," the dragon grumbled, his voice a rumbling rockfall. "He was detained. I am called Redfang the Terrible. You will find me a suitable opponent in his stead, I trust?"

"Is the deal still on?"

"Alas, I fear not," the dragon chortled. "The fight is regrettably to the death."

There was no running away—the beast would be upon me in a heartbeat. There was only one thing for it.

"Then let's rumble," I said, and charged.

Having never faced a dragon of any stripe before, let alone the deadliest kind, I could only default on the Guild's textbook training. Dragons have poor peripheral vision, so avoid a direct line of attack. My big-ass kite shield would afford me some protection against the blasts of hot plasma, so long as I avoided standing near anything flammable. Once its breath had ignited, it took about two minutes for the dragon to recharge. With no chance to get near the beast's belly, my best bet was to leap onto his back and aim blows at his neck. And if there was any to be found nearby, my best defense was—

—water. That was it. Enveloped by the darkness of my impending death, I saw yet one small sliver of light: If I could get to the Glittering

Cave, the river might absorb the worst of the flames. And if I had my history right, the cave might give me an even greater advantage.

The dragon wasted no time on parlay. Redfang reared back, unhinged his jaw, and let fly a blazing plasma tornado. The full-throated roar was deafening. I hit the dirt and cowered under my shield, which grew red-hot in my gloved hands.

Every bush and tree within twenty feet of me exploded into flames. When the fires subsided, I noticed my hair burning beneath my helm. I cast the helm aside, swatted down the flames, and leaped back up.

"Try again, shitbird!" I bellowed, and then charged the beast again. The dragon rose from his perch, his great, tattered pterodactyl-wings beating the air. As Redfang soared over my head, he swung around and smote me with his great spiked tail. I flew sprawling. Axe and shield spun out of my hands.

Rolling to my feet, I grabbed the axe. Before I could make it to the shield, the dragon landed on it—those fucking lizards don't play by gentleman's rules. To the dragon's left, about a hundred chains away, lay my goal: the mouth of the Glittering Cave, into which the Black-guard flowed on its long journey underground. I sprinted toward it. If I didn't make it inside, I was fucked.

I risked a look over my shoulder. The dragon reared up again—and then shrieked in pain as two arrows pierced the soft wattle beneath his plated neck. Those would come from James. Then came Phoebes driving his horse over a small defile, reigns in one hand and trident held aloft in the other. As the dragon whipsawed around, Phoebes drove the trident into his side and spurred his steed away.

Skidding to a halt, I raised my axe on high.

"Back off!" I cried. "He's mine!" At the sound of my voice, the dragon wheeled about. I made sure he saw me.

"That's right, hot pocket," I growled. "Come and get it."

As the dragon took flight, Phoebes drew up his steed—good. Whoever set me up thought I stood no chance against a red dragon. Of that notion, I aimed to disabuse him.

Plunging head-first into the river, I swam into the cavemouth dragging my axe along with its leather strap in my teeth. Behind me, the cave exploded in dragonfire. I dove deeper beneath the water's surface, the river boiling above me, and swam close enough to the bank to find my footing and pop up again. As a defensive position, the cave was good enough; the river would presumably save me from immolation, while the low roof would keep the dragon grounded.

And then, the turn: Fishing into my belt pouch, I whipped out the *Raise Undead* scroll that Amabored had so casually tossed to me lo those many years ago when we were adventuring outside Redhauke. I unrolled it and read the incantation. The parchment, made from human flesh, turned black and disintegrated in my hands.

Around me, the cave floor rumbled. Clods of rock and dirt exploded like boils popping. Bony, decayed hands clawed out of long-silent graves. The clacking of bone on bone was maddening. Then, I was surrounded: my own skeleton army, two hundred strong, the long-dead bannermen of King Margordon II lining both banks of the river. They raised over their rotting skulls the rusted and pitted swords and shields they had last raised in doomed defense against an imp horde. Grimly eying the dragon from the dark recesses of their black eye-sockets, the army awaited my command.

Redfang the Terrible entered the cave, smelling my blood. Gripping the haft of my axe, I stared into the lizard's merciless eyes.

"Bring it, bitch," I snarled.

15

I could recount every dodge, parry, and thrust of my epic battle with Redfang the Terrible, but what's the point? You know how it turned out. When I'm in a reminiscing mood, like now, I imagine how heroic I looked to the cheering onlookers when, battered and slimed black with the dragon's blood, I staggered from the cave dragging his severed head behind me. Had the villagers known that a skeleton army turned the tide, would it have lessened their admiration? If you think it was easy cutting off that fucking beast's head, then I invite you to tangle with one yourself.

At the time, vanquishing Redfang the Terrible did more for my rep than any other line on my resume. I became known as a big swinging dick. Had there been any fair maidens in Falcastle, or even not-so-fair ones, I could have had my pick. Instead, all I had was the pick of my hands. Even from onanism I abstained, however, as I was obsessed over Zereth and Tarkin, those treacherous cockmonglers. Who the fuck were they? Why try to kill me, and with such an elaborate scheme? Was it Melinda? Jaspin? Maybe even Koschei himself?

That it was my own father behind the bushwhack, driven as he was by his compulsive need to test me, to temper my steel for future rule or destroy me in the process, never occurred to me. Had it, I would have commenced promptly with the long journey back to Tradewind to cut off his head and drag it also through the streets.

"Put the word out," I advised Phoebes. "Anybody who locates those two assholes and brings them to me alive will win a chest of auratae and the protection of my shield."

"Whoever did this, they kind of did you a favor," James said. "Get yourself an agent and make some hay out of it. You might pay for your keep from sponsorships alone."

And so, I did. After receiving my Lordship along with a commemorative Tenth-Level staff, I purchased a plot of land on credit near Stallion Rock, a horse-head-shaped granite hillock on the Kenwood frontier. Pledging vassaldom to Princess Arianna's father, King Argentine III, I hired a contractor, and within a year was toasting the King's health at a grand fete in my new castle, which I dubbed Redfang Keep. The dragon's head I stuffed and mounted over the fireplace. When I was off campaigning, Phoebes, now ensconced as my steward, would charge the locals admission to look at it. He also made a mint selling off the scales, the teeth, the organs, and anything else that any superstitious twit was convinced would bring good health or make his prick hard.

That year was the eye of the hurricane, one of those verdant periods in life when you can almost convince yourself that the good times are here to stay. I longed to share my good fortune with Cassie, who was back in Collanna defending the family estate in the wake of her father's death at the hands of the Plague Knights. Since the fall of Helene, the Chaos Hordes had fallen quiet; other than skirmishes along the frontier between what remained of the Free Kingdoms and the lands that Koschei had once again enslaved, we could almost be forgiven for shirking the Quest to concentrate on leveling up. Complacency is an evil curse; it creeps up on you, diverts your attention to the trivial, and wraps a layer of fat around your heart. Cassie wasn't complacent, and her bitterness at my own lack of urgency became a wall between us. She wanted to love me, but I made it so fucking hard on her that she didn't dare—until I breached that wall, and I made her mine.

AFTER FALLING IN LOVE WITH CASSIE, WHICH HAPPENED THE MOMENT I left our first lunch together, I began to perceive Melinda not as my wife, but rather as a treacherous jailor from whom I longed to escape. Melinda hadn't changed; she was still the same strong-willed, pure-hearted woman for whom I had pretended to fall five years earlier. Still, everything about her now bugged me. Her habits, once endearing, now grated. I turned sullen. Never mind that Melinda was equally tired of my indifference, my stink, my utter uselessness as a partner; she still loved me enough to forgive. I had become a raving narcissist, incapable of sympathy, empathy, or compassion. Nothing mattered to me but my own craven needs.

The meltdown didn't begin until I began to turn away from her in the bedroom. What can you do when your wife expects a good shagging, but the entirety of your desire is bent upon another? I wanted to fake it, believe me. I tried. Little Elberon brooked no dishonesty, however, and refused to rise to the challenge.

"Maybe you should see an apothecary," Melinda said, sitting cross-legged on the bed beside me after our latest pathetic attempt at lovemaking. My back was to her. I felt like a runny stream of troll diarrhea.

"I'll be fine," I said. "I'm just freaked out about the Skull, that's all. I'm never going to be rid of the fucking thing."

"We've had sex no more than a handful of times the entire year," Melinda said. "What does that have to do with the Skull? You know I want to try for another baby. Don't you? Don't you want me anymore?"

No, I thought grimly. *I don't.* "Look, I just need some breathing room, that's all. I'm stressed out."

"I'll give you breathing room!" Melinda cried. She jumped out of bed, grabbed her robe, and stormed out of the bedroom. I didn't go after her. Instead, I lay in our marriage bed, breathed a sigh of relief, and turned my thoughts to Cassiopeia.

16

Six months later, I'd have more breathing room than I dared wish for. For nearly six years, Redhauke had been my home. During the fallow times when dungeon-scouring opportunities dried up, I would spend the afternoons wandering from one end of the sprawling city to the other: perched on the Mere Wall watching the stately processional of merchant ships on the Everdeep awaiting entry into the Under-Canals; braving the press of humanity in the Bazaar while on the lookout for some thoughtful trinket to bring home to Melinda; gambling in the Pit at one of the Guild casinos; strolling along the Grand Promenade with Melinda on midsummer's eve, the air sultry and redolent with spice as the dying sunlight plated the city spires in gold. Tradewind was my home, and always would be; I missed it desperately. If Tradewind was my mother, however, then Redhauke was my lover. Live long enough in a place, and it gets in your bones.

Imagine my surprise when it appeared as if I would be leaving the city for good by being catapulted over the Shield Wall into the clutches of a ravenous army of ten thousand imps, Chaos dwarfs, and Plague Knights beating their war drums outside the city walls. That

I've been in tighter spots still speaks only to my dizzying procession of poor life-choices.

Bound hand and foot, I now lay in the shallow bowl of a catapult. The Screaming Skull lay next to me, linked to my girdle by a chain. A year earlier, we had told the city fathers everything we knew about both the Skull and the Girdle; after the lemming imp incident, the Lord Mayor had instructed us to lay low, say nothing of the Phylaxes, and wait until we were contacted with instructions. As the months passed, we presumed that the city fathers had forgotten about us. We were wrong, of course—and the night before my impending execution, Farbrimm had dispatched the Guard to capture me as I attempted to flee the city through the Under-Canals.

The guards tossed me into a dungeon cell beneath Shorestone Palace, where the late Lord Mayor had resided until he rode out to meet Lord Eckberd that afternoon and found his head spinning away from his neck via a single swing of Borg Hammerfell's axe. Bad luck for him. How could anyone know that this time the horde outside the city walls was real, and not another illusion concocted by that treacherous fuckwad Jaspin Spellbinder? Eckberd had the Mayor's head mounted on a stake near the Shield Wall, where the Bully Boyz threw so much shit at it that it now looked like a chocolate basketball.

Despite the death of old Sklaar the night before, the remaining students and faculty at the School of Thaumaturgy still wielded sorcery powerful enough to turn the city into an impregnable fortress. That insurance wasn't good enough for Phineas Bramann, the Chief Administrator, a spineless twerp who was, thanks to the deaths of the Lord Mayor, Farbrimm, and Sklaar, the last remaining authority in the city. He planned to follow the late Mayor's plan by tossing me over the wall and into the waiting hands of Lord Eckberd. Could I blame him, really? I'd have done the same thing.

For good measure, the Guard had nabbed my friends as well. Now Amabored, Lithaine, and Redulfo each lay bound in the bowls of catapults lined up next to mine in the palace courtyard. Did they blame me for their predicament? Bet your ass they did.

"This is all your fault for finding that fucking Skull in the first place!" Amabored called over.

"I didn't find shit," I said. "It found me, remember?"

"Then it's your mother's fault for squirting you out of her twat!"

"Did Elberon ever really have a choice but to find the Skull?" Redulfo mused.

"Don't start that shit again," Lithaine said.

"If I get out of here, I'm going to cut off your goddamned head," Amabored called to me.

"Empty words from a dead man."

"Then I'll kill you in the next life, brother."

"Cease this pointless blather!" called Phineas Bramann. "Spend your last moments making peace with your gods. Guards! Prepare to launch the prisoners!"

A guard stepped forward next to each catapult. Each one raised his sword, ready to slice the ropes and send us vaulting over the wall and into the arms of the waiting hordes. Overhead, storm clouds roiled. Outside the palace walls, the assembled throngs of city dwellers chanted for our deaths: *Over the top! Over the top!* I closed my eyes.

When I heard a gurgling cry, I opened them again. The guard nearest me now sprouted a crossbow bolt in his gullet. He collapsed, blood bubbles spurting from his lips. Across the way, the guards preparing to launch my mates fell also with bolts to the eye, heart, or throat.

Phineas whirled around wildly, his eyes bulging with surprise. "Wha—!" he began. A giant silver hammer coalesced out of the air above his head and bashed in his skull before disappearing again. He dropped like a drunk in the gutter. A spell—but from who?

Beside me, Wilberd appeared with knife in hand. Giving me the thumbs up, he sliced through the ropes binding my wrists.

"Wilberd!" I cried. My hands free, I scooped up the monk in a bear hug. "Praise Odin. Where's Cassie?"

"Here!" Cassie called, as the monk raced over to free the others. She stood on the roof of the palace armory decked out in Athenian war-maiden garb and clutching a morning star. Her blonde hair flowed like spun gold from beneath her quilted cap. "You didn't think I was going to let you off the hook, did you?"

And then, from the opposite side of the courtyard, another woman's voice: "Who the hell is Cassie?"

I wheeled around. Atop the courtyard wall stood Melinda, flanked by seven of her personal guard. Beside her stood Fiona, her Second, with a glint of knowing triumph in her eyes. She had been spying on me for months.

"I am Cassiopeia, Shield Maiden of the Temple Athena," Cassie called to Melinda. "And you are?"

"Melinda the Blade, Over-Boss of the Thieves Guild. How do you know my husband?"

Cassie turned furiously to me. Her face burned crimson.

"*Husband?*" she spat. "This woman is your *wife?*"

"Catfight!" said Amabored.

17

G ive me a choice between facing Koschei the Deathless himself or the wrath of those two women, and I'll choose Koschei every time. What's more dangerous than a woman scorned? Certainly not an evil dark lord bent on world domination. Compared to these gals, he was a creampuff.

I was in this pickle because of Jaspin; it had always been Jaspin. Had I known that I'd spend most of my career as a pawn in a chess match between Jaspin Spellbinder and my own father, I'd have spent the rest of my life as a hermit. The friendly barkeep, retired adventurer, brewer of Flaming Telepaths, and sage counsel was all along in league with the Crimson Hand. He had started out in the employ of my father, was turned by the Hand via some unknown process, and then planted in Redhauke as a secret agent with one goal: to find the Screaming Skull before I did. Even though he disappeared after the Showdown at the Blue Falcon, he kept turning up again to fuck with us, like a scorching case of herpes. No one was happier than me to learn that Amabored had nailed that fucker to a cross; a more fitting end for him I couldn't devise.

When Malacoda appeared in Hundred Fountain Square a year earlier, however, we had no idea that Jaspin was involved. We even met at his former inn to decide what to do about the curse the devil had placed upon the city.

On a bed on the third floor of the Suds 'n Shade writhed Melinda, attended by her trusted physicians. The miscarriage had ravaged her body; she was corpse-white from blood loss and carrying a high fever. She radiated heat like a forge. The physicians set blood-engorged leeches on her and cast the *Reversal* charms. The leeches began to pump their stored blood supply back into her veins. Slumping beside her like a poisonous mushroom, I held her hand for several hours. Then Amabored called up the stairs.

"Come down," the barbarian called. "We have a plan."

Not until her breathing steadied and her fever broke did I go downstairs. I found the droogs sprawled around the bar, their faces drawn. The flotsam of the wedding party lay scattered about. The candlesticks were burnt down to nubs. Lithaine slid a mug of ale down the countertop toward me. I drained it in one go.

"She's out of the woods?" Redulfo asked.

"I think so. Sleeping, anyway. She scared the shit out of me."

"Thank the gods for that," Amabored said. "That woman is tough as dragon scales, Elberon. Why she fancies you is a mystery."

"It's my enormous prick, of course. What's the plan?"

The plan was to commit suicide. Malacoda had called us out, and we had to answer him. What we couldn't figure was why the devil thought I still had the Skull. I wracked my brain for memories of our battle, but they remained elusive. I knew only that I had beaten him, and that the Skull was gone. Once a devil proclaimed a curse, however, then that was fucking that. If we didn't produce the Phylax, then Malacoda would use Redhauke for a toilet.

Twelve hours after the devil vanished in a thunderclap, he punctuated his curse. From the Stonesong Hills west of the city there came a low rumbling, which sent the Guard racing to the walls. While I sat with Melinda upstairs and Amabored stood guard below, Lithaine and Redulfo tore through the crowd clogging Fountain Avenue near the Dragon Gate. Bribing a guard, they climbed the crooked stone steps to the parapets, pushed past the grunts, and cast their gazes across the shallow valley bathed in silver starlight. Fires from the outlying villages flickered in the distance.

Then, from out of the foothills, they came. At first, Lithaine and Redulfo could see only a black line on the dim horizon, growing thicker as the vanguard approached. Above the bass rumble of the marching horde, they heard now a high, keening buzz, like the complaints of a million angry hornets. The lights from the villages winked out, one by one. Then came the screams.

"Fuck me," said one of the nearby guards. "Would you look at that."

The horde approached the perimeter of the city's torch line, where they stood revealed: lemming imps—ten thousand of them. We knew of them only by legend; Koschei had bred them, the tales told, to lay waste to rebellious towns and villages within his conquered lands. Lemming imps bore no weapons and indeed had no arms to hold them. No eyes, either. They stood waist high, gnome-size, and consisted almost entirely of mouth and fangs. They spoke in buzzing, guttural Hell-speech impossible to decipher.

All lemming imps do is eat. If they continued their march unmolested, they would eat every living thing within sight: every man, woman, child, horse, dog, and rat within range of their jaws. The pit devil had set upon us a plague of locusts—and if we didn't produce the Phylaxes, they would surge over the walls and strip the city bare.

Elf and wizard slipped back to the bar to relay the bad news. Hours later, I heard the plan: We would seek an audience with the Lord Mayor of Redhauke, tell him our story, and volunteer to lead the imps away from the city walls. The Mayor would need only agree to a diversionary attack by the Guard to give us a chance to escape.

Even if the plan worked, the odds favored a single outcome. The imps would find us, and we would die screaming.

"I can leave on my own," I told the others. "No point in all of you getting eaten."

"If I thought it would work, I'd throw you over the wall myself,"

Amabored said, "but everyone knows we're mates. They'd toss us all out anyway."

"Elberon, are you sure you don't know where the Skull is?" asked Redulfo. "The simplest way out of this bind is to give them what they came for."

"I haven't seen the thing in three years," I said. "Melinda nearly died helping me get rid of it. If my death can save her now, then she's got it."

18

The next morning, we dragged our asses out of bed to enact our laughable plan. As Melinda had yet to wake, I asked Fiona to get word to the Mayor that we needed a meeting. That afternoon, a phalanx of expressionless Redhauke Guards arrived at Lady Haag's house to escort the four of us to the palace.

The streets were deserted. An exodus of fishing trawlers, merchant ships, and barges drifted out of the Grand Canal, through the Harbor, and into the safe waters of the Everdeep. For the remaining citizens, there was no escape. Some wags had secured perches on the walls to watch helplessly as the horde of lemming imps buzzed and milled about outside the walls. Everyone else now cowered in cellars or in the Under-Canals, hoping to ride out the storm.

We were led through the Shorestone Gate and into the palace courtyard, where a platoon of peacock-channeling guards relieved the soldiers and perp-walked us into the palace itself. At our first sight of Shorestone Palace, we turned slack-jawed: The place would have impressed enough on its own without the added decor provided by the scores of chests, boxes, and barrels filled with coins, gems, gold, silver, and treasure stacked everywhere and more than man-high. As the guards led us on a winding path through the treasure, several brawny men entered through a side door and dumped more booty into the room.

"The fucking nobles are bugging out," Amabored whispered.

Through the foyer, up a staircase that descended from the mezzanine like a marble waterfall, along the broad balcony festooned with portraits of the mayors of old, into a library stacked to the rafters with musty first editions, and we found ourselves standing before the three most powerful men in the city: the Lord Mayor himself; Sklaar, the Dean of the School of Thaumaturgy; and Lord Marshall Farbrimm, commander of the Redhauke Guard. If ever you've stood before truly powerful men, then you know what an unmanning experience it can be. As soon as we stepped into the room, our pricks shriveled to noodles and our balls ran screaming from our sacks.

The guards shoved us forward. We huddled together like a litter of newborn pups.

"You're here under the protection of Melinda the Blade," the Lord Mayor said, scrutinizing us from beneath his massive brow, "and that is the only reason you're here. Speak now and make it short."

We looked at each other. Then Lithaine pushed me forward.

"It's about the devil's curse, my Lord," I finally said. "The devil demands the Screaming Skull and the Girdle of Gargantua. Both items have been in my possession. The Girdle I still possess, but the Skull is lost."

The wizard Sklaar stepped forward. Yes, he wore a beard and pointy hat.

"You've found two of the Phylaxes?" the wizard cried. He turned to Redulfo. "You—apprentice. Can this news be true?"

"We believe so, my Lord," Redulfo said. "Koschei's Rune is inscribed on both."

"Tell us everything," the Lord Mayor commanded. "If you lie or leave something out, Sklaar will incinerate you."

And so, we told them everything—and our lack of incineration meant that the lords believed us. I'd gladly turn over both relics to them, I explained. The Girdle was now fused to my torso, however—

an after-effect of wielding the Skull beneath the Blue Falcon—and the Skull was lost in the Hellmouth. So, we offered our simple proposal: If the lemming imps saw us flee the city, they would assume that we possessed both relics still, and turn aside from the city to pursue us. We just needed the Guard to execute a feint, so we could enjoy a sufficient head start.

The three lords nodded solemnly and then conferred together out of earshot. When they returned, the Mayor motioned to the guard captain.

"Seize them and lash them to the catapults," the Mayor ordered. "Launch them over the walls."

"Sold out!" Amabored cried. "I'll rip off your balls, you mother-fucking—"

"Stay your hand, Lord Mayor," Sklaar said. "There may be a better way." The wizard stepped to a heavy tapestry covering one wall of the library and drew it back. The tapestry concealed not a wall, but rather a balcony, overlooking the palace courtyard. From beyond the Shield Wall came the distant buzzing cacophony of the imps.

"We shouldn't be so hasty to turn these fellows over to the devil," said Sklaar. "If the rumors are true and Lord Eckberd has risen again, then Koschei himself may be directing his old warlord's actions. That this fellow here possesses the Girdle means he may yet have some part to play. Mayhap these men, as useless as they now appear, will form the foundation of the next Quest to throw down the Deathless One."

"Confound your mysterious pronouncements, wizard," said the Lord Marshall, "These cretins couldn't overthrow a gnome birthday party, let alone a dark lord. What are you driving at?"

"The lemming imps take orders only from their queen," Sklaar continued. "I propose that we send these chaps out behind a street-sweeper to find and slay her. If they succeed, we may be assured that Fate guides their hand. If they fall, then the devil gets his due, and the city may yet be saved."

"Aye, 'tis sporting enough," said Lord Farbrimm. "And while this lot are dying beyond the walls, we can spirit our booty out the back door. But what about the Girdle of Gargantua? We're to just hand it over to the devil with our compliments?"

"Absolutely," said the Lord Mayor. "Even if we could get it off this fool without cutting off his head, I certainly wouldn't want to possess it. I doubt either of you wants it, either. It's no threat to Woerth without the other Phylaxes, and those were lost in the Dread Wars centuries ago. Even if the Skull turns up again, the devil won't be able to use it for more than a paperweight." He turned his gaze to us. "What say you, lads? Would you care to go down fighting?"

"Hold on a minute," said Amabored, oblivious as always to the proprieties of status or rank. "If these things are Phylaxes, why don't you noble lords protect them? Why don't you form a Quest of your own to find the others? If the Dread Wars are to return, shouldn't you wise men be working to destroy the Phylaxes and save the Free Kingdoms?"

There was a beat while the three lords absorbed Amabored's mini-tirade. Then they all burst into laughter. Sklaar himself patted Amabored's shoulder.

"Allow me to let you in on a little secret," said Sklaar, his eyes squinching impishly beneath his bushy white brows. "There's a reason why the Wise in these tales always send a pack of nobodies to destroy the dark lord. It's called *hedging your bet*."

"That's right," said the Lord Mayor. "Now get out there and kill that queen, lads. There is no other way."

"Thank you, my lords," I said. "If need be, we'll honor you with our deaths."

"That's but little honor indeed," said the Mayor. "But we appreciate the sentiment."

19

It's supposed to be every man's fantasy: two hot babes fighting over him. Even if I were worth fighting over, however, I gave neither Melinda nor Cassiopeia the chance to do so—after all, I was lying my ass off to them both. To each woman, I had sold a phantasm: a standup, considerate, monogamous, easy-going chap who, even if he failed to provide a blazingly inventive sex life, could at least offer them a measure of comfort and security. At times, I even believed in this ghost myself.

AFTER A MONTH OF SNEAKING OUT ON MELINDA TO SEE CASSIE, I hardly recognized me. I lied to Melinda about where I'd been; I lied to Cassie about where I was going. I lied to my mates about what I was up to. I lied to myself about everything. Each night has my head hit the pillow, I turned my back on the woman who loved me to dream of the woman I loved. I wanted her, no matter the cost.

It didn't help, mind you, that time with Cassie was a day at the beach, while time with Melinda was like shoveling shit in the stables. Melinda had become consumed with running the Guild: fending off challenges, keeping the Under-Bosses in line, stopping the odd gang war, shifting the Guild businesses away from slavery and assassination to honest vices like gambling and brothels. She had become so dour and humorless that every moment spent with her became an effort of will. Cassie, meanwhile, knew how to party; those Greek pagans all pay fealty to Bacchus. The woman could drink any man I knew under the table, and it became a challenge just to keep up with her. Combine world-class imbibing skills with wit that sparkled like champagne and beauty that could stop your heart in its tracks, and you have a woman I was helpless to resist, even as she made no effort to snare me. Melinda never stood a chance.

One bitter hour in the dark of night, after Melinda had blown up at me yet again for the contempt with which I so obviously regarded her, I said a prayer. Thanks to Wilberd's counsel, I was a newly minted follower of Odin; that night, I challenged the All-Father to show himself.

As Melinda slept next to me curled in a ball, I left our bed and slipped into the common room. I lit a candle, placed it on the hearth, and then knelt before it.

Okay, All-Father, I prayed silently with head bowed. *I want the woman Cassiopeia. I want her more than I've ever wanted anything. I want her more than wealth, more than fame. And yet it's impossible to believe that I'll end up with her. So, give her to me, All-Father. Give me this woman, and I'll know that you exist. I'll believe in you to the end of my days.*

And guess what? He did. And not via showy miracles, either. Rather, the prayer implanted in my mind the notion that if I just stayed the course, if I continued to lie my ass off, then things would work out in my favor. It could have ended otherwise, with both women telling me to go fuck myself. By all rights, I should have wound up alone. The Quest took care of that possibility; I was always meant to win Cassie. To win her, I had only to stab Melinda in the heart.

Having seen my prayer answered, I did believe in the All-Father—

until sixteen years later, when I held Cassie's hand while she died. Then I knew there was no All-Father, after all. If I was wrong and he did exist, then I vowed to find him in the afterlife and gut that merciless fucker like a river trout. Real or not, Odin can go fuck himself.

20

When Cassie and Melinda confronted each other for the first time, I could see, even as I was lashed to a catapult, the thunderstorm of emotions in Melinda's eyes. Time froze. She stood poised atop the courtyard wall, crossbow at the ready, auburn hair flowing, green eyes blazing. Behind those eyes lay confusion, jealousy, sadness, and rage, all locked in a death-struggle for mastery of her heart. Across the way, the same emotions warred in Cassie's eyes. The enormity of the betrayal I had wreaked upon these two women fell upon me like a cliff face sheering away from a mountainside.

"You'd better haul ass," Lithaine was saying to me, as we jumped down from the catapults. "Those women want your balls on a plate."

Before either of them could produce the garden shears, the air assault began. Life is, after all, entirely dependent on timing.

Outside the city walls, the Plague Horde waited—but waiting was all they could do. With the wizards at the School holding fast despite Sklaar's demise, anything that touched the city walls from the wrong side would be incinerated. Should the magical shielding fail, five thousand hard-case Redhauke Guards waited on the battlements giddy to avenge Farbrimm's assassination by wetting their blades in

Plague Knight blood. Should Eckberd prevail and sack the city, his forces would be so depleted that the Free Kingdoms would quickly retake it. The city faced not imminent destruction, but rather the slow strangulation of a prolonged siege. Could Redhauke hold out until relief came? The city could be resupplied by water for a time, but Eckberd's navy would no doubt soon arrive to blockade the Everdeep and tighten the noose. With winter capering just over the horizon, the outlook was dire.

Eckberd the Pestilent, Lord of the Plague Knights, had in mind a simpler solution to the standoff. For all his power and wisdom, Sklaar was a surprisingly two-dimensional tactician; his opponent suffered not from such shortcomings.

Before I could adjust to my newfound freedom, Melinda raised her crossbow in my direction. The woman could shoot the wings off a fairy at fifty chains—if she wanted me dead, then dead I would be. I scrambled for cover and found none. Then the thought came to me: *I deserve this*. Once I had vowed to pay my debt to her with my life; now was as good a time as any. So, I stood straight, found her gaze with mine, and waited for the shaft to pierce my heart.

Melinda didn't murder me. Instead, she aimed the crossbow above my head and speared a Chaos dwarf piloting a steam-powered ornithopter. The machine banked sharply downward and crashed into the palace in a horrendous crunch of wood, brass fittings, and hide-sewn bat wings. The sky was filled with such machines, from which their dwarf pilots dropped onto the city streets hundreds of silvered glass spears. These shattered upon impact and released billowing blooms of scarlet light.

"What the hell are those things?" I asked Redulfo.

"Sorcery dampeners," the wizard shouted above the din. "Eckberd is shutting down Sklaar's magical defenses—and without Sklaar, our own ornithopters are useless. You know what comes next."

"He'll rain fire on the city," said Amabored. "Burn us out."

"Then there's only one thing for it," I said. My three friends strode to my side. We stood together, four comrades bound not by blood nor even honor, but rather by the shared desire to save our asses. "We leave by the front door. Take the Skull and Girdle to Eckberd."

"And when we find him," said Lithaine, "we filet him."

"You got that right," said Amabored.

"Perhaps he doesn't," said Redulfo.

"No!" came Cassie's voice, ringing across the courtyard.

She strode forward, an Athenian warrior-priestess with mace at the ready, and she looked as hot as a demon's tit. When she reached me, she pulled off her mailed glove and rocked me across the chops with it.

"Are you that fucking stupid?" she asked. "You all heard what the Ki-Rin told me. It's not just the fate of this city at stake, or your lives. It's the fate of the Woerth! You must find those Phylaxes, and you must start looking now. March out there with your dicks swinging, and it's not just the end of you, as if anyone would give a shit. It's the end of everything! So, find a way to sneak out of this city and do your fucking jobs, you miserable pieces of shit."

There was no answer we could give to that speech, so we gave none. Redulfo responded for all of us by saying, "There's only one problem: there's no way out of the city."

"I know a way." Having descended from her perch, Melinda stepped forward. I saw her, too, as if for the first time: the most powerful woman in Redhauke, with five thousand rogues at her command. Jesus, I never stood a chance against either of these women. What the fuck was I thinking?

"It's inside the palace," Melinda continued. "We'll have to get through the guards. And then we'll have to make it down to the catacombs."

"The catacombs?" asked Lithaine. "I'd rather face the Plague Knights."

"What happens after that?" Redulfo asked. "We don't have the slightest idea where to go."

"If we can get you out through the catacombs, a boat will be waiting to take you to a ship," Melinda said. "The ship is called *The Bilge Rat*, and the Captain is a friend of mine. I reached out to him

through the aether in case we needed to flee the city. His ship should
be anchored somewhere between the city and the mouth of the
Whitehorse River—and he'll agree to transport the lot of you down-
river and to the bay. He's also the greatest treasure hunter in the free
kingdoms. If he can't track down the Phylaxes, then no one can."

"I'll go with you, as far as the boat," said Cassie. "I can at least
make sure you live long enough to escape the city. After that, you're
on your own."

We all nodded our heads like a bunch of dumb fucks. The women
were in charge now, and we were just happy to have a chance to
escape the city with our miserable lives. Melinda sent Fiona off to
make sure the boat was in position, and then we headed for the
palace.

I took Melinda by the shoulders. "You'd do this for us? After what
I've done?"

"I'm not doing it for you," Melinda said. "Now take your hands off
me, and let's go."

21

The Palace guards turned out to be less of a problem than we anticipated; they had all fled the palace, taking with them every transportable object of value. Our dearly departed Lord Mayor had taken no chances, despite his certainty that the army camped outside the city was just another illusion. Fortunately, the armory hadn't been looted; a few moments within, and we were all armed for battle.

Our footfalls echoed madly through the empty marble halls as Melinda led us through the palace, down several staircases, and finally into the catacombs below. We paused at the top of a stone staircase to get some torches going. Melinda's wide face was set to a determined scowl. She was Melinda the Blade now, and I had seen the last of whatever love for me she had once harbored.

"You'd all best draw steel," Melinda told us. "Fiona has been in contact with the warden of the catacombs, and he tells us that the Rat King has mobilized his troops. We'll need to find him and parlay for passage."

To most of the city, the Rat King was just a rumor trumped up by rat catchers to make their job seem more glamorous than it was. The truth was far more terrifying. For all its wealth, power, and military might, Redhauke thrived only at the pleasure of the rats, who outnumbered the city's humanoid population ten to one, and who could lay waste to it anytime they pleased via pestilence and massed attack. The city fathers had long ago made peace with the rodent kingdom: The rats suffered the city's population to live, and Redhauke's succession of mayors allowed the rats to feast on the city's offal, its old and sick, and the occasional infant plucked from its crib. The rat catchers were paid agents of the Rat King, spying on the populace for their verminous liege. The last war between the city's humanoid and rodent factions occurred a century ago when Lord Mayor Fractulus had imported ten thousand cats into the catacombs to rid the city of its vermin for good. Ten days later, Fractulus's steward found the mayor's skeleton in bed, stripped clean of every scrap of flesh as if it had been prepared for an anatomy class. Since then, both sides had kept the peace.

These thoughts in mind, we descended into the catacombs single file: Melinda in front, Amabored behind, then Cassie, Redulfo, and Lithaine, with me guarding the rear. The staircase descended for what seemed like a league. The stone walls grew slimy. Eventually, we left the stairs behind and entered a low-ceilinged tunnel bisected by a stinking stream filled with waste. We turned south, aiming in the general direction of the Whitehorse, hoping to intersect one of the Under-Canals.

That tunnel dead-ended into another, and that one into another, each tunnel becoming taller, broader, and descending lower, until at last we found ourselves in a vast, high-columned gallery through which flowed a canal broad enough to float a fair-sized dinghy. We continued south to the sounds of filthy waterfalls plummeting from side-tunnels high above our heads. Shafts of dirty light speared down from apertures hidden somewhere above.

And then, we saw the first rat. It was a garden-variety gray rodent, the kind you'd shoo out of your kitchen with a dust broom. Perched atop an ancient wine barrel tucked into an alcove off the main gallery, it sat on its hindquarters blinking at us and sniffing the air. Then it leaped off the barrel and vanished into a crevice.

"That was a scout," whispered Melinda. "We may expect the vanguard presently."

Continuing forward, we saw more rats lurking atop rubble, creeping along the low crenelated wall that topped the gallery, and lining the path before us. A dozen rats became two dozen, ten score, a hundred score. Soon the entire gallery before us teemed with the scurrying, scampering, squirming bodies of ten thousand vermin ranging in size from church mice to german shepherds. They chattered together in their verminous tongue, and the sound was such to drive us mad.

We stopped. There was no going farther until the rats made their intentions clear.

"If they attack, toss the torches on the ground in front of us," said Amabored, his hand drifting to his sword hilt. "That will buy us some time. Redulfo, how many can you incinerate before they reach us?"

"I have a couple of mystical missiles and a fireball ready to go," said the wizard. "Maybe a few hundred."

"Don't be daft," said Melinda. "If they want us dead, then dead we'll be. Let's wait and see what they want."

At the far end of the gallery, obscured by the murky gloom, a shadow filled the canal. It grew larger as whatever object casting it neared. We heard the lap of water against wood, and large creatures dog-paddling.

Only they weren't dogs. The light revealed a team of a dozen humongous rats, each as big as a Shetland pony, paddling together in the canal. Harnesses tied them to a makeshift barge constructed of driftwood, scraps of iron, pieces of furniture, and wine barrels. Atop the barge stood a throne made from human bones. Atop the throne writhed something that bent our minds sideways.

Was it a single creature, or something more terrifying still? It looked like a thousand or more rats all entwined together in a squirming mass of coils: long pinkish tails wound tightly in knots, rat bodies fused like conjoined twins, huge clumps and clots of dozens of rats knotted together with matted fur tangled in disgusting plates. Each individual rat was still alive. Rat-limbs worked furiously, jagged rat-teeth chomped, beady rat-eyes regarded us with menace. Together, these fused clumps of rats made up the thing's torso, its limbs, and something approaching its head. Within the massive, teeming ball of rats that made up the latter, a pair of torch-like red eyes gleamed at us.

"The Rat King, I believe," Melinda said.

Up to that point, it was the most fucked up thing I ever saw.

22

W hich moment was more terrifying: seeing the Rat King for the first time, or watching the Chimera Gate open on the sea of lemming imps through which we were expected to wade to find their queen? In retrospect, neither moment makes my all-time list of most scared-shitless encounters. Contenders for the top spot include the moment I unmasked Garrin Grimm-reaper, or the moment we got our first look at the Violet Queen on her home turf—but the former moment was too surreal, and the latter too abstract, to qualify. For Number One, I have to give it up for Koschei. That asshole knew how to throw a party.

NINETEEN YEARS HAD PASSED SINCE I FIRST FOUND THE GIRDLE OF Gargantua in the cavern beneath Chasm Falls. How was I to know that Jaspin had placed it there, at my father's command, for me to find? Had I known that detail, do you think I would have touched the fucking thing? I would have run screaming out of that cave and never looked back.

Down what a torturous path that seminal event sent my mates and me: fleeing Redhauke for our lives, charged with finding the remaining Phylaxes in a new Quest of the Dread Plain; seeing Redulfo, Malcolm, and Bellasa come to bitter ends; essaying epic journeys high in the mountains to cloud giant lairs, and far below the Woerth's surface to subterranean oceans that never knew sunlight. We led great armies into battle. We fought and killed every manner of foul beast and denizen of evil that exists on this godforsaken rock. We journeyed to Hell and back. We were lost in other universes. As for me, I played the role of buccaneer, hero, warlord, spy, and slave, among many others. At the Quest's end, that greenhorn fifteen-year-old kid who found the Girdle so long ago was as dead and buried as his most distant ancestors.

Once we reached the Dread Plain, we survived everything Koschei could throw at us: Harvesters, Plague Knights, the Bridge of Terrors, and finally the hellspawn that guarded the Dread Gate itself. We fought our way through the Deathless One's psychic assault, the united Phylaxes pulling us inexorably forward as the walls of the Dread Keep melted and flowed around us, forcing us to wade through blood and piss and suppurating flesh, the faces of the thousands of children whose souls Koschei had consumed crying out to us from the walls, the ceilings, the floors. Only our faith in our fellowship kept us moving forward. Had any one of us doubted that bond, our defenses would have collapsed. We would have been lost to madness and death, and the Woerth would have followed soon thereafter.

When at last we reached Koschei himself, what did we see? A dread evil Lord in the full majesty of his powers, cloaked in dark glory, before whom it took every ounce of our will not to bend our knees and quail before him? Nope—we found a fucking kid.

Overcoming every horror, we found ourselves at last in the Chamber of Eternity, Koschei's seat of power on Woerth. The Chamber was an island of Law in a sea of Chaos, for even the Deathless One required a platform upon which to wage his wars for the annihilation of Woerth.

"Come in, come in, friends, welcome," Koschei said as we entered the Chamber. It was appointed as a modest wizard's quarters: tall shelves lined with books and tomes, wooden globe of the Woerth in one corner, a wide desk stacked with scrolls, quills, and pots of ink. In the center of the room stood a simple upholstered throne positioned over the eight-pointed Star of Chaos made of marble and inlaid in the polished wooden floor. On the throne sat a child.

At least, he appeared as a child, of no more than five or six years, with the androgynous features of a cherub rendered in oils. He wore a simple tunic and sandals. In one hand he bore a goblet, from which he sipped primly. As we crept into the Chamber, the child greeted us with a cold smile and a piercing gaze brimming with wry good humor.

We spread out into the room, we survivors: Amabored, Lithaine, James, Andrigan, Lindar, and me. Cassie remained outside the Keep, for entering this fountainhead of Chaos would have warped our gestating son—had the boy lived at all, he would have been born a monster. Wilberd had remained with her. We didn't bother to draw steel, as this wasn't to be a fight with conventional weapons. It was psychic warfare: our collective wills locked in mortal combat with the will of a sorcerer who had last lived on Woerth five hundred years ago, whose consciousness now spanned a thousand universes and ten thousand centuries.

"Shall we have a toast, then, to our parlay?" Koschei asked in the high, innocent voice of the child whose body he possessed. Our hands now held goblets of warm spiced brandy. The Dread Lord noted our wariness.

"Surely you don't suspect something as prosaic as poison?" Koschei asked, grinning his cherub's grin. "Fear not, for our battle will be joined shortly—assuming, of course, that you mean to kill me. But our inevitable clash is no reason to forgo courtesy."

"To your health, then," Amabored said, and raised his cup. We drank. It was good stuff. The ability to manipulate raw Hellfire had its advantages.

"Now then, let's to business," Koschei said, stepping down from his throne. His little feet dangled above the floor for a moment, and I nearly laughed at the absurdity of it. Shouldn't I just bend the little shit over my knee and spank his ass? Could it be that simple?

"If I read our situation aright, then I may summarize it thusly," Koschei continued. "I aim to give this world over to Chaos, and you five men aim to stop me. A simple, timeless dilemma enacted in infinite scenarios across the vast expanse of the Multiverse over many long millennia. Do I have it right?"

"Master of the obvious," said Lithaine.

"As you are master of the cliché, young elf," said Koschei. Then the child paused, passing a hand across his brow. Was this a moment of weakness? Reaching into his tunic, Koschei pulled out a pack of cigarettes—Marlboro Reds. He tucked a smoke between his lips and lit it with a snap of his little fingers. After a few puffs, he spoke.

"Look," Koschei said, and his voice had changed—still childlike, but possessed now of a decidedly jaded ennui. "Do you chumps know how sick I am of this scene? How many times I've given this same ridiculous speech?"

"How many times?" asked Lindar. "If it's confusion you're sewing, Dread Lord, then you'll need to do better than that."

"Again with the dime-store quips," Koschei said, drawing on his red. He smoked it so fast that he had to light a new one with the butt of the first. "We can do this all night, or we can make it easy. Here's the truth: You think that killing me will restore peace and plenty to the Free Kingdoms—but it won't. Killing me won't save the Woerth; killing me will destroy it."

That last bit gave us pause. "Okay, we'll bite," Amabored said. "Tell us how killing you will destroy the Woerth. If we don't buy your story, then I promise you that I will eat you and shit you out again right here in this room."

"So mote it be," said Koschei. Throughout this exchange, I had remained silent; now Koschei pointed to me and motioned me forward. I now bore nine of the ten Phylaxes that would allow me to wrest Koschei's power from him: the Screaming Skull sat once again on my shoulders; the Crown of Chaos sat upon the Skull's brow; the Horrible Heart beat in my chest; Soulreaver, taken from the Grimmreaper himself, rested in its sheath at my side. Etcetera. We lacked only the Awful Orbs, which we assumed were staring at us from the child's cherubic face. Duly outfitted, I stepped forward.

"Look at you," Koschei said. "Do you know how ridiculous you look? Seriously, you look like an idiot. What did you think was going to happen here, Elberon? Did you think that you would yank the Orbs out of my head and then destroy me?"

"UM... YEAH, I GUESS SO," I said in the Skull's booming voice.

"What about the sacrifice?" Koschei asked. "The friends you've lost, the family members, the lovers, all the nameless soldiers who gave their lives in the war to get you six sorry-ass losers to me—you think that was the end of it? The victory is only as great as the sacrifice required to achieve it, Elberon—that's how these stories work. This doesn't end with you standing victorious over my corpse. It ends with you dead."

"Bullshit," Amabored said. "He's bluffing."

"Jesus, how dense are you morons?" Koschei asked, shaking his cherub's head. "Here's what happens: To find the Orbs and gain the power of the Phylaxes, you need to step through this."

With that, Koschei waved his hand. Behind his little throne, a pair of velvet curtains parted to reveal the Black Mirror—the same Black Mirror Andrigan, Wilberd and I would find in Lindar's cave more than twenty-five years later. Immediately, we were filled with that same nauseating sense of wrongness that we felt when we first encountered the Violet Queen on the road to slay Redulfo the Black. We all took an instinctive step away from it. Whatever this mirror was, whatever horrors lay behind the negative space held within its obsidian frame, it didn't belong in this universe.

"Step through this, and you'll find Her," Koschei said. "You know who I'm talking about. She has the Orbs. Before anything else happens, you'll need them."

"We'll get them," said Lithaine, "and then we cut off your fucking head."

"No. NO! WRONG!" said Koschei, pistoning his little arms around. "You don't. As soon as Elberon returns through the Black

Mirror, then I'm no longer trapped in this little package." He slapped himself on the chest. "I become HIM. Don't you see? HE becomes ME."

And then, as suddenly as if Koschei had flipped a light switch—had there been such a thing as light switches in our world—I did see. I saw. I knew what Koschei meant by sacrifice. By the looks on the mugs of my mates, they knew it, too.

"Oh," said James.

"Ah," said Andrigan.

"Yeah," said Amabored. "Okay." The barbarian turned to me. "Look, Elberon, I told you outside the Blue Falcon that I would, you know... if you needed me to."

'YES. I UNDERSTAND," I said in the Skull's voice. "THANK YOU, BROTHER. IT DOESN'T CHANGE WHAT WE HAVE TO DO."

"Ah—but it does. It DOES." Koschei stepped forward, animated, his smoke bouncing up and down between his fat little lips. "There's another way—a way we can end this whole stupid charade once and for all. We can all go home happy."

"Do tell," Lithaine said.

"Easier to show you." The Dread Lord stepped to me, took my hand in his tiny one, and led me before the Black Mirror. "Just take a look, Elberon, and everything will become clear. You'll learn the identity of our true Enemy. And you'll know that I'm not it. You'll learn that we're both on the same side."

The child stepped aside and bowed low, like a carnival barker inviting a skeptical audience to step into the tent and see the freak show. We all looked at each other. Then I shrugged and stepped forward.

"ALL RIGHT, WIZARD," I said. "IF THIS IS A TRICK, I'LL FIND THOSE EYEBALLS AND SEND YOU BACK TO THE VOID WHERE YOU BELONG."

"Yeah, kid. Sure thing," Koschei said, and motioned me forward. Stepping before the opaque surface of the Black Mirror, I stared into its featureless depths. At first, I saw nothing but my own reflection: a haggard, gaunt, bearded bloke rocking the thousand-yard stare. Nothing I hadn't seen before. It was me.

Then the reflection rippled before my eyes, as if I had dropped a pebble onto the surface of a black pond. The image twisted and swirled like pulled taffy, clouding up and then resolving itself again. The reflection became a window, through which natural light bathed me.

Then I saw myself—only it wasn't the Me I had just seen in the Mirror's black surface. It was the real me. I saw myself for who I really was.

And I screamed.

23

W hen the Chimera Gate opened on ten-thousand hungry lemming imps carpeting the landscape outside the city, I also had the urge to scream. None of us had any illusions that we could stand against them long enough to find and slay their queen. We would die, and the pit devil would have the Girdle. We could hope only that the city would be spared destruction.

A detail of Redhauke Guards had helped outfit us for battle. They had wheeled out a big steam-powered street sweeper, one of the same machines we had seen quash the riots in Doomtown five years earlier. The crawler bore man-high iron wheels wrapped in thick spiked treads, an iron-shod dozer blade ringed with sharp teeth forged of tempered steel, and four crossbows mounted on a high platform protected by steel-mesh nets lined with oversized fishhooks. There was a bridge with a clutch, accelerator, and steering wheel at the bow, a short mast with crows' nest amidships, and a coalhouse topped by twin smokestacks at the stern. It was a badass piece of equipment. We would have jizzed ourselves at the opportunity to ride it into battle, if doing so would prolong our lives for more than a few hours.

One of the guards showed us how to drive it by standing with

Redulfo on the bridge while the wizard piloted it around Chimera Plaza. When the guard was satisfied that Redulfo could at least maneuver the crawler through the gate, he hopped down and motioned us aboard.

"We'll remember you lads in song," the guard promised, with the air of a prison chaplain comforting a condemned convict. "Take as many hellspawn with you as you can."

"You have our word," said Amabored. The barbarian hoisted himself onto the crawler. For a man about to be devoured by a ravenous horde, he was in good spirits. Falling in blood-soaked battle was certainly the preferred fate for fighting men; had I already chosen Odin as my deity, I might at least have looked forward to hoisting a flagon in Valhalla. As I was still an agnostic, I could look forward only to the oblivion of the grave.

"You must enjoy the irony of dying out there with us when you could be chilling on the throne back in Helene," I said to Lithaine as we climbed aboard the crawler.

"I wouldn't say I'm enjoying it, no," said Lithaine.

"You girls need to pull yourselves together," said Amabored, grinning like a wolf at the sight of a lame deer. "How would you rather go out? Sitting on the toilet? Today is as good a day to die as any."

"Yes, I'd rather die sitting on the toilet than being eaten alive," said Redulfo. "But that's just me."

"Say, listen, your majesty," Amabored said to Lithaine, placing a familiar arm on the elf's shoulder. "I know how you feel about me. If you'd like to go to some quiet place for a few minutes where we could be alone, I'm game. I'd like to make your last moments on Woerth happy ones."

"Suck a bag of dicks, asshole," Lithaine said, pulling away.

"Do you have a bag of dicks I could borrow? Because, you know, you look like the kind of fellow that would have a couple of bags of dicks lying around."

"Let's get this over with," I said. Hopping onto the crawler, I examined our arsenal, which lay stored in a pair of large chests bolted to the platform. To aid us in our futile mission, the guards had procured for us an impressive array: Molotov cocktails, incendiary grenades, *Holocaust* potions, and a dozen spell scrolls requested by Redulfo. Lithaine had ten quivers of arrows at the ready—and if every arrow found its mark, his kill total would be no more than a rounding error.

Redulfo positioned himself at the wheel, then nodded to the guards in the gate tower. They saluted us and cranked up the portcullis. When the wizard hit the gas, the crawler lurched forward belching steam from the stacks. The portcullis fully retracted, he nudged the crawler forward. Through the open gate we saw only darkness.

The teeth-rattling clang of the portcullis dropping behind us foretold our doom. We could see no lemming imps, but despite the ear-pounding growl of the crawler engine, we could hear them: the high-pitched, buzzing whine of ten thousand hungry mouths all chattering at once like a swarm of angry mutant wasps. Fear rose in my throat like stomach bile.

"BUTT-SCRATCHER!!!" cried Amabored, shouting one of the many non-sequitur oaths he brought from the North. He twirled his sword in a broad circle over his head.

"We're doomed," said Redulfo. He gunned the motor.

24

No more than ten yards beyond the gate, the roiling see of
lemming imps attacked. It was the beginning of six hours
of hell.

It was past midnight; a hunter's moon hung in the sky, which we
took as a good omen. First up: Redulfo, set to cast a *Force Shield* spell
inscribed on one of the scrolls tucked into his shoulder pouch. He
sang the incantation and blew the spell's melody on his flute. Then
the requisite sound of tearing paper as our universe collided with
another, and the crawler was encased within a blue translucent
globe.

We slaughtered the imps inside the shield in short order. As
Redulfo gunned the crawler forward and the snapping horde threw
itself against the force shield, we started in with missile weapons,
Amabored and I manning crossbows while Lithaine rocked his longbow. We couldn't miss. We dropped scores of them, piling one corpse
on another until the corpses blotted out the moon.

The shield afforded us progress away from the city walls; when it
dissipated, we suffered the downside—a rain of snarling imps falling
on our heads. Taking a few nasty bites, we chopped up about fifty or

so. Then Redulfo cracked open one of the *Holocaust* potions, and the detonation incinerated every lemming imp within a hundred yards.

"Cast the *Detect Chaos* spell!" I called. "Let's see where we are."

The scroll was a secret weapon of sorts, a gift to us from Sklaar himself. Most *Detect Chaos* spells were limited to a radius of ten chains or so, but Sklaar had extended this one to a one-league radius. Since lemming imps lacked free will, any strong Chaos source in the vicinity ought to emanate from their queen.

As the imps surged forward again, Redulfo cast the spell. We rained fire with crossbows again until the bodies began to pile up near the platform. Redulfo detonated the second *Holocaust* potion, which took out maybe another hundred. Small potatoes, but the blast cleared our sightlines enough that we could make out, far in the distance hovering over an abandoned farmhouse, a smoky nebula of fluorescent green light.

"Bingo!" cried Amabored. "Gun it, wizard—let's kill that bitch and go have breakfast."

Redulfo pushed the throttle forward, and the crawler plowed into the morass of imps. Those in our path were ground to hamburger beneath the tracks; soon the bottom half of the crawler was dripping with their black blood. Those that made it to the top of the machine were caught in the nets and hooks, allowing us to run them through with steel and push their corpses back into the pool. The few making it onto the platform itself, we swatted like flies.

The combined might of the crawler, Redulfo's sorcery, and our steel afforded us slow but steady progress toward the farmhouse. Hours passed. A glimmer of dawn glowed above the eastern horizon. Hope whispered to me that we might make it through this night alive.

That moment, of course, was when the dozer conked out.

"That figures," said Redulfo.

Lithaine checked the coal forge and found the fire still burning. When Redulfo tried the throttle, the gears ground together. The entire machine began to rattle ominously. No steam belched from the stacks, which meant that—

"She's going to blow!" Lithaine cried.

We were surrounded by a grumbling, buzzing carpet of lemming imps extending in every direction as far as we could see. Drawing back to a perimeter around the crawler, they gnashed their fangs, licked their chops, and awaited our next move. We had two choices: stay on the crawler and die in the explosion, or wade into the imps and kill as many as possible before they devoured us.

I extended my hand to Amabored. "It's been an honor fighting at your side, brother," I said.

"Likewise, Elberon of the Isles," Amabored said.

Lithaine and Redulfo joined us. Together we drew our swords, the wizard raising his flute, and we saluted one another. If I had to die, I was happy to die with these men.

Jumping from the rattling, smoking crawler with sword drawn, I felt only the dull acceptance of a cow in the slaughter pen, waiting my turn for the killing bolt. And then: For the briefest of intervals—no more than a fraction of a second—every lemming imp around us vanished. I saw clearly the empty farmland around the city: the fields unsullied, the farmhouses still and quiet in the pastel dawn, the untrammeled road leading back to the city. The horrid earsplitting buzz from the lemming horde likewise blinked out.

It happened so fast that it barely registered in my brain. The pastoral scene vanished in an instant, and the noisome sea of snarling imps once again surrounded us.

Blinking, I glanced at my fellows. "Did you guys see that?" I asked.

"Close your eyes!" Redulfo ordered. "Try to picture the scene again in your mind—imagine that the imps are gone!"

We did so. In my head, I conjured a vision of the empty land-scape. No sea of imps. No trail of dead ones behind us. The buzzing of the horde receded, as if I had dipped my head into a pool of water —and then the sound ceased altogether.

"Now open your eyes," Redulfo said.

We opened them. Lo and behold, the lemming imp horde had vanished. The landscape appeared again just as we had briefly seen it, looking for all the world as if the horde had never existed. The crawler too, was now clean, with no traces of the imps' black blood that had coated it only moments before. The cuts, bruises, and bites we had taken in battle were likewise gone.

"What. The. Fuck?" I asked.

"It was all a goddamn fucking illusion!" Amabored said, whirling around to take in the full view of our surroundings. "A fucking spell!"

"Then what have we been fighting?" I asked, still slow on the draw. "Nothing?"

"Nothing is exactly what we've been fighting," Redulfo said. "This was all high-level sorcery, the work of a master illusionist. Whoever he is, he'd have to be at least Fifteenth Level to pull this off."

Lithaine pointed toward the distant farmhouse. "Then he must be over there."

The amorphous green cloud of Chaos still hung over the farmhouse. While there might be no imp queen there, the presence of Chaos was no illusion—and whoever had pulled this trick was still there.

The front door of the farmhouse opened, and a cloaked figure ran into the garden. He was too far away to make out his face. The figure crouched down, and then blasted upward into the sky like a roman candle, moving so fast that he left a small sonic boom in his wake. Within a second, he had vanished into the clouds.

Before we could process this turn of events, we were startled out of our stupor by the broken-down crawler, now rattling like an avalanche of scrap iron. That hadn't been an illusion, either. The immense steam pressure began to pop the rivets, which whistled past our ears like bullets.

"Run for your lives!" Lithaine shouted. We ran. With an ear-crunching *RHUMP!*, the crawler blew. We hit the dirt as twisted iron plating, gears, wheels, pieces of tread, and flaming coals rained down around us. The dozer blade thudded into the ground two feet from Amabored's head.

A moment passed before we felt safe enough to rise. We stared at each other, still unsure of what had happened or why. Then Amabored rolled to his feet.

"Well, that was fun," he said. "Let's get back to the city. Who wants grub?"

25

The wizard rocketing into the stratosphere was Jaspin, of course. Three years after the fall of the Blue Falcon, he had reappeared to fuck with us. It was always Jaspin. Years after the lemming imp incident—which led the Lord Mayor to lock us in the tollbooth for a week until he was satisfied that we hadn't pulled it off ourselves—we still wondered why the wizard had bothered. Why fake out the entire city with a phantasm? Why make us fight nothing for six hours? What was the point?

It had all been an elaborate bluff. Jaspin thought that my father had somehow returned the Skull to me, and he followed the devil's very real threat with a bullshit ruse designed to trick me into donning the Skull again. Even the most powerful wizards have their blind spots; Jaspin's mistake was in thinking that I had a fucking clue.

THE RAT KING, WHICH WE FOUND OURSELVES FACING IN THE REDHAUKE sewers just a year later, was not an illusion. How happy we would have been to find out that it was.

For once, we were able to hang back and let someone else stare down the beast. This was Melinda's show, and we knew it. As we stood crowded around one of the alcoves, swords drawn but useless, Melinda stepped forward to confront the King. Reflected torchlight capered in the eyes of ten thousand rats crouching on every available surface in the dank, dripping stone gallery. The vermin horde was silent, expectant, waiting only a word from their abominable liege to overwhelm us. Their sheer numbers reminded me of the lemming imp episode; squeezing my eyes shut, I imagined the rats gone, just as we had done with Jaspin's phantasm. When I opened them, the fuckers were still there.

The Rat King slumped on its barge and awaited Melinda's approach. Within the foul mass of fused rat-flesh constituting its body, two red eyes lingered on her. The thing radiated a malevolent intelligence that was not so much evil as indifferent; it bore us no more regard than we bore any rat we might see scurrying around the refuse of the city.

"Greetings, Lord of Vermin," Melinda announced, bowing low. "I am Melinda the Blade, Over-Boss of the Thieves Guild. I come to treat with you. We seek your permission to pass through these tunnels and flee the city."

When the monstrous hive of ratness spoke, its voice was the sound of a thousand rats squeaking words in unison. Gooseflesh rose on my arms.

"*You may not pass,*" the Rat King said. "*We are charged with keeping this gate closed.*"

"Charged by whom?" Melinda asked. Respect paid, she stood straight to regard the foul king as its equal. "Surely the Vermin Lord submits to no master."

"*We serve none,*" the Rat King squealed. "*But we are allied with the Lord of Pestilence, who commands the army above.*"

"You ally with the invaders? To what end?"

"*The Pestilent One asks us to spread coughing-death to the two-legs above. Should we do this, he grants that we may feast on the flesh of the dead. We will feast as none have on the Woerth. We will take our place as rulers of the above.*"

We all pondered this for a moment. If the rats released a plague upon the city, Eckberd would need do no more than wait a few weeks, walk through the front door, and set his slaves to sweeping up the bones.

"Surely, you are prepared to leave the city after the feast," said Melinda.

"We will not leave the city. We will rule. We are the Vermin Lord."

"What will you eat when all the two-legs are dead? Has Lord Eckberd promised to tend the fields outside the city? To raise the cattle? To cast fishing nets into the Everdeep? Surely, he has promised you these things."

"He has not promised these things."

"Then your great host will take on these tasks? You will no longer subsist on the leavings of the two-legs? Shall the vermin scavenge no more?"

"You speak ill of us. We are the Vermin Lord. The great host brings tribute. This is the way of it."

"Really? Then the feast you propose is naught but a last supper. For when the two-legs are dead, soon thereafter will the Lord of Vermin surely die."

"You dare say so!"

"That is the way of it," Melinda said. She shrugged, breaking eye contact with the King. "It need not be so. Long have the two-legs ruled the city together with the Vermin Lord. Two-legs rule above, and the vermin rule below. The vermin feast on the fruits of this partnership. So it may be until the end of days."

"How may it be so?" the Rat King asked. It leaned forward on its throne to tower over Melinda, who stood her ground. *"The Lord of Pestilence is powerful. He will take the city by force. The Vermin Lord would die with the two-legs. We must ally with him or perish."*

Then Melinda turned to look at the rest of us, and her eyes met mine. She motioned me forward. When I stepped up, the Rat King reared back, its thousands of rat-mouths hissing and squealing in unison.

"Put away your sword, you idiot!" Melinda whispered. I did so, trying hard to will the blood away from my face. The Rat King settled down.

"Lord Eckberd wants only this man here," Melinda said to the Rat King. She pointed at me. "We cannot give him this man, or all things on Woerth will end, including the Vermin Lord." She glanced at me again, her eyes narrowing to slits. "I would that it were not so, for I would freely turn him over."

"*You say it is so,*" said the Rat King, "*and yet the Pestilent One promises us life.*"

"Eckberd is the empty vessel into which the Deathless One pours his worthless words," said Melinda. "If you help us spirit this man and his companions away from the city, I tell you now that he will turn his army aside, for his master is not yet strong enough to draw the Free Kingdoms into open war."

"*What is this to us? We care nothing for Free Kingdoms.*"

"It may be so. But you care yet for your horde, I think. Know this, Lord Verminous: The Lord Mayor is dead. The Redhauke Guard are broken. Sklaar himself has fallen. But I am Melinda the Blade, Over-Boss of the Thieves Guild and the last seat of authority in this city. Redhauke is mine. And I make this promise to you: Help this man escape, and together we shall rule the city—two-legs above, and the vermin below, as it has always been. The horde will want for nothing."

The Rat King collapsed back onto its throne. Its component rats conspired together, whispering rat lips to rat ear, rubbing their tiny pink paws together, their knotted tails writhing like a wall of pink earthworms. Gathering itself together again, it regarded Melinda with the glowing coals of its eyes.

"*The Blade will give us your infants? Your young ones?*" it asked. "*We desire the taste of their flesh. The Pestilent One promises us this. Will you also?*"

"No," Melinda said. "Our young ones are precious to us, just as yours are to you. But you will eat well. That, I can assure you."

Silence again, but for the conclave of whispering rats. We were all afraid to breathe.

"*You speak well and true,*" said the Rat King to Melinda. "*It will be as you say. Follow us.*"

Melinda turned back to us. Her look of relief told us how close we had come to disaster.

"Let's go," she said.

26

The Rat King's barge pulled away, hauled by a second team of giant water-treading rats pointed in the opposite direction. The attendant rat horde scurried back to their holes like filaments of iron repelled by a magnet. We followed behind: Amabored, Lithaine, Redulfo, Wilberd, Cassie, and me. Cassie refused to look at me. The snub catching his eye, Amabored sidled over.

"Don't sweat it, man," the barbarian whispered. "You're already in there."

"The only place she wants to see me is in a grave," I hissed back.

"You're a known liar now," he said. "That makes you a bad boy. Chicks love bad boys. Before, she was only considering fucking you. Now, she's trying to figure out how to let you fuck her without it looking like she's forgiven you."

"You really are a total douchebag."

"Card-carrying." Amabored slapped me on the back and moved up to take point.

Heading east, we cut through the sewers for about a quarter-league. Then the Rat King turned south, where the tunnels narrowed, and it was forced to relinquish the barge. The foul mischief of intertwined rats surged forward through knee-deep sewage, spilled forth to fill the tunnel, scurried along dripping stone walls, and crawled inverted on the ceiling with red eyes gleaming in the dark.

At last, we saw dim light ahead. Melinda turned to address us.

"There's a sluice gate ahead that leads to the Whitehorse," she said. "My friends will be waiting for you with a few small boats. If there's trouble, this is where we'll find it."

And so, we did. The light brightened, then resolved into partitions of daylight: the gate. Before the gate stood a figure in silhouette. We could make out no details other than the outline of a broad, black cloak and hood. A few more steps, and we saw a black scythe inverted, its point resting on the ground, its pommel gripped by the figure's leather-gloved hands.

"Say, isn't that...?" Lithaine began.

"...the fucker who was leading the pit devil around on a chain?" Amabored finished. "Yeah, I think so. Elberon?"

It was him. Our first encounter came beneath the Blue Falcon —and so explosive was that encounter that the quantum shock wave destroyed that legendary inn. Our second encounter came three years later, when he appeared in Hundred Fountain Square with Malacoda in tow. In both cases, I had felt him mark me from somewhere behind the impenetrable darkness of his cowl. Thrice now this man had appeared to thwart me—and while I might have a hundred questions for him, every one of those questions could be answered by watching his head roll away from his twitching corpse.

"Let's grease that cocksucker," I said.

Lithaine, Odin love him, stepped up and launched a trio of arrows at the figure. The asshole merely raised a medium-sized kite shield— or, as it appeared to us, a kite-shield-shaped negative space—and the arrows disappeared into its black, fathomless depths. Then Redulfo blew an arpeggio on his flute and cast a massive fireball. It rocketed high over the squirming mass of the Rat King, exploded at the end of the tunnel, and engulfed the figure in a hellstorm of flame. When the flames died down, we saw him crouching unharmed behind his shield.

"What the hell are you doing?" Cassie cried. "You're giving away our position!"

She was right—but it was too late for recriminations. The figure rose and stretched forth a gloved hand. The perimeter of the shield glowed red, like neon tubing. The Rat King, which until that moment seemed prepared to overwhelm the cloaked figure, stopped cold. Every rat within its mass turned to look back at us. Somewhere deep within the twisted mess of vermin, the red eyes of the Rat King narrowed to slits. It charged toward us, an avalanche of rat flesh, a crumbling wall of gnashing teeth and rending claws.

"Holy fuck!" I cried. We turned to run. Then, racing forth from the back of the party, came Wilberd. We had forgotten all about him, which was easy to do since he never spoke. He ran straight for the dark nucleus of the Rat King. The mass of vermin rolled over him like a wave rolling into a half-pipe. For a moment, the monk disappeared, and we feared him dead.

There came the horrid, ear-splitting awfulness of a thousand rats all screaming at once. Wilberd rolled out of the rat-mass and into the sewer water. In his hands he held a throbbing, blood-engorged mass of rat-flesh about the size of prize-winning pumpkin. Making eye-contact with me, he lobbed the rat-pumpkin in my direction.

I knew what to do. Swinging my axe in a deadly parabola, I sliced through the rat-pumpkin, cutting it in twain. Another horrible echoing shriek, and the Rat King collapsed in a crashing, thunderous rain of rodents. Those vermin that could get away scurried into any hole they could find. The remainder of the Vermin Lord lay in twitching, clotted clumps of dying rats.

That left the cloaked guy—time to take his measure. Shouting an oath, I ran toward him with axe raised. The cloaked figure swung up his own rune-covered blade to absorb my blow.

Our blades connected. There was a thunderclap and a flash of blue-white lightning. I flew backward until I crashed into my companions and sent them flying like bowling pins.

We all rose to our feet. Acrid smoke filled the clammy air. The tunnel gate was open; the cloaked figure was gone.

"That fellow has some bag of tricks," Redulfo said, pushing his glasses up his nose. "Who was he?"

"I don't know," I said, slinging my axe across my back. "But I'll see him again."

27

We stood at the open gate, waiting for the boats to come in. There was no more trouble; Redulfo's fireball had gone unnoticed. My mates gathered together to light their pipes, which gave me leave to step over to Cassie.

"Come with us," I said. "We need a cleric. We'll all be dead in a fortnight if you don't come."

Her face was red and pinched, full of rage. Not for the last time, I found myself burning with guilt and shame. If she had just told me to go fuck myself, her road would have been far smoother. Even then, I knew she couldn't.

"Hire one from the port towns," she said, not looking at me. "My place is at the temple."

"You told us yourself how important this Quest is. The Ki-Rin chose you, remember? You're the one who got us off our asses. We'll be lost without you." I touched her chin, turned her face toward mine. "I need you. Come with me."

She pushed my hand away. "You ask this now? In front of *her*?"

"He's right. You should go," said Melinda, stepping forward. Her anguish was now held at bay by renewed resolve. She was becoming more than just the Over-Boss of the Thieves Guild; she was becoming a leader of men.

"I don't know you, and I have no feeling for you," Melinda said to Cassie. "But if this piece of shit and his friends really are the only hope we have of saving the Woerth, then go with them. Make sure these dipshits finish what they started. And when the job is done, do with him what you will."

For the first time that day, Cassie smiled. "You have some balls on you, I'll give you that," she said to Melinda. "You saved our asses back here, and I won't soon forget it. I'm only sorry we didn't meet under better circumstances."

Melinda bowed. As Cassie turned away, I stepped over to my soon-to-be-ex-wife, determined to end our time together with some small measure of grace.

"Thank you," I said. "The words can't mean shit to you, but I'll say them anyway: I'm sorry. I never thought you'd be just a minor character in my story, or I a minor one in yours. I thought we'd walk through the tale together."

"Stuff your apology up your ass," Melinda said. Although she looked up at me, she seemed somehow taller. "Just do your job. I'll do mine. I'm the only authority left in this city, and it's my job to see that Redhauke survives the wars to come."

"If there's anything you need from me, just send word."

"I need nothing from you. Don't ever step foot in Redhauke again while I'm alive."

Her eyes dismissed me. My head was filled with more bullshit, everything I wanted to say to her to justify my wretched behavior. At the end, silence was the best option. She turned away, heading back into the tunnels alone until the darkness swallowed her. I haven't seen her since—and I never even learned her real name.

Amabored called over. "The boats are here. Let's go."

Outside the gate floated a pair of dinghies, each crewed by two scruffy sailors sitting the oars. In the closer boat, a squat, barrel-shaped man in a blue captain's uniform stood puffing on a pipe, his booted foot resting on the gunwale. He bore a close-cropped white beard and wore a billed cap pushed down on his head. He smiled broadly at us.

"Captain Quid Saltwind at your service, my lords and lady," The captain said. "If you'd be so kind as to board these boats, we'll slip out into the Whitehorse Estuary, where the *Bilge Rat* awaits."

"The *Bilge Rat*?" Lithaine asked. "As if we haven't had enough of rats already."

"Ah, but the *Bilge Rat* isn't just any rat, my eldritch friend," said the Captain. "She mayn't look like much, but she's as fast as a horse-lord and as sturdy as a hill troll. She'll do just fine for our purposes. Now, if you please."

We boarded the boats. As we slipped away from the Shield Wall, I sat staring into the tunnel mouth, hoping that Melinda might yet emerge, might wave, might grant me some sign that she wouldn't hate me forever. If it was hatred she chose, however, then I had certainly earned it. Her path was now her own.

So I left the city of my dreams, never to return.

BOOK IV

Showdown at the Blue Falcom

1

The Showdown at the Blue Falcon, as historians would dub it, featured multiple takes on the theme of loss. Young Redulfo suffered his own future death. Nine years later, those of us who assaulted the Workshop of Telescopes suffered the second and final loss of our friend. In the catacombs below the inn, I suffered the loss of the woman I pretended to love. And, for a moment, my friends thought they had lost me.

With my mother dying too soon for me to recall her love, the first great loss of my life was the loss of the city I loved. The *Remembrance* potion provides me with perfect recall of Redhauke despite last stepping foot in the place forty years ago. The city spires pastel in the dawn mist; toothless merchants smelling of cardamom and rum, calling prices across the packed labyrinth of the Bazaar; the salted stink of the stevedores unloading fish on the docks; the Grand Promenade, lush with fruit trees growing in marble pots carved with images of the great merchant princes of old; at the first brush of dawn, the calls to prayer from the temples, mosques, and churches crowding for attention along the Godsway. I could lose myself still in the streets of the city, wandering along its marbled bridges, ancient cobblestones, and narrow dirt alleys in search of my wasted youth. It is well that men forget—if we could live always in the rosy past, who among us would bother to live in the present?

To tell this tale fully, then—to make you understand why, in just a few days, I'm going to murder everyone I love—I must dwell also in the desert of my memory, lest I dwell only its green fields. In that wasteland, my father looms large.

ELDERON AND I WERE JUST A FEW YEARS OUT OF DIAPERS WHEN WE figured out that Olderon was out of his mind. His madness was forged in the Horst mines, where he suffered the tortures of the damned, and I might forgive him for it if he didn't seem to relish the crazy so much. If history is made by men with iron balls, then Olderon's package was forged by Weiland, the Smith of the Gods. For years, he plotted his revenge while slaving in the mines for his Talon masters: saving scraps of steel, recruiting allies, scouting an escape path, and stashing caches of supplies. To construct weapons, he built a secret forge in the deepest, most dangerous section of the mines. Then he led his men in a revolt that would soon pass into legend: hacking apart an entire legion of guards, fleeing Gorm on a pirated bireme, losing the pursuing Talony fleet in the labyrinthine channels of the southern islands, making landfall on Hydra Rock, slaughtering every native on the island, founding a city, methodically conquering the other islands, building a kingdom, and defending it against invaders for thirty years. Who could measure up to that resume? Not me.

The constant trauma and stress, however, put a kink in his brain. On one particularly fine midsummer's day on the high grasslands overlooking Tradewind, my father and Jorren, his Master-at-Arms, took my brother and me to drill with our swords in the tall meadow. Elderon was ten; I was eight. When our ponies crested the ridge, we saw a small open tent billowing in the wind. Beside the tent stood a rack of short swords. Inside the tent burned a small brazier. Someone had thrust an iron brand into the coals.

We tied up our ponies. Master Jorren, a squat, one-eyed veteran campaigner who wore the traditional spiked and jeweled mohawk of House Panterian, led us to the sword rack and ordered us to choose a blade. Elderon and I traded wary gazes. If only we had learned to become allies against Olderon, it might have turned out differently for my brother—it might be his fat ass warming the throne today instead of mine. And yet here I sit, while he rots in the grave with his skull resting on his ribcage. I don't apologize for it; I avenged his death, for fuck's sake. The asshole is no doubt sitting a bar stool in Valhalla right now, still stewing with resentment.

Swords in hand, wooden bucklers strapped to our opposing fore-arms, we turned to face each other. My brother's face flushed red with rising adrenalin; I suppose mine did as well. Master Jorren stepped forward.

"Today's lesson is about fear," Jorren said to us. "Fear leads to inaction. Inaction leads to death. Properly crewed and captained, however, fear can become the ship that carries you to new conquests." He gestured toward the tent. "Within the tent you see a brand. You will fight to the first blood. The winner, as judged by your Lord Father, will brand the loser."

In the shocked-white expression of my brother, I saw the mirror image of my own face. Elderon swallowed hard.

"You think this a cruel test, and so it is," said Jorren. "But now you know fear. One of you will master it, and one of you will be marked by your failure to do so. The winner, therefore, has nothing to fear. You will begin on my mark."

Jorren was right—fear burned in Elderon's eyes, as it did in my own. When I turned my gaze upon Olderon, watching us through lidded eyes like an old lion in the shade, I felt something else—an emotion stronger than fear. It was hate. I hated the old bastard, and I knew then that my brother would have to kill me before I'd let him put that iron on me.

"Begin," called Jorren.

"For the Lordship!" I cried, and charged at Elderon. He flung up his shield, and the battle was joined.

For twenty minutes, we tried our best to murder each other. Our fear and rage ebbed and flowed across the high plain as the older men watched. Elderon was bigger, and for a while his strength carried the day. When he saw the hate in my eyes, however, his fear crippled him. Raining blows as my anger swelled into fury, I drove him back. After I took care of my brother, I vowed silently, I would turn to the old man and stick this sword in his belly.

I sent Elderon's sword spinning from his hand. Ducking around his shield, I dug my sword point into his arm. He cried out, tripped backwards over his own feet, and fell hard on his ass. I thrust my blade under his chin.

"Yield," I said. Elderon's eyes, burning with acid tears of shame, rolled wildly over to our father's expressionless face. There, he found no succor.

Jorren stomped over, grabbed the boy by the armpits, and wrestled him to his feet. Then he turned to me.

"Fetch the brand, boy," he said.

With my brother's pleas ringing in my ears, I turned toward the tent. He may as well have begged for mercy from the pitiless stars. Anger now writhing in my stomach like a nest of maggots, I pulled the red-hot brand from the coals and walked it over.

Elderon twisted and pulled in Jorren's iron grip. His eyes were those of a horse trapped in a burning stable.

"Father, don't let him burn me! Please!" my brother cried.

Holding the brand aloft, I looked now to my father and Jorren. Their faces betrayed nothing. My brother's gaze was locked on the burning red end of the brand. He had also wet himself.

That did it. With my gaze still locked on my father's, I cast the brand on the ground at Jorren's feet.

"Have you lost your senses, boy?" Jorren asked. "Pick up the brand and finish the lesson. Your king and father commands it!"

To this day, when the nightmares come in the deep hours of the dark, Olderon's is the face I see. It wasn't fear that I rode into battle; it was hatred for the man from whose seed I came. If love is this most powerful force in the Multiverse, then hate is its dark mirror; hate can command armies, raise monuments, inspire great art. And yet, hate is a parasitic muse, taking so much more from your soul than it gives, until it leaves you lying in the gutter soaked in your own piss and shit. From this vantage point in time, I can see the hard wisdom inherent in the lesson. For an eight-year-old boy, it was a heavy load to bear.

"No," I said to the two old men.

Elderon's fear broke, and he collapsed crying in Jorren's arms. Ignoring his eldest son, Olderon strode forward to tower over me. His thick brows narrowed together. For a long, silent moment, he regarded me coldly. Then he turned away.

"My younger son has chosen dishonor," he said to Jorren. "Toss him in the dungeon until he learns wisdom."

2

For three days, I languished in my father's dungeon with only a crust of bread and a cup of water per day to sustain me. On the third day, the heavy door finally opened. The cell flooded with light. Two gaolers entered bearing a brazier burning with red coals. They placed it in one corner and thrust a brand into the fire. I shrank back into the opposite corner, ready to go straight for the balls of the first one to come after me. Then Olderon strode in.

He stared at me down the slope of his nose. I expected to find only cruelty in his gaze. Behind the hard flint in his eyes, there was something else: a mewling, hairless runt of an emotion, grasping blindly for a teat. I dare not call it love, for of love Olderon knew nothing. Better to call it pride—but did it burn for me, or for himself? Had he even then begun the long con designed to trick me into becoming one of the greatest heroes of my age?

"You're a stubborn lad," Olderon said, "but you come by it honestly. There's a debt still to be paid for losing the duel. If you won't brand your brother as I command, then you may take the brand in his stead. The choice is yours."

The scar is old and weathered now, eroded by time. After such a sacrifice, you might think that Elderon would learn to love me.

Instead, it cemented his contempt. Whenever we swam the surf on Diamond Beach or grappled shirtless in a game of Crush the Kobold, the brand on my arm was a livid reminder to my brother that I had kicked his ass. Our hatred burns brightest for those who show us mercy.

3

My own hatred is but a feeble flame compared to the great inferno of hatred that Lithaine must bear for me now. Even now, the elf—or whatever he has become since he merged with Madrigel—must have already taken ship from the Were Coast. When he arrives with his host, any day now, he will put my crops to the torch and my subjects to the sword. Then he'll come for me. Should I sound the Conch of Battle, summon my admirals, and command them to muster their fleets? That would mean only the end of my fleets. Lithaine means to finish me. Was it my fault that the fucking Fire Die rolled his name? It could have just as easily been Amabored's name, or Malcolm's, or mine. We're all slaves to Fate—everyone but me, that is. Should my ultimate plan bear fruit, then I'll make Fate my bitch.

Lithaine never grasped Madrigel's plan until it was too late. The minute he realized that Starfall was really the Celestial returned, he should have run for the fucking hills. Instead, he fell in love with her. You don't need a wizened sage to remind you that fucking an angel is going to get you burned.

When Starfall first spoke her challenge to the Violet Queen, halfway along our journey to Redulfo's lair, we didn't know what to expect. We understood the Queen no more than the ant comprehends the boot. So, we lay prostrate on the ground, our hands mashed over our ears, trying to keep out the Queen's maddening voice even as it emerged from inside our skulls. Lithaine still held the sword aloft, his hands fused to the hilt. As the Queen approached, his boots left the ground. He was carried forward, floating, toward the monstrosity. The sword was running the show; Lithaine was merely a useless appendage.

"PREPARE YOURSELF FOR THE VOID, CHAOS-BITCH," the sword cried.

"THE VOID HOLDS NO TERROR FOR ME, CELESTIAL," the Queen said. She surged forward, her horrid purple torso towering far above the tree line atop legs that seemed to quaver in and out of existence. All around us, the black sky was torn apart by shards of unholy violet light as the Last Universe collided with our own. We had no idea what she wanted then, and I still don't today; even when we confronted her again in her Palace of Webs, where the Word holds no sway, we could not divine her will. *"I AM THE DEVOURER OF WORLDS. SOON THIS UNIVERSE WILL PERISH, AND SHE WILL BE FREE FROM HER PRISON AT LAST."*

"BOASTFUL WORDS, WHEN THIS UNIVERSE IS UNDER MY BANNER. BACK TO YOUR HOLE, BITCH!"

And then Starfall blazed white—a white of such blinding intensity that only later did we realize that we had witnessed pure industrial-grade *logos*, the ultimate expression of Law in the Multiverse. Her blade was now an impossibly blue and bright rectangle that seemed to expand in all directions at once, until it became a portal into another world—the Celestial Kingdom itself. From deep within the portal came the faint echoes of Heavenly choirs. For a moment, the Violet Queen seemed to hesitate.

From somewhere deep within the maelstrom of white, blue, and purple light, Lithaine's voice called faintly: "Are you assholes going to help me out here or what?"

Though my head seemed to weigh as much as a small mountain, I managed to raise it and direct a questioning gaze to Amabored, prostrate nearby. The barbarian merely shrugged.

"That goddamn sword is his problem," Amabored said. "I told him not to pick it up."

From the sword-blade-turned-portal, now a blue rhombus blazing in the sky, emerged Madrigel herself. No longer was she the ghostly child we had seen first outside of Doomtown, and later at the Blue Falcon; she was a woman now, and her white face bore the flawless beauty of the *Elohim*. The silver crown of her choir gleamed. Blinding *logos* streamed in long comet-tails from her white wings tattooed with sonnets to El. As her blue-white Celestial essence merged with the spectral wrongness of the Violet Queen, both angel and arachnid were consumed by the light. They collided, and the earth shook from a monstrous tremor that lifted us all from the ground and slammed us down again. Then came the Queen's horrid wail—a cosmic shriek of fury that echoed unto the Void itself—and the entire scene winked out of existence.

Lithaine fell to the ground in a heap. Still he clutched Starfall, but the sword was inert—just cold, pale steel. The elf was unconscious. The rest of us rose warily to our feet. We were alone again in the mountain forest now slumbering under a black sky. The spiders were gone. No sound remained but the wind soothing the frightened trees. After a long moment, the crickets resumed their night music.

Malcolm knelt beside his fallen liege. "Thank the Star Maiden, he lives still," said the paladin.

"Praise Jesus," said Amabored, reaching for his flask. "Who wants to get blotto?" he called out.

"Who doesn't?" I asked.

4

L ithaine remembered nothing after Starfall began her dance with the Violet Queen. He was dazed, paler than usual, but otherwise unharmed. He returned Starfall to her scabbard, where she rested quietly. Then he poured a flask of brandy down his throat and said nothing more. The rest of us knew well enough to leave him to his thoughts.

Having taken a near-fatal blow from the spider assault, Wilberd wasn't going anywhere. So, we gathered firewood, built a fire, left him a few days' rations and another *Holocaust* potion, and then wasted no time in vacating that forest. We were reduced now to four fighters: Amabored, Lithaine, Malcolm, and me. Did we have enough fire-power to take down Redulfo, with no sorcery to aid us? To ask the question was to answer it.

Dawn bled over the horizon before we finally stopped for rest. A small, flat patch of land midway down the slope of the forested hill-side served as our campsite. Before us loomed the Valley of Sorcerers, clinging to the flanks of the Shadow Mountains and shrouded in mist. Untold men had perished assaulting that valley. Their ghosts lingered still, their wails carried by the bitter mountain winds, their souls borne by the ravens that stood in serried ranks atop the pines.

Many thousands more would die here in the next few years. Were the spirits haunting this land those of soldiers long dead, or those of soldiers yet to die? Who the hell can say?

The Valley was originally the home of Gygax the Great and his partner Rigsby, until the two arch-mages, having been bosom companions since Koschei the Deathless was still Koschei of the Verdant Vale, came to blows over an unknown dispute that nearly leveled the Shadow Mountains from the force of the sorcerous duel that commenced. After the duel, one wizard had vanished, while the other had presumably died—and no one knew for certain which was which. What argument had precipitated this divorce, no one knew—not even Sklaar, who had been among the first apprentices trained by the two wizards.

With the Workshop of Telescopes now deserted, the local Baronies made repeated attempts to march upon it and claim it for themselves—but not a single man-jack sent into the Valley ever returned alive. And so, the Valley remained deserted—until Redulfo the Black, newly resurrected by the Crimson Hand after we greased him, descended upon the Workshop and claimed it as his own. The dragon had then holed up in the valley for months, doing—what, exactly? Building an army, constructing a super-weapon, conducting research, hibernating, jerking off—who knew? We knew only that the Bad Brain was ensconced in the dragon's skull, and that the only way to get it out of said skull was to cut off Redulfo's head. Killing our friend a second time was a shit assignment, but what could we do? We were all pawns, and pawns are made to be sacrificed.

We dozed, choked down some breakfast, and then began the long descent into the mist-shrouded Valley. The mist itself was cold, tinged yellow, with a sulfurous odor betraying its sorcerous origins, and we could only tremble at the thought of the horrors it contained. Still, our path was clear and danger-free—until we found the Rockfall. That thing sure wasn't on any fucking map.

We crested a crumbling ridge, the last obstacle before we entered the Valley proper. Once over the crest, we found our way blocked by a massive chasm—a jagged axe-wound spanning the valley's width, its depth impossible to determine, its gaping maw filled with swirling mist stabbed through with sharp, rocky peaks and crumbling hillocks rising from the chasm floor. Or at least that's what we thought—until one of the hills moved. All of them moved, in fact. They weren't peaks or hillocks; they were giant rocks, boulders and shards of granite, all floating in the mist and rocking ever so slightly, like giant fishing-bobbers on a fog-bound lake. Occasionally the giant rocks and boulders collided, raining debris into the chasm below. Thanks to the mist, we had no idea if the rocks floated sixty feet above the ground, or six thousand.

"Should be simple enough to get across," Amabored said, scratching his head. "The rocks are close enough to jump from one to the next, all the way to the other side."

"Too simple," I said. "If this thing isn't a trap, then I'm a gnome's ass."

"You've got fucking wings, dipshit," Lithaine said to Amabored. "Just fly us to the other side."

"If you weren't pulling taffy instead of listening to the Ki-Rin's briefing, you'd remember that nothing magical flies in the Valley but the dragon," Amabored said. "Clean the shit out of your ears."

"Why don't you suck it out?"

Lithaine was back to normal, at least. Malcolm stepped to the lip of the chasm, where an elephant-sized rock bobbed like a cork in the mist, close enough to touch. Extending a leg, he touched the rock with his boot. The rock bobbled and twisted harmlessly in midair.

"Well lads, what do you say?" Malcolm asked, turning back to face us. "Do we belabor our next move, or do we simply charge ahead? We shan't rest until we hoist—"

5

"The cup of victory!"

Nine years earlier, Malcolm stood resolutely before us on Halberd Street. His mailed hand rested on his sword pommel. His raven hair was blown by unfelt winds. Across the plaza waited the Blue Falcon, its towers thrust into the darkening sky, its black windows harboring malevolence.

Yes, the paladin used the same words on both occasions. The two events are forever linked in my mind—initially, at least, because in both cases we were assaulting a fortified position with a suicidal lack of manpower. Thanks to Redulfo's mirrors, the two events were also literally linked together. I'm still not sure if the time loop logic holds up to scrutiny, or why the resulting paradoxes didn't collapse the universe. Best not to think too hard about these things.

We were still recovering from the shock of Malcolm's revelation. If we were to believe the paladin, then Lithaine was none other than the missing High King of Helene, chosen at birth by the Star Council as the true avatar of the Star Maiden. The council had snatched him from his natural parents, raised him as a living god, and then drilled him in the arts of elven sorcery, statecraft, and war. On his twenty-fifth birthday, they dragged him to the foot of the Tree of Illumination and set the Sapphire Crown on his head. At that moment, he became the absolute ruler of elvendom throughout the Free Kingdoms.

We were gobsmacked. This was Lithaine, remember: an elf perpetually one misfired synapse away from uncontrollable battle rage, who needed no more reason to put an arrow into your heart than not liking the cut of your jib. You may as well put a rabid weasel on the throne. On the other hand, Lithaine's will was indomitable; set him in motion, and he wouldn't stop until the job was done, or he was dead. Unlike Alexander, Lithaine wouldn't have wept when he ran out of lands to conquer; he'd simply find a reason to get pissed at his vassals and then reconquer all the lands behind him. The truth is that I loved the guy, more than I loved my own brother, and I knew he was damned sure better off on the road than on the throne.

One night, about ten years or so after he was crowned, Lithaine sat at his desk beside the White Throne, shuffling morosely through the stack of trade agreements, treaties, and bills awaiting signature. Sighing, he set down his quill. He took a brief, longing look through a palace window at the rising full moon. Then he stood. From a stash behind the throne, he retrieved a short sword, a longbow, and a supply satchel. Flipping the bird to his guards, he launched himself headlong through the glass window and into the night.

That was the last anyone in Helene saw of Lithaine; for fifteen years, the elf had wandered the Woerth in self-imposed exile. The Star Council sent their best knights questing for him. Malcolm was among these, scouring the Free Kingdoms for his missing liege, running down every rumor, turning aside at every dead end. Eventually, he became the last knight errant on a perpetual and fruitless quest to find his king, until he arrived in Redhauke, took a room, pinned his business card to the Guild bulletin board, and waited for paid sword work. By selling his services, he hoped to uncover some sign of Lithaine—and so he did.

"If you think I'm going to let up on you, then your head is so far up your ass that it's back on your shoulders," Amabored said, poking the elf in the chest. Like me, he was mostly excited by the rich, unexplored veins of comedy unearthed by this news.

"Let's get this straight," Lithaine said. "I'm no king. I never asked to be a king. Anybody who calls me a king will find himself short a head." He wheeled to face Malcolm. "That goes for you too. Call me your king again, or mention me to anyone, and I'll cut your fucking balls off."

"As I rather value my testicles, young Lithaine," said Malcolm, "You have my word that we shall not speak of it again, unless you speak it first."

"He may keep quiet, but I plan to win a lot of bar bets," I said. "We'll split the pot."

"You can say whatever you want," said Lithaine, "because nobody gives a shit what you say."

Ultimatums drawn, we found ourselves back to the task at hand. Melinda knew as much as anyone about Storm Stonegorm's haunted masterpiece, but she knew next to nothing about its defenses. Saggon, however, knew less—other than the well-trod path from his tower apartments to the larders, he never explored the place. As every door, window, crawlspace, crevice, and trapdoor within would be guarded by both sorcery and steel, the front door was as good a place to try as any.

Whatever happened, I hoped to delay wearing the Skull as long as possible. If you possessed the skull of an evil demi-god, how eager would you be to put it on your shoulders? We had no idea what it would do to me, either. Would I be incinerated? Would it give me extra health points? Plus-enchantments on my weapons or armor? Extra strength, dexterity, or endurance? Or would I have to roll a saving throw to shake a curse? We cultivated pessimism as a survival skill, and this philosophy told me that the chance of something bad happening when I donned that Skull was as certain as anything could be in a probabilistic Multiverse.

Our loins girded and our nerves more or less steeled, we paused to regard the Falcon, looming before us across Halberd Street. The stone gatehouse stood open, its darkened windows black and silent as a tomb. No guards barred entry. Perched on either side of the spiked wrought-iron gate, a pair of vultures regarded us. They chortled together, rustling their wings to herald our presence.

"Vultures?" Redulfo asked. "Seriously?"

"Saggon knows we're coming," Melinda said. She squeezed my hand. "You ready to rustle a pit devil, cowboy?"

"I've already shit my pants, so I guess I am."

"What's the worst that could happen? You get your heart ripped out by the devil and spend eternity in Hell. Big deal."

"Why don't you wear it?"

"If I could do it for you, I would."

"That's what we guys say about childbirth."

"I know."

6

W e drew steel and started across the street. The silence was deafening. The bustle and din of Redhauke life had vanished: Every street empty, every door shut, every window dark and shrouded. Overhead, the clouds roiled. Before us loomed the Blue Falcon, its tower windows now glowing from some fell light within, its black spires stabbing the sky. The building's long wings were outstretched arms, beckoning us into a fatal embrace.

"The air is thick with melodrama," Malcolm proffered, glancing around the street.

"You get used to it," I said. Even as it lay secure in a pouch lashed to my belt, I could sense the Skull leering at me. *You're its slave*, a voice told me, and I couldn't say if the voice came from inside my head, or from the Skull itself. *No shit*, I thought, *but I'm not the one riding in a pouch*. There was no fucking way I wanted to put that thing on my shoulders, not even if Koschei himself gave me a reach-around.

We arrived at the gate. The vultures watched us. Lithaine put an arrow through one. It squawked and died while the other vulture flew off, cawing in protest.

"Vultures," Redulfo said, shaking his head.

Inside the gate, the Falcon's grounds stood dark and barren. Across the cobblestoned courtyard, the stables lay silent, no sign of horse or man within. The guardhouse was deserted. Lined with unlit oil lamps, the broad stone walkway led in a wide semicircle around the statue of Arturus's Falcon to the main entrance. There, the twin iron-shod oak doors stood open.

"Fucker's thrown out the welcome mat," said Amabored. "It's all for show. He's afraid of us."

"The guy has an army of imps and a pit devil inside," I said, "and he's afraid of us?"

"He's not afraid of you," said Melinda. "He's afraid of losing the Skull when it's close at hand. Of course, he's inviting us in."

"Fear not, my good lady," Malcolm said, unsheathing his sword. "I serve at the pleasure of the Star Maiden whose shield protects the servants of *logos*."

"That and a copper will get you a hand job down at the Pit," I said.

The courtyard around us exploded, as giant geysers of stone and earth burst in a chain reaction like ripe blackheads. Shards of cobblestone and clods of dirt rained down on us. We threw up our shields to absorb the blows. The clearing dust revealed rows of coffins, thrust up from the earth in crooked ranks. From each coffin emerged a raging, frothing zombie—arms outstretched, clawed fingers grasping, eyes devoid of pupil, pale gray corpse-flesh glistening with grave-sweat.

There were two hundred of them, at least. It might have ended there—but Malcolm, Paladin Knight of the White Rose, was on the case.

"Stand back!" He cried, raising sword and shield as he faced the zombie horde. "Turn aside, foul denizens, or perish in the Void!"

The white rose emblazoned on Malcolm's shield glowed blindingly, until it launched forth a massive spectral assault. Lances of multi-hued light mowed through the zombies as a scythe mows through meadow grass. Two-thirds fell cleft in twain or thirds. Those closest to us were consumed by the holy light and melted away screaming. Within a minute, we were once again alone in the court-yard coated in dust and picking our way through the rubble.

"That's a hell of a trick," said Amabored to the paladin. "Can you do it again?"

"Not today," said Malcolm as he wiped the dust from his paul-drons. "I've spent my seed, so to speak. Just as well—it's impressive, but not nearly as enjoyable as sword work. Shall we step inside and see what else there is to slay?"

"I'm warming up to that guy," Amabored said to Lithaine as we headed for the door. "He looks a hell of a lot more like a king than you do. How did you come into your crown? You won a sweepstakes?"

"If we make it out of this place alive," said Lithaine, "I'm going to kill you."

"Get in line."

7

Our plan, such as it was, would now be executed by three teams. Melinda and I would enter the catacombs below the Falcon; she would taunt the devil while I found the children, freed them, donned the Skull, shoved the devil into the Hellmouth and tossed the Skull into Hell with him. Meanwhile, Amabored and Lithaine would ascend Saggon's tower, find that fat fuck, and cut off his head. That left Malcolm and Redulfo to fight a rearguard action to thwart any attempt to trap us inside.

It was a dumb, dangerous plan reeking of failure. Our only comfort lay in knowing that Saggon faced his own challenge: He wanted the Skull, and he could get it only by taking it from my twitching corpse. Would the Skull infuse me with enough power to take on both the devil and whatever else Saggon sent after me? To find out, I planned to wait as long as I possibly could.

On any other day, Saggon would have planted enough soldiers inside the Falcon to kill us before we got one toe past the threshold. On this day, we stepped unmolested into the Grand Foyer: an opulent, decaying space of vaulted ceilings festooned with shadows, with winding staircases of polished marble and lacquered mahogany that led up or down into the vast interior labyrinth. Dozens of doors led hither and yon. Faded oil paintings hung forlorn, dusty statuary pondered us from recessed displays, and massive tapestries draped rotten with neglect. On a normal day, the Foyer teemed with visiting supplicants, appointment-seekers, job hunters, beggars, whores, and public officials seeking Saggon's favor. This evening, it was empty and silent. Only dim torchlight flickering from the wall sconces kept the foyer from darkness. Normally drafty, the room seemed unusually cold—colder even than the cool spring air outside—and our breath bloomed in ghostly clouds before us. We spread out with weapons drawn.

"How disappointing," said Malcolm. "One expects a welcoming committee. Shall we march in and free those children, then? We may still have time for a late—"

The paladin's quip died in his throat, as the high shadow-draped ceiling erupted in hellish shrieks, and an army of imps rained down upon us. Not garden-variety imps, either, the kind we had slain by the hundreds during our adventuring careers—these were Ur-imps, bred in the forsaken pits of Malebolge to serve as cannon fodder in Hell's armies. Driven by torment, their souls burn with no desire other than to die gloriously in battle. Their size ranges from dwarf to troll, their color from green to black to red. Their flesh they carve deep with spells formed from Hell-runes; their extremities they self-mutilate with piercings, insertions, and ritual debasements. Splintered horns curve from their skulls, cloven hooves depend from their cat-jointed legs, and their barbed tails lash out like bull whips.

In short, they looked like any gang of youths you'd see lounging around Redhauke on a Friday night. Black venom flying from their forked tongues, they fell upon us.

We learned soon enough that their hides were impervious to steel —the shock of my blade caroming off an imp's thick skin nearly dislocated my shoulder. Neither Amabored nor Malcolm fared better. Lithaine shot a few arrows into a few eye sockets, while Melinda scored with a dagger to an open maw, but we were only playing defense. The imps rained blows upon us, until we fell back toward the front door.

"Uh-oh," Amabored called out. "I gotta take a shit."

"Now?" I cried.

"Yeah, now. Have to move some merchandise."

"I told you to lay off the burritos, dumb-ass," said Lithaine, as he loosed an arrow.

"Sorry boys. Back in a flash." Amabored fell back, then sprinted down a nearby hallway.

"I'll cover you," cried Redulfo. He blew a short run of notes on his flute, holstered the instrument, and stretched out his hands. Out of the aether, a weapon materialized—a trigger-fired, barreled contraption with a wooden grip and stock and a round magazine. Stepping forward, the wizard squeezed the trigger, and slugs of hot lead leapt from the barrel. The imps squealed as the slugs penetrated their hellish hides—a most pleasant sound indeed. Black, brackish blood flew from their wounds. Those that died exploded in jets of hellfire that set the tapestries ablaze.

That got their attention. The imps fell back to regroup, which gave us our opening. Lithaine emptied half his quiver into the horde, gave us a nod, and then fell back down the hallway after Amabored. That meant Saggon was dead meat.

Melinda grabbed my hand. "Now!" She said, pointing to a nearby descending staircase. I nodded. Redulfo was busy mowing down imps, so we threw thumbs up to Malcolm.

"Godspeed!" the paladin called to us. "Remember, we shan't rest until we hoist—"

8

"The cup of victory!"

Nine years later, Malcolm finished his oath, stepped fully onto the massive floating island of rock upon which his boot had been resting, and disappeared. An echoing crack of thunder accompanied his vanishment as air rushed to fill the vacuum.

"Holy smoking shit!" I cried.

"Is he dead?" Amabored wondered.

"Only one way to find out," Lithaine said, and leapt onto the boulder. Another loud crack, and he vanished.

"Fucking hell," Amabored said to me, after a few seconds had passed. "That cocksucking elf always narrows our choices down to one. Shall we?"

"It's either follow them or go home," I said, gripping my axe-haft in my gloved hands. "After you, cupcake."

"Eat my ass, fuckface," Amabored said, grinning. Then he, too, leapt onto the boulder and was gone.

That left me. I didn't consider turning around, despite what you may think. Okay, maybe for a second, I did. But I jumped all the same.

There was no sensation involved, no dematerialization or deconstruction—I simply left my universe and appeared in another one. I stood now in a vast orange desert. Rippled dunes like the scales of some long-dead würm stretched in every direction. A burning wind clawed at my flesh and licked my face like tongues of flame. The sky was purple and violent, with bruised clouds skidding toward the horizon. The light was low, diffused and ominous; somewhere behind my back, a sun might have recently set.

I searched for my companions. Then came Amabored's frantic cry: "DUCK!"

I was tackled from behind, my face plowing into alien orange sand. I rolled over, sputtering, to find Amabored rolling off to my side. Above my head, what looked like a giant winged scorpion soared past—about the length of three men, constructed of armored bone segments, with claws the size of ponies and mandibles big enough to snap your neck like a chicken bone. It swooped upward, shrieking with rage, its stinger-shod tail missing my nose by an inch. Three more of the creatures followed in formation behind. As they sailed past, Amabored pulled me to my feet.

"Where the hell are we?" I asked.

"Somewhere else," the barbarian answered.

"Ho, gents! This way!" came Malcolm's voice, from somewhere nearby. We found him about thirty chains away. He was pointing at a more distant object, a rectangular shape thrust up cockeyed from a tall sand dune.

"What is it?" Amabored shouted above the wind.

"Perhaps a way back!" Malcolm called.

"Fore!" came Lithaine's voice. The scorpion squadron had banked back around and was now bearing down on us with stingers locked and loaded. Lithaine stood a short distance away with his bow cocked. We hit the dirt, and the elf let fly three arrows with Oswaldian speed and accuracy. They clattered harmlessly off the scorpions' armored plating. Two of the monsters peeled off formation and flew towards Lithaine, their wings beating the air like war drums.

"Oh shit!" he cried, and took off running, plowing through the dunes toward Malcolm.

We all raced toward the paladin. He stood with legs splayed, blade at the ready, as the other two scorpions barrel-rolled over our heads and rocketed toward him. He managed one swing before they were upon him. One of the beasts snared him in its barbed crab-claws and carried him off into the sky.

"Goddamn it!" Amabored snarled. "There goes our paladin."

The barbarian spoke too soon. We saw only a frenzy of blurred motion as Malcolm battled the beast in midair. There came a horrid, cawing shriek, and the thing plummeted straight for the ground with Malcolm's sword wedged between its armored plating. As its body convulsed, the paladin planted his boots on its underbelly, grabbed his sword hilt, and yanked hard. Beast and elf flew apart. The scorpion crashed in a clattering heap with its green blood spraying out in a glorious money shot. Malcolm hit the ground rolling, performed a double-somersault, and vaulted to his feet with sword in hand.

"Fuck, yes, that's how you do it!" I shouted, pumping a fist in the air.

Lithaine kept running, blowing right past Malcolm and barreling toward the paladin's distant rectangle. Cawing angrily for their dead brother, the three remaining scorpions flew in a wide ascending arc. Malcolm had scared them off—but not for long.

"Now, lads, while our luck holds!" The paladin called. He ran after Lithaine, and we ran after him.

We gathered together at the rectangular object. It was a mirror, as it turned out: man-high and man-wide, with a simple frame of porous gray stone. The mirrored surface, polished to a high gloss, threw fear and uncertainty back in our faces.

"Convention would dictate that this is—" said Malcolm.

"—a portal," finished Amabored.

"A portal to where?" I asked.

"Only one way to find out," Lithaine said. He flung himself head-first at the mirror. His body melted into the glass, from head to booted feet, until he vanished.

"Has he ever once stopped to consider the consequences of his actions?" I asked Malcolm.

"Not in my experience," said Malcolm, sheathing his sword. "Shall we?"

We stepped through the glass in turn and vanished forever from the desert world. Only a single dead beast remained to tell that we had ever been there at all. What effect its death would have on that world, we couldn't say.

9

We appeared back on the same rock from which we had vanished, the floating boulder now bobbing precipitously under our feet. We clung to it and waited for it to steady. After a long moment, we stood warily. The vast, mist-filled crevasse lay yawning open, two hundred chains wide, filled with floating mountains, hillocks, boulders and rocks. Somewhere on the other side of that crevasse, Redulfo waited. It would be easy for him to sally forth from the Workshop and swoop down upon us—so why didn't he?

"He's chickenshit," said Amabored.

"It's more than that," I said. "He thinks this is all part of some clockwork motion of the universe that none of us can alter. If he thought attacking us now would change the outcome, he'd do it. He knows that we're meant to confront him."

"Why attack us with bugbears and spiders?" asked Malcolm. "Why not invite us in through the front door?"

"We lost two men in those fights. Maybe we were supposed to."

"Spare us the dime-store metaphysics," said Lithaine. "Let's go kill that fucking dragon."

I pointed to the closest boulder, about the size of a small keep, floating a few feet away. "Your move," I said to Lithaine.

The elf allowed a smile. He took a few running steps, leapt the short distance across to the next boulder, and vanished with another loud crack.

"You don't suppose this next world will be populated by naked serving wenches and covered in oceans of beer, do you?" I asked.

"Not a chance," said Amabored, and made the leap.

10

You may rest assured that the next world was even more heinous than the last. So it went: With each step across the chasm, we entered another universe. Each time, we fought for our lives to reach the exit portal and return to our own world. Sometimes, the portal was nearby; other times, we traversed vast stretches of jungle, climbed mountain ranges, or sailed across churning seas to reach it. The shit that went down in these places could fill another book. We were often separated and forced to undertake solo quests; during this time, I was enslaved as a galley oarsman, appointed a queen's champion, briefly ruled a small mountain kingdom, captained a pirate galley, and lived the same day over and again for about six years until I achieved enlightenment. Finally, I'd find the exit-mirror and return to my own world, precisely when I left it.

These are tales for another time. If Redulfo hoped for our deaths in one of these other universes, then that was bad luck for him. In fact, the plan backfired—thanks to the amount of ass we kicked, we all went up a level. As Redulfo certainly foresaw this outcome, he must have wanted it this way. Or rather, he knew it was supposed to happen this way. To Redulfo, absolutely nothing could happen that hadn't been preordained since the birth of the Multiverse; only morbid curiosity got him out of bed in the morning. Fate preordained or not, when we finally reached the opposite edge of the chasm and began our descent into the valley, we were ready.

REDULFO'S UNSHAKEABLE DETERMINISM USED TO DRIVE CASSIE INSANE —especially when the rest of us used him as cover, like we did when, five years before we killed Redulfo the Black, she told us about the latest appearance of Jo Ki-Rin. Even as Plague Knights marched on the city, we hid behind the wizard's skirt. Okay, so we were supposed to save the world—but what was the hurry?

"You have to move. Now!" Cassie told us. We stood on the battlements atop the Butcher's Wall. Before us on the plain outside the city walls marched, to the ear-destroying heavy metal conjured by Eckberd's war-bards, an army of ten thousand or more: mounted Plague Knights, Chaos dwarfs, war-ghouls, battle-trolls, a dozen imp tribes hoisting high their garish banners, great horned beasts pulling massive siege engines, iron-shod battering rams carved deep with fell runes, gargantuan catapults loaded with brimstone to rain fire upon the free city. Soon they would lay siege to Redhauke—and, if the siege broke, the Chaos army would rape the city's women and put its men to the sword. Unless the city fathers gave us up, that is. Or more specifically, gave me up.

Until that moment, I had managed to keep Cassie inside a hermetically sealed bubble built by my deceit. I only saw her alone; my crew knew nothing of her existence. Melinda was entrenched in my old life, which had become torture to me, and therefore torture to her. Of my new life, Cassie was the sole occupant. It was a universe made only for we two; slipping into it made me feel like the man I was always meant to be. These two worlds were matter and anti-matter, headed for a cataclysm of my own design.

Now, Cassie stood before my mates, who regarded her with bald suspicion. She had just recounted a tale we could scarcely believe— Jo Ki-Rin appearing before her, blowing her mind in that black-light-poster way of his as he revealed the ten Phylaxes to her and proclaimed that the fate of the Woerth rested in the hands of my friends and me. Other than for its comedic potential, my mates didn't give two shits about me keeping a woman on the side. But who the fuck was this blonde chick telling them to get off their asses and save the world?

"So, you drank too much temple wine and hallucinated the apocalypse," said Amabored. "How is that our problem?"

Forty years later, Amabored would hallucinate his own apocalypse and start crucifying wizards. The interesting thing about irony is that it also works in reverse. Just to be an asshole, he also failed to mention that he had first heard of Phylaxes and quests when he encountered the dark elf Hamara on the steps leading to Saggon's lair, four years earlier. Had he forgotten? Not a chance.

"It wasn't a hallucination," I said. "I saw the Ki-Rin, too. Twice I saw that pain in the ass."

"Once after drinking a Flaming Telepath, and once after nearly dying," Amabored said.

"The Ki-Rin gave me the choice to die, or to do what needs to be done. And now the bill has come due. I believe her."

"Of course, you'd say that. You're fucking her."

"I'm not fucking her!"

Cassie, Odin bless her, got up immediately into Amabored's grill, even though he towered over her by a foot. "Listen, asshole," she said, "I don't give a fuck what kind of shit-eating persona you've constructed for yourself. You can kiss my ass. But that army out there will raze this city to the ground if the city fathers don't give you up. What do you think they're going to do, genius?"

Amabored only grinned. It was Redulfo who answered. "Nothing," said the wizard. "At least, not for a while. With Sklaar manning the defenses, the walls will stand against anything they can throw at us."

"And the Mayor owes us for that lemming imp business," said Amabored. "He told us they'd contact us with our next move. Why shouldn't we hold tight?"

"An army ten thousand strong approaches," said Cassie, "and you think the Mayor or Sklaar give one holy fuck about what they owe you?"

"Premature action vastly increases the number of universes branching off from ours," Redulfo said. "It increases our possible futures, in many of which we fail. Success becomes probable only when our path becomes constrained—when we have no other choice. In this case, procrastination is a virtue."

"Your path is already constrained, you dumbfuck. What choice do you have now?"

"Time out," I said. "Look, I'm all for bold action, but stepping outside these walls now is suicide." I turned to Lithaine. "What do you think, elf?"

"You don't want to know what I think."

"We don't need to think," said Amabored. "We can protect the Phylaxes here until Sklaar helps us figure out how to get rid of them. Fuck finding all ten of them. Let Sklaar deal with it. He's a Fifteenth-Level wizard, for crying out loud. He's supposed to be saving the world, not us."

The barbarian motioned to Sklaar's tower, thrust up near the Stranger's Wall far above the vast sea of rooftops. At that moment, the entire top of the tower exploded in a thunderous gout of rubble, smoke, and flame. A half-second later, we heard the boom of the explosion, followed by screams as the avalanche of debris rained down onto the school campus. We all stared horrified at the spot on the skyline where Sklaar's tower had stood.

Cassie turned to Amabored. "You were saying?"

11

In heroic adventure, as in everything else, it's the women who make the hard choices. Men take the easy way out. Oh, we'll advance civilization, launch wars, and build pyramids, if there are chicks involved. Give us a chance to keep our asses glued to the couch, however, and we'll take it every time. Only a woman's scorn can spur most of us into action.

IT WAS MELINDA, FOR INSTANCE, WHO KEPT ME ON POINT BENEATH THE Blue Falcon. Four years earlier, she and I raced down rough-hewn steps leading to the bowels of the inn. The stairs dropped us into a long stone hallway lit by capering torch flames. Iron-shod wooden doors lined either side of the hallway as far as we could see, until the hall shrank to a dark vanishing point. It was impossibly long, a funhouse hallway. It could lead to nowhere, we thought, or it could lead to Hell.

"Any idea where we're going?" I whispered to Melinda. It seemed dangerous to speak aloud.

"Not exactly." She squeezed my hand. "We have to keep going down."

We pushed on. The farther down the hall we ran, the longer it became, leaping away from us like a dark gazelle. We ran for a good fifteen minutes, and still we found no end to it. There were no turns or tributaries—just doors. Hundreds of doors. We ran until we felt stupid for running. Then we stopped, panting like sheepdogs.

"The Falcon is working against us," Melinda said. "It doesn't want us to succeed."

"For fuck's sake, it's just a building," I said. "It's wood and stone. I'm packing the strength of a goddamned stone giant. There isn't a door or a wall here that I can't get through. Hear me, you fucking mule barn?" I shouted to the walls.

"Give it a rest." Melinda glanced around. "Let's start trying doors."

I stepped before one of the oak doors and pulled the iron ring bolted to it. The door swung in abruptly, yanking me forward. My boots dragged across the threshold—and found nothing beneath them but a black abyss. I plummeted. Blessed instinct kept my hand gripping the ring, which became my new best friend, and the force of the fall nearly pulled my arm from the socket. Thank every god in the Multiverse for that girdle.

"Odin's balls!" I cried.

Below my feet and two million light years away, a spiral galaxy turned in a bed of stardust. The deep immensity of the universe lay beneath me. If I let go of the door, that galaxy was my next stop.

"Throw up your sword!" Melinda shouted. I hadn't realized I was still holding it. I tossed it up. Melinda fed a thin line of elvish rope through the door ring and dropped the end down to me. With my free hand, I pulled the line through the girdle and knotted it tight. She ran to a door across the hall, fed the other end of the rope through that door's ring, and then lashed it to my blade. Within a minute, she was hauling me back up with a makeshift pulley. The rope dragged me across the threshold. We slammed the door shut again and fell panting to the floor.

"It's hopeless," Melinda said. "I'm not even sure we can go back the way we came."

"Not so fast," I said, pointing. Farther down the hall, a dark-haired girl in a white dress stood near an open door. She glowed palely, as if spun from moonlight, the doorframe visible through her translucent body. She motioned to us to follow her. I glanced at Melinda. "Should we?" I asked.

"I don't have a better idea," Melinda said.

The girl disappeared through the door. We ran after her, and in a minute were through the door and charging down another rough-hewn stone hallway that sloped downwards at a fast clip. There was no sign of the apparition.

We paused to take stock. "We'll see her again, I wager," Melinda said. She noticed the look in my eyes. "You've seen her before?"

"No," I said. "But I think Lithaine did. She must be the one who told him about the kids down here, when she appeared to him in Doomtown."

"Then she's on our side. Let's go."

We raced on. The slope sharpened, until we struggled not to remain upright. When we stopped to shore up our balance, the floor itself lurched forward. We toppled over and bounced down the hallway like a couple of drunken hedgehogs. With nothing to stop our fall, we continued thus until we finally fell, bruised and battered, into a deep stone pit.

We sat up, took stock of our injuries, and collected our wits. A mass of hard, brittle, splintered sticks had broken our fall. We didn't need the dim light from the torches far above to know that we had fallen onto a towering pile of bones.

"Jesus, is that girl trying to kill us?" I asked, reaching for Melinda's hand. Her lip was bloody, her legs bruised and scraped through her torn breaches. I had a gash on my forehead and a bloody knee. Holding hands, we waded down through the musty, clattering fall of skulls, ribcages, and thigh bones until we reached the bottom of the pit. As far as we could tell, we were alone.

"Where do you suppose that tunnel leads?" Melinda asked, pointing behind me, where a rough, man-high tube snaked away into the bedrock.

"Nowhere good," I said. "I want to know what cleaned the meat from these bones." I picked up a shin bone and examined it. "Some of them are still fresh."

Then a ghastly, deafening shriek shredded the air. Lurid red light, faint but gathering in strength, filled the tunnel. The stench of brimstone wafted from it. From deep within the rock tube came a loud, sickening burble, as of brackish oil bubbling in a pit. Some pale beast burning with Hellfire slouched through the tunnel towards us. The girl had led us into a trap.

Melinda squeezed my arm, hard. "Wear the Skull," she said. "It's time."

"No reason to be hasty," I said. "Maybe we can kill it, whatever it is."

"We'll die if you don't put it on. You know it as well as I."

So, here it was—my date with destiny. What would Redulfo say, four years anon, about success becoming probable only when success is your last option? This was as tight a fucking spot as he could hope for. We had to keep swimming or drown.

I took the Screaming Skull from its pouch. As I detached it from its chain, it grinned at me. As I brought it up to my face, it radiated malicious glee. In the black hollows of its eye sockets lay hidden my secret shame, those cold thoughts of humiliation that crept through my mind on little cat-feet in the dark hours of the night. Even as the Skull lusted for me, even as it feared me, still it mocked me. It dared me to be anything other than the wretched failure of a man I was.

Something hard within me still, some nugget of self-esteem buried deep inside, kept me from going down the rabbit hole. *Fuck it,* I thought.

As I brought the Screaming Skull toward my face, the black chasms of its eye sockets filled my vision. Then I fell, plummeting into that darkness in free fall, losing myself. Had the Skull cast me into the Void? Would my mind wander, untethered from time and space, for eternity? Was this the Ki-Rin's plan all along? Was it Saggon's?

After what seemed an Age, I beheld an atom of light in the darkness. It grew in my vision until it became a cold emerald flame, capering in the darkness. That flame was my goal. I came to it, or it came to me. It grew brighter and yet colder, until my soul lay exposed and frozen before it, until I merged with it. My soul and that flame were united, and I became one with the Deathless.

12

Earlier, on the Falcon's ground floor, Amabored emerged from the shitter to find Lithaine waiting for him. I know this because I've combined the *Remembrance* potions with long sojourns gazing into the Astral Telescope. Through it, I've explored the nooks and crannies of this story to make certain that I'm doing right by killing my friends in nine days. Thanks to Redulfo the Black, I now believe in chance—and I dare leave nothing to it.

"Proud of yourself?" Lithaine asked. Back down the hallway, the ricochets from Redulfo's sorcerous machine gun rattled and jumped.

"It was an emotional shit," said Amabored. "It changed me, like Saul on the road to Damascus. You want to see it?"

"If you're done admiring yourself, then let's go grease that fat fuck."

"Lead the way, sweetheart."

Down the dark, deserted hallway they jogged, until they entered the Great Hall with weapons drawn—but the vast ballroom was deserted. Upon the long oak tables lay the detritus of a recent feast: dirty plates piled high, half-eaten haunches of meat flung across platters, half-drunk flagons of ale standing at attention. In the fire pits, the coals still smoldered. Normally toasty from the combined heat of the half-dozen great fireplaces lining the walls, the hall was even colder than the Grand Foyer.

"Stay squirrelly," Amabored said. "We won't get into that tower without a fight."

"That's some astute analysis."

"Lick my balls, magic boy."

"Put 'em on the table."

Banter thus exchanged, the two men crept toward the far end of the hall, where the entrance to Saggon's Tower lurked. Though they expected imps or worse to bound around every column or burst through every door, they encountered nothing. When they reached the iron-banded double doors that led to the tower, they found them standing open. The ogre doorman was gone. Through the doors, darkness beckoned.

"Why hasn't he thrown more shit at us?" asked Amabored.

"Maybe he's not here," said Lithaine.

"He's here. This is a showdown, and he knows it. Up the stairs, then."

Amabored thrust a torch into the coals and got it going. Thus, they started up the twisting stone staircase that wound up the tower to Saggon's lair: Lithaine in front with bow locked and loaded; Amabored behind, guarding their six. Each time they passed an unlit torch, Amabored lit it with his own brand. Soon, nervous torchlight flung restless shadows against the walls. Now even colder than below, the air clung to their skin like wet leather.

Barbarian and elf crept upward, their silence complete. When they rounded a curve in the staircase three stories up, they saw the first set of eyes: red, slitted, harboring malice. Then came the growl. Something hulking and inhuman lurked ahead.

That something vaulted over the steps, its hulking silhouette filling their frame of vision. Lithaine put three arrows into it before it hit them. It struck the elf at full force, throwing him back into the barbarian, and the three of them rolled down the steps. The creature twisted around and attacked Lithaine with jaws snapping. Hot spittle lashed the elf's face.

Then the beast's head was jerked back. Amabored's blade flashed. The head sheared away from the torso in a fabulous spray of black blood.

It was a wolf's head: its jaws locked in a snarl, its double row of fangs dripping saliva. The torso was humanoid, covered in a thick gray-brown fur. Amabored kicked over the corpse.

"A fucking werewolf!" the barbarian said. He tossed the head down the staircase.

They had no time to ponder this news, for at that moment an entire pack of werewolves leapt around the curved walls. These were no puppy-dogs, either. They were 'roided-out nightmares: teeth like saw blades, claws like iron hooks, muscles like pythons roped around their limbs. Before he even knew what hit him, Lithaine took a bite in the arm that tore flesh from bone. His bow clattered to the steps.

Behind him, Amabored split the skull of a werewolf, splattering the walls with blood and brains. If you've never split a skull with sword or axe, you should seek out the opportunity. I've split the skulls of men and beasts; of Chaos dwarfs, shadow elves, and red gnomes; of zombies, animated skeletons, ghasts and ghouls; of plague knights, harvesters, and crimson monks; of kobolds, goblins, trolls, and giants. Pretty much everything that has a skull, I've split it in twain at one point or another, and it never gets old. Ten years at least have passed since my axe last tasted blood and brains, and with each passing year I grow farther from myself. When I wander over to my trophy hall and grip the haft of my trusty Rod of Lordly Might, the feeling is strange, as if my hands and my axe haft are magnets of opposite polarity. That's why this *Remembrance* potion is so dangerous. When you have the choice of reliving those golden yesterdays, when your youth burned as brightly as a comet romancing the sun, or of wandering through the bleak present, bereft of even the faintest starlight—who wouldn't choose the past? Even as Amabored's sword blade crashes through that werewolf's skull, so long ago and far away on the vast wheel of time, I feel what he felt. We are one.

"COOOOORRRNN-HOOOOLE!" the barbarian cried, as the dead monster fell away from him. Then the wave of beasts crashed down upon them.

13

For an hour on that staircase, they fought for their lives. Sometimes they gained ground, and sometimes they gave it back. They killed dozens of the shapeshifters, until their corpses clogged the steps, and the remaining werewolves were forced to tear through their own dead to reach their prey. Still more came. The stairs grew so slick with blood and gore that the two men were forced to fight from their knees.

It wasn't often that we lost serious health points; the dirty secret of the adventuring trade is that it really isn't all that difficult. For the most part, you don't meet anything you can't handle. If you do, it's pretty easy to just run like hell. Those dungeon traps, meanwhile, aren't exactly designed by diabolical geniuses. Adventuring is easy money, though you'll never hear an adventurer say it. Yeah, we lost a lot of clerics; we lost them at the rate of rock 'n roll drummers. And Malcolm, we lost him. And Redulfo. And Bellasa. And my father and brother. And, finally, Cassie. For the most part, though, it was the tits.

The assault on the Blue Falcon was one of the bad nights. On the staircase, blood mingled with sweat to drip into the eyes of our heroes. A werewolf broke through Lithaine's frantic sword work and buried its fangs in his throat. The elf dropped like a gnome at an eleventy-first birthday party.

Amabored drove his sword into the beast's heart—and a dozen more rounded the corner. The barbarian knew he had come to it. He might slay one or two more, but the rest would gut him. And since he was alone, unaware that decades later I would be watching him at this very moment, I get to see him face death. As far as I know, there's been no moment in Amabored's life that he's failed to find ridiculous —not even this one. And I'm happy to report that, at the moment of his impending demise, the fucker laughed.

Then salvation came, as it always does, from out of the blue. Suddenly, leaping blades of violet light arced past Amabored's head to smite the werewolves. Eldritch sorcery engulfed the beasts, and a raging firestorm turned them into bone and ash. Those not incinerated bounded down the staircase with their tails between their legs, presumably to hide somewhere until dawn.

The savior was Saggon's secretary: the shadow elf who ignored us whenever we ascended the tower to report to the Over-Boss. Racing down the staircase toward the two men, she was dressed for battle with a tight leather cuirass bound to her torso and twin hand-crossbows holstered on her broad hips. She also carried a harp—she was a war bard like Lindar, which meant she could chop off your head or fry you with sorcery, depending on her mood. She kind of terrified me.

Ignoring the barbarian, she leapt over him to the dying Lithaine. As the elf's life spilled from his savaged throat, she pulled his head into her lap, uncorked a potion, and poured the liquid over his wound. Then she plucked a mournful melody on her harp, her voice filling the tower with melancholy. Lithaine's throat glowed neon blue. When his wound was closed, she poured another potion into his mouth. Then she turned her attention to Amabored.

"It was stupid to attack this place without a priest," she said. Her skin was the deep blue of dusk, her eyes like violet nebulae.

"That may be true," said Amabored. "But what we lack in brains, we make up for with recklessness. Why are you helping us? Aren't you Saggon's girl?"

"I'm nobody's girl. And that isn't Saggon upstairs."

"Then who is it?"

"Something else."

"But you don't know what else."

"No. But it's something worse than Saggon, I can assure you."

"Thanks for the tip. But you still haven't said why you helped us."

The dark elf stood, slinging her harp back over her shoulder. "Because we are the Watchers," she said.

"The Watchers?"

"The *Tarkailya*. We are tasked with guarding the Phylaxes and ensuring that the Quest succeeds. So it has always been."

"Quest? What Quest?"

"It is seldom useful to ask questions until you know what questions to ask, barbarian," said the dark elf. "Merely thank me, and trust that all will become clear."

"Okay. Thanks it is, then," said Amabored. He kicked a dismembered were-corpse out of the way, sat down, took out his flask and offered it to the dark elf. She declined. He shrugged and drank deeply himself. His hand was shaking.

"You were afraid for him," the dark elf said, her voice softening.

"I was." He drank again.

"You love him, then."

"It's the other way around—he yearns for me tragically. If he was awake, he'd say so himself."

"No doubt." The elf made a pillow of Lithaine's cloak and laid his head upon it. Then she stood. Amabored stood with her. She smiled, and you might guess that Amabored felt a stirring in his loins. She motioned back up the steps. "The thing that is not Saggon awaits. Send it to the Void."

"My Lady Watcher, on that you have my word," Amabored said, drawing a sword-cloth from his pack to clean the gore from his blade. "At least tell me your name."

"My villa overlooks the Sunless Sea in the great city of Night," she said. "If you find me there, I'll tell you my name." She turned and leapt down the staircase, disappearing into the darkness.

14

In the Grand Foyer, the imps had regrouped. Malcolm and Redulfo gave ground slowly, the paladin parrying scimitar blows with sword and shield while the wizard laid waste with his sorcerous Tommy gun. Imps leaped at them by the dozens. Finally, the spectral weapon grew so hot in Redulfo's hands that he cried out in battle rage. The spell finally ignited in his hands, and he was forced to banish the weapon back into the aether.

"I'm out!" The wizard cried.

"Fall back—up the steps!" said the paladin. The two men raced up the nearest marble staircase. Along the way, they flung over statuary, broke vases, and ripped down tapestries—anything to slow down the onrushing hoard of hellspawn.

At the top of the staircase, Malcolm planted his feet wide, set his shield, and gripped his sword pommel. His raven hair was blown by unseen winds. His jaw jutted at an impeccable angle. He looked damned good, despite the imminent peril, and I'm not too uptight to admit it. The paladin could have had any woman in the Free Kingdoms, but he had taken the vow of the Star Maiden and thus committed himself to celibacy. That is, until the Empress Wilomina got her hands on him and started working his joint like a squeezebox.

Pledging your life to the Star Maiden did, however, have its advantages. As the imps scrambled up the staircase, their forked tongues lolling, the paladin drew his sword and raised the pommel to his heart. A prayer formed on his lips.

"Star Maiden, thou art blessed above all mothers in the universe," began the paladin. His eyes were closed, and a veneer of calm lay upon his face. "Thy raiment of stardust is my armor. Thy loving gaze is my shield. Thy laughter is my blade. Bless my steel, oh Lady of *logos*, that I might rid the Woerth of this filth."

It was just as Wilberd would spell it out to me, four years later: Call on your deity once per battle, and there's a five percent chance the god will answer your prayer. Malcolm rolled the proverbial pair of percentile dice—and the fucker rolled a five. Opening his eyes, he found his blade glowing. The light swelled brighter, until the sword shimmered in a luminous scabbard of silver light.

"Not bad," Redulfo said. "You're a true believer. That's rare."

"I place my faith in the Maiden, 'tis true," said Malcolm. He assumed his batting stance, sword cocked high over his shoulder. "And she places her faith in my steel."

"As do I," said Redulfo. "Hold them here. Saggon must have a stash of enchanted weapons around somewhere. I'll find something that can bring the heat, and then meet you back."

"Not a single hellspawn shall pass this staircase."

Redulfo saluted and tore away down the long balcony. The first imps reached Malcolm. His blade a blue comet, the paladin swung. Two imp heads popped free from their bodies and bounced away down the steps. Torrents of black blood geysered from their severed necks.

"Blessed be the Maiden," said Malcolm, and went to work.

15

I see Redulfo, speeding down the hallway. He's impossibly young; it's hard now to believe that any of us were ever that young. Spectacles perched on his nose, pointed chin thrust forward, his gait driven by frantic purpose, the wizard clutches his flute in one hand and carries a torch in the other. He's listening for the music, for all enchantments sing to those who can hear.

It all happened over forty years ago. Memory is water; it ebbs and flows, flooding your brain with emotions long submerged, sweeping you along its currents, until its branches evaporate, and what was once as vivid as a thunderstorm becomes as barren as a drought-parched stream bed. It was long ago; thanks to the Astral Telescope, it is also now. Time is my bitch.

FOR ALL HIS FAULTS, JASPIN WAS AN ABLE PHILOSOPHER; I often wondered how he seemed to know so much, given his humble origins as the son of shopkeepers in Hardcastle. He once described time to me as akin to the grooves on a record album—and once he explained to me what a record album was, I kind of got it. Like the grooves on a record, all time exists at once: From the distant past to the far future, the path of time is already recorded. Looking down on the record, you can see the entire stream of time in whole. Most of us, however, experience time as the needle: bouncing along the peaks and valleys of the groove, moving ever forward, with the future stretched out before us as the past recedes behind.

Time travel merely allows you to pick up the needle and drop it on another part of the record. For the most part, you don't have to worry about negating your own existence by going back in time and killing your grandfather, because your birth and his death are happening at the same instant. Concepts such as past, present and future are meaningless—human conceits necessary for us to process the universe, nothing more. Everything that has ever happened, or ever will happen, is happening now.

"Stare at the night sky," said Jaspin, as we sat smoking pipes on the back porch of the Suds 'N Shade. He thrust the stem of his pipe up at the starry canopy over Redhauke. Around us the city lay dreaming, oblivious to the dance of creation whirling over their heads—the dance that begins in the First Universe, where the Machine Elves perform their merry jig. "You're staring into the past. That star, the bright blue one, is a dozen light-years away. That means its light left the star a dozen years ago. You're seeing it as it looked then. And yet, there it is, right in front of you. The past exists now—you can see it. If your arms were long enough, you could touch it."

"That's the Eternalist view," said Melinda. "What about entropy? What about the Second Law of Thermodynamics? Doesn't that prove the arrow of time is real?"

"If your understanding is limited to a single universe, then perhaps," said Jaspin. "But all you're saying is that entropy occupies a specific region of spacetime, which we perceive as 'the future.' Entropy exists simultaneously with non-entropy. If you know the way, you can journey through entropy in reverse."

"And don't forget about probability," said Redulfo. "According to quantum theory, only the act of observing something makes it real. You can say that all time exists all at once, but it's equally true to say that it doesn't exist at all—at least, not until we observe it. Until then, everything is probability."

"If only the act of observing something makes it real," I said, already sensing the headache that inevitably followed one of these conversations, "What happens if there's no observer?"

"Now you're getting to it," said Redulfo. "If there were no life in the Multiverse, would the Multiverse exist? I say no. If anything outside our sphere of observation exists only as probability, then that goes for time as well. The past is no more or less probable than the future, and the present is whatever we observe. If there is no observer, then there is no reality."

"But observation at what level?" I asked. "Must it be an intelligent observer? A dog can figure things out well enough. Can a plant observe the universe? Can an amoeba?"

"Maybe nothing exists outside the life of the mind," said Amabored, his eyes red from pipeweed smoke. "Maybe mind is all that exists."

"Or maybe the Multiverse itself exists only in the mind of El," said Redulfo, "and we're nothing more than his fleeting thoughts."

"Then El is the only thing that exists," said Lithaine. "It kind of lets you off the hook, doesn't it?"

"There is more than just El," said Jaspin. "There is another."

Honestly, it could go on like this for hours. Suffice it to say that when you mess around with time, you run the risk of encountering paradoxes within conundrums wrapped around ironies. It can turn your brain into tapioca if you think about it too hard. That's where Redulfo's determinism served him well—nothing unexpected could happen to him, because he knew that he was meant to experience it.

So, we may forgive the wizard his lack of surprise when this next thing happened. As he strode down the hallway deeper into the Blue Falcon, Redulfo heard the distant, ethereal echoes of music heralding the presence of strong enchantments. Somewhere close by, a store of magical items lay hidden behind a door or wall. Behind him, he heard the ringing clang of Malcolm's sword as it cleaved through imp armor, muscle and bone.

A few more twists and turns took him past bedrooms, studies, alcoves and staircases. The music swelled. The magic was close by. Redulfo scanned a blank wall in front of him, searching for some sign of the secret door he knew must be there. Somewhere behind that wall lay a wizard's study. Or so he may have been thinking. What the hell do I know? I'm just an observer.

That is, until I'm a participant. At that moment, a hidden panel in the wall slid open, and I stepped out of the Red Library—Jaspin's secret magical treasure-trove within the Blue Falcon. Only it wasn't the Me simultaneously donning the Screaming Skull, far below in the bowels of the great inn. It was the Me of nine years later—the Me on my way to kill Redulfo in his future incarnation as a black dragon. It was Future-Me.

"Get in here," I said to Redulfo, and pulled him inside.

16

S o, here's how that happened.

Fast-forward nine years, to the Valley of Sorcerers. The wind raged cold out of the Shadow Mountains, careening through the valley in great eddies and swirls, sighing through the tall mountain pines, moaning through the high grass, flowing into the crevices of our armor, where its icy fingers sought our bones. We stood huddled together at the edge of the Wilderness of Mirrors, pondering our next move.

The Wilderness of Mirrors was Gygax's and Rigby's most diabolical defense mechanism. Before us stretched the vast forest of mirrors, which marched in serried ranks from the lip of the valley down toward the Workshop of Telescopes, towering at its center. There were tall mirrors and short mirrors; round mirrors and square ones; mirrors of silvered glass and polished metals; mirrors with frames of wood, brass, gold, or marble. Because of the mirrors, no army had ever successfully assaulted the wizards' fortress. You'd think that a force of foot-soldiers could simply march into the valley, smashing mirrors as they went—and you'd be wrong. There was but a single path through those mirrors, a path that required trespassers to step through each correct mirror in sequence. Failure to follow that path led to one's instant incineration. We knew this only because Jo Ki-Rin had told us; otherwise we'd have all died again that very day, and he wasn't much in the mood to resurrect us again.

Beyond the mirrors, Redulfo lay in wait. The wind had blown the mist away from the valley floor, revealing the Workshop in all its baroque glory: a castle of jagged spires and glowering domes, garishly colored, like a fading casino lurking in the forgotten nether regions of Las Vegas. The castle stood on the face of a massive sidereal time-piece: a clock one mile in diameter, with gargantuan gears buried in the earth that rotated the face in time with the Woerth's rotation. Even now, from a good distance, we felt the low grumbling of the ground beneath our feet as the great clockworks turned below. As we stood there, fruitlessly trying to keep our pipes lit while we wasted time, the castle itself made a quarter-turn around the valley.

We didn't know what else to do but keep watching. If we walked through the wrong mirror, then we were dead meat. The Ki-Rin had told us that much. Why he didn't just give us a map showing the correct path is beyond me. Sometimes I think that fucker wanted us to fail.

"He said we'd know the right mirror when we saw it," said Lithaine.

"There must be over five thousand mirrors in this valley," said Amabored.

"Why don't we just sit on our asses and wait for Redulfo to come out?" I asked. "He can't stay in there forever."

"You forget who you're talking about," said Malcolm.

"You're right," said Amabored. "He'll stay in there until we all starve if he thinks we're supposed to come in after him."

He wasn't waiting for us to come in, however, because out he came. From one of the castle's many retractable domes, a dark, slender beast rose into the sky, its ragged bat-wings beating the wind with slow oarsmen's strokes. The beast soared high, turning in tight spirals, until it was just a black dot against the blue sky.

"Goddamned showoff," Amabored grumbled.

The beast banked hard left and rocketed toward us. We

unsheathed our weapons. We had all taken the *Antidote* potions designed to protect us from the dragon's acid cloud, but that was cold comfort; Redulfo could kill the lot of us with tooth, tail, or claw.

He didn't attack. A few pirouettes later, he landed with a flourish before us amidst a great cloud of dust that the wind quickly took away. His body, as big as an elephant's, was armored in thick obsidian scales. His neck, as slender as a serpent's, was outstretched, so that he towered five chains above us. Atop the neck perched the dragon's head, elongated and narrow, with rows of razored fangs and two green eyes glowing like emeralds in firelight.

"Hey, welcome," said the dragon. The voice was graveled, layered in echoes, but unmistakably Redulfo's. "It's great to see you guys again."

Was it Redulfo, really? We couldn't be sure. The poor bastard had his brain replaced by the Bad Brain in the Temple of Pain Eternal, lurking on an island in the middle of the Sunless Sea. After we killed him, the Crimson Hand kept the Brain alive—presumably with Redulfo's soul, neural patterns, or ghost along for the ride—by inserting it into the skull of this big fucking lizard. What was left of Redulfo, exactly? Nothing but his neuroses.

"It's great to be seen," said Amabored. "You know why we're here?"

"I do," said the dragon. "You can't have it."

"Why not?" I asked. "Save us all a lot of trouble."

"Because I'm using it."

"Really, my good würm, what sort of life is it?" asked Malcolm. "Is life as a reptile really so grand? Head full of Hellfire magic, no friends, and only a burning sense of resentment to keep one warm at night. I should rather welcome a clean death."

"It's ironic, me being back in this place," Redulfo said, black vapor spewing from his nostrils. "The Workshop is the greatest observatory on Woerth. Through its telescopes, one can peer into thousands of worlds. And yet, thanks to the Brain, I don't need them. I see everywhere and everything. I can see all the way to the End—where She lives. Where She waits."

"Who, your mom?" asked Lithaine.

"What you encountered before was just her avatar," Redulfo said. "She can't exist in our universe; she can only consume it. Eventually, you'll see her, because you'll need the Orbs. But you won't return from that encounter, I'm afraid."

At the mention of the Violet Queen, Lithaine blanched. Redulfo knew what buttons to push. He wasn't as merciless about it as Amabored, but he was subtler.

"That big-ass spider?" I asked. "She works for you?"

"It's the other way around," said the dragon. "She meant to lure the Celestial from Starfall, because it's the only weapon you had that could have killed me. Believe me, I would rather she hadn't done it."

"Try us anyway," said Amabored. "We're here to party, not chit-chat."

"I want to show you something first," said Redulfo. "Call it a demonstration."

The dragon launched his great bulk into the air, his wings thundering and snapping like the sails of a great trireme. We hit the dirt. Redulfo flew back toward the Workshop, still turning slowly atop its vast clockworks pedestal. The castle's portcullis clanked upward, and a column of pikemen marched forth—a mixed force of hobgoblins and trolls, by the looks of them. As their drummers beat a tattoo, the pikemen spread out into tight, regimented lines across the great timepiece, while Redulfo circled above. After this short march, the army stood at attention, shoulder to shoulder, polearms held high. For a Chaos army, it was a decent display of discipline. What was in it for them, I often wondered? What made your average hobgoblin want to leave hearth and home to kill and die at the command of some would-be dark lord? Don't they want to stay home and fuck and eat and watch television like the rest of us? I've never bothered to ask one, because it's a lot more fun to cut off their heads. Don't the more reflective among them sometimes question the meaning of it all?

Redulfo flew one final circle above his army, banked sharply, and then swooped down. His shadow fell upon the soldiers. The dragon shrieked, and a bilious black acid cloud issued from deep within his throat to fall upon his army. They didn't break ranks until the first of them started screaming: their armor and helms melting like wax, flesh running like heavy cream, bones shrinking into charred twigs. Those who didn't die immediately dropped their pikes and scrambled for the safety of the castle.

Redulfo rode them down and spewed acid on them, burning them alive where they ran. Their screams echoed off the mountain walls. On any other day, the sight of so many hobgoblins and trolls dying in agony would have had us dancing a jig. Why would the dragon destroy his own army? The sheer dumb-fuckery of it astounded us.

"Is he trying to make a point?" Amabored asked.

"One almost feels sorry for the poor blighters," said Malcolm.

"Almost," I said.

After Redulfo had turned most of his army into smoking goo, he chased down the stragglers and broke their backs in his jaws. Within ten minutes, five thousand burning, broken corpses lay strewn in obscene piles across the clock face.

The dragon flew back to us, landed smartly, and craned his serpent's neck on high. He regarded us with a gaze of cold appraisal.

"You may wonder if I'm trying to make a point," Redulfo said. "I spent six months building that army for the Hand; I was to lead it forth and lay waste to the Baronies, Arrendell, Kilcastle, and every kingdom that borders the Shadow Mountains. But my knowledge of the full scope of the Violet Queen's game tells me that this war is nothing more than a game of chess played on the deck of a sinking ship. It's all pointless, you see. That army was pointless. Their lives were pointless; they were meant to die. Koschei's war of conquest is pointless; it always has been. Your quest is pointless, and always has been. That's my point. And it, too, is pointless."

"Are we going to tangle?" asked Lithaine. "Or are you going to keep running your mouth?"

The dragon waved a languid claw. A low rumble sprang up beneath our feet, and every single mirror in the valley vanished beneath the ground as if yanked down by subterranean hands—

every mirror, save one. It stood alone now, a few dozen yards distant: a simple glass rectangle in a blue wooden frame, unadorned but for a carving on top.

"As I said, you currently have no weapon that can kill me," Redulfo continued. "But kill me you must, or your quest will fail, pointless though it is, and this universe will die. It will die anyway, but you may at least save it from the Queen's gullet. I once said that your chance of success increases only when your choices are constrained—and your choices, my friends and bosom companions, have been reduced to one."

"Look, we don't miss your goddamned lectures one bit," Amabored said, "Give us the short version."

"For countless centuries, I've believed that free will in this universe is most definitely an illusion—for this universe, unlike all others, is removed from the laws of probability. Causality is a function of spacetime branching like lightning to form the Multiverse, but this universe cannot bear offspring," said the dragon. "So, if our every action has been preordained since this universe began, and you're meant to kill me, then there's no action I can take that will alter my fate. Conversely, if you're meant to fail, then you can take no action that will succeed."

"Your trash talk needs some work," I said.

"But now—and here I confess to feeling a certain excitement that I haven't felt in at least five thousand years—I've come to believe that the opposite is true, and that ours is the only universe in which free will is more than an illusion. We may, in fact, be able to alter the fate of this universe by a simple purposeful act. I plan to test this hypothesis."

"How so, lizard?" asked Lithaine.

"By granting you the means to kill me. As my possession of the Bad Brain renders suicide impossible, success would mean that we are, all of us, truly free agents in this universe."

"So, you want us to go through that mirror and retrieve a weapon to take you out?" Amabored said. "How do we know it isn't a trap?"

"As I could kill you where you stand, I don't need a trap to do it."

The dragon motioned to the mirror. "Step through that mirror, and you'll find an old friend—one who can help you kill me. You'll need to bring him back here. You'll also need to retrieve a particular weapon, the nature of which I'll reveal to you shortly. Do these things, and you'll have your battle. If you kill me because I chose to arm you, then I will have purposefully orchestrated my own death, despite the Bad Brain preventing me from doing so—and I'll have proven my hypothesis that free will does exist in this universe. That knowledge itself would be worth dying for."

The dragon motioned us to follow. We walked behind him as he slithered toward the lone remaining mirror, his black wings folded across his sinuous spine. Later, when we had time to reflect on the dragon's words, we understood that he hadn't been conning us; this whole episode was indeed Redulfo's way of killing himself. He despised what he had become: twice-dead, reborn a monster, with the brain of an evil demigod lodged in his skull. Surely, he preferred death to such an existence. The Bad Brain wouldn't allow him to off himself, however; the Hand wanted to collect the Phylaxes before we did, and the Brain wanted them to succeed where we failed. To ensure the ultimate success of the Quest by killing himself, Redulfo needed to outwit the brain he now shared with Koschei.

"You're not so different from the old Redulfo," I said to the dragon. "Do you regret opening that egg? If you had it to do over again, would you do it differently?"

With one taloned claw, the dragon pointed to the mirror. We saw that the carving atop its frame was in the shape of a bird. Not just any bird—it was a falcon. A blue falcon, in fact.

Redulfo spread his jaws into a shape approximating a smile. "I don't know," he said. "Why don't you ask me?"

17

Nine years earlier back at the Blue Falcon, the night just kept getting weirder. On the second floor of the inn, four heroes crept through the mirror outside the Workshop of Telescopes in the year 3965 and found themselves inside the Falcon's Red Library in the year 3956. At that same moment, Amabored sat on the steps midway up Saggon's Tower, watching the dark elf's ass as she turned to descend. On the balcony overlooking the Grand Foyer, Malcolm stood with legs planted in front of the staircase, carving up the onrushing horde of imps with his blessed sword. In a second-floor hallway, the non-dragon Redulfo listened to the spell-music growing louder as he neared that same Library.

Where was I? That depends on your point of view. When I was thirty, I was up in the Red Library with the boys. When I was twenty-one, I was trapped in some extra-dimensional space far below in the bowels of the Falcon, starring at my own skull as I held it in my hands.

It's an odd thing, regarding your own skull. I wouldn't recommend it. Your first thought is wonderment at how delicate a thing it is; I could easily have shattered it against the wall like a clay pot. Studying its contours, I tried to make some connection between the reflection I saw in mirrors and the skull's sharp cheekbones, the smooth curves of the eye sockets deepening into shadow, the slightly crooked teeth embedded in the jaw. The sight of it drove me careening between love and revulsion. It wasn't quite the same thing as seeing your own soul exposed—a treat that Koschei himself would provide, a dozen or so years later—but it was a fair precursor. No one can say that I don't know myself.

Beside me stood Melinda, adrift in her own churning sea of love and revulsion. With a little effort, I found that I could project my sight outside of my body and see myself as she saw me—as a monster. Where my own head had once been sat a horned skull blazing with cold blue flames, the rune of Koschei glowing bright red in the center of its forehead. My body had expanded with rippling muscle, tearing my tunic to shreds, turning my studded leather armor into confetti. Around my burgeoning torso, my girdle glowed like gold melting in a forge.

Centering my vision once again, I handed my skull to Melissa. When I spoke, the voice broadcast from the Screaming Skull was a deep baritone, amplified beyond all reason and projected straight from my burning brain. Something told me I should speak in short sentences.

"TAKE THIS. KEEP IT SAFE," I said.

Her eyes wide, Melinda nodded. She tucked my skull inside the Screaming Skull's padded box, and then placed the box into her satchel. She took a few steps back, her eyes searching for an escape path, though a blood worm in fact blocked the only exit. I felt momentarily bad for scaring her so, though the emotion was accompanied by a curious Zen detachment. I thought I might comfort her, if my touch wouldn't make her scream.

There was no time for further reflection. The worm emerged from the tunnel, shrieking its unholy cry of hunger and pain. Blood worms begin life about the same size as your pinky. Only by consuming the blood of living things do they grow—and they can grow as large as a brontosaurus. This one oozed out of the tunnel in repulsive waves, its massive bird-beaked jaws snapping and its multi-tentacled tongue undulating wildly at the smell of blood.

"STAND BACK," I said to Melinda. My voice boomed off the pit walls, and the beast recoiled. Sizing me up as its most immediate threat, it then leapt forward with surprising speed, its jaws descending upon the Skull. I pistoned out my arms to seize the worm's beak with my now-massive hands.

The worm's sheer strength forced me back into the pile of bones, causing an avalanche that sent Melinda scurrying back against the wall. Then I got my feet planted under me, and we got down to business.

With all the strength my cartoonish muscles could supply, I forced the worm's jaws wider apart. It thrust its tongue-tentacles at me, seeking purchase, but my flesh had become rock-hard and impenetrable. Really, the beast didn't stand a chance. I bore the power of the Deathless One, drawn from the wellspring of Hellfire channeled through a thousand different worlds. Who did this slimy piece of shit think it was?

The worm's jaws began to tear open from the pressure, its black, viscous blood flowing over my fingers and running down my arms. Its shrieks of pain were poison to our ears. It began to surge backward, into the tunnel, fighting for its life to break free.

And then, the *coup de grace*: The blue flames cavorting around the Skull grew brighter, bathing the pit in neon. Bright, arcing tines of lighting burst forth from the Skull's eye sockets. The lightning leapt straight down the worm's gullet, lighting it up like a fluorescent tube. The whole beast grew rigid, its bloated length caught in mid-undulation. Then it exploded.

Blood, tissue, and entrails spewed from the tunnel in a massive torrent, bathing Melinda and me in slime and putrescence. Hunks of worm-meat rained down on our heads. The walls of the pit dripped with wet filth. Melinda wiped the gore out of her eyes and stepped toward me. She was smiling.

"Neat trick, that," she said. "Now let's see what you can do to that devil."

Creeping through the slimy tunnel, we emerged into another long tunnel-like corridor hewn from natural rock. To our left, the tunnel swiftly vanished into utter darkness. To our right, a strange reddish-orange glow beckoned. As light trumps dark, we turned right.

The orange light grew brighter as we jogged forward. Soon the natural stone of the tunnel walls gave way to something far stranger: a glistening, fleshy surface that seemed somehow to pulse with obscene life. The orange glow radiated from this surface, suffusing the tunnel with lurid luminescence. Wearing the Skull, I could sense knowledge unbidden invade my mind, and I knew that we were leaving the Falcon proper and entering some twilight realm between Hell and Woerth.

Ahead of me, Melinda stepped over to the walls for a closer look. I moved beside her. We could see beneath the fleshy surface branching violet and red lines coursing this way and that—veins and arteries, through which the blood of some abominable life flowed. Had I a real mouth, I would have vomited. As we stared, there appeared suddenly a horror-stricken face—bloodshot eyes, bulbous nose, and gaping mouth—bulging from the flesh-wall. Then it spoke in a terror-stricken, hoarse moan.

"Bitchgotwhatshedeserved... onlymeanttoscareher... whydidn'tsheloved-herlovedHER..."

Melinda jumped back as if the wall had reached out a hand to slap her. She looked to me, searching for a sign of humanity within the monster I had become.

"Souls," she whispered. "These walls are made of damned souls, Elberon. The Hellmouth is close."

"I KNOW," my Skull-voice boomed. "BE CAREFUL."

And then—the sound of a child crying, somewhere farther down the flesh-tunnel. Melinda's head snapped around, and she took off running. I followed. Another hundred yards or so, and we found the treasure we had sought: the children still trapped here, waiting for the devil to feed.

There were seven of them: five boys and two girls, appearing to range in age from six to twelve. From the flesh-walls, a dozen or so pairs of human arms had sprouted to bind the children to them, with spindly, skeletal fingers wrapped tightly around their limbs, torsos, and throats. Their bare feet dangled above the tunnel floor. All appeared comatose, with mouths agape and blank eyes staring at nothing—but for one little blonde girl, who turned her head to mark our approach. When she did so, a hellish hand gripped her throat more tightly.

"Thirsty," the girl moaned to us, her voice scarcely a whisper. "So thirsty."

Melinda burst into tears. Yanking her canteen from her belt, she stepped forward and held it up to the girl's dry and cracked lips.

"We're here, honey," Melinda sobbed to the girl as she swallowed a few drops of canteen water. "We're here. You'll be free soon. I swear to you, you'll be free." Then she turned to me, her eyes filled with righteous anger behind her tears. "Free them, Elberon! NOW!"

"RIGHT," I said. Stepping up, I took one of the wall-arms into my two meaty mitts and pulled hard. With the combined power of the girdle and Skull, I was able to rip the arm from the wall with a crunching, ripping sound and a gout of ruby-red blood that sizzled as it drenched me. The remainder of the arms writhed and undulated, squeezing the children in a death-embrace. Still awake, the thirsty girl screamed.

"Do something else!" Melinda cried. "The wall is killing them!"

Without even consciously thinking about it, I did something else. From the Skull's eye sockets emerged the same blinding blue flames that had preceded the blood worm's demise. Lightning arced again, striking the wall-arms in a dozen places and turning them to ash. The moans and shrieks of the damned souls trapped within filled the tunnel with madness. The children, freed at last from their hellish grasp, collapsed onto the floor.

Melinda rushed over to them, dropping to her knees to tend to them with her canteen. One by one, they sat up, dazed and blinking like kittens bathed in sudden sunlight. Spying me, their eyes widened —but not with fear, oddly enough. Despite my monstrous appearance, they seemed to know that I was a friend.

"Gather yourselves, children," Melinda told them, making sure each one could see her smile. "We're leaving this place."

At that moment, a bellowing, chortling laugh rattled the tunnel. The sound sent the flesh-walls writhing with undulating life. The children screamed and cowered behind us. From the far end of the tunnel, silhouetted against a backdrop of nauseating orange light, appeared a towering, hulking figure dragging behind it a heavy iron chain. The light grew brighter, and behind the figure there appeared a pair of massive, obsidian, iron-shod doors, five men tall and carved with deep runes glowing red with Hellfire: The doors of the Hell-mouth, through which Arturus had banished Beelzebub's hellspawn army five hundred years ago, revealed to us at last.

"NOT SO FAST," said Malacoda, Dire Malebranche of the Eighth Circle of Hell. *"FIRST, WE'RE GOING TO HAVE US A LITTLE PARLAY."*

And then, unbidden, there came a voice in my head. It was a familiar voice, projected into my mind from somewhere else.

"There's still time to change things," the voice said to me. *"Stop her. Take her out of the city. Start the Quest now, just the two of you, together. You don't have to hurt her."*

"Who the fuck are you?" I thought.

18

As it turned out, I wasn't the only one who got to have a conversation with himself. Far above the catacombs, Amabored was helping Lithaine to his feet. Reaching negative health points takes a lot out of a fellow, and the elf would need a moment. Time was short, however, not to mention fluid—so the barbarian allowed the elf only a few swigs of grog before forcing him up the steps.

By their step count, they should have been midway up the tower. The spiral staircase wrapped around the inside of the tower wall, the diameter of which was wide enough for them to see the dim light from the Great Hall far below. This wasn't just any tower, however—it was the tallest tower in Storm Stonegorm's multi-dimensional masterpiece. So, as they raced up the steps, expecting at any moment to reach the summit and enter the maze that led to Saggon's lair, the steps just kept coming. First dozens, then scores, then hundreds. Soon, their confident leaps turned into leaden staggering. Finally, they stopped.

"Jupiter's ball sack!" said the barbarian, doubled over with fatigue. "We should be a hundred stories up by now."

"Fuck this. It's useless," said Lithaine. "Let's go back down." As an elf, he was engineered to look untroubled by earthly cares, and only a slight increase in the pace of his breath hinted at his exhaustion. It was maddening, I tell you, and more than once I wanted to break his nose for it.

"You got it," said Amabored, sheathing his sword. "Saggon isn't the prize. If he dares come out of his hole, we'll gut him."

There came at that moment a gust of frigid wind swirling up from below, followed by the great rustle and flap of large wings. Then something swift and strong seized the two men by their wrists and dragged them into the air.

Great wings beating the darkness, it hauled them upward through the tower. They alighted in the small vestibule outside the labyrinth on the top floor. The kidnapper dumped the two men onto the stone floor. Rolling to their feet, they leapt up with weapons drawn to confront—

—Amabored.

Not just any Amabored, mind you. It was nine-years-older Amabored, the same Amabored who stepped through Redulfo the Black's mirror outside the Workshop of Telescopes and into the Red Library that very night.

Imagine finding yourself face-to-face with yourself, only nine years older, or younger. Is your first reaction one of recognition? Revulsion? Love at first sight? If first impressions matter, then your first impression upon meeting yourself at a bend in time would be revealing, would it not? Most people couldn't bear it.

First, there was a moment of silence as the three men took stock of each other. Amabored the Elder grinned, pleased at the effect his presence had on the other two. The two barbarians looked much the same, provided that you ignored their complete dissimilarity. The younger Amabored was bare-chested, wearing his usual leopard-skin loincloth, his white hair flowing in the traditional Nomad mullet, his frame devoid of accouterments but for the scabbard strapped across his lean, lanky torso. The elder Amabored was dressed for the mountains in full studded leather armor, his frame bigger, his face fuller, his beard wilder, and his hair flowing past his shoulders like the mane of a rock star. And then there were the wings—full, luxurious, with thick down and feathers as long as your arm. Imagine wondering where those came from.

Lithaine looked from one barbarian to the other. "Whoa," said the elf.

"Who the fuck are you?" asked Amabored the Younger, thrusting the point of his sword under Amabored the Elder's chin. The latter just widened his grin.

"I'm you, you dumb shit," said Amabored the Elder. "I'm future-you. Nearly a decade older than you, in fact, so you'd best show respect. And get this knitting needle out of my face." Elder pushed Younger's blade aside with the tip of his finger.

"Is that so? Well, I've certainly gotten uglier," said Younger. "And obviously more stupid. Touch my blade again and see where it gets you."

Elder laughed. "If I touch it again, it'll be to shove it up your ass." From its scabbard he drew the legendary Stormcrow, forged by the dwarf smiths of the Goldspur Highlands, its blade traced with fine filigree runes, its pommel wrapped with gold wire and topped with a blazing ruby.

"Now here's a sword," said Elder. "What are you, Fourth Level? Thirty-something health points? You couldn't even lift this sword, Junior."

"Ten years older, you say?" asked Younger. "What does that make you? Pushing forty? You're on the downward spiral, brother. I'll bet your reaction time is already for shite. Bet your recovery time is longer, too. Me, I'm in the full flower of youth."

"If you suck my cock, does that make it masturbation?"

"If I skull-fuck your corpse, does that mean I'll have ten years to live?"

"If I cut off your fucking head, will I cease to exist? Let's find out!" Elder swung his sword in a swift arc aimed at Younger's neck. Younger brought up his own blade to deflect the stroke. The clash of steel echoed in descending notes down the length of the tower.

"Knock this shit off!" said Lithaine, stepping between the two men. They both fell back, wearing nearly identical grins. The elf turned to the older Amabored. "Where did you come from? And where did you get those wings?"

"It's a long story," said Elder. "The short version is that I brought you both up here to do your job, because I knew you'd pussy out. That thing inside is waiting, and you need something he has. You two need to take care of business. It's part of the Quest."

"Quest? What quest?" asked Amabored the Younger. "That's the second time someone has mentioned that word to me."

"Never mind what Quest. Just listen. You need to retrieve the petrified dragon-dick hanging above Saggon's mantel. You know the one?"

The two younger men glanced at each other. "Yeah, sure," said Lithaine. "Why do you need it? Somebody going to peg you with it later?"

"Yeah, your mom," said Elder. "Never mind why I need it. Just get in there and grease that fat fuck."

"If it's so important, why don't you do it?" asked Younger. "You must be Ninth or Tenth Level by now."

"I'm busy, that's why," said Elder. "I have to grab Redulfo, take him back to my time, help him kill himself again, and then bring him back here. So, man up, youngsters. Just do what comes naturally."

The younger men exchanged another glance, then nodded. Elder extended his hand to his younger self. As the latter accepted his handshake, Elder's face split once again into a wide grin.

"You'll be all right, kid," Elder said. "Trust me. I'm standing here, aren't I?"

"Anything we should know before we go in there?" asked Younger.

"I remember it being pretty damned cold in Saggon's office," said Elder. "You might want to start a fire in the hearth. Use this." He took a glass vial from his pouch. It was empty, save for a small portion of red liquid at the bottom. Younger took it with a questioning glance.

"*Holocaust* potion," continued Elder. "Just a few drops—that's all you'll need. And now, ladies, I must be off. Try not to trip over your skirts. And you, magic boy—" with this, Elder pointed to Lithaine —"You told me to tell you to go fuck yourself."

With that, the older Amabored launched himself down into the tower headfirst, his great wings spreading wide as he plunged into the darkness. The two friends stared after him.

"Could this night get any more fucked up?" asked Lithaine.

"I'm starting to like that guy," Amabored said. "He reminds me of me."

19

Amabored had snagged the *Holocaust* potion from Jaspin's stash in the Red Library—the very place that young Redulfo was headed before we black-bagged him. Even amongst the wise of today, no one knows exactly who created the time loop that resulted in Redulfo killing himself; could it have been Gygax and Rigsby themselves? After all, the wizards founded the Workshop of Telescopes, and then created the Wilderness of Mirrors to defend it from assault. In that Wilderness, they included a mirror that would send anyone who stepped through it to the Blue Falcon on the precise night that we were assaulting it. After they helped kill Koschei during the first Quest, the wizards were instrumental in hiding the Bad Brain where, five hundred years later, Redulfo would find and become possessed by it, be killed by his mates, and then be reincarnated as a black dragon by the Crimson Hand, which then sent him to reoccupy their former haunt. That same Redulfo the Black then returned us to the Blue Falcon—through the mirror that Gygax and Rigsby created—to find the young Redulfo and wield him as the weapon that effectively allowed the older Redulfo to kill himself. Redulfo's second death was a key milestone in the Quest that brought down both Koschei and the Hand. Had the two wizards known all along that Koschei would return, and booby-trapped time to ensure his downfall? Who the hell knew?

Seriously, reread that last paragraph. Does it make a lick of fucking sense? But that's as good an explanation as any for how it went down.

That night, it didn't take long for those of us who went through the mirror to decide that facing a black dragon was preferable to running for our lives in the Blue Falcon. The massive fortress-inn was already threatening to implode around our older selves, the great stone walls and thick oaken beams of the Red Library quaking from the force of the quantum tremors unleashed by the conflict far below. I grabbed young Redulfo by the shoulders and yanked him through the secret door, where the four of us—Amabored, Lithaine, Malcolm and me—regarded him with the shock of recognition seared onto our faces.

For his part, Redulfo the Younger merely squinted through his spectacles. "How did you all get in here? You look... different. Where the heck did those wings come from, Amabored?"

"Never mind that," I said. "We're here from the future, and unless you want us to fuck you up with some crazy-ass future-shit, just shut up and listen. Got it?"

"Got it," said Redulfo. Behind me, my three older companions loomed ominously, ready to fuck up Redulfo with some crazy-ass future-shit, should the need arise.

"Good," I said. "Right now, your version of Amabored and Lithaine is about to run into an ice-golem masquerading as Saggon." We knew this because Redulfo the Black had told us so, right before we stepped through his mirror. "That fat fuck has something that we need to kill a black dragon. So, we need something that'll help them take out the golem. See anything in here they can use?"

Redulfo looked around the Red Library, burgeoning as it was with shelves crammed full of all manner of tomes, scrolls, stacks of parchment, and magical bric-a-brac. Later, we'd learn that it was Jaspin's own secret stash of magical booty, stored here for the day he rubbed out Saggon for good and assumed control of the Blue Falcon himself.

His gaze settled on a bookcase stuffed full of sealed jars, vials, and tubes stacked on their sides. Spying one containing a small portion of red liquid, he snagged it and handed it to me.

"*Holocaust* potion," said the younger wizard. "Just a few drops. Heat the place up and the golem's ice armor will melt. Or at least, that's what I've read."

I tossed the potion to Amabored. "You on it?" I asked.

"On it. Any words for your younger self?" the barbarian asked Lithaine.

"Tell him I said to go fuck himself."

"If you guys are from the future, why don't you just all go kill the ice-golem yourselves?" Redulfo asked.

"Because we need to stay here and guard you," I told him. "Interested parties might want to stop this little event from happening."

When Redulfo the Black explained what would happen when we stepped through the mirror into the Blue Falcon, and what we would need to do when we got there, we huddled briefly to discuss the ramifications. Should we help our younger selves? What else should we do, or not do, to change things? Being time-novices, and certain that the dragon was going to fuck us somehow, we decided to say as little as possible.

As we sat on Redulfo the younger in the Red Library, waiting for Amabored to return with the petrified dragon phallus, I couldn't help but think of my own younger self, about to wage the battle of his young life against a foe with whom he had no business tangling. Nine years of my life vanished in an instant, ripping open the emotional scars from my past to leave fresh wounds now raw and red. I saw Melinda, and my life in Redhauke, lost to the Quest. Melinda was about to sacrifice herself—could I save her the pain and psychic scars of her time in Hell? My mind's eye found the scene in my memory—and suddenly the two me's collided in time and space. I was up here; I was down there. I was down here; I was up there. We were me.

I knew then that there was still a chance to change her fate and mine, regardless of what Redulfo believed. All I had to do was give

myself a heads-up. Did I want to? If I had a chance to do things differently, would I? There was only one way to find out.

"*There's still time to change things.*" I projected the thought to my
younger self. "*Stop her. Take her out of the city. Start the Quest now, just
the two of you, together. You don't have to hurt her.*"

"*Who the fuck are you?*" my younger mind projected.

"*Your fucking conscience, that's who. Just listen to me. Stop Melinda.
Now.*"

Just as I could see young Elberon's future, so could he now see my
past. He saw it all: Melinda's fall and rebirth; my betrayal of her, and
the furious pain in her eyes as she turned away from me in the
Under-Canals. He saw her pregnancy, and its loss. He saw Cassie and
me, us, making love under the Star Maiden's hem in the lush olive
groves of Collanna, the summer breezes caressing our sweat-limned
flesh. I took first one and then the other of her nipples in my mouth.
They were ripe pink olives, tasting of salt and sweat.

"*And give up the chance to nail the hot blonde?*" the younger me asked
the older me. "*No fucking way.*"

"*No, seriously. You've seen how much pain we cause Melinda. Don't you
want the chance to save her from it?*"

"*If you love Cassie, then isn't it worth it? Wasn't it meant to be?*"

"*That's what I don't know. Did I have a choice to hurt Melinda? Maybe
not. But now you have one. Now that you know how it turns out, you can
choose not to do it.*"

"*But we don't know how it turns out, do we? Will the Quest succeed?
Will you marry Cassie? Will she bear your child? If so, dare I deprive that
child of life? That's a lot of fucking pressure to put on me, asshole. It's not
my place to change the future. I'm as beholden to it as I am to the past.*"

"*It's a fair point,*" I said. "*Look, I had to ask. So just go take down that
fucking devil. And for Odin's sake, don't forget to scream.*"

The spell broke. I snapped back to the present—but the hurt, the
loss, the guilt, the exhilaration, and my love for the woman for whom
I betrayed another, remained constant. *No matter where you go in the
Multiverse*, I thought—

20

You always carry the same baggage with you.

Below and nine years earlier, the connection broke. The Hellmouth sprang back into existence. The massive iron-shod obsidian doors, carved from the souls of great kings, once again loomed before me. Before the doors stood Malacoda, Dire Malebranche of the Eighth Circle of Hell, a vicious piece of shit who had been condemned by Beelzebub to guard the Hellmouth for eternity as punishment for his failure to vanquish Arturus. Now, he passed his time by eating the souls of the children Saggon sent to him—and for that, he had to die.

"WELL?" asked the devil, his black tongue lolling. "ARE WE GOING TO PARLAY, OR PARTY?"

"Watch the children, Elberon," Melinda whispered to me. "When he's distracted, lead them out of here."

With that, Melinda stepped forward to confront the devil. Sheathing her sword, she curtsied low, sweeping her arm out before her.

"Your Satanic Highness," Melinda began. "All praise to your cruelness and malice. We thank thee for treating with us."

"SAVE IT, BITCH," said Malacoda. "I DON'T WANT YOU. I WANT

HIM." The devil extended a hooked talon and pointed it in my direction.

Startled, Melinda looked back to me. Her gaze met mine, and she nodded. Then she shrank back against the writhing flesh-wall to allow me passage forward. I took five steps toward the devil and planted my feet.

"OKAY," I bellowed in my booming skull-voice. "I'M HERE."

Malacoda roared with laughter. *"TWO PHYLAXES, AND YOU THINK YOU CAN TAKE ME,"* the devil said. *"FAT CHANCE."*

"TWO PHYLAXES?" I asked. "WHAT ARE YOU TALKING ABOUT?"

"EVEN FOR A MORTAL, YOU'RE ESPECIALLY DENSE," said the devil. *"HERE'S THE SKINNY: I GAVE THE SKULL TO THE GIRL FOR KICKS. NOW INTERESTED PARTIES NEED IT BACK. SO, HAND IT OVER, AND I'LL ONLY KILL BOTH OF YOU AND EAT THE KIDS QUICK. GIVE ME ANY LIP, AND I'LL NOT ONLY EAT THEM, BUT I'LL ALSO PLAY WITH THEM FIRST—FOR A FEW HUNDRED YEARS."*

"I'D LIKE TO ACCOMMODATE YOU," I said. "BUT I'M USING THE SKULL—TO RIP YOUR OWN SKULL OFF YOUR FUCKING SHOULDERS. YOU EAT KIDS, YOU DIE. SORRY, BUT THAT'S THE WAY IT IS."

With that, I stretched forth my hand—an instinctual move, as wearing the Skull seemed to fill me with knowledge of how to manipulate Chaos. At my command, the doors to the Hellmouth parted with a great ratcheting groan, revealing a thin line of light that seemed to glow white and black at the same time. As they began to swing wider, I felt for a moment at one with Arturus, the greatest hero Woerth had ever known, as he banished the hellspawn and sealed the Hellmouth, so long ago.

The feeling didn't last. Suddenly the doors ground to a halt. Then, even more swiftly than I had opened them, they slammed shut again.

"YOU'RE NOT FIT TO LICK ARTURUS'S BALLS, MORTAL," the devil said. *"NOW, LET'S TANGO."*

With that pronouncement, Malacoda strained forward with

rippling black muscles against the immense iron chains binding him to the Hellmouth. For a moment, it appeared the chains would hold. Then, with great cracking pops, two of the links broke, and the devil was free. On his great hawk-talons, he galloped toward me—and before I knew what hit me, I was fighting for my life with a live pit devil. How many Fourth-Level fighters can say that?

His black, spell-carved arms outstretched, the remnants of his binding chains still dangling from his manacles, the devil's talons gripped the horns of the Screaming Skull as he tried to wrench it from my shoulders. My own hands, now grown massive with fingers like links of polish sausage, were wrapped around the devil's throat. His yellow eyes bore into my brain like a Mindworm of Tarsus.

The devil was as tall as three men. In my current incarnation, I matched him inch for inch. The Skull and the Girdle together had filled me with enough power to go toe-to-toe with this Fallen asshole. What would a guy be able to do if he managed to collect all ten Phylaxes? Forget about untold riches or world domination, because who needs it? Let's just say I'd be popular with the ladies.

The more immediate question: Could I stop this particular fuck-face, here and now? We were encased in Hellfire—the untrammeled essence of Chaos born when El divided himself, mated with Tiamat, and emanated the Multiverse—leaping from our entwined forms like solar flares. The power of it shook the very bedrock under the city, sending towers swaying from the Chimera Gate to the Harbor. Beyond the flesh-walls, the natural tunnel leading to the Hellmouth began to collapse, with massive shards of granite sheering from the cave roof. Somewhere nearby, Melinda raised up my shield as scant protection against the avalanche. The terrified children cowered around her.

No cavefall touched we combatants; we fought in a pocket universe built just for us, one in which only one of us could live. There was no need for words—we could read each other's thoughts just fine.

"*Go home, mortal,*" the devil's mind told me. "*Hang it up. Chill out for a while. You've earned some time off. Don't make me use your spine to pick your bits out of my teeth."*

"Sorry, chum," I answered. *"You have to answer for those kids. You're a sick motherfucker, and I'm some motherfucking penicillin, motherfucker. I'm going to tear off your motherfucking head and shove it up your motherfucking ass."*

"I'm not your chum, pal."

"I'm not your pal, friend."

"WHAT IS THIS—CANADA?" the devil hissed aloud. Malacoda shoved me back, and a great pimple of Hellfire burst forth from our broken union to shower the fleshy, dripping walls of the tunnel with a suppuration of flame. The souls trapped within cried out, their screams ricocheting in my mind as I flew back a hundred yards and crashed into the ruins of the blood worm's tunnel.

I leapt up. Rubble fell from my shoulders.

"OK, NOW YOU'RE PISSING ME OFF," I said aloud. I drew my sword, and the blade burst into cold blue flames. The power of the Screaming Skull filled me with the opiate pleasures of madness. I would take a piece out of this fucker's hide—that was that.

I advanced. The devil, now wielding a massive two-headed battle-mace carved deep with runes of necromancy, raced forward to meet me. His black hide capered with yellow flames. His bullish face spread in a leering rictus. His fangs dripped red with the blood of innocents. By the standards of Hell, he was quite stylish.

Out of the corner of whatever passed for my eye at that moment, I spied Melinda, attempting to slip past us leading a chain of children linking hands behind her. The children wore expressions that foretold a lifetime of haunted memories, should they survive the night. She got them halfway down the long tunnel before the damned souls trapped within the walls began to shriek the alarm, and the devil spied her.

"TRYING TO MAKE OFF WITH MY DINNER, ARE WE?" Malacoda roared, as the children shrieked with terror. *"THINK AGAIN, MILDRED."* The devil's horns glowed magma-red as fingers of Hellfire arched from their tips to seize the children, tear them from

Melinda's grasp, and drag them screaming back toward the Hell-mouth doors.

"Elberon—stop him!" Melinda cried out.

Though her voice was distant, hobbled by whatever dark energy surrounded me, I caught her meaning. Cocking my arm back, I drove it with full force into the devil's right eye. His bull-head rocked back —and as black blood spurted from the fresh cut above his brow, he laughed.

"TRY HARDER!" The devil bellowed with lunatic mirth. He jerked back his horns, and the tendrils of Hellfire enveloping the children flung them toward the Hellmouth doors with sudden and over-whelming force. As the children's frail bodies rocketed toward the closed obsidian doors, the grasping, corpse-colored arms of scores of damned souls trapped within them reached out to seize the limbs of the screaming children. One by one, the children were pulled into the doors: their little bodies melting into them, their skinny limbs waving frantically until they vanished, their agape mouths and rolling white eyes melting also into them. All seven children vanished, until only the echoes of their screams remained.

"NO!" Melinda cried, as she raced for the Hellmouth doors. She flung herself against them as if her fury were all she needed to fling them open. Then she turned to me again.

"Open the doors!" she cried.

All right, then. *"What are you gonna do with that mace, imp?"* my mind projected into the devil's head.

No mortal man calls an Arch-Devil like Malacoda an imp and gets away with it. These High Lords of Hell, with legions of Fallen at their command, take that shit seriously. But I was by now no mere mortal. Thanks to the Skull, I had become some strange mashup of Elberon and Koschei, powered by the wellsprings of Chaos from a thousand other worlds. Would it be enough juice to tear off this devil's fat melon head?

Malacoda roared, swung his mace on high, and brought it down. I raised up my sword to parry. The force of the devil's blow snapped the blade at the hilt. I held up the sword pommel to regard the space where my sword once was. *Fucking hell.*

"Oh, you'll be fucking Hell, all right," came Malacoda in my head. *"I'll see to it personally. You'll be fucking Hell for the foreseeable future."*

The devil readied another blow. The mace head caught me square on the side of the Skull. While it wasn't the skull I was born with, this one was definitely connected to my nervous system. Pain burst in my head like popcorn. Everything went white, then black. The tunnel floor leaped up and punched me in the teeth. The tormented souls in the floor cried their lamentations and tore at my mind and body with grasping, ragged claws.

There came the echo of footfalls, and then pain as the devil ground a hooked talon into my back. His laugh was a black rain that fell on my soul.

"As you know, I like my souls fresh, as the Lord of Flies commands," the devil said. *"But for you, I'll make an exception. I'll murder you here, and after you spend the next thousand years as my personal bitch, I'll eat your soul. I'll sauté it with some onions and garlic and serve it over rice. The Void awaits you, Elberon of the Isles."*

So, this was how it was all going to end? The children lost, Melinda left to die, the Quest over before it began? I had just communed with my older self—didn't that mean I lived through this? Or had it all been a fever dream, a final jest of the Skull?

Suddenly I knew what I had to do. Was it the Skull itself that imparted to me knowledge of Infernal decorum—knowledge of which I had been heretofore ignorant? Or was it the Ki-Rin again? It didn't matter. I knew now how to make Malacoda delay ripping my heart out of my chest.

"I CHALLENGE HIS SATANIC HIGHNESS MALACODA, DIRE MALEBRANCHE OF MALEBOLGE AND VASSAL OF BEELZE-BUB, KING OF THE EIGHTH CIRCLE AND LORD OF FLIES, TO THE JUDGEMENT OF MINOS!" I cried out loud.

The devil lifted his talon from my back. I was able to roll over and stand up, more or less, with the Skull still sheathed in blue flame and sitting on my shoulders. Malacoda regarded me through narrow, contemptuous eyes. Far down the corridor, the Hellmouth doors now stood open again, framing a high rectangle of black-white light.

"*SO, YOU WANT TO PLAY GAMES, LITTLE MAN?*" Malacoda roared. "*ALL RIGHT—LET'S PARTY.*"

"AFTER YOU, TOUGH GUY," I said.

The devil reached out to touch my arm—and we both vanished from Woerth.

21

U p above, Malcolm stood on the staircase in the Grand Foyer waist-deep in imp corpses. Though the Star Maiden's blessing had proven true, it wasn't without cost; the paladin now bled from a dozen wounds. He healed the ones he could, until his store of *Health* blessings was spent; from that point he gave ground stubbornly, one step at a time, still drawing the never-ending horde of imps away from both Saggon's tower and the catacombs below. As he did so, the quantum earthquake engendered by my battle with Malacoda rocked the Blue Falcon, sending splintering cracks racing across the foyer's tiled floor as the walls rippled like sheets on a clothesline. If Malcolm prayed again to the Star Maiden, he did so silently.

Farther above, atop Saggon's tower, the younger Amabored and Lithaine found themselves emerging from the labyrinth outside the Over-Boss's office, having avoided the sentient Black Sand pit, as well as the myriad other spring-loaded traps, spikes, and missiles lining the narrow stone passages. They brushed the debris from their shoulders created by the recurring tremors now rocking the Falcon. Entering the lobby, they found the dark elf's desk upended, the bookshelves overturned, and the file cabinets vomiting parchment and scrolls. On the opposite wall, the large oaken door to Saggon's office stood ajar; from the office interior came only dim candlelight, silence, and a cold so intense that the breath of the two men billowed before them like the sails of a trireme.

The two men shared a glance. Amabored drew his blade, while Lithaine nocked arrow to string.

"Lord Saggon?" Amabored called out. "A word with you, sir?"

No answer came. Amabored shrugged at the elf, and the two men approached the door. Stepping inside the Over-Boss's office, they found it much as they had found the lobby: in utter disarray, with tables and shelves overturned, books and scrolls scattered everywhere, pots and mugs shattered, and the stuffed heads of Saggon's victims laying hither and yon. At his desk scribbling on a piece of parchment with quill and ink, looking for all the world as if nothing was amiss, sat Saggon the Large—bloated, corpulent, his multiple chins quivering, his pasty flesh shining as if slathered in lamp oil. From the twin stone bear-heads protruding from the wall over his desk, arctic air blew into the room. The Over-Boss glanced up to regard his visitors.

"Tommy, Dick," said Saggon. "Come in, boys. You hungry? I'll have my girl bring in some sausages. I get the best, from a dwarf butcher I know near the Stranger's Wall. Some mulled wine, then? Have a seat."

Lithaine responded by letting his arrow fly. The arrowhead bounced harmlessly off Saggon's forehead, the shaft splitting as the arrow clattered to the ground.

"What gives?" asked Saggon, looking aggrieved. He lumbered to his feet like an avalanche of round, fleshy boulders running in reverse. "You boys got some sack on you, I'll give you that."

"Fuck this," said Amabored, and charged at the Over-Boss with sword cocked. The barbarian charged only until he didn't—after he had covered a few feet of distance, the frigid cold pierced his flesh, entered his muscles, and turned them to stone. Amabored froze in place, his sword still raised. Beside him, Lithaine had likewise frozen solid. His face now a leering, inhuman rictus, Saggon trundled around his desk to approach the two frozen men.

"It's my lucky day, boys," the Over-Boss said. "Looks like I'm having a few friends for dinner."

22

Nine years later in the time stream, Amabored, Lithaine, and Malcolm emerged stumbling again through the mirror that had transported them to the Blue Falcon. They rolled into a tumbling heap on the grass, disentangled their limbs, and leaped to their feet with weapons drawn. Across the plain loomed the Workshop, still rotating slowly atop its great timepiece foundation. There was no sign of Redulfo the Black. There was also no sign of me, nor of Redulfo the Younger, whom I was supposed to be dragging with me through the mirror.

"Where the hell are they?" Amabored asked, scowling. In his hand he held the petrified dragon phallus from Saggon's mantel. "We don't have time to fuck around!"

"I'll check," Lithaine said, and flung himself at the mirror. Instead of sailing through it back to the Blue Falcon, the elf bounced off it, stumbling back to fall on his ass.

"That usually works," Lithaine said, as Malcolm helped him up.

"Sorry, gents—it was a single-trip ticket," came a rumbling voice from above. "Now that you've returned, our battle can begin." The three men cast their gazes skyward to spy Redulfo the Black spiraling fifty feet or so above their heads. Swooping down with alarming speed, the dragon loosed his jaws to spew forth upon them a firehose-strength stream of black acid. Were it not for the *Antidote* potions we had swallowed that morning, the acid would have turned all three of them into smoking pink goo. Instead, the hot solution drenched them and turned a wide, winding path of grass into sizzling black ash.

"Nice try, you fucking ass-cactus!" Lithaine called.

"My liege, the length of your sojourn in the company of low men has degraded the quality of your discourse," Malcolm said, acid dripping from his nose. "Perhaps a higher quality of jape is in order?"

"Oh, yeah?" Lithaine asked. "Give it a shot, Lawful Good."

"You're no dragon, good Redulfo!" Malcolm called up. "You're naught but a mandrake mymmerkin!"

Amabored and Lithaine burst into laughter, which sent the paladin's chest puffing with pride. Before Malcolm could figure out that they were laughing at him and not with him, the ground below the three men began to quake—and before they could blink, they were surrounded by a score or more of mirrors that had suddenly thrust themselves up from below. Outside the circle of mirrors, Redulfo glided to a smooth landing.

"A mandrake mymmerkin I may be, good paladin," said Redulfo the Black, "but I'm a still-living one. As I see you're missing a certain young wizard required to vanquish me, I'm afraid that's more than I'll be able to say for you."

From the mirrors there emerged, one after another, dozens of scarlet-cloaked and hooded men—dressed identically, in fact, to the assassins who had attacked me on the streets of Redhauke five years earlier, when that mysterious dwarf presented the Screaming Skull to me again. As the cloaked figures raced toward our heroes, and just as they had done when they attacked me, they changed. Their torsos and limbs split open like hot sausages, spraying gouts of blood and tissue as insectoid mandibles, thoraxes, and segmented legs burst from their bodies. Casting aside their cloaks, they were now revealed as man-sized, beetle-like creatures with gleaming black carapaces and leg-segments tattooed with blood-red rings. The first of them crashed into the three men, who fell back towards each other swinging their blades wildly.

"Just the appetizer, gentlemen," Redulfo the Black said, picking at his fangs with one taloned claw. "Finish it, and I promise that you'll enjoy the entrée even more."

23

The insectoid attackers were Assassin Bugs sent by the Crimson Hand to stop us from extracting the Bad Brain from Redulfo the Black's staved-in skull. Given that the dragon had just wiped out his own army as a demonstration, we may surmise that he didn't ask for their help. Rather, the Hand had insisted on it.

It was the second time they had attacked me. The first time was on the streets of Redhauke, right after a mysterious dwarf messenger returned to me the very same Screaming Skull that I had previously tossed into a lake of Hellfire. I had no fucking idea then who they were. Even now, years later, we knew little about the Hand; they were mostly a rumor, a secret cabal of mysterious origins with spies and assassins ensconced in power centers throughout the Free Kingdoms. Later, we would learn the truth: They had come from the Penultimate Universe, where they worshipped an avatar of the Violet Queen, to further the Queen's plan to consume Woerth. In that aim they were sometimes allied with Koschei, and sometimes they worked at cross-purposes. Nearly 150 years earlier, the very fabric of the Woerth itself was rent by the sudden appearance of their Sky Ship in the upper atmosphere; the force of its appearance shook the foundations of the Shadow Mountains, damaged their craft, and sent it crash-landing into the Pustiu Waste several hundred leagues to the west of the borderlands. I've seen the Sky Ship in person—walked its corridors, marveled at its vast machinery of mind-bending construction and purpose, and fought terrified against the fearsome mechanical soldiers that defended it. We nearly lost the race against the Hand to recover the black mirror from the ship's hold. If Cassie hadn't found a way to convince the spirit of the ship's captain, still haunting the vessel, to aid us, I'd be dictating this tome from Valhalla.

The Hand also armed and trained Garrin, the Grimmreaper, whose fell purpose seemed to include the dark annihilation of my soul. At every inflection point on our Quest, he appeared to test me. Armed as he was with Soulreaver and the Shield of Sorrow, he was, to most mortals, effectively invincible. To me, his adversary, however, he was most strangely and evenly matched. No matter how many times we clashed, neither of us could ever get the drop on the other—not until I finally cut off his fucking head before the Black Mirror itself.

That night in the Blue Falcon, the motherfucker appeared twice: once to my twenty-one-year-old self, after I had vanquished Malacoda in the Halls of Minos; and simultaneously to my thirty-year-old self, in the Red Library, as I was about to drag Redulfo the younger through the mirror to help murder his future dragon incarnation. Thanks to the Astral Telescope, I can see now that the Grimmreaper had slipped through the same mirror through which we had traveled to reach the Blue Falcon—he was ordered to do so by the Hand, so that their attack on the Quest occurred simultaneously in both timelines. I can assume only that they had ordered the hit on my younger self as well—tipped off by that fucking douche-canoe Jaspin, no doubt.

As my younger self stood before the Hellmouth in the catacombs below the Blue Falcon, I was still reeling from Melinda's sacrifice.

Now that it appeared as if we had pulled off the impossible—Mala-coda vanquished, the Skull trapped in Hell, the Saggon-golem dead, and the Blue Falcon itself shuddering through its death-throes—Melinda's sudden decision to remain in Hell to save the souls of those poor kids sent my world crumbling into ruin around me along with Storm Stonegorm's architectural triumph.

I love you, she had mouthed to me as the Hellmouth doors slammed shut for the final time. And there he was: the dark figure I would later know as the Grimmreaper, his face concealed within his black cowl and his black scythe drawn. As it was our first encounter, I thought him at first some lackey of Saggon's fleeing for his life before the catacombs collapsed. Then I heard his voice, echoing inside my head, and I *knew*—though we had never met, this dark figure was destined to become my mortal enemy, to haunt my nightmares, and to stand as the most fearsome harbinger of my doom.

"Too late for the Skull," came the figure's voice. "But I'll have that girdle off your stinking corpse, shitstain."

"Come and get it, assclown," I said.

The cloaked figure charged forward, his scythe a deadly whirling cuisinart in his gloved hands. I launched my own blade skyward to meet his blow. As our blades clashed, red sparks flew—and the resulting shock from our impossible meeting in this universe sent us both flying in opposite directions. I crashed into the now-inert doors of the Hellmouth, bounced off them, and rolled to a heap.

Leaping up, I found a tremor in spacetime itself now roiling the catacombs. Around me, the fleshy, soul-laden walls of the Hellmouth rippled wildly, as if some cosmic giant had dropped a stone onto the surface of reality itself. So massive was the shockwave that its force echoed back and forth in time, forcing tremors to rock the building throughout our assault of it.

Snarling furiously, the cloaked figure leaped up and raced toward me, only to find himself falling back as the catacomb ceiling collapsed in a thunderstorm of falling rock. We had one moment to glare at one another—though his face was hidden in shadow, I could feel his gaze branding me with enmity—and then the avalanche of rock sealed the tunnel, separating us for good. A rolling tumble of jagged boulders overcame me, and a large dog-sized rock caromed off my own now-ordinary skull. I saw blossoming star-flowers, and then utter darkness as I knew no more.

24

U p above and simultaneously, my nine-years-older self stood in the Red Library watching first Amabored, then Lithaine, and then Malcolm step through the mirror portal, presumably to return to the Wilderness of Mirrors to face down Redulfo the Black. My right hand gripped the upper arm of Redulfo the Younger, who stood blinking behind his spectacles as if he had just been bitch-slapped by a brontosaurus. In his free hand, he clutched his flute, having been told by us to prep a *Magnet* spell and be prepared to do what we told him.

"Remember, don't ask any questions," I told the young wizard. "The less you know, the better."

"Chances are, I won't even know what questions to ask," said Redulfo. "Where did you say we're going, again?"

"That was a question," I said, and turned to lead the wizard through the mirror—and then *he* was there.

Perversely, I felt a thrill of recognition at once again seeing him, dressed as always in the red and black colors of the Hand. His face lay still concealed in the shadows within his cowl. In his right hand he wielded Soulreaver, the wicked ebony scythe with which Koschei had returned from his own sojourn into Hell. To his left forearm was

strapped the Shield of Sorrow, which, should I roll a critical fumble
in my duel against the assassin, would see me sucked immediately
into its black depths and my soul cast irretrievably into the Void. It
had been a year since I had seen him last, after he caused us so much
grief in Helene; before that, on the Goldvale, where he poisoned the
mind of Bellasa's father, the Cloud Chief Hoyadi; before that, in the
sewers below Redhauke, after Melinda talked down the Rat King;
before that, in Hundred Fountain Square, leading Malacoda himself
on a leash; and, the first time—nine years earlier, this very night in
the Blue Falcon. Suddenly, I remembered: Even as I confronted him
here, in the Library, I was also confronting him far below, before the
Hellmouth.

As if to punctuate this revelation, the Library shook suddenly
from a great tremor. The floor of the room itself undulated even as
the walls danced a jig and the high vaulted ceiling splintered asunder
in an exploding web of jagged cracks. The force of the tremor sent the
three of us sprawling—Redulfo rolling across the heaving floor still
clutching his flute; me flung backwards into a display case, sending a
ceramic bust of Elvis Presley thumping across the heaving floor; and
Garrin back into the mirror portal, which flipped over with a crash as
his shield skidded across the room.

Before I could locate my wits, the assassin was upon me, his
scythe arcing down towards my neck. I found the haft of my battle-
axe and blocked the blow, just as I had blocked his blow nine years
ago on this very night. Calling up strength from the Girdle, I planned
to flip the asshole backwards and then drive the spiked end of my
axe-haft into that negative space where his face should be. Imagine
my surprise when I found that he was able to match my strength, and
he began to push the pointed tip of his rune-covered scythe-blade
back toward my own face. As the black tip approached my eyeball, I
allowed myself a small measure of panic.

"You think that girdle will help you?" came Garrin's terrifyingly
familiar voice, filling my head with spite. "You're too much of a
fucking pussy to beat me, you goddamned queef biscuit."

"You think so, you cock-juggling thundercunt?" No way I was

going to back down from this shithead. Bending my will to the Girdle, I summoned from it every ounce of sorcerous strength it could muster, until the veins stood livid on my arms and forehead, and my muscles burned as if they were being deep-fried. Slowly, the assassin gave ground. Then, just as slowly and inexorably, he gained it back. His head closed with mine—and still, even though I could feel his hot stink-breath washing over my face, I could see nothing within that ominous leather cowl but the utter blackness of the Void. There we remained, two mortal enemies poised on the precipice of destroying the other, and yet neither of us able to summon the final act of strength required.

"Who the fuck *ARE* you?" I cried.

"Everything you're not," Garrin returned.

We might have remained there forever—or at least until the Blue Falcon finally imploded around us—but for young Redulfo, the resourceful good egg. Even as I raged against Garrin, I felt the assassin's strength suddenly abate. He had frozen in place. Struggling mightily to comprehend my good fortune, I yanked myself away from him, leaped up, and readied an axe-blow designed to separate his head from his shoulders.

"Don't bother," came Redulfo's voice. The wizard cowered in a corner, clutching his flute with both hands. "It's a *Petrify* spell. You have about five minutes, but you won't be able to kill him. His skin will be as hard as dragon scales."

"Hot tuna!" I cried, running over to clap the wizard on the back. "That's using the ole coconut." Then I raced over to the mirror now lying flat on its face. Was it smashed to pieces, as I assumed it would be, thereby trapping me in the same time-space as my nine-years'-younger self?

No, it was not. My luck had held, and I wasn't about to give Odin time to wake up from his nap to start fucking with me. "Wizard!" I cried. "Over here—through the mirror. Now!"

Redulfo complied. The wizard stepped one foot gingerly toward the mirror as if dipping a toe into an icy river. When his boot dissolved into the glass, he looked back to me, unsure.

"Am I going to come back from this?" he asked.

"No questions, remember?" I said. "But since you asked—probably not."

Redulfo blinked. Then he nodded. "Okay, then," the wizard said, and stepped through the glass. Before I too, stepped through, I turned once again to regard my foe, still frozen and clutching his deadly scythe.

"See you around, Freddie," I said. At that moment, another massive explosion rocked the Falcon—this one from somewhere far above. *Probably Saggon's tower*, I thought. Knowing that my younger self was now trapped in the bowels of the dying inn, I paused to send him my best wishes. Then I stepped through the mirror and left myself behind forever.

25

The explosion had indeed come from Saggon's Tower, which had finally imploded in a horrific mushroom cloud. It was the final movement in the symphony of destruction that would bring to an ignominious end the long and storied legacy of Redhauke's world-famous Blue Falcon Inn. Ten minutes or so prior to this violent allegro, Amabored and Lithaine found themselves frozen solid in Saggon's office as the Over-Boss—or whatever the hell he was—trundled toward them. The office air was now so cold that every surface and object within was coated in a thin layer of frost.

"It's my lucky day, boys," the Over-Boss said. "Looks like I'm having a few friends for dinner."

As the icy tendrils of Death Frost worked their way through their armor and garments toward their hearts, the boys could only stare with their unmoving eyes as Saggon changed. His exposed blubbery skin took on a corpse-white sheen. The pupils of his eyes turned ice-blue. When he spoke, his voice remained as gruff and course as ever—but its cadence had changed.

"Do you think you ever stood a chance against me?" the Saggon-thing growled. "I, who have stood on the shores of Woerth before the first life even formed in its oceans? I, who have traversed the farthest reaches of the Multiverse? I, who have bowed before the Queen of Chaos Herself? Even now, seconds before your death, your Quest has failed. Your friends are dead or will soon die. The Skull and Girdle will be ours, and you will perish, your souls consigned to the Void."

Who was now speaking through the Saggon-golem, we would later vigorously debate. The consensus view was that the words had come from Koschei himself. Amabored, however, was convinced that it was Jaspin, as the illusionist must have been controlling the ice-golem that replaced the real Over-Boss. I'm still not sure I buy it—why would Jaspin spout off nonsense about bowing before the Violet Queen? Sure, he was working for the Hand, but it wasn't as if he was a Twentieth-Level sorcerer, for cripes' sake. Illusionists are low-rent wizards, bottom-feeders content to impress the chicks with their cute little phantasms instead of mastering truly badass sorcery. Why do you think the guy gave up adventuring to tend bar?

As for Amabored and Lithaine, we can only imagine the colorful retorts trapped behind their frozen lips as the Over-Boss approached. Another tremor rocked the tower—this one so strong that a fault line erupted in the office floor, sending shards of wood exploding into the air. Still frozen stiff, both men toppled over—and the *Holocaust* potion Amabored was holding in his motionless fingers slipped out. With one-half of the office floor now jutting upward at a thirty-degree angle, the vial bounced past the Saggon-thing, rolled under his desk, and then shattered against the iron grating of the great stone fireplace jutting from the curved rear wall.

The explosion was massive and instantaneous. Had the Death Frost not already frozen solid the two men, they would surely have been killed instantly—either incinerated in the fireball or crushed to death as the top of the tower exploded, sending a thundering avalanche of stone and wood raining down upon Halberd and Chain-mail streets far below. Across the city, gawking onlookers witnessed the explosion. Within minutes, a phalanx of Redhauke Guards assembled outside the East Barracks to march on the Blue Falcon, while over at the Wizards' College, Sklaar ordered a squadron of ornithopters to blast the area with sorcery dampeners. The city hadn't seen such excitement since we sent a herd of terrified cattle stampeding through the Chimera Gate two years earlier—and had the city fathers any inkling of our culpability for both events, they would have hunted us down like rats.

Atop the tower, the explosion had vaporized the turreted roof and much of the top floor. Miraculously, the outer wall and fireplace survived, but the rest of the office was gone. The remainder of Saggon's lair was now engulfed in fire, with dragon-sized tongues of flame stabbing the star-strewn night sky. Rather than vaporize our heroes, the *Holocaust* potion had instead dispelled the Death Frost, allowing them to rise to their feet singed, bloody, and shaken.

"Just a few drops—isn't that what you told us?" asked Lithaine.

"Not my fault, magic-boy," said the barbarian. "Got us free, didn't it? Let's find that dragon-dick and get the fuck out of here."

"*Urp—!*" said Lithaine, as the Saggon-thing wrapped a massive paw around the elf's throat and hoisted him high. The intense heat now found the Over-Boss's flesh melting, running like beef tallow in a hot frying pan, dripping from his limbs in great looping gobs, his multiple chins sloughing away from his face to slide down his leather cuirass. As the thing strangled Lithaine, its face bubbled, popped, and then ran dripping away from the now-exposed skull, which glowed green with fell necromancy.

Amabored might have taken a beat to marvel at this strange turn, but for the alarming purple shade his friend's face had turned. Swiftly retrieving his sword, the barbarian charged.

"COOOOORNHOLE!" he bellowed, and then brought his blade down on the golem's arm. Instead of hacking off the limb above the elbow, the blade stuck fast in the gooey mass of burbling flesh.

"*Uuurgh—!*" said Lithaine, his eyes bulging like bloodshot marbles.

"Motherfucker!" Amabored cried. Bellowing inchoate war-cries, he pulled a dagger from his belt and threw himself at the Saggon-thing. Slashing and stabbing at its leather armor, he soon found himself stuck as well, the golem's melting flesh capturing him in its deadly, asphyxiating embrace. The Over-Boss now resembled less an obese crime lord and more a gigantic, quivering mass of flesh-colored pudding. The mass closed around the barbarian. In its eagerness to crush the life from him it released Lithaine, who dropped to the floor and rolled away wheezing for his life.

Slow to recover, the elf could only watch as the Saggon-thing absorbed his friend. A moment passed as the undulating mass burbled and belched, digesting its prey. The heat from the fire was becoming too much to bear; in a moment, the elf would be forced to abandon Amabored and fling himself back down the remaining tower stairs before the whole thing came down.

The elf didn't flee. Instead, his eyes narrowed to slits. His jaw set, and he unsheathed his sword. Still gasping for air through his brutal-ized throat, the elf stumbled toward the golem.

And then: The great blubbery pile of Saggon-flesh rent asunder as Amabored's knife-blade slashed through it. With a ragged cry, the barbarian hauled himself from the thing's grasp, his muscles straining against the flesh now pulling like taffy as it attempted to haul him back. In his right hand, he held his knife. In his left, he now clutched a head-sized, pulsing, bloody mass—Saggon's heart.

From within the quivering mass of flesh came the surprising and muffled sound of Saggon's voice: "No hard feelings, fellahs! Let's call up for some brandy, from my personal cellar. It's from Collanna, they make the best. We'll have it with a charcuterie board, my treat."

Amabored's knife-hand was held back by ropes of gooey flesh. His left hand, however, was free. With a glance to Lithaine, he tossed the bloody heart at him. The elf swung his blade—and cleaved the flying organ in twain.

The effect was immediate. The towering pile of flesh that was once the Over-Boss collapsed in a splashing, bloody pool of goo that then began to boil away from the heat. Whether the thing had always been Saggon, or whether the real Saggon was dead and replaced by the ice-golem at some unknown point in the past, we couldn't say. Either way, the result was the same: The notorious Saggon the Large, who once consolidated underworld power by executing twenty-three key crime family heads during the Feast of the Fountains in 3930, was no more. His days of feeding children to Malacoda like so many pickled herring were over.

Freed from the goo, Amabored fell forward, caught himself, and stumbled to his feet. "Now that's some fucking teamwork!" the barbarian allowed, fist-bumping Lithaine. "That's twice I saved your life tonight. That's worth a lifetime supply of beer on your credit, elf."

"Your ass—seems like I just saved your life," Lithaine said, allowing a rare grin. "Better stick a crowbar in your wallet and pony up."

"Fat chance. Let's get that dragon-dick and get it back to me," said Amabored. The two men turned—and found Amabored the Elder standing before them. In his hands he bounced the petrified dragon phallus once mounted above Saggon's mantel.

"No need, boys," said Amabored the Elder. "For a couple of pikers, you did good. I'll take it from here."

"You were watching the whole time?" asked Amabored the Younger. "Why the hell didn't you do something?"

"You pussies want me to do everything for you?" asked the Elder, grinning. "Now get the fuck out of here and let the grown-ups take care of business." With that, the elder barbarian spread his wings, ran for the precipice of the now-exposed tower floor, and launched himself through the flames and into the night. With one great flap of his wings, he was gone.

"Those wings are badass," said Amabored. "Bet they smell like a wet sheepdog, though."

"As if you need another reason to jerk yourself off," said Lithaine. "Ready, asswipe?"

"Ready, Jerky. Let's hope a few of our friends are still alive."

26

Nine years later, Redulfo the Younger and I tumbled through the mirror in the Red Library and back to my present in the Wilderness of Mirrors. Immediately, we were assaulted by Hand assassins. Only my considerably older and more sharpened reflexes prevented one of the bugs from decapitating the young wizard as I instead shaved off the creature's head with my axe-blade. My three companions stood in a rough triangle around the mirror as they fought off the onrushing horde of enemies with bow and blade. More of them were now emerging from the mirrors—so many that, absent divine intervention, we were as dead as Dillinger.

"Ho, gents!" said Malcolm, calling back over his shoulder as he sliced a bug in half from crown to tail. "We feared you had been irretrievably delayed."

"Ran into an old friend!" I called back, shoving Redulfo the Younger behind me as five assassin bugs rushed into axe-range. "Stay behind me, youngster," I told the wizard. "With your paltry supply of health points, you won't last five minutes out here."

"Where are we?" the wizard asked as he cowered behind me.

"We're right here," I said, and swung my axe. My blade bit into an insect head and sent it exploding like a ripe melon tossed from a parapet. Goddamn it, it felt good to go to work.

Far above, Redulfo the Black flew in descending spirals toward our hopelessly outmatched party. When he spied Redulfo the Younger hiding behind my skirt, he flew over—and if a dragon could entirely replicate human expression, his face would have mirrored the withering disdain that his human incarnation reserved for such irony-laden situations.

"Redulfo, my good fellow!" the dragon called. "So glad you could accept my invitation."

"Invitation?" The young wizard called back. "To my funeral, I suppose."

"In a sense, yes," said the dragon. "As I mentioned to your older companions, my possession of the Bad Brain renders suicide impossible, as much as I might wish it. Given the rather singular nature of this universe, however, I have developed a hypothesis that you will help me test."

At that moment, every single assassin bug currently attempting to disembowel us stopped dead, frozen in place. We four fighters glanced around, panting and bleeding from our various wounds, unable to keep pace with the continually shifting tactical situation. Stepping around from behind me, Redulfo the Younger regarded his older dragon incarnation, now hovering in place about thirty feet above our heads.

"Hypothesis?" asked the wizard, his interest piqued.

"Indeed," said the dragon. "As I mentioned, the Bad Brain prevents me from taking my own life. I have, however, engineered an encounter in which my death is inevitable. Either you will kill me, thereby completing my suicide attempt, or I will kill you, and negate my own existence. Either way, there's nothing this universe can do to prevent my death. I will have proven that, after five thousand years of clockwork causality, free will now exists on Woerth. An elegant experiment, wouldn't you agree?"

"What does he mean, 'negate my own existence?'" Redulfo whispered to me.

Before I could answer, the dragon chimed in. "When attempting private conversation, good Redulfo, you must account for a dragon's acute hearing. To answer your question: In five years' time, by your own timeline, you will encounter a treasure egg in the Temple of Pain Eternal, on the Sunless Sea. You will wonder whether you should open that egg. My advice to you: Open it."

"I'll take it under advisement," Redulfo said.

"You're forgetting one thing, dragon," called Amabored. "To get to the wizard, you have to go through us. You can't kill him if we kill you first."

"Ah—empty bravado," said the dragon. "I had so forgotten its peculiar odor. My retort, friend barbarian: It's you who have forgotten 'one thing.' For, while the four of you have imbibed a potion that protects you from my breath-weapon, our young wizard here has not."

At that moment, two things happened simultaneously: Released from the dragon's glamour, the frozen assassin bugs un-froze, and began their assault anew; and Redulfo the Black swooped down on Redulfo the Younger's position to launch at him a blistering stream of black acid. It all happened so quickly that I could only wait for my sluggish brain to alert my limbs to do something, anything, to protect the young wizard.

As insufferable as they mostly are, elves do possess a few useful traits. One of these is an innate ability to seize the initiative. Malcolm, for example, launched himself at Redulfo and tackled the young wizard, raising his kite shield over them both to deflect the torrent of hot acid now pouring like sizzling oil over the shield. Lithaine, meanwhile, bounded over and rocked me across the chops.

"Wake up!" The elf shouted in my face. "And give me a lift. A power lift—you got me?"

Miraculously, I got him. I dropped my hands into a cup, and the elf dropped his boot into my cupped hands. Calling up strength from the Girdle, I flung him skyward. Lithaine intercepted the dragon in mid-flight and wrapped his arms around his neck. As the beast rose higher, the elf twisted, wrapping his legs around also while mostly avoiding the beast's razored spines. The dragon whip-sawed his long neck to and fro, attempting to unseat the elf, but Lithaine went nowhere. Instead, he crept forward toward the dragon's head with one arm gripping the neck. With the other, he drew an arrow from his quiver.

From a position near me, Amabored stopped killing bugs long enough to toss toward Malcolm a long, red, and barbed piece of stone —the dragon-phallus, procured from Saggon's mantel nine years earlier. Malcolm caught it.

"Give it to the wizard and tell him to stand by!" Amabored called.

"It will be done!" the paladin called back. Emerging from beneath Malcolm's shield, Redulfo the Younger patted the un-burnt grass in search of his spectacles. Finding them, he wrapped the wire temples around his ears. Malcolm then handed him the stone phallus, which the wizard regarded with mild distaste.

"I know how it must look, young wizard," Malcolm told him. "Unfortunately, this is the only object available to us that can penetrate a dragon's hide. Now, be a good chap and stand behind me." Three more bug-assassins slammed into the paladin, who ducked beneath their swinging scimitars and sliced open their black thoraxes with his own blade.

While we fended off the insectoid assault, Lithaine worked his way to the crown of the dragon's head. The dragon flew straight up, paused majestically so that his slender frame and outstretched wings were silhouetted against the setting sun, and then flipped over 180 degrees to descend screaming toward the ground. Gripping a handful of the dragon's jagged spines so tightly that his hand bled, Lithaine raised up the arrow in his other hand—and then drove the arrowhead directly into the dragon's right eyeball.

So terrifying was the dragon's piercing shriek that the Hand's attack stumbled to a halt. Seeking the scream's source, the insectoids trained their bulbous compound eyes upward. The dragon flipped around again, arresting his screaming descent, and then flew skyward with two great flaps of his ragged bat-wings. The force of the torque flung Lithaine from the beast's neck to crash into a swarm of assassin bugs and scatter them like bowling pins. Still shrieking, the dragon raced upward, one foreclaw swiping at the arrow shaft protruding from his oozing eyeball.

"NOW!" bellowed Amabored, waving his arms at young Redulfo. "Cast the spell and hold up the dragon-dick!"

Malcolm gave a small bow to the wizard. "If you would indulge us, young sieur. Cast your spell, and once you've done so, hold the phallus aloft, like so." The paladin demonstrated with his sword, hoisting it high over his head with both hands.

Shrugging with exquisite indifference, Redulfo the Younger tucked the dragon-phallus under his arm, took out his flute, and blew a short run of notes. The air around him began to shimmer. Before he could vamoose to a safe distance, Malcolm's sword and shield were ripped from his hands and captured by the invisible magnetic sphere that had formed around the wizard.

High above the ground, another magnetic field appeared as a shimmering bubble around the shrieking black dragon. Redulfo the Black stopped suddenly in mid-flight—and for a moment, the dragon hung there resplendent, his dark wings stretched taught like full-bellied outer jibs.

And so, back to my original point: Why does my swollen prostate make me think of the day we slayed Redulfo the Black? Because my apothecary did the same thing to me that the dragon's younger incarnation did to him—shove something so far up my ass that it had to come out somewhere else. The first time one of my apothecaries shoved his fist up my bunghole to check my prostate, I kicked his ass right there in his office and threw him into my dungeon for a week. While I never got used to the procedure, I did come to accept it; I wished only that one of my many healers and clerics had bought me dinner first.

To Redulfo the Black, however, we only had to do it once. The spell did its job, manifesting two opposing magnetic fields that wanted nothing more than to race toward each other at ridonkulous speeds. Holding the phallus aloft per Malcom's direction, the wizard launched from the ground like a Saturn V, racing at a blistering pace toward the dragon. The dragon, meanwhile, was flung ass-first at the wizard. Below, all of us—men, elves, and insects—watched with stunned wonder.

When the two opposing objects met, the result was both predictable and wildly astounding: Redulfo the Younger drove the dragon-phallus directly up Redulfo the Black's black-dragon asshole. There was an explosive gout of black blood and gore as both phallus and wizard disappeared into the dragon's bowels—and then another geyser of blood as the wizard rocketed out again through the dragon's upper chest, directly above his heart.

"Bullseye!" cried Amabored.

The force of the impact dispelled the magnetic fields. His momentum arrested, the poor gore-drenched wizard now flailed wildly in a ragged parabola back toward the ground, where he crashed into another knot of insectoids and sent them flying. The fatally-wounded dragon, meanwhile, tumbled head-over-tail, plummeting straight down, until he landed with a sickening thud about fifty chains away from our position.

For a moment, nothing moved. Then the remaining insectoid assassins renewed their attack—but only for a moment. The dragon moved his head briefly, and the bugs froze again. With scimitars poised, they stood utterly still amongst the bodies of their dead comrades littering the field, now a pop-art cacophony of congealed red and black blood, grass blackened by acid, and lonely patches of undisturbed green.

Meanwhile, a bruised and battered Lithaine climbed to his feet, a bloodied Malcolm retrieved his sword and shield, and a gore-slimed Amabored wrapped bandages around his savaged forearm. Across the field, Redulfo the Younger also rose unsteadily. As the least-wounded amongst us, I took it upon myself to jog over to him.

"That was surprisingly effective," I said. Robes matted and slimed with black dragon blood and entrails, the young wizard was searching the ground for his spectacles, only to give up when he realized that he must have lost them when he was rocketing through a black dragon's guts at Mach Five. He shrugged.

"I'd say that was the most unpleasant thing that will ever happen to me," said Redulfo, "but I'm pretty sure I'd be wrong."

"Look on the bright side," I said, hooking a thumb over my shoulder. "You could have been him."

I walked the wizard across the field to where the dragon now lay in a jumbled, angular heap. The others gathered also, until we stood together in a rough semicircle around the bloody mess. Redulfo the Black, erstwhile Lord of the Valley and Master of the Workshop of Telescopes, was still alive, if barely. From top to bottom, the würm was a bloody horror. As the dragon's shallow, ragged breath rose and fell, the gaping hole in his upper chest oozed black magma. Stretched out on the grass, his long neck curled around to the thin, tapered head and snout, also caked with blood. Lithaine's arrow protruded still from one eye. He looked asleep—until he opened his good eye to regard us with surprising warmth.

"Well done, fellows," Redulfo the Black croaked. "Well done indeed, young Redulfo. It appears that my hypothesis was correct, and my experiment a success."

"You know we had no choice," I said to the lizard. "It's not personal. We just need your brain."

"Why the elaborate plot?" asked Amabored. "Why the bugbears, why the spiders, why the time travel, if all you wanted to do was die? You could have made it a hell of a lot easier on us."

"In my previous incarnation, I might have told you that none of us ever had a choice in our actions," said the dragon. "I have, however, proven that notion incorrect. There is a lesson for you here, my friends, should you choose to learn it. For five thousand years, we have been trapped in a universe in which time was immutable, and life preordained. As I have just proven, however, that this proscription is no longer true. You live now in a universe in which anything is possible. You have free will. I suggest you use it."

"We will," I said. "Now, we have to get young Redulfo here back to the Blue Falcon before the whole place implodes." I glanced around at the frozen assassin bugs. "What about these guys?" I asked the dragon. "Why did you stop them from killing us? Aren't you on the same side?"

"While possessing Koschei's brain makes one necessarily Lawful Evil, I'm pleased to report that imminent death has released me from the stringent requirements of alignment—allowing me to help you," said the dragon. "You see, here at the end of my life, I find that I want you to succeed, friend Elberon. I want you to complete the Quest."

"Now he tells us," said Lithaine.

"Once I expire, the spell restraining the Hand will dissipate within an hour," the dragon continued. "I suggest you retreat to the Workshop, where the castle's defensive charms will prevent them from following you. There, you'll find the pathway to resume your Quest."

"Then we'd better get moving," said Amabored. "We're going to need that brain of yours, you know, pretty soon."

"Do you mind if I take a minute?" asked Redulfo the Younger. He glanced back at the dying dragon. "Now that I've killed him, I'd like to get to know him a little better."

"Sure thing, kid," Amabored said, clapping the wizard on the back. "Five minutes." He turned to the dragon. "The less he knows, the better, right?"

While dragons can't necessarily smile, this dragon gave a convincing approximation of one. "There's nothing this young wizard can learn from me that he doesn't already know," said Redulfo the Black.

While we searched for the mirror that would send the wizard back to his own time, Redulfo communed with the dragon. Ostensibly, they were the same person, incarnations separated only by a short span of time. Again, I wondered: Just how much of our friend was left in the dragon? Wasn't Redulfo gone well before we killed him this second time? The thought filled me with inestimable sadness— for the loss of my friend, and for losses yet to come. Even living as I was in the full glory of my youth, I had come to understand one of life's eternal truths: Live long enough, and life becomes mostly about loss. Live long enough, and everything you love dies, changes irrevocably, or becomes a brutal parody of itself. Like I said before: It's all a steaming bowl of shit soup.

I wasn't alone in my melancholy. Having at last located the blue-framed mirror that led back to the Red Library, we returned to gather up Redulfo the Younger and found that Redulfo the Black had finally died. The wizard had placed a gentle hand on the dragon's blood-caked snout. When he turned to us, we saw the tears streaming down his face.

"I would have liked to have known him longer," said Redulfo. "I think all he really needed was a friend."

Malcolm knelt beside the wizard. He placed his own hand alongside Redulfo's on the dragon's snout.

"My good wizard, we were his friends, to the last," said the paladin. "We gave him that for which he longed the most: We released him from his pain."

27

A s I hear Malcolm say those words again, I wonder still if they're true. Did Redulfo long most for relief from this world? We all bear our measure of pain; I sometimes justify my own often-terrible behavior by convincing myself that the pain I've endured is more than most people could handle. And yet, I say this while sitting atop the riches of a kingdom entire. No matter how badly you think you have it, there's always someone who has it worse than you.

THE CONFLAGRATION OF QUANTUM FORCES ERUPTING WITHIN AND beneath the Blue Falcon had sent the famous inn and fortress shuddering through its final death rattle. My battle with Malacoda, my first explosive interaction with Garrin, the detonation of the *Holocaust* potion, and the kinetic energy released by the clashing timelines had proven too much for the inn, which was now imploding into slow-motion ruin. Outside the Falcon's high courtyard walls, the Redhauke Guard and the gawping onlookers could only watch in horror as stone, bricks, wood, and debris began to rotate madly around the inn's expansive courtyard in a strengthening chaotic cyclone.

It was one thing to observe the destruction from the outside; it was quite another to be trapped within. The young Redulfo, still reeling from his brief sojourn through a dragon's colon, emerged flying out of the mirror portal to find the Red Library disintegrating around him. Dodging a hailstorm of flying tomes, jars, and sorcerous artifacts, the wizard raced out into the hallway, where he nearly collided with Amabored and Lithaine fleeing from the collapsing remains of Saggon's tower.

"Redulfo! Thank the gods you're alive!" said Amabored, grabbing the wizard's shoulders. "What happened to your glasses? Have you seen the others?"

"Those are more complicated question than you might think," said the wizard, who had mostly cleaned off the dragon's blood and guts before his older friends sent him back. "If by 'the others,' you mean the others we came here with—then no, not recently. I left Malcolm in the Grand Foyer. I haven't seen Elberon and Melinda since they descended below. I'm pretty sure they're okay, though. Call it a feeling."

"I know what you mean," Amabored allowed, narrowing his eyes at the wizard. "I know I make it out of here, at least. Can't say the same for the elf, though."

"If we don't leave now, then we're all going to die," said Lithaine.

"You're right," the barbarian allowed. "Best not to chance it."

As the wooden floor of the long corridor bucked and split while the plaster walls exploded in successive gouts of dust and debris, the three men bolted for the staircase leading down to the Grand Foyer. They arrived there to find the staircase collapsed into a heap of rubble. Peering down from the mezzanine into the wide hall, they saw amidst the overturned long tables and shards of smashed crockery a wide, tall, bloody and suppurating mound of dead imps— most of them missing limbs, a good many missing heads. Of Malcolm, they saw no sign.

"Christ, that paladin took care of business," Amabored shouted over the din of the Falcon's demise.

Taking a few steps back, Lithaine jumped from the balcony to land with a sickening thud on the pile of corpses. He slid down them, causing a small avalanche of severed limbs and headless torsos, and then bounced away onto the floor of the hall. He glanced up, waiting for the others to follow suit.

They did so, sending more corpses sliding and rolling down the corpse-mound. When they arrived at the bottom, the three men turned toward the pile—and saw a hand, now exposed from within and clutching a sword hilt. It was Malcolm's sword.

"Holy shit!" Amabored exclaimed. "It's our paladin!"

The three men rushed the pile and began pulling out corpses to expose more of Malcolm. Soon they had exposed his head—and their fear of his death vanished when the paladin, be-slimed with blood and gore, sneezed explosively to clear the dripping black goo from his sinuses.

"Thank the Star Maiden!" Lithaine cried with uncharacteristic alacrity. Together, he and Amabored hauled the paladin from the pile. By the time Malcolm had recovered enough to stand wobbly, Lithaine had restored his façade of insufferable ennui.

"Hogging all the glory for yourself, I see," the elf said.

"Forgive me, my liege," Malcolm said, smiling through the dried blood caking his face. He retrieved his kite shield from the corpse-pile as he spoke. "'Twas not my intention. As I had promised your wizard friend that I would guard the staircase, however, I was bound to slay these foul hellspawn until there were no more to slay."

"You've earned your stripes, paladin, there's no doubt," said Amabored. "Enough with the jerking off—we have to find Melinda and Elberon."

At that moment, the inn gave a great shuddering groan as the walls and ceiling of the Grand Foyer began to give way. Wooden beams and jagged sheets of plaster and lathe broke free to sail past the heads of the four men. The debris was sucked into a quantum vortex forming around an eye located somewhere near the center of the inn's footprint. Within a minute, the flying debris field became so intense that it threatened to decapitate or impale them.

"Run away!" Amabored cried, and they all broke for the exit.

Dodging missiles of brick and stone, they serpentined through the foyer and then out through the front entrance, just as the mighty oaken door-halves were ripped from their hinges and sucked into the vortex. Once in the courtyard, they each dived for cover—Amabored into an open zombie-grave, Lithaine and Redulfo under a pile of stone debris, and Malcolm beneath his shield. From their separate vantage points, they watched the Blue Falcon die: the burning remains of the tower now imploding, the walls and ceilings of the great inn breaking apart, the furniture, tapestries, and possessions collected over the long centuries of the inn's lifespan vanishing into the whirling vortex. The tornado of debris increased in intensity, spinning ever faster, condensing into a neutron star of quantum destruction. Finally, the remains of the vast inn vanished in an orgasmic release of force that flattened bystanders and broke windows from the Thieves Quarter to Shorestone Palace. Out in the harbor, the chop grew so fierce that smaller boats were swamped or capsized. Every bird flying over the city was killed instantly.

After that, there was silence—until the crowd gathered outside the walls finally overcame their shock and exploded into a raucous hubbub of excitement and disbelief. Within the courtyard, the four men emerged from their cover.

"That was intense," said Lithaine, dusting himself off.

"We sure as hell know how to throw a party," said Amabored. "We need to scram before the guards grow balls big enough to come in here."

"Your friends," said Malcolm. "The woman, and the fighter. What of them?"

"Jesus, you're right," said Amabored. "They're trapped below, or they're dead. FUUUCCK!" the barbarian bellowed.

"I don't know about Melinda," said Redulfo, "but Elberon is still alive."

"How do you know, good wizard?" asked Malcolm.

"Trust me."

"Okay, he's alive," said Amabored, glancing around at the smoking hole where the inn had been. The inn had sat atop a vast

warren of dungeons and catacombs which was now entirely exposed
—and entirely buried beneath a massive, smoking pile of stone and
brick debris. "How the fuck do we find him?"

"Follow her," said Lithaine. Amabored spun to find the elf
pointing to a figure standing off in the middle distance of the courtyard—the glowing form of a barefoot, raven-haired young girl
wearing a white gown. She beckoned to the men to approach her.

"That's her?" Amabored whispered, as he perhaps wondered to
himself why he was whispering. "The girl from Doomtown?"

Lithaine sighed. "Yep. That's her."

"An apparition—marvelous!" said Malcolm, clearly enchanted.
"She's no tool of Chaos. In fact, the light of the Star Maiden shines
brightly from her. Whatever she is, we may trust her."

The paladin's endorsement was good enough for Amabored, who
shoved Lithaine forward with a hand on his back. The elf approached
the girl warily as the others followed. The ghost allowed them to
close, and then darted into the inn's carriage house. The slate roof of
that building had been sucked into the vortex along with its three
sets of tall wooden barn doors. The girl stood at the middle archway
of the barn, motioning them again to follow her inside. As the men
approached, she slipped into the shadows of the ruined building.

Once inside, the men found the girl hovering over a stone well
long since gone dry. She motioned them to descend into it. Then she
quickly faded and was gone.

"You first, cupcake," Amabored said to Lithaine.

The elf tied a rope to the bars of one of the horse stalls, then
dropped the other end into the well. Malcolm found a torch, lit it
from his tinder pack, and tossed it into the well after the rope. Then
Lithaine climbed into the pit, and the others followed.

So it went, with the apparition guiding them at each stage of their
journey: through the dark dungeons beneath the former inn and
down the endless stone staircases, until the man-made tunnels gave
way to natural stone catacombs enlarged and reinforced over the
centuries. Along the way, Redulfo paused intermittently to mark with
Light charms the path of their return.

They came at last to a narrow crevice in the rock through which they could only squeeze single-file. Through it they went, until they found themselves within the Chamber of Malacoda itself, where the shit had gone down. At one end of this high cavern stood the immense obsidian doors of the Hellmouth; their carved runes, once glowing red with Hellfire, were now dark. The opposite end was now sealed by a wall of jumbled stone. And there I was, lying inert on the ground before the Hellmouth doors.

Redulfo dropped to my side and felt for my pulse. He looked up and nodded—I was still alive. Amabored turned to the translucent girl, still shimmering nearby.

"Whoever you are, thank you," said Amabored. "Thank you for finding our friend."

"Your Quest must yet be born," said the girl, and her voice sounded as if it came from the end of a long tunnel. *"And by ending the devil's terrible hunger, you have each proven your worth."* She turned to Lithaine, standing uncomfortably nearby. *"Until we meet again, my beloved."*

"Stop calling me that!" Lithaine snarled.

"What is your name, young maiden?" asked Malcolm.

"I am the Glorious Song of El," said the girl, bowing before the men. *"You may call me Madrigel."*

Before Amabored could summon a suitable insult with which to jab Lithaine, the girl vanished. Malcolm dropped to one knee and clutched his sword pommel to his breast.

"A true herald of the Star Maiden!" the paladin exclaimed. "My liege, you are truly blessed to have the favor of a Celestial."

"If anyone mentions that girl to me again, I'll shank you in the belly."

"Duly noted," said Amabored. Then the men turned their attention turned to me as I moaned and attempted to roll over. They helped me to sit up. My headache was immense, as if some malevolent god had dropped a planet on my head, and it would be some time before I could even begin to piece together the events that had transpired after I donned the Screaming Skull.

"Elberon, what happened?" Amabored said. "Where's Melinda? The Skull—is it gone?"

I took several beats, and then the enormity of Melinda's sacrifice fell upon me like a sudden fever. Leaping up, I seized Amabored's shoulders.

"We have to save her!" I cried.

"Save her?" asked Amabored. "Save Melinda? Where is she?"

I pointed to the Hellmouth doors. "She sacrificed herself. For those kids. I have to save her, Amabored. If I have to cross the Nine Circles myself to find her, then by the gods, I will."

28

Another nine years would pass before I could fulfill my promise to save Melinda—and yet only six months would pass until she returned to Redhauke in a litter borne by a phalanx of Cloud Riders. If that paradox doesn't twist your brain into a pretzel, it should.

If even a single strand of the web of events supporting the Quest would have failed, then the entire enterprise would have collapsed. As the Celestial sent to Woerth to stand against the Violet Queen, Madrigel's chosen mission was to ensure that no strand did fail. She had appeared to Lithaine in Doomtown so that we would end Malacoda's slaughter of innocents—and, in so doing, I would enter the city, meet Melinda, and come to possess the Skull. Two years later, she led my friends to find me in the devil's chamber so that I would, nine years hence, descend into Hell to save Melinda—even if she also ended up saving me. Had Melinda died, then she wouldn't have been around to parlay with the Rat King. Both Skull and Girdle would have fallen into the hands of Lord Eckberd, and we would all have died on his gibbet. In turn, Koschei would have conquered the Free Kingdoms, thrown down the Celestial Stairway, and opened the pathway for the Violet Queen to devour Woerth. You'll have to forgive us for feeling like pawns.

As essential as Melinda was to the Quest, so too was Cassiopeia. I never understood why that fucking Ki-Rin appeared to her, and not to me. Hadn't he revealed to me that my destiny was to complete the Quest? Hadn't he resurrected my friends and me and told me that we were each essential to its completion? Thanks to the Astral Telescope, I can now watch that asshole reveal the Quest to Cassie. In so doing, I learn the truth: The Ki-Rin didn't trust me. He knew me too well; I was insufferably lazy and an unrepentant procrastinator. Had he left me to my own devices, Koschei would have conquered three-quarters of the Free Kingdoms before I decided to do something about it. I needed a woman to light a fire under my ass—so he found one to do it.

It was the day before Cassie confronted us, and we watched Sklaar's tower explode when Garrin assassinated him with a satchel full of dwarf boom-clay hidden under the old wizard's desk. Cassie was practicing her mace-work in the olive garden outside the Temple of Athena when the Ki-Rin appeared, accompanied by overwrought pyrotechnics and a musical score entirely suited to his bourgeois sensibilities. Momentarily terrified, Cassie hit the dirt and covered her head. Only after the Ki-Rin spoke did she stand and face him.

"Behold!" the Ki-Ri said, appearing as he had to me in a vision, reposed on a green hill beneath a blue sky with fluffy white clouds skidding behind him. His voice boomed off the walls of the Temple courtyard. His lion-mane rippled in the breeze. His white teeth gleamed. "I bring you tidings, fair shield-maiden. You have been chosen to fulfil a great mission. Athena herself commands it."

"Um... who are you?" asked Cassie, recovering her gumption.

"I am the Herald. You have been chosen. Prepare now to receive enlightenment, and to take up your sacred Quest!"

"Look, pal, I'm pretty busy. Take it somewhere else."

The Ki-Rin broke character. "No—you look, lady," he said, his ringing orchestral accompaniment decreasing in volume. "How about you just let me get through this? I spent hours working on this presentation. There's a lot of exposition to get through. I don't want to be here any more than you do, so let's just make the best of it, shall we?"

Considering this plea, Cassie nodded her consent. The Ki-Rin faded from view to be replaced by a vision of the Dread Keep itself, towering over the blasted ruins of the Dread Plain.

"This is the Dread Keep," said the Ki-Rin. "Home of Koschei the Deathless. You've heard of him?"

"Of course," said Cassie.

"After five hundred years of sleep, the Dread Lord has awoken," said the Ki-Rin. "Tomorrow, his army will arrive outside this city. His warlord will demand the head of someone you know—the fighter Elberon. You must not allow this to happen. You must help him get out of the city alive."

"What's Elberon got to do with Koschei? Is this about that skull he keeps talking about?"

"Elberon and his friends are the chosen ones charged with completing the new Quest of the Dread Plain to throw down the Deathless One." At Cassie's look, the Ki-Rin nodded. "Yes, I know— hard to believe. In fact, I can't imagine any lot less qualified. That's why we need you to guide them. Otherwise, Woerth is screwed."

"Okay. Let's say I buy what you're selling. What do I have to do?"

"Ah—glad you asked! Prepare to be dazzled." At that, the image of the Dread Keep faded and was replaced by an image of Koschei himself—a figure cloaked in black and bearing fell weapons. As Cassie watched, the figure broke apart into ten separate objects.

"These are the Ten Phylaxes of Koschei the Deathless," the Ki-Rin continued.

"Ten Horcruxes? What are those?" Cassie interrupted.

"Not Horcruxes, for crying out loud. Phylaxes," said the Ki-Rin. "Five of Koschei's preserved body parts. Five of his most powerful weapons and relics. Each one bears a piece of the Deathless One's soul. You must find each of them before your enemies do. Only by collecting all of them can you hope to destroy him. Let's review."

As Koschei introduced each Phylax, its image rotated forward and grew to fill the frame of the Ki-Rin's display. First, a jeweled, horned skull rotated forward.

"The Screaming Skull," the Ki-Rin intoned. "Elberon possesses it already. Keep it out of Eckberd's hands."

The Skull was replaced by an image of a warrior's jeweled leather girdle. "The Girdle of Gargantua," the Ki-Rin continued. "Elberon has it also. Ditto on keeping it away from the bad guys."

Next, there appeared an image of a long, black, rune-covered scythe. "The Scythe of Souls, also known as Soulreaver. It's already in the hands of your enemy, so you'll want to get it back—if you can."

Next, an image of an utterly black kite shield. "The Shield of Sorrow—likewise in your enemy's hands."

"The Bad Brain," the Ki-Rin continued, as the shield was replaced by a pulsing green brain. "It lies in the Temple of Pain Eternal, on the Sunless Sea."

Then came the image of a pair of glowing eyeballs with red pupils shaped like cat-eyes. "The Awful Orbs. They're lost—but you must find them."

"The Horrible Heart." Cassie next saw the image of a black, beating heart. "It beats within the chest of Lord Eckberd himself. Good luck getting it from him."

An image of a red, throbbing man-organ, the sight of which made Cassie visibly nauseous. "The Fell Phallus. I'd stay away from it, if I were you."

Then, an image of a black ceremonial mace with rune-covered flanges and an ebony shaft topped with the snarling head of a lion. "The Mace of Malice. You'll need to pry it from the dead hand of the Empress Wilomina. Good luck with that."

And, finally, the image of a gleaming golden crown studded with diamonds and rubies. "And, last but certainly not least," the Ki-Rin concluded, "The Crown of Chaos. Also lost—though the Wise may know where it can be found."

The image of the crown faded, and the Ki-Rin appeared again, visibly pleased with himself. "Find these Phylaxes you must, before your enemies find them, or kill you," he said. "This is your charge. Without you, Elberon and his friends will never complete this Quest, and the Woerth will be lost."

For a moment, Cassie was silent. Then something within her seemed to stiffen, and she stood taller. "Okay, friend. When we've collected all ten of these Phylaxes, what do we do with them?"

"Let's not get ahead of ourselves," said the Ki-Rin. "Your odds of success are so low that it's best to take this thing one stage at a time. Get the Phylaxes, and then we'll talk."

With that, the Ki-Rin bowed theatrically. The unseen orchestra swelled again to a crescendo. With a final flourish of trumpets and timpani, the Ki-Rin vanished, leaving Cassie alone again in the olive grove to contemplate her misfortune.

"Fucking hell," she said to herself, and headed back to the temple.

29

Had Garrin not greased Sklaar that following day, things might have turned out very differently—or they might not have, depending on your point of view. We might have tried to turn over the Skull and Girdle to Sklaar, despite Cassie's dire proclamations; once the wizard learned that both were irrevocably tied to my fate, he might have waxed me where I stood. Or, it might be that every aspect of the Quest was preordained, with a chain of causality stretching back to the earliest movements of the Machine Elves in the First Universe. Who the hell knows? Redulfo the Black told us that he had proven free will was now built into the fabric of Woerth, but what did that mean in practical terms? How could we use that knowledge to save the world?

WHETHER OR NOT FREE WILL EXISTS, THERE WERE CERTAIN INFLECTION points along the path of the Quest where the fate of Woerth truly did hang in the balance—points at which the outcome was not preordained. As the young Redulfo told us, success becomes possible only when all other options have been exhausted. My final confrontation with the Arch-Devil Malacoda was such a moment.

Had I not prevailed, the Woerth would have become the Violet Queen's lunch.

"I CHALLENGE HIS SATANIC HIGHNESS MALACODA, DIRE MALEBRANCHE OF MALEBOLGE AND VASSAL OF BEELZE-BUB, KING OF THE EIGHTH CIRCLE AND LORD OF FLIES, TO THE JUDGEMENT OF MINOS!" I had cried out, as the caverns around the Hellmouth collapsed around us.

"SO, YOU WANT TO PLAY GAMES, LITTLE MAN?" Malacoda had roared. "ALL RIGHT—LET'S PARTY."

The devil had touched my arm—and I found myself standing in an arena in Limbo, the First Circle of Hell.

Later, I would become well-versed in the geography of the Infernal Realm. At the time, I could only guess that, by invoking the Judgement of Minos, I had given Malacoda the power to transport me there. As to where he had taken me, or why, I couldn't begin to under-stand. Shit, I didn't even know what judgement I had invoked. I knew only that, by invoking it, I had momentarily prevented the devil from making me his bitch.

I was still wearing the Skull, which provided the hyper-clarity of total awareness even as it beclouded my vision within a veil of blue Hellfire. I stood at the center of a massive arena, around which loomed the towers, columns, and battlements of what I would one day come to know as the great city Hades, the capital of Limbo. Above the city and the extended landscape of Limbo loomed a black sun, like a permanent eclipse in the sky, bathing the land in a pale corpse-light that illuminated the city while providing scant warmth. This orb, I would later learn, was the Black Sun of Hell, a gift of light and time from Kronos to Lucifer. During my later sojourn there, I would come to lust after and loathe that cursed orb like a lover scorned.

Across the field from me stood Malacoda, still clutching his mace, still leering at me with the utter certainly of impending victory. Around us, the stands of the oval arena were full of demons, devils, and the damned, all gathered together to watch whatever entertain-ment we were about to provide. On the ornate gallery at the center of

the *ima cavea* sat the high nobility of Limbo: lords and ladies of the
Fallen, gloriously bedecked in their finest raiments, the various hues
of their corrupted flesh carved with runes proclaiming their house
allegiances, complemented by their jeweled horns, and debased by
their ritualistic piercings. Before this crowd, three High Princes of
Hell sat at a long marble table. The first was a fierce devil with
massive horns, a leering tongue, and red rune-carved skin; the
second, a giant-sized man with obsidian skin, black feathered wings,
and eyes glowing with Hellfire; the third, an immense green-skinned
demon with a mummified lower body, bearing a crook and flail and
wearing a white crown topped with ostrich feathers. Behind this lot
was a tall, black throne. On that throne sat the most immense being I
had ever beheld: fully thirty feet tall, a pale king with a Grecian beard
and a muscular, alabaster body. Instead of legs, a long, scaled
serpent's tale depended from his torso and coiled around the throne.
On his brow sat a silver crown so large that I could see the damned
souls attending to this being from within its carved chambers. This, I
could at least surmise, was Minos—King of Limbo and Judge of the
Damned.

From the gallery there came the peal of trumpets, as to whatever
ceremony I had committed myself commenced. The middle demon
stood, outstretching his black wings, and spoke. Though he stood at
least fifty chains from me, his voice boomed and echoed throughout
the wide arena.

"My lords and ladies of Limbo," said the demon prince, "Welcome
to the Field of Judgement. As a High Judge of the damned, I, Prince
Rhadamanthus, have the honor of addressing you today on behalf of
his Royal Satanic Highness, the great King Minos, Lord of Limbo,
Royal Patron of House Sathariel, and Master of the great city of
Hades. We are gathered here this day to witness the final judgement
of Minos regarding the enmity between His Satanic Highness Malacoda, Dire Malebranche of the Eighth Circle of Malebolge, and
Prince Elberon of Woerth."

At the announcement of his name and title, Malacoda bowed
before the King, so I figured I should do likewise. A low thrum and

buzz came from the crowd. Seated on his throne, King Minos remained silent and immobile; he might have been a statue, were it not for the blazing white light emanating from his eyes.

"Lord Malacoda, Prince Elberon," continued Rhadamanthus, "Do you both accept the Doom of Minos, should it befall you?"

"BETCHYER ASS," said Malacoda.

"I DO," I said, through my booming Skull-voice.

"So mote it be," continued the judge. "As neither of you are counted among the damned, to be bound by the judgement of Minos you must each serve at the pleasure of an editor. Is there someone here who will serve as the editor of Malacoda? If so, let him now speak."

On the gallery, the assembled nobles rose and stepped aside to allow passage for what I can describe only as a giant, black, hairy, loathsome housefly. Supporting himself with a black scepter, the giant fly-devil shuffled forward on his hind segmented legs. A small red crown sat askew atop his bulbous head.

"I will sponsor Lord Malacoda," said the devil-fly. "Although he long ago failed me on the field of battle against the mortal man Arturus, he has remained a faithful vassal to House Golachab. Should he prevail today, I will release him from his long prison."

"Very well, King Beelzebub," said Rhadamanthus. "Lord Malacoda, do you accept your King's charge?"

"WITH PLEASURE," said Malacoda. He bowed before Beelzebub. *"MAY YOU BATHE FOREVER IN THE BLOOD OF INNOCENTS, MY KING."*

"So mote it be," said the winged demon. "Who now will sponsor Prince Elberon in this contest?"

Crickets—I got crickets. Not one being in the great arena spoke on my behalf. Finally, there came another voice from the gallery—one I recognized. Jo Ki-Rin stepped forward from his seat near the rear.

"I'll sponsor the kid," the Ki-Rin said.

There was more hubbub from the crowd. The three judges conferred together, and then Rhadamanthus spoke.

"You are indeed an honored guest of Hell, Lord Jo," said Rhadamanthus. "King Asmodai of Sheol has granted you the Right of Passage. And yet you hold no power here. What can you pledge to Beelzebub, should Prince Elberon fall?"

"My life," said Jo Ki-Rin. "If the kid loses, my life will become forfeit to Beelzebub. Good enough?"

More crowd-buzz and another judges' conference later, and Rhadamanthus bowed to the Ki-Rin. "King Minos has accepted your offer of editorship. Your grace, will you accept the Ki-Rin's pledge of his life to you?"

"Oh, indeed I do," said Beelzebub, his fly-body bowing obscenely to the Ki-Rin.

"So mote it be," said Rhadamanthus. The prince turned to my opponent. "Lord Malacoda, as the challenged party, you hold the right to name the form of combat. Do you accept this challenge?"

"BETCHYER ASS," Malacoda repeated.

"Very well. Name your preferred form of combat."

For some reason, at that moment, I thought of my father. Two years ago, I had fought for my pride against the old man. Now, I was fighting for my life. In truth, I was in both cases fighting for the same thing: freedom. For without freedom—the true, unfettered power to enact one's will, free from every constraint, be it a father's wrath or the clockwork machinations of the Multiverse—there was no life. There was only slavery.

Unfortunately, the psychic link between the devil and me persisted, and Malacoda divined my thoughts. I heard again the fell echo of his voice in my head.

"Thanks for giving away the game, pal," the devil's voice said. *"Nothing like beating you with your own fear."* Malacoda then spoke aloud, and his voice rang like my doom across the great arena. *"I HAVE CHOSEN THE MANNER OF OUR CONTEST, OH GREAT JUDGE OF THE DAMNED. I CHOOSE... CRUSH THE KOBOLD. ONE GAME, WINNER TAKE ALL."*

Anticipating the excitement to follow, the crowd went nuts. The nobles gathered on the gallery hubbubbed together. *Holy fucking shit, I thought. Are you kidding me?*

"*No, I'm not kidding,*" the devil's voice answered in my mind. "*Prepare to be ass-raped, puny mortal.*"

"Prince Elberon," Rhadamanthus called down to me from the gallery. "Your opponent has chosen the manner of contest: Crush the Kobold, one game, winner take all. Do you accept his choice?"

I paused—not out of fear, mind you. Perhaps it was for dramatic effect.

"BETCHYER ASS," I said.

30

"So mote it be," proclaimed Rhadamanthus, as the winds of Limbo roared. "The battle is to the death, until the first player scores, or until one player yields to the victor. May the Great Satan, Lucifer the Morning Star, have mercy on your souls."

Anon, two tall goals appeared at either side of the stadium, along with a spike-studded metal ball—no live kobold this time—that now appeared on the ground at the fifty-yard line. Across the pitch from one another, the devil and I squared off: he wielding his massive battle-mace, me my trusty and yet sadly pathetic +2 longsword. I was a lowly Fourth-Level fighter, about to engage in mortal combat with a devil that could easily murder fighters of twice my experience level. I had the girdle, and bore the Skull—but what would these items avail, given that I had already fallen once to the devil? Malacoda seemed to think that choosing my family's game would enhance my fear and thus give him an edge—but what sharper edge did he require?

A gong gonged, signaling the start of the match. Malacoda then revealed his game plan—for there appeared, materializing out of the aether, four-score of the devil's infernal henchmen, ready to join the fray. There were minor pit devils, armored war trolls, ghastly ghouls, ghoulish ghasts, muscled Ur-imps, skeleton warriors, even a vampire or two. Instead of facing a single opponent, I was facing a small army.

Devils are liars and cheats—I should have seen it coming. As the vanguard was already racing for the spiked ball, there was nothing else for it. Girding my loins, I ran for the ball with my sword cocked over my shoulder, bellowing the war cries of the Lordship.

An imp got to the ball first. I arrived in time to shear off the fucker's head. With no way to both carry the ball and defend myself from the horde, my play was to guard the ball while taking out as many of Malacoda's minions as I could. As the girdle and Skull provided me with strength and endurance far beyond my scrawny mortal abilities, I could take out a lot of them.

Malacoda, meanwhile, was content to hang back, waiting for his minions to do his work for him. As I stacked up bodies, the crowd grew rowdier. They hadn't expected me to last for more than a minute. At the sight of a mortal man giving an army of infernals what-for, they began to rally to my cause, cheering every time I fried a hellspawn with Skull-lightning or rammed my blade through an infernal's black heart. Chafing at the loss of his home-field advantage, Malacoda grew wroth. Raising his mace high over his horned head, he called down from the roiling sky above Hades a blast of lightning, which exploded like an incendiary grenade in the arena, sending me and every one of Malacoda's minions flat on our bellies.

As I stood, acrid vapor filled my lungs. The smoke cleared, and I could see now filling the arena a fresh army of infernals. Hundreds of them—slavering, rattling their bent scimitars and curved hooks, snorting smoke and flame from their nostrils. Now, I realized the truth: Malacoda was smarter than me. He had trapped me after all, and I would die screaming.

Wait a minute, I thought. *Screaming.*

Oh, you'll be screaming, all right, the devil's voice taunted in my head. *For the next ten thousand years, I reckon.*

And then came another voice in my head—my own. It was the voice of my future self, speaking to me before our mental connection broke during the showdown at the Blue Falcon.

Go take down that fucking devil, I had told me. *And for Odin's sake, don't forget to scream.*

Some mental switching station in my brain at last clacked into life, and I understood. I was no longer just Elberon, lowly Fourth-Level fighter. In part, I was also Koschei the Deathless, the most powerful sorcerer ever to walk the Woerth. Koschei had imbued his own skull with the ability to summon allies, I knew, because I had slain scores of them during my possession of that cursed relic. Before, I had no control over it. Now that I wore the Screaming Skull as my own, what allies might it summon? Reaching out to find the devil's mind, I locked onto it—and realized that I was right. Malacoda had hung back not out of confidence that his minions would best me, but rather out of fear. Fear of the Skull. Fear of its power.

I've got you now, pal, I thought.

I'm not your pal, buddy.

I'm not your buddy, asshole.

I'm not your asshole, fucknut.

You're right—I am fucking nuts, and you're about to get fucked, I thought. Then I opened the Skull's jaw, and let it scream.

The sound sent every demon and devil in the arena running for cover. Even the three High Judges of Hell ducked, while King Minos remained as immobile and impassive as the Sphinx. Atop my shoulders, the Skull now burned with a blinding aura of blue flames. Around me, the arena faded from view, and I found myself seemingly floating in utter black emptiness—a void that was yet filled with a foaming sea of glowing bubbles that swelled and collided and formed new bubbles that sometimes popped like a silent surprise. Each bubble, the Koschei in me knew, was a separate universe. I had only to extend my mind into one of those bubbles, and I could see with perfect clarity its connection to the pure blood of Barbēlō, she who is called Tiamat, the Mother of Chaos. To wield her power, I had only to reach out my hand.

One of the universe-bubbles swelled in size before me. Within its curvature, I saw a small blue-green planet rife with the spawn of Chaos. Extending my thoughts into this world, I found on a vast plain a horde of fur-clad horsemen galloping toward a crowd of panicked villagers screaming for their lives. I reached out—

—and now the horde of Mongols appeared in the arena in Limbo, twirling scimitars above their heads and charging straight toward the vanguard of Malacoda's minions. Their eyes wide with shock and terror, the hellspawn broke and ran. The Mongols rode them down, swinging their swords in tight arcs that sent heads popping from torsos.

At this turn of events, Malacoda hesitated—but only for a moment. Then he raised his mace again. Another lightning flash, and there appeared in the arena a herd of war-mammoths topped by wooden towers manned with bowmen. The Mongols' charge broke against the line of these great beasts. From their perches atop the mammoths, Malacoda's bowmen rained death upon the horde.

Just the appetizer, I thought, and reached out my mind again. I summoned a line of ballistae manned by armored crews. The war machines hurled massive barbed bolts at the mammoths, which trumpeted their pain and alarm as their line broke, and they stumbled backwards to trample the devil's minions. Malacoda summoned a dozen trebuchets loaded with flaming brimstone missiles that smashed into my ballistae. To counter, I called forth a double-line of armored triceratops ridden by Atlantean war-maidens; these barreled into the trebuchets and smashed them to bits.

So the battle raged, with the devil and I in turn summoning creatures of Chaos and machines of war to smite the other's forces. I threw at Malacoda three brigades of fusiliers. When they died, I countered by pulling the 26th North Carolina regiment from McPherson's Ridge and throwing them into the fray. Following the Confederates came a line of 7.7cm FK 16 German field guns. Then a division of Panzer IIs supported by a battalion of Waffen SS and a squadron of Stukas. When the Stukas began dive-bombing the arena, the devil got pissed, and I had to bring out the heavier stuff: Bell AH-1 Cobra gunships, complete with "Ride of the Valkyries" accompaniment; Merkava Mark IVs, their 12.7mm swivel-mount machine guns and 60mm grenade launchers laying waste to Malacoda's lines; MQ-9

Reapers raining appropriately-named Hellfire missiles; a squad of Battle Angel mechs armed with 60 kilowatt las-cannons and pulse grenades; three Deatheater 6000 dreadnoughts complete with nano-fighters to attack the nanobots Malacoda had sent after my troops; more and more advanced war machines, the abilities and construction of which I couldn't begin to understand, but which nevertheless obeyed my summons to rain death with impunity upon the devil's minions.

And I was prevailing. Behind my forces I came, carrying the game ball, waiting for an opening to find Malacoda and rip his fat bull's head from his shoulders before I marched across the goal line to win this fucking game. Then, a rookie mistake. For the briefest moment, I wondered what my father would think of my impending victory, and I allowed myself a measure of pride.

Pride, as the Wise know, is the Original Sin—the only sin, the proto-sin, in which we assume that we can achieve a balance that exists apart from El. None see this truth more clearly than the Fallen. Sensing my thoughts through the battlefield carnage, the devil roared with laughter.

"SO, YOU THINK YOUR FATHER WOULD BE PROUD OF YOU?" The devil asked aloud, and despite the din of combat his voice rang throughout the arena.

"WHAT BUSINESS IS THAT OF YOURS, IMP?" I roared back. "COME AND TAKE YOUR MEDICINE."

"HERE'S WHAT YOUR FATHER THOUGHT OF YOU, SHITBIRD," said the devil. *"YOU THINK HE DIDN'T KNOW YOU WERE PACKING THAT GIRDLE WHEN YOU TOOK HIM OUT? HE'S THE ONE WHO FUCKING PUT IT IN THAT CAVE FOR YOU TO FIND! HE'S THE ONE WHO STARTED YOU ON THIS GODFORSAKEN QUEST. HE LET YOU WIN, DUMBASS! YOU HADN'T FIGURED THAT OUT?"*

Malacoda belched laughter again, and then the devil invaded my mind with knowledge unbidden. As a waking dream, images of the past unspooled before me. Olderon laughing maniacally on the bridge of his flagship as the sea drakes destroyed the Talony's fleet in the Battle of Hydra Bay. Olderon again standing on the deck over two captive wizards—and one of them, I was flabbergasted to learn, was our old pal Jaspin Spellbinder. The other wizard, I didn't recognize. My father and Jaspin? What the fucking fuck?

The movie continued: bound in magic-dampening chains and facing execution, Jaspin and his companion pledging themselves to Olderon's service, taking the Oath of Binding to seal their bargain and save their lives; Olderon watching my brother and I grow to manhood, secretly doubting that either of us were fit to rule his hard-won kingdom; deciding finally that my brother was too weak to reign, Olderon calling in his marker on the two wizards to help him devise a quest that would test my own fitness to rule the Lordship. Next, I saw the cave under Chasm Falls—the same cave where I had discovered my magic girdle. I watched Jaspin and his companion teleport into the cave and carefully place the Girdle over the corpse. To give me an extra shock when I later found it, Jaspin cast a *Fear* charm on the corpse. Then they vanished again.

The images raced by so swiftly that I scarcely had time to process them. Even so, I could perceive the truth: Olderon had himself launched me on the path to what I would later think of as the Quest, and Jaspin had helped him do it. It was Jaspin who had been searching for the Skull all along. Arriving in Redhauke ahead of my exile, he had murdered Saggon, replaced the Over-Boss with an ice-golem under his control, and set to digging for it beneath the Blue Falcon. Malacoda had mucked up the plan by tossing it to Melinda—but it came to me anyway. Thus came to me the second revelation: What the devil had told me earlier was true.

TWO PHYLAXES, AND YOU THINK YOU CAN TAKE ME, the devil had said.

The Phylaxes are drawn to each other, like magnets, Redulfo had said. *Once the first one is found, the others will be, too.*

Fuck me, I thought. I possessed not one of Koschei's Phylaxes; I possessed two. The Girdle and the Skull. Olderon knew all along that I wore the Girdle, because he ordered Jaspin to hide it in the cave for me to find. He also knew that I wore it during our match, and he hadn't done a thing about it. He let me beat him, so he could banish me from his kingdom and send me on my way to undertake a quest of his devising, all so I could prove to him my fitness to rule—and even then, he doubted me enough to let me cheat.

So stunning was this deluge of knowledge that I fell to my knees. Before I could recover, Malacoda was upon me. Seizing the Screaming Skull by its horns, he yanked upward, lifting me bodily from the ground.

"YOU SEE IT NOW, DON'T YOU?" the devil bellowed. *"YOU'RE NOTHING. YOUR OLD MAN KNEW YOU WERE CHICKENSHIT. HE KNEW YOU WOULD FAIL WITHOUT HIS HELP. SO, HE RIGGED THE GAME. YOU'RE NOT FIT TO WEAR THIS SKULL, AND I'M GOING TO RIP THE FUCKING THING OFF YOUR SHOULDERS. RIGHT. NOW."*

Around us, the mayhem of battle faded. Like ice water in my veins, fear flowed through me. Not just fear of immediate death, but rather all the fear I had ever felt, or ever would feel: fear of the Quest, fear of failing my friends, fear of women, fear of love, fear of embarrassment and failure and inaction. Ruling over it all, like some cruel despot with an iron grip on the kingdom of fear that had conquered my heart, was fear of my father. Fear of loving him. Fear of hating him. Fear of becoming him. The devil had found my weakness, and he would use it to destroy me.

Then, there came unbidden to my mind's eye an image of my brother and me facing each other on the grassy, windswept plateau above Tradewind with swords drawn. Within the nearby tent, a red-hot brand waited in a bed of coals for one of us to scar the other.

You think this a cruel test, and so it is, Jorren, my father's master-of-arms, had told us. *But now you know fear. One of you will master it, and one of you will be marked by your failure to do so. The winner, therefore, has nothing to fear.*

Yes, I thought. *That's right. I mastered my fear. I beat my brother, and yet I took the brand.*

What did you say? I heard Malacoda say in my head.

I ignored the devil. The arena, the two armies still laying waste to one another, the assembled crowd, Malacoda himself still attempting to wrench the Skull from my shoulders—it all faded away. I found myself once again in the moat outside of Castle Kraken, my head submerged beneath the filthy water as Olderon drove his thumbs into my throat.

This was the moment when I had called upon the Girdle to save my ass. It wasn't a memory. I was there again, and with an epiphany that perhaps shook the very foundations of Woerth, I realized that this moment—not the battle with Malacoda—was the true inflection point. Even though I had yet no real inkling of the Quest, I understood that the course of my life depended on my actions here, and now. Knowing now how the old man doubted me, I would spend the rest of my life doubting myself—and self-doubt, I knew, was a terminal condition. The match had already happened—and yet here I was again, with the power to change it. All I had to do was beat the old man square.

As Olderon closed off my windpipe, I saw stars. To my thoughts I summoned the look in his eye as, three days after I had cast the brand at his feet and refused to maim my brother, I took the branding myself. Though I was but eight years old, I had in some unspoken and yet mutually understandable way beaten the old bastard. At that moment, he realized he would one day die. He realized he would need me to carry on his legacy—and he hated me for it.

That was all I needed to know. With no help from the Girdle at all, I summoned my rage and flipped him over into the drink. I let him flail about for a moment. Then I pulled him sputtering from the moat.

"Yield, old man!" I cried.

"I'll see you in Hell first!" Olderon raged.

I gave him another taste of the moat. "Yield! You are finished here!"

"You'll have to kill me!"

I flipped him over so I could see his face. "I don't want to kill you!" I bellowed. "I want my freedom!"

We locked gazes. The gleam of triumph in his eyes that I remembered was now gone—replaced with fear. For only the second time in his life, Olderon was afraid. He threw up his hands.

"I yield!" King Olderon cried. "Prince Elberon is the victor!"

Only it wasn't King Olderon who had yielded—it was the devil. I was back in the arena in Limbo. Our armies were gone; though warfare had raged for an indeterminate time across the playing field, there was no sign of it. There was only we two. My cartoonishly-muscled arms were wrapped around the devil's head and neck as he clawed at them in a futile attempt to free himself. He could struggle for eternity for all I cared—I was still going to choke him out, and he knew it.

"*I YIELD!*" Malacoda, Dire Malebranche of the Eighth Circle and loyal vassal to Beelzebub, cried out. "*PRINCE ELBERON IS THE VICTOR!*"

With that pronouncement, I dropped the devil like a bad sandwich. I walked over to grab the game ball, laying on the ground nearby. Picking it up, I walked it over to the goal line, stepped across it, and flung the ball to the ground. Then I looked up to the gallery.

"The judgement of Minos is final and inviolate," said Rhadamanthus, standing from behind the long judge's table. "Prince Elberon has won."

"BETCHYER ASS," I said.

31

"EL-BER-*RON*! EL-BER-*RON*! EL-BER-*RON*!"

Across the vast expanse of the arena, Fallen and damned alike roared their approval at my victory. Demons approved because they saw it as the triumph of Law over Chaos, devils because they enjoy seeing anything get fucked up, and the damned because they saw me as one of their own. Black roses fell as a soft rain upon the field, tossed by the Fallen ladies from the gallery. For a short while, I rocked the attention, rotating in a slow circle to absorb the cheers. I looked up to find the Ki-Rin in the gallery—but Jo was gone. Goddamned fickle Celestial. I was now in his fucking pocket, and he knew it. The only question was when the bill would come due.

Behind me, Malacoda lay prostrate, supplicating himself to his Lord and King Beelzebub, who sat grimly in the gallery with his grotesque fly wings vibrating in short fits. Then the Lord of Flies stood, balancing himself on his little royal staff.

"Thrice thou hast failed me, Malebranche," said Beelzebub, his gurgling voice quieting the crowd. "Thy failure is utter, and thy failure is complete." The devil turned to face King Minos, who sat his throne with cosmic impassivity. "King Minos, as a guest in your realm

I of course defer to your authority over my vassal Malacoda. I ask your blessing to adjudicate his fate myself."

Rhadamanthus spoke for his king. "King Minos is pleased to grant you leave, King Beelzebub."

Now Beelzebub turned to his groveling vassal. "To the Arch-Devil Malacoda, I say unto thee: As is my right as thy King and right hand of the Satan Lucifer, I hereby strip thee of thy lands, titles, and duties as Dire Malebranche of the Eighth Circle. Thou art now among the lowest of the Fallen. Thou shalt serve as my slave, until such time as I consign thee to the Void."

"So mote it be," said Rhadamanthus. From the near end of the arena a portcullis rose, and two massive, muscled and horned demons bearing the sigil of House Sathariel emerged from a brimstone tunnel leading back to the arena's staging areas. Seizing Malacoda by the arms, they dragged him back toward the tunnel. As they did so, the devil dropped all pretense of humility and thrust a taloned claw in my direction.

"YOU THINK THIS IS OVER?" Malacoda roared at me. *"I'LL FIND YOU, FUCKSTICK! YOU HEAR ME? I'LL HUNT YOU FROM THE FIRST UNIVERSE UNTO THE LAST, AND WHEN I FIND YOU, I'LL FUCK YOU FOREVER! DO YOU HEAR ME, MORTAL? DO YOU—"*

The portcullis slammed shut, and the devil's oaths dissolved into reverberating noise. That was the last I saw of Malacoda, former Dire Malebranche of the Eighth Circle of Hell, until he appeared on the end of a chain in Hundred Fountain Square three years later calling for my head. How Garrin had captured the devil, I wouldn't learn for many years—until Malacoda came perilously close to fulfilling his promise to me.

For the nonce, I was finally rid of that asshole. Standing in the arena, I was unsure of what to do next. I was in trapped in Hell, I now possessed two of Koschei's Phylaxes, and now knew that both my own father and Jaspin Spellbinder had been playing me like a goddamned squeezebox. Could life get any more fucked up? Fortunately, Rhadamanthus came to my rescue.

"Prince Elberon of Woerth," said Rhadamanthus, resuming his

spot at the Table of Judgement, "You victory is well won, but it appears your editor has taken his leave. If you will allow me, I will serve as editor in his stead. You may ask a boon of me, if you so desire."

I did so desire. Lifting my hands to the Skull still burning like a butane torch atop my shoulders, I touched it, wondering how in hell I was ever going to get my own skull back again. Lucky for me, touching it was all that was required. My vision filled with light, descended into utter blackness, and then slowly resolved into the surrounding arena again—only this time, I was seeing it with my own eyes. Somehow, my own skull, which Melinda had been holding for me, had reappeared on my shoulders, complete with the rest of my head. In my hands, the Screaming Skull now stared up at me, leering at me with its fanged grin, laughing at me behind the shadows of its eye sockets. I had wielded the thing, but I hadn't mastered it—and the Skull knew I was its bitch.

"The Skull. The Girdle I wear," I called up to Rhadamanthus. "These are the tools of Koschei the Deathless, and I do not wish them to become my doom. I beg your leave to destroy them—or, if they cannot be destroyed, I ask that you allow me to leave them here, in the safekeeping of King Minos of Limbo."

There was a pause as Rhadamanthus communed silently with his pale King, still sitting his throne with utter passivity. Then a crack appeared before me in the hard, dusty sand of the arena floor. Ugly crimson light spilled from this crack, which widened until a small lake of raw Hellfire burned at my feet.

"These things cannot be destroyed here, Prince Elberon," said Rhadamanthus, "But King Minos does grant your second request. You may imprison these Phylaxes in Hellfire, if you wish."

Bowing low before King Minos, I took a final look at the Skull, wished it a silent *fuck you*, and then tossed it into the burning lake. It bobbled there in the magma for a moment in silent reproach. Then it slipped beneath the surface and was gone.

Next, I moved to doff the Girdle for good. No more stone-giant strength, which was a bummer. Better to be a weakling again than to possess any relic of the Deathless. My hands grasped the buckles—

—and the Girdle tightened around me like a python. *What the fuck?* I thought.

I grabbed it by the straps and pulled, and it pulled right back, threatening to crush my ribcage. Goddamn it, the thing wasn't going anywhere. It was mine, whether or not I wanted it—and it meant that whatever doom my father had set in motion, when he ensured that I found the thing beneath Chasm Falls five years earlier, still loomed before me. The Quest was my fate, and no amount of free will was going to change it.

Looking up to Rhadamanthus again, I shrugged. "One out of two, right?" I said. "And now, your Satanic Highness, if there's a way to, you know—"

Before I could finish the sentence, I found myself once again standing before the Hellmouth in the catacombs below the Blue Falcon. The very foundations of those catacombs were now bucking and twisting as the quantum vortex tore them apart. I whirled around —and saw Melinda standing behind the closing doors of the Hellmouth, prepared to sacrifice herself to save the souls of the innocent.

"Come back!" I cried.

32

T hose words echoed in my mind as, nine years later, I stood staring at the Astral Telescope for the first time. On the telescope—a simple contraption that belied its abilities as perhaps the most powerful spying device on Woerth—hung a note written on parchment, presumably by Redulfo the Black, although how a fat-fingered dragon could handle a quill, I couldn't say. My three friends and I read the note together. It said:

Your Quest continues here. Unless you rescue her, she won't be able to rescue you. If she doesn't rescue you, you won't be here, and your Quest will end. Use this telescope to find her, and then step through the mirror. Remember, you have the power to change this universe. If you don't change it, you can't save it.

"We need Redulfo here to tell us what the hell this means," said Amabored.

He wasn't wrong. We had left our friend behind twice: once when we sent young Redulfo back through the blue mirror to rejoin our younger selves nine years earlier; and once again when we left the desecrated carcass of Redulfo the Black lying on the field of battle. It's bad enough when a friend dies; watching him die twice by your own hand is a little less enjoyable than drinking a bucket of warm piss.

Leaving the dragon behind with our hearts burdened, we navi-
gated our way around the dead insectoids and found the stone path
leading down from the Wilderness of Mirrors to the great, slowly-
rotating platform upon which stood the Workshop of Telescopes,
surrounded by the smoking remains of the dragon's army. That architectural, scientific, and sorcerous masterpiece, constructed by the
wizards Gygax and Rigsby five hundred years ago, truly astounded.
Its ornate, garishly-painted towers, spires, and domes loomed over
our heads as we stepped onto its timepiece foundation and entered
through its main gatehouse, which had been left yawning open after
the dragon's doomed army had marched through it.

Once inside, we were flabbergasted. We saw a vast interior observatory supporting scores of platforms large and small, upon which
stood hundreds of telescopes ranging in size from nautical spyglasses
trained on individual universes to gargantuan lenses designed to peer
deep into the Multiverse. A hundred feet overhead, the massive
domed ceiling was pierced by a multitude of sliding panels that
allowed the telescopes access to the sky. This network of telescopes,
platforms, and panels was connected by an elaborate system of gears,
chains, and pullies designed to rotate any telescope to any position
within the observatory. The young Redulfo would have had his mind
blown by the Workshop; were he ever to see it, he might devote the
rest of his life to mastering it. By the time he did see it, what little
remained of the wizard was living too hellish an existence to appreciate its wonders. As we wandered aimlessly through the observatory,
we silently pondered the cruel machinations of the universe that had
led us to twice kill our friend.

In a satchel depending from Malcolm's shoulder rested a jar
containing the Bad Brain, floating in a solution of water, vinegar, and
salt. Despite its current state, the vile green organ pulsed with
undying malevolence. I had convinced each of the others to take a
turn carrying it, rather than saddling me with it for who-the-hell-
knew how long. Why should I have all the fun?

Despite our success in capturing the Brain, we were each fully aware of our utter failure thus far in fulfilling the Ki-Rin's charge. In the five years since Jo had appeared to Cassie, we had managed to procure only five of the ten Phylaxes: The Girdle and Skull, the Fell Phallus, the Horrible Heart, and now the Bad Brain. The Skull and Phallus were stored safely in the Bilge Rat's hold under the protection of Quid Saltwind. We needed to get the Brain to the ship as well, which meant a long and perilous journey back to the Were Coast, the thought of which left me antsy. Sure, I wanted to save the Woerth— but I also wanted back in Cassie's pants. Our parting in Collanna three years prior had been bitter, after she had laid into me for soft-pedaling the Quest. With real progress to report, I might have a shot at her forgiveness—but business came first.

Before we could travel again, we needed to heal and rest. Fortunately, the Hand had afforded us the opportunity; when the dragon's *Paralyzation* spell had worn off, the insectoids had not assaulted the Workshop, opting instead to return through their mirrors to wherever they holed up. Tomorrow, we would dispatch Lithaine and Malcolm to retrieve James and Wilberd, assuming they were still alive. Amabored and I would remain at the Workshop to guard the place from intruders. First, however, we needed a meal and a fresh store of supplies. With whatever servants who tended the Workshop now gone, that need sent us exploring the place—until we found the Astral Telescope, and the note that Redulfo had left behind.

I read the note again. The events of nine years earlier came flooding back to me, as vividly then as the *Remembrance* potion allows today: the battle with Malacoda, the children disappearing into the Hellmouth, and Melinda's determination to save them. Six months later, she had reappeared to me as if from the dead, carried to Redhauke on a litter borne by Cloud Riders. What had happened to her during those six months? Of the time between the Hellmouth doors closing and her awakening at the feet of the Celestial Stairway, she could recall nothing. And yet somehow, she had returned alive.

Unless you rescue her, she won't be able to rescue you. If she doesn't rescue you, you won't be here, and your Quest will end.

I understood—or at least, I thought I did. I'm not actually very bright, as my father would never tire of telling you. I did, however, have my moments. Stepping forward, I pressed my eye to the telescope's eyepiece.

At first, I saw nothing but a reflection of my own eyelashes. Then the image cleared, and I saw two figures—a man and a woman—on a road approaching a great city slumbering beneath a black sun motionless in a pallid sky. The man I didn't recognize. Of the woman's identity, however, there could be no mistake: It was Melinda. The city I didn't recognize either, but the sight of that motionless black sun jolted my memory, and I understood: Melinda was in Hell. I was watching her on her journey through the Infernal Realm to rescue the souls of the seven children lost to Malacoda.

I stepped back from the telescope. Just as I thought—opposite it stood a mirror, through which pale light emanated. That mirror, I knew, was a one-way ticket to Hell. If I didn't step through it to aid Melinda in her quest, then our own Quest would end here.

If Redulfo the Black wanted to prove that free will exists, then how would he explain this path, which eliminated all possibility of another? We couldn't ask him, because he was dead. At seeing Limbo again, the time I spent in Hell came back to me—the Crush the Kobold match, defeating Malacoda, and my opportunity to beat my old man clean. Perhaps *that* was the proof. By changing history, had I introduced the free will that the dragon had been so determined to prove? Who the hell knew?

I took a moment to explain the situation to my mates. They listened as if I was recounting my plan to grow an extra head. Despite their best efforts, however, they couldn't deny the path that now lay before us.

"I have to go," I told them. "You don't. You can continue the Quest without me."

"And miss the chance to slay hellspawn on their home ground?" asked Malcolm. "Surely you jest, friend Elberon."

"Without us to save your ass, you won't last five minutes in Hell," said Amabored.

"You got that right," said Lithaine.

Amabored thrust out a gloved hand. In turn, each of us also extended our hands, until the four of us stood together, one hand atop another, united in our mission.

"Let's go save the ex-wife who probably wishes you were dead," said Amabored.

33

They were my brothers and best friends, these men. I could ask for none better. As I sit here today, mulling their end from the safety of my throne, it's hard to believe that we ever mattered so much to one another. In the long years after the Quest, we survivors drifted inexorably apart, our lives intersecting ever less, until our infrequent reunions served only to remind us of how far apart we had grown. And yet, on that day, and throughout the long years of the Quest, I would gladly have died to save any one of them.

Now, in nine days, they'll have the opportunity to die for me.

You're wondering now why I want to kill them. Have I truly gone mad? Or is it all part of some secret plan to thwart you? Yes, I know you're reading, even as my scribe records my tale in real time. If the Seven are meant to destroy the Woerth in ten days, as Amabored's prophecy promises, then killing my friends seems pointless, no? And yet I mean to do it anyway. To jump-start my plan, I've dispatched the gnome Xingo on a mission, and aren't you dying to know what that mission is?

You've no choice but to keep listening, therefore, in the hope that I'll reveal some clue that will help you divine my plan. And listen you will, because I've more tale to tell. It's a tale of epic high adventure. In it, we'll descend into Mormant and stand on the shore of the Sunless Sea. We'll march with the Knights of the White Rose as Eckberd's Chaos Army threatens to destroy the Tall Tree of Helene. We'll journey from the ruins of the Sky Ship in the Pustiu Waste to the court of the Empress Wilomina; from the Four Winds Bar at the Nexus to the halls of the Violet Queen; and from the high plains of the Goldvale to the blasted wasteland of the Dread Plain itself. We'll journey to Hell and back.

We'll journey together, you and I, because our fates are intertwined. And I'll tell you this: I know who you are, fucker. To find out how I know, and what I plan to do about it, you'll just have to keep listening, won't you?

They call me a hero. They call me a leader of men. The truth is that I was never really a hero; I only pretended to be one. Is there time yet to become one? We'll see. Perhaps this decrepit, broken-down adventurer has a few surprises left in him yet.

THE END

The Chronicles of Elberon continue in Vol. II:
The Mace of Malice

If you like The Screaming Skull, please leave a review!

Reviews are the lifeblood of any independent author, and yours *will be much appreciated. You know the drill: If you loved this book, please leave a review—and if you hated it, don't feel obliged to leave a review at all (jk, we love all reviews). To leave a review, please visit www.phabulousity.com/product/the-screaming-skull and click on the Amazon link. It's free and relatively painless!*

A HELPFUL TIMELINE

Yr. 3935: Elberon is born.

Yr. 3943: Elberon (age 8) and Elderon fight a duel at Olderon's behest.

Yr. 3951: Elberon (16) finds a magic girdle in a cave outside of Tradewind.

Yr. 3954: The Crush the Kobold match. Elberon (19) is banished from the Tradewind Lordship by his father. He journeys to Redhauke and meets Amabored, Lithaine, and Redulfo. He enters the city. He meets Jaspin Spellbinder.

Yr. 3955: Elberon (20) meets Melinda the Blade. He drinks a Flaming Telepath. He comes to possess the Screaming Skull. The Hydra Incident.

Yr. 3956: The Showdown at the Blue Falcon. Elberon (21) meets Malcolm. He meets Garrin Grimmreaper. He defeats Malacoda in Hell.

Yr. 3957: Melinda returns from Hell to Redhauke, born by Cloud Riders. Elberon (22) finds the Rod of Lordly Might.

Yr. 3959: Elberon (24) and Melinda marry. He re-encounters Garrin and Malacoda. The Lemming Imp Incident.

Yr. 3960: Elberon (25) re-encounters the Screaming Skull. He is attacked by the Crimson Hand. He meets Cassiopeia and Wilberd. Cassiopeia receives a vision from Jo Ki-Rin. Elberon flees Redhauke for good. The Dread Wars begin on Woerth.

Yr. 3961: Elberon (26) meets Xingo Lightfingers. Father Jethro of Tull falls in the Sorrowful Pass.

Yr. 3962: The Quest winters with the Cloud Riders. Amabored meets Bellasa. Lithaine finds Starfall. Redulfo encounters the Bad Brain, dies, and is resurrected as Redulfo the Black.

Yr. 3963: Amabored marries Bellasa and receives his wings.

Yr. 3964: The Siege and Fall of Helene. Elberon (29) meets Andrigan, James, and Lindar. Lindar dies in battle and is resurrected by the Quest.

Yr. 3965: Elberon (30) defeats Redfang the Terrible. He builds Redfang Keep. The Quest enters the Valley of Sorcerers. They journey back to the year 3956 to participate in the Showdown at the Blue Falcon. The death of Redulfo the Black.

Yr. 3966: The Quest begins the journey to the Sky Ship in the Pustiu Wastes. They have a campfire discussion about politics.

Yr. 3967: Garrin Grimmreaper assassinates all rulers of the Free Kingdoms, including Olderon, Elderon, and Bellasa. Elberon (32) confronts Garrin atop the Crimson Citadel.

Yr. 3969: The Quest crosses the Coldsoul Abyss. Malcolm is slain by Lithaine and falls to his doom. Elberon (34) learns that Cassiopeia is pregnant. The Quest enters the Chamber of Eternity. The fall of Koschei and end of the Dread Wars. Elberon encounters the Black Mirror. Lithaine is imprisoned in Hell.

Yr. 3970: Elberon (35) and Cassiopeia are married. Alderon, son of Elberon, is born. James marries Queen Arianna of Kenwood.

Yr. 3976: The death of Cassiopeia.

Yr. 3978: Elberon (43) marries the Lady Astrid of the Talon Republic.

Yr. 3996: Elberon (61) re-encounters Lindar along with Andrigan and Wilberd. He re-encounters the Black Mirror. Amabored loses the 12th Battle of Oxcipius Plain. Amabored receives a vision from the Archangel Metatron.

Yr. 3998. Elberon (63) and James visit Amabored in the Beradon Forest. They learn of the death of Jaspin Spellbinder. Amabored gives Elberon the Time Stone. Xingo attempts to assassinate Elberon and James. Elberon imprisons Xingo in the dungeons of the Kraken.

Yr. 3999: Lithaine escapes from Hell. Wilberd tells Elberon (64) that he will die on the toilet in sixty-five years. Elberon prepares for his sixty-fifth birthday party. He begins dictating *The Chronicles of Elberon* to his scribe.

JOIN THE ADVENTURER'S GUILD

Join the Phabulousity Press **Adventurer's Guild** by providing your email address, and you'll receive a **FREE sneak preview of Part I of** *The Mace of Malice*, Vol. II in *The Chronicles of Elberon* trilogy!

You'll also be **automatically entered into a drawing to have your favorite fantasy role-playing character written into** *The Mace of Malice*! Adventurer's Guild members can become beta readers, receive exclusive short stories featuring Lord Elberon and his crew, and be entered into other contests and drawings. It's free and relatively painless!

To join the Adventurer's Guild, just visit this link:

www.phabulousity.com/adventurersguild

ABOUT THE AUTHOR

Rick Ferguson is a globally recognized marketing expert with appearances in the *New York Times*, the *Wall Street Journal*, *Advertising Age*, *Fast Company*, the *Globe & Mail in* Canada, the *Guardian in the United Kingdom*, the *Financial Times in India*, MSNBC, and the Fox Business Channel. He has delivered keynote speeches on marketing principles and best practices on six continents. He is also a master of time, space, and dimension. He lives in Cincinnati, Ohio with his wife Allison, son Ian, and cat Penny.

UPCOMING BOOKS BY PHABULOUSITY PRESS

The saga of Lord Elberon of the Isles continues in the second and third volumes of *The Chronicles of Elberon*:

The Mace of Malice (to be published in the fall of 2019)

The Crown of Chaos (to be published in the fall of 2020)

For more information on these books, as well as other books by Phabulousity Press, please visit www.phabulousity.com.

ACKNOWLEDGMENTS

Despite the reality of writing as a solitary occupation, no book is written in isolation. First and foremost, love and thanks to my wife, Allison Cripps Ferguson, for her unwavering support and encouragement during the book's completion. Special thanks to Ian for being awesome. Thanks also to Obsidian Abnormal for the fantastic cover and interior art; to Kate Shepherd for her essential editing job; and to my beta readers for their necessary assurances that I hadn't wasted my time. And, lest I forget, thanks to you for reading. If you like the book, be sure to tell your friends!

Made in the USA
Middletown, DE
04 November 2019